Blood Money

Also by Clive Egleton

Blood Money

Clive Egleton

St. Martin's Press ❧ New York

Library of Congress Cataloging-in-Publication Data

Egleton, Clive.
  Blood money / Clive Egleton.
    p.   cm.
    ISBN 0-312-18540-5
    I. Title.
  PR6055.G55B58   1998
  823'.914—dc21   98-16335
                                                                  CIP

First published in Great Britain by Hodder and Stoughton, a division of
Hodder Headline PLC

First U.S. Edition: August 1998

10 9 8 7 6 5 4 3 2

FIC

One more time
for Robert Low Donaldson

CHAPTER 1

It was a truly horrendous breakfast – four rashers of bacon, fried bread, two pork sausages, a slice of black pudding, baked beans and fried potatoes. Annette Jukes could scarcely bring herself to look at the already overcrowded dinner plate as she endeavoured to find room for a solitary grilled tomato. Of all the house guests she had catered for, the one with far and away the biggest appetite was Larry Rossitor. Considering how little exercise he took, it was a miracle he wasn't as fat as a barrel. Annette supposed it had everything to do with his metabolism; some people could eat like a horse and never put on as much as an ounce of spare flesh, while others got by on one meal a day and still fought a losing battle with the waistline.

That certainly wasn't true of Rossitor's colleague. Sharon Cartwright might breakfast off a slice of brown toast and a cup of black coffee without sugar but she did so from choice and not because she needed to diet. Sharon would retain her lithe figure no matter what she did; in twenty years' time she would look the same as she did now and a lot of men would think her still a dishy twenty-four-year-old.

Annette picked up the overfull plate and carried it into the dining room. Last night she had laid a table for four but so far only Larry Rossitor and Sharon had put in an appearance. Inigo, of course, was invariably late for breakfast, but she had hoped that Mr Harvey Yeo would have recovered sufficiently to leave his sick-bed. Three days ago he has woken up with a sore throat on top of a heavy cold and had decided to isolate himself from the others in case he had flu. The hoarse voice had disappeared yesterday, leaving him with just a snuffly nose and a temperature slightly above normal.

'That looks great,' Rossitor said, eyeing the plate Annette had

1

put in front of him. 'I only hope I can do it justice.'

'I'm sure you will,' Sharon told him with a touch of acerbity.

'Well, I need to keep up my strength, I'm a growing lad.' Rossitor winked at Annette. 'Isn't that right, Miss Jukes?'

'I'm sure I don't know, Mr Rossitor,' Annette said, and edged towards the door. She didn't mean to sound prim and mealy-mouthed but she found their childish banter very wearying. She could feel one of her migraines coming on and wanted nothing more than to escape to her kitchen and find relief in two para-cetamol washed down with a glass of water.

'How's your father this morning?' Sharon called after her.

'Much the same as usual,' Annette said in a brittle voice.

Gus was suffering from advanced multiple sclerosis and could no longer feed himself. Six months ago she had moved his bed into the study off the hall because the stairs had become too much for him, and she had put out her back trying to assist him. It wasn't much of a life for Gus but he was seventy-five and had been lucky enough to live it to the full except for the last eight years. Annette's own life had become something of a drudgery at the age of twenty-nine when, at Gus's bidding, she had given up her job in order to look after her invalid mother. It wasn't fair but she was single and, as an only child, it had been expected of her.

Annette filled a tumbler under the cold tap, then reached for the plastic container she kept on the windowledge. Although the throb-bing ache was confined to the right side of her head, it affected the vision in both eyes. Her face screwed up and whimpering with pain and frustration, she wrestled with the childproof cap which it seemed only adults found difficult to prise off. Wholly dependent on her sense of touch, she eventually managed to line up the raised portion on the cap with the one on the neck of the container and release the paracetamol. In a frenzy to find some relief, she tapped four tablets into the palm of her left hand and swallowed them one by one between sips of water.

The hammer blows inside her skull gradually eased to the point where at least the pain was tolerable. As she stood there at the kitchen sink, massaging her temples, Annette heard footsteps on the staircase and knew instinctively that it wasn't Harvey Yeo. Inigo usually had two hard-boiled eggs for breakfast but there was always the possibility that he would like something different for a change. A little unsteady on her feet, she went out into the hall to intercept him before he disappeared into the dining room. Suddenly a darkness closed in around her and she felt herself toppling into a yawning chasm which opened beneath her feet. She thrust out a hand to break her fall and swept a vase containing a large bouquet of imitation roses from the hall table on to the floor.

Although Inigo had only just entered the room, Rossitor, seated, was the quicker to react. While the other man was still thinking about it, he left the table, pushed past him and went out into the hall. Annette Jukes was lying face down on the parquet floor among the shattered fragments of the fake Ming vase. The artificial roses formed a sort of halo above her head, which was turned over on to the left cheek so that she was facing the staircase. Her eyes were glazed and there had been some slight bleeding from the nose and mouth. Bending down, Rossitor pressed a finger against the jugular but could detect no pulse.

'Has she fainted?' Sharon asked.

'It's more serious than that. Annette's in a deep coma and I think she could have had a massive haemorrhage.'

'Oh, my God.'

'You'd better phone the Emergency Services and tell them to send an ambulance.'

'Right.'

'Then I'd be grateful if you would let Harvey Yeo know what's happened.'

'What about Mr Jukes? Should I tell him?'

'You've got enough on your plate,' Rossitor told her. 'I'll handle it.'

But only after he had contacted London and appraised them of the situation. It wasn't just a case of London providing another housekeeper; they would need to think about finding a full-time nurse to look after Gus Jukes.

'Is it serious, her illness?'

Rossitor looked up to find Inigo hovering in the doorway.

'Very serious, I'm afraid, possibly fatal,' he said, and got to his feet.

'That is unfortunate.'

'Yes, it is.'

'So who will boil my eggs now?'

'That's what I like about you, Inigo,' Rossitor said grimly, 'you're all heart.'

Roy Kelso had held the appointment of Assistant Director, Administration, longer than his peer group in the Secret Intelligence Service cared to remember. His empire comprised the Financial Branch, the Motor Transport and General Stores Section plus the Security Vetting and Technical Services Division. He was responsible for claims and expenses, control of expenditure, internal audits, Boards of Inquiry, clerical support and the provision of stationery. Behind his back, Kelso was referred to as the officer in charge of paperclips.

To run such a diverse and semiautonomous organisation as the Admin Wing required a sense of humour, an attribute which Roy Kelso sadly lacked. He had been promoted to Assistant Director a week after his thirty-ninth birthday and had convinced himself that he was destined to go right to the top. Ten years later it was evident that he had been passed over and was stuck in the proverbial rut. Consequently, Kelso had become a tired, disappointed, small-minded and deeply embittered man. He had let it be known to all and sundry that he couldn't wait for his fifty-fifth birthday to arrive, when he would be eligible for early retirement. Now, with severance less than nine months away, the thought of leaving the SIS before he had to dismayed Kelso, and he hoped the Director General would allow him to withdraw his application.

The DG was Victor Hazelwood, and they didn't really get on. Kelso could not forget that in 1990, Hazelwood had merely been a senior Intelligence officer in charge of the Russian Desk and in view of the fact that they were the same age, Kelso had assumed Victor would go no farther. Then the Head of the Eastern Bloc Department had suddenly dropped dead and Hazelwood had been moved upstairs. Barely eighteen months later, the newly appointed Director General, Stuart Dunglass, who'd spent the greater part of his service in the Far East, had invited him to become his deputy.

The onset of cancer of the prostate had forced Dunglass into early retirement and Hazelwood, who had been keeping the chair warm for him on and off while he was recovering from the effects of chemotherapy, had been confirmed in the post by a reluctant Foreign Secretary.

Kelso read the letter he had written to the DG a third time to satisfy himself that it struck exactly the right note. Any hint of obsequiousness on his part and Hazelwood would turn down the application flat. Flattery only aroused his ire, and antagonising him was the last thing Kelso wanted. But even if Hazelwood did support his request to continue in the service, the Treasury could still prove a stumbling block. Keen to cut every establishment to the bone except their own, they had suggested that in view of reduced commitments worldwide, the next head of the Admin Wing should be a Grade I Intelligence officer, thereby saving Her Majesty's Government the princely sum of nine thousand two hundred and seventy-five pounds a year, a cheese-paring, contemptible economy in his view. As he mentally groped for a suitable expletive that would adequately express his feelings on the subject, the telephone rang and interrupted his train of thought. Snatching the receiver from the cradle, he answered the call with a curt 'Yes?'

'This is Rossitor,' an equally curt voice informed him. 'Just how discreet are you?'

'Discreet?'

'Do you have a secure speech facility?'

'Of course I do,' Kelso said indignantly.

'Then switch it on.'

Rossitor was a Grade II Intelligence officer, which meant he was some way down in the pecking order. Too surprised to ask him who he thought he was talking to, Kelso meekly complied.

'It's on,' he muttered.

'We've got a problem,' Rossitor said tersely. 'Annette Jukes collapsed this morning and was pronounced dead on arrival at York District Hospital. We need a replacement urgently, preferably some-one with nursing experience. If it's any help, Harvey Yeo reckons he will be finished with Inigo come Friday.'

'Does Benton know about this?' Kelso asked.

Roger Benton was the Assistant Director responsible for the Pacific Basin and Rest of the World Department and Inigo was really his pigeon.

'He's down at Amberley Lodge lecturing to the induction course and his deputy is off sick. And before you ask, yes I have spoken to the appropriate desk officer and naturally he referred me to you. OK?'

'Yes.'

Kelso didn't like his attitude and was about to give him a piece of his mind when Rossitor asked if he would kindly let him know the outcome and then hung up.

'Rude young devil,' Kelso said to himself, and replaced the receiver which automatically switched off the secure speech facility. The problem Rossitor had dumped in his lap was definitely one for the DG. However, before going upstairs, he opened the combination safe in his office and took out the register of safe houses. When you were dealing with Hazelwood, you needed to be sure of your facts and more than sixteen months had elapsed since the last guest of the SIS had stayed at The Firs in Naburn. His memory refreshed, Kelso locked the file away and rode one of the lifts up to the top floor.

The whole of Vauxhall Cross was supposed to be a smoke-free zone. The ban had come into force when Hazelwood had been the Deputy Director and the SIS was still using Century House. Being the sort of man he was, the then DG, Stuart Dunglass, had agreed that the restriction would not apply to Hazelwood. Despite the fact that the SIS was about to move into Vauxhall Cross, the Property Services Agency had been authorised to install an extractor fan in his office, the bill for which had been passed to the Admin Wing for settlement out of the contingency fund. An invoice for a second extractor fan had appeared in Kelso's in-tray following their re-location in the new premises: it was followed by a third after Hazelwood moved up the corridor on assuming the appointment of Director General.

Kelso supposed it was almost inevitable that Hazelwood should be enjoying one of his foul-smelling Burma cheroots when he entered the Director's office. A committed smoker, Hazelwood kept a supply of them in an ornately carved wooden cigar box he had bought on a field trip to India. From the number of stubs in the cut-down shell case which served as an ashtray, it was evident that Victor paid little attention to government health warnings.

'What can I do for you, Roy?' he asked, and simultaneously waved him to sit down in the nearest of three leather armchairs provided for visitors.

'We have a problem,' Kelso told him, repeating what Rossitor had said, then going on to recount their subsequent conversation word for word.

'I don't know where we are going to find another housekeeper at short notice, Roy.'

'I thought you might send Harriet Ashton.'

'Her husband's in America.'

'Yes, that's why I thought of her.'

'Peter is due back tomorrow morning.'

'We could get one of the duty officers to meet him at Heathrow and explain where she is.'

'Harriet has a son who's only eight months old . . .'

'And her parents live in Lincoln, which is on the way to Naburn.' Kelso paused, then put the knife in. 'I don't know how we can justify paying Harriet a retainer of ten thousand per annum if we are never going to employ her.'

'But she has no nursing experience,' Hazelwood protested, clutching at a straw.

'What about the first-aid course Harriet did when she was with MI5? Doesn't that count for something?'

Kelso knew he had Hazelwood on the rack and was hard-pressed to conceal his elation. Victor had a soft spot for Peter Ashton; their friendship dated from 1988 when the younger man had been assigned to the Russian Desk to work under his direction, and Kelso had a score to settle with Hazelwood's protégé. He could not forget how Ashton had made him feel small when he had been running the Security Vetting and Technical Services Division. He had been a very difficult subordinate, forever undermining his authority.

'Remind me,' Hazelwood said. 'When did Harvey Yeo say he would be finished with Inigo?'

'Friday, three days from now. After that we can replace Harriet with a trained nurse to look after Gus Jukes, assuming we want to retain The Firs on our books?'

'Why should we want to cancel the tenancy agreement?'

'Well, as you know, Gus has multiple sclerosis and by all accounts his condition is deteriorating rapidly. The time is coming when he will have to go into a nursing home.'

'Not as long as I'm the Director,' Hazelwood said angrily. 'Gus was with the Special Operations Executive in World War Two.' When Churchill had asked the SOE to set Europe ablaze, Gus Jukes had been one of the agents who had done just that, winning a DSO, an MC and the Croix de Guerre in the process. Hazelwood could not forget that. 'If any Treasury official looking to make yet further cuts in our budget suggests we get rid of The Firs, refer him to me. I promise you, Roy, he'll be sorry he even thought of it.'

'What about, Harriet?' Kelso asked. 'Are we going to send her?'

'Do we have any choice?'

'Not really.'

'Well then, there's your answer.'

'Shall I tell her or will you?'

'I think she will take it better coming from me,' Hazelwood said with no great confidence.

The fir trees had disappeared in '87 when the council had reluctantly given permission for them to be felled. According to Gus Jukes they'd had no choice considering the roots were in danger of undermining the foundations and the trees were already dying. All that now remained of the evergreens that had given the house its name were three stumps some four feet high. In spring Annette used to plant sweet peas at the base of each one and train them to grow up through the chickenwire she had wrapped around the trunks. Old man Jukes had told Larry Rossitor that the garden had been her pride and joy and that what she had created would not have disgraced the Chelsea Flower Show. Rossitor could only take his word for that; in late January, with a carpet of snow hiding all but a few tufts of grass, the garden looked totally barren. On the

8

ornamental pond, a solitary blackbird pecked at the ice in the forlorn hope of reaching the water below.

'Admiring the view?' Sharon asked behind him.

Rossitor flinched at the sound of her voice and turned swiftly about. 'I didn't hear you come into the room,' he said accusingly.

'You were obviously daydreaming; it took you long enough to answer the phone a while back.'

'I figured that was your job; you were the one who was on duty.'

'Harvey Yeo wanted me to sit in on the interrogation.'

'You should have told me; if I had known that, I would have picked up the phone a lot sooner.'

'Who was calling?'

'Roy Kelso.'

Sharon grinned at him. 'And he gave you a piece of his mind for keeping him waiting?'

'He was just getting his own back. I was pretty short with him this morning.'

'So who is he sending us?'

'Harriet Ashton. Her name was Egan when she was seconded to the SIS from MI5.'

'What's she like?'

Rossitor hesitated. He could say that Harriet was half an inch under six feet, a fact of life which at one time she had tried to disguise by wearing low heels and walking with a slight stoop. He could add that although she had a good figure, it was the perfect symmetry of her face which remained firmly imprinted on people's minds. He could enlarge on this by stating that she was in fact quite beautiful, though she herself was unaware of it. But he knew this was not the sort of thing Sharon wanted to hear. 'Harriet was one of the best,' he said.

'Was?'

'Some of the stuffing was knocked out of her when she was injured in a riot.'

'I see. Do you think she will be able to cope with Gus?'

Jukes had been totally devastated when Rossitor had told him that Annette was dead. The old man had cried out like a wounded animal and had been inconsolable ever since. When Rossitor had

9

looked in on him half an hour ago he had been sleeping fitfully, exhausted by the frequent bouts of weeping.

'We'll find out soon enough; according to Kelso, Harriet reckons she'll arrive here before seven.'

'That gives me about four hours.'

'To do what?' Rossitor asked.

'To go into York and get my hair done, see a film at the multiplex – whatever. I just need to get away from this house for an hour or two. OK?'

'No, you're still on duty.'

'Only until 14.00 hours, then it's your turn.' Sharon checked her wristwatch. 'I make it five to; by the time I've changed into something halfway decent, you'll be well and truly in the chair.'

'What does Harvey have to say about you going into York?'

'Nothing, I haven't bothered to consult him.'

'I think you should.'

'Why? Harvey is so entranced with Inigo he won't even miss me.' Sharon opened the door, then turned about. 'Matter of fact, Larry, he'll be relieved that I'm not around to question the veracity of the info we're getting from Inigo. Personally, I think the guy is a fraud.'

It was an opinion Sharon had expressed to him more than once and to some extent he too had his doubts about Inigo. But whereas her judgement owed everything to intuition, he was not prepared to go public until such time as he could support the allegation with some kind of proof.

Rossitor walked over to the bookcase, found an old copy of John Masters' *Bhowani Junction*, which was more to his liking than the novel he had been reading, and settled down in one of the armchairs to enjoy it. Some fifteen minutes later he heard the clack of high heels on the parquet flooring in the hall and Sharon called out that she was borrowing the MG Maestro. Then the front door slammed behind her and peace of a kind returned to the house.

Sharon Cartwright was roughly halfway between Naburn and the junction of the B1222 with the A19 south of York when she heard the urgent pap, pap, pap of a horn and saw a blue Ford Transit in her rear-view mirror. The hazard warning lights on the van were also flashing and from the way the driver was gesticulating, she gathered there was something seriously wrong with the Maestro. Responding to the hand signals, she pulled into the grass verge and stopped. As she eased the gear stick into neutral, the transit overtook the Maestro and pulled up in front. All last summer the newspapers had carried stories of road rage, of drivers assaulting one another for no apparent reason, but the young man who alighted from the van and walked towards the Maestro was not the least bit menacing, and Sharon liked the way he smiled at her.

'I think your tank has sprung a leak,' he said when she lowered the window a fraction. 'You're leaving a trail of petrol behind you. Come and see for yourself.'

Sharon released the seat belt, got out of the car and started to follow him. A hinge squeaked behind her and she looked back over her shoulder to see two men leap out of the Ford Transit. In that same instant, the affable young man swung round and drove a fist into her stomach. The pain was agonising, her legs gave way and her vision blurred as the world started to revolve.

One of the men caught Sharon before she hit the ground, carried her over to the Transit and dumped her in the back. While one man forced a ball gag into her mouth, the other lashed both wrists to her ankles, then a drawstring bag enveloped her head, shutting out the light.

CHAPTER 2

Harriet leaned forward until her chest was almost pressing against the steering wheel as she strove to penetrate the darkness beyond the largely ineffective full beams. She didn't like driving at night, particularly when it was snowing heavily and the flakes driven by a headwind were splattering against the windscreen, reducing visibility to less than thirty yards. She had made good time to her parents' house in Ferris Drive opposite Lincoln Cathedral but thereafter everything had gone to pot. She had hoped to be on her way again by 5 p.m. at the latest but she had encountered an unforeseen delay due to her mother, who had asked her a hundred and one questions about Edward as though having a baby in the house were a completely new experience for her.

It had started to snow as she headed west on the A57 out of Lincoln to pick up the Great North Road at Markham Moor. Long before she left the trunk road, it was apparent that she was going to be at least forty-five minutes later than the estimated time of arrival Rossitor had been given. She had tried to call The Firs several times on her Cellnet to give him a revised ETA but had got an unobtainable signal on each occasion. Never one to give up easily, she had asked for an operator-assisted call and had fared no better.

The tyres suddenly lost their purchase and the Vauxhall Cavalier fishtailed to the right; putting the wheel over, Harriet turned into the skid and straightened up. 'Not good, not good at all,' she breathed and eased her foot on the accelerator.

It seemed to her that the visibility was definitely getting worse; furthermore, the snow now appeared to be bouncing the glare from the headlights back into her eyes. She dipped the main beams and for a while was convinced she could see a lot better, but then an oncoming vehicle blared a warning and, realising she had drifted across the centre line, she hastily took avoiding action. Unnerved by the near miss she dropped down another gear into second. Within a matter of yards, the car did yet another shimmy. Too much damned torque, she told herself, move back up into third, take some of the traction off the rear wheels and give the engine just enough revs to keep it from stalling in the higher gear.

Harriet glanced at the odometer, couldn't believe that it had only registered a mere three miles since the last time she had checked it. The instrument couldn't be accurate; it was probably worn out like the wiper blades which tended to scratch the glass. The Vauxhall Cavalier had given Ashton sterling service but it was time he bought himself a new car or a more up-to-date second-hand model.

Given the odometer wasn't functioning properly was it possible that she had overshot The Firs? Hazelwood had said the house was on the outskirts of Naburn but neither he nor Kelso, who had phoned her later to pass on more detailed instructions, had indicated whether The Firs lay east or west of the village. Was the house on the left- or right-hand side of the road? Blowed if she could re-member. There was a river a little way over to her left and Kelso had told her The Firs stood on a two-acre plot, so it had to be on the right.

Out of the corner of her eye, Harriet spotted a gap in the hedge-row and stamped on the footbrake a split second before depressing the clutch. The wheels locked, the engine stalled and the back end slewed round leaving the vehicle broadside on across the road. As she hurriedly cranked the engine into life, it occurred to her that the left rear footbrake had responded before the right, which was one more reason why Ashton should part-exchange the car. Shifting into reverse, Harriet backed up, locking the wheel over to bring the Cavalier back on to the correct side of the road, then she tripped the indicator and went through the gap in the hedgerow.

The Firs was a typical stone-built manor house with a slate root and an imposing front porch. A flat stone four feet below the roofline recorded that it had been completed in 1845 and there was no reason to suppose it wouldn't still look pretty much the same in another hundred and fifty years.

The original sashcord windows had been retained upstairs; downstairs they had been replaced with something more modern and far less pleasing to the eye. Had anyone asked Harriet to describe the building, solid would have been the first adjective which sprang to her mind.

Roy Kelso had The Firs listed as a Grade II house, a classification that denoted its security status as opposed to the building's architectural merit. Burglar alarms were fitted to all the windows and the immediate surrounds were monitored by TV cameras concealed in the eaves. The anti-intruder systems were not however linked to the nearest police station, nor were the grounds patrolled by guard dogs and their handlers as was the case with a Grade I safe house.

Harriet got out of the Vauxhall, crossed the drive and rang the front doorbell. Although the curtains were drawn in the rooms either side of the porch and the lights were obviously on downstairs, nobody came to the door. She stepped back and looked up at the glimmer of light showing in the room above the porch. Feeling distinctly uneasy, she tried the bell again and this time kept her finger on the button long enough to rouse even the heaviest of catnappers. There was nothing wrong with the bell; it wasn't out of order like the telephone. So how could Sharon Cartwright, Larry Rossitor and Harvey Yeo fail to hear its strident summons?

Harriet didn't like the possible explanations which occurred to her. Returning to the car, she picked up the Cellnet phone lying on the front seat and stuffed it into her coat pocket, then opened the glove compartment and took out the small but powerful flashlight which Peter had bought for emergencies. She switched it on only to find that the batteries had run down, leaving her with a flicker of light which barely illuminated the ground at her feet.

'Well done, Peter,' she murmured to herself. 'Just wait until you're back home again.'

She circled the house, looking for signs of a forced entry. There were no footprints but that was hardly surprising; enough snow had fallen in the last two hours to cover any tracks that had been made before six o'clock. Harriet trudged on, her feet sinking ankle-deep and getting colder with every stride. She saw nothing untoward on the west side of the house; round the back it was a very different story. The right-hand side window in the kitchen had been smashed to pieces with such venom that some of the jagged shards were embedded in the far skirting board. Even if the alarm system had been malfunctioning, Harriet couldn't understand how anyone could have failed to hear the noise the intruder must have made. She also noticed that there were still enough jagged splinters left in the windowframe to inflict a nasty gash on anyone who inadvertently brushed against them.

'So watch yourself, my girl,' Harriet said aloud.

She reached inside and raised the latch, did the same with the catch and then opened the window as far as it would go. That done, she took off her coat, folded it in four and used it to sweep the shards of glass from the worktop on to the kitchen floor. The windowsill was about three feet above the ground, which posed no problem for someone who was only half an inch under six feet. Still holding the torch in one hand, she turned sideways, her back to the shattered window, and balancing on the right leg, raised the left and slipped it through to kneel on the coat which she had left on the worktop. At the same time, she hunched her shoulders and ducked her head under the frame. Lifting the right leg through the frame was the trickiest part of all and she almost lost her balance and fell on to the floor.

Harriet stepped down from her precarious perch, retrieved her coat and slipped it on before opening the door into the hall. 'Hello there,' she called out. 'Is anyone at home?'

It was the sort of thing one said automatically, even though it was self-evident that the query would go unanswered. Knowing the lights were on in the rooms at the front, she decided to check them out first. Heart thumping, she walked towards the front door.

The dining room on the left was empty and undisturbed; the study to the right looked as if it had been hit by a bomb. Gus Jukes was lying on the carpet, at least Harriet assumed the blood-spattered corpse with a face that had been smashed in was he – it was too old to be anyone else.

The ferocity of the attack unnerved her and she could feel the bile rising in her throat. Her stomach churning, Harriet backed out of the room.

If Gus Jukes had been brutally murdered, what about the others – Harvey Yeo, Larry Rossitor, Sharon Cartwright and Inigo? She found the light switch for the landing in the hall by the front door and put it on. Kelso had said there were seven bedrooms, one of which had been turned into an interview room after Gus Jukes had moved into the study. The one above the porch served as the control room and should now be manned by whichever duty officer happened to be on the night shift. Taking a deep breath, Harriet threw the door open, uncertain what she would find inside.

There were four 18-inch screens, each one linked to a camera and video recorder. All four monitors were active. On the north-facing screen, Harriet could see the snow-capped Vauxhall Cavalier, and her footprints leading to the porch, then on round to the east side of the house to stop outside the kitchen window. The fourth camera covered the western aspect and showed virgin snow and a wooden outbuilding-cum-garage, both doors of which had been left wide open. The secure speech facility had been disconnected, which explained why she had got an unobtainable signal. From the briefing she had received, Harriet knew the anti-intruder alarm system was controlled by a master switch hidden inside the fitted wardrobe. Even with the lights on, finding it was not easy and she would never have thought to look at the underside of the shelf above the hanging rail without prior knowledge.

Harriet tried the switch. A high-pitched, nerve-grinding warble immediately assaulted her ears, making her flinch, and she hurriedly cut the switch.

Get on with it, she mentally urged herself. You know what has to be done and you can't put it off any longer.

She moved anticlockwise around the landing – number 2 bedroom unoccupied, undisturbed; bathroom; number 3 bedroom – contents of chest of drawers tipped out on to the floor – tights, several bras, underwear. Number 4 bedroom converted to an interview room – table and two upright chairs overturned, smashed carafe of water lying on soddened carpet next to the battered and bloody corpse of Harvey Yeo. Bloodstains on the floor, the wallpaper, and even the ceiling. What in God's name had they beaten him with? An iron bar?

Harriet backed out of the room, took a few moments to compose herself, then carried on with the search. Number 5 bedroom occupied, contents of wardrobe and chest of drawers piled higgledy-piggledy on the divan bed – no sign of the occupant. Number 6 occupied but undisturbed, contents of wardrobe suggested the room had been allocated to the mysterious Inigo. Second bathroom, number 7 bedroom unoccupied and undisturbed. So where the hell were the other three?

There was only one other place in the house where she hadn't looked. Slowly and very reluctantly, Harriet made her way downstairs and went into the drawing room. She had heard it said that there was a limit to the amount of carnage the mind could absorb and that when confronted with a surfeit of it, the horror of it all ceased to register and the beholder became callously indifferent. It was the reason why she could now look at the smashed pumpkin that had once been a face and feel nothing.

Three accounted for, two missing. Harriet walked into the kitchen, opened the back door and trudged over to the wooden outbuilding on the west side of the house. The feeble beam from the flashlight revealed a Range Rover and an H registration Ford Granada. Recent oil stains on the concrete floor led her to suppose there had been a third vehicle. It could be that Sharon Cartwright and Inigo had driven off in the missing car, though she personally doubted it.

Harriet returned to the house, fixed herself a stiff brandy and ginger from the drinks cupboard in the kitchen and carried the tumbler up to the control room. Setting the glass down, she reconnected the secure speech telephone by shoving the bayonet lead into the socket and got a reassuring continuous burr when she held the receiver to her ear. Satisfied that the phone was in working order, she punched out Hazelwood's home number.

'I'm calling from The Firs,' she told him when he answered, 'and all is not well.'

'You want to switch to secure?'

'I don't think I can, Victor. The phone was disconnected.'

The secure speech facility she was holding was the static version of the Mozart Peter had been issued with. It was therefore crypto-protected, which meant that an electronic strip had been passed through the jaws of the cipher input which resembled a small vice. Unlike the early scramblers, the crypto coding on the Mozart was routinely changed every seven days; the one fly in the ointment was that if for any reason the telephone was disconnected from the power source, the crypto input was automatically wiped out.

'What about the current input tape?' Hazelwood asked.

'I don't know what they have done with it. I imagine there is a safe somewhere in the house, but I haven't been given the combination.'

There was a significant pause and she could picture Hazelwood sitting there in his study, a Burma cheroot burning down between the fingers of his left hand, forehead creased in a frown as he weighed the risks of holding an open conversation. No amateur eavesdropper equipped with a scanner could home in on them but even friendly powers snoop on one another. And since Hazelwood's private address was known to a number of Intelligence agencies, it was possible that his house in Hampstead had been targeted.

'All right,' he said presently, 'let's have it in plain language.'

In a few brief sentences, Harriet told him what had happened to the occupants of The Firs – who was dead, who was missing. 'It was an inside job,' she continued. 'Somebody told them where to find the master switch; then the kitchen window was smashed to make us think they had simply broken into the house. I believe they had a key.'

'You keep saying "they".'

'One man on his own couldn't have committed such mayhem, Victor.'

'Are the monitors still running?'

'Yes, but I believe they have been doctored.'

'Would you care to enlarge on that statement?'

'There's a four-hour tape in each video recorder. Three of the cassettes have been running for between eighty-one and eighty-four minutes; the fourth has just eleven minutes remaining. In other words, they wiped out all the pictures relating to the northern, eastern and southern aspects of the house, then reloaded the VCRs and set them running again.'

'Why do you think they did that?' Hazelwood asked.

'I don't know. There's something like two weeks supply of used tapes here. Maybe they decided there were just too many to take away and destroy, so they merely dealt with the three which affected them.'

'I'd like you to view the latter three, Harriet.'

'And then what? Do I phone the police or should I get the hell out of here?' Harriet moved up to the window, drew one of the curtains aside and looked out. 'That is, assuming the roads are still passable.'

'Phone the police: if they ask what you're doing at The Firs, tell them you work for Household Services and were hired by Mr Jukes.'

'Is there such a firm, Victor?'

'Yes, it's in Warwick Lane. The number is 0171-784-5797. Better make a note of it.'

'I already have.'

'Good. Don't let the police shake your story. Rest assured, I'll straighten things out with the appropriate Chief Constable just as soon as I can.'

'Thanks, Victor,' she said drily, but he had already put the phone down. Harriet followed his example, took some time out to drink her brandy and ginger, then viewed the cassettes, using fast forward whenever nothing was happening. As she had anticipated, the videos only showed her arriving at the house and walking round to the back. The on-going time appeared in the top left-hand corner of the picture which could make life pretty difficult for her, unless she did something about it.

William Zenker was one of seven Deputy Undersecretaries of State at the Home Office. To his peers in that select band he was next to God, God himself being the Permanent Undersecretary of State, who at the moment happened to be on leave, skiing at Arosa. As the senior Deputy, Zenker was therefore in charge of the ministry in the absence of his superior. He knew Hazelwood only by reputation as a risk taker who believed in making things happen. Some twenty-five minutes ago Zenker had also discovered that he was a man with the hide of a rhinoceros. He had tried to explain that he and

Diane were hosting a rather important dinner party and Hazelwood had told him bluntly that what they needed to discuss was a problem that couldn't wait until tomorrow.

Diane had been furious when he'd told her that Hazelwood was on his way to their town house in South Audley Street, and had asked their guests to excuse him. In retrospect, he could have put it better because the assembled company had assumed that he wanted them to leave. That they hadn't done so was largely due to Diane, who had persuaded them that this was the very last thing he'd meant or wanted. But the damage had already been done. Although everybody had stayed on for a bit, it wasn't long before Diane's brother-in-law had looked at his wristwatch and said, 'Good Lord, is that really the time?' and had thereby triggered a general exodus.

Diane, of course, had blown a fuse and had stalked off to bed after telling him in no uncertain terms that, thanks to him, her dinner party had been ruined. It had been *her* dinner party as opposed to *theirs* because Diane didn't want him to forget it was her money which paid for their life style and the more-than-comfortable roof over their heads.

And where was the villain of the piece right now? Why, he was somewhere between Willow Walk and South Audley Street. The time he was taking, anybody would think Hampstead was in Outer Mongolia, rather than six to eight miles across town. In the oppressive silence, Zenker heard a car drive slowly past the house and hoped it was Hazelwood looking for a parking space.

Five minutes went by, then ten and still no sign of the bloody man; he walked over to the drinks trolley and poured himself another treble whisky. He'd had several too many already but what the hell did it matter if he got pissed as arseholes? He was going to spend the night in one of the spare rooms, locked out of the conjugal bed by Ms frigid vagina rich bitch Diane.

For someone who fancied herself as the arbiter of good taste, the carillons she had chosen would have offended nine out of ten householders on a council estate. And that wasn't snobbishness on his part; it was simply a fact.

The carillons chimed a second time and were accompanied by a shrill voice upstairs; swallowing the rest of his drink, Zenker left the empty glass on the trolley and lurched out into the hall. 'Hold your horses,' he mumbled, 'I'm coming.'

He'd heard it said that Hazelwood was a big man in more than one sense of the word. If physical appearances were anything to go by, the DG of the SIS was certainly intimidating. While not particularly tall, he was broad-shouldered and looked as if he'd been hewn out of granite.

'Sorry I'm a bit late, William,' he said, shaking hands with a bone-crushing grip, 'but I had to leave the Rover in the Hyde Park underground garage. Couldn't find a space for it round here.'

Without waiting to be invited, Hazelwood stepped inside the hall, shucked off his overcoat and draped it over the hall chair. 'OK if I leave it there?' he asked belatedly.

Zenker wasn't sure whether he had pointed to the drawing room or whether Hazelwood, observing that the first door on the right happened to be half-open, had merely anticipated this. It was the same with his Christian name; he couldn't recall inviting Hazelwood to call him William.

'Is it Bill or William?' Hazelwood asked, as if reading his thoughts.

'It's William,' Zenker told him.

'Good, I'm glad I got that right.' Hazelwood reached inside his jacket and produced a cigar case. 'Mind if I smoke?'

Zenker hesitated. Ordinarily he would have politely stated his objection. If there was one thing Diane couldn't stand it was the smell of stale tobacco smoke, but tonight he felt like getting his own back. 'Please do,' he said and fetched a Spode coffee saucer from the display cupboard for Hazelwood to use as an ashtray.

'I need your help,' Hazelwood told him, drawing on a pungent-smelling cheroot. 'There's been some unpleasantness at one of our safe houses.'

After listening to Hazelwood, Zenker thought unpleasantness was a masterly understatement. Three people had been bludgeoned to death and two were unaccounted for. The incident had been or was about to be reported to the police by a Mrs Peter Ashton.

'Well if that's so,' Zenker said, 'what is it you want from me?'

'That's easy, William. I'd like the police to treat the incident as a normal murder inquiry. I don't want the investigating officers to know that there is an SIS involvement. At least, not at this stage.'

'So?'

'So I'd like you to have a word with the Chief Constable of the North Yorkshire Police.'

'I'm sorry . . . er . . .'

'Victor,' Hazelwood said, 'please call me Victor.'

'Right. Well, Victor, I'm afraid you will have to tell me a great deal more about this dreadful incident than you have done so far.'

'We are missing two people: Sharon Cartwright, who is an SIS officer, and a source whose codename is Inigo.'

Inigo had walked into the British Embassy on the Avenida el Bosque Norte, Santiago, Chile, and asked for political asylum on the grounds that gunmen from one of the drug cartels were stalking him and his life was in great danger. Inigo had let it be known that he had intended to seek the protection of the US Embassy but the hit team had got there ahead of him.

'He told our people in Santiago that he'd believed the information he had would be of more interest to the Americans than us.' Hazelwood smiled fleetingly. 'Personally, I thought he was peddling a load of bullshit.'

'But now you've changed your mind?' Zenker suggested.

'Three dead men is a powerful argument for re-evaluating an asset. Now, could you please have a word with the Chief Constable of North Yorkshire?'

'I don't know his home number.'

'I bet one of the resident clerks at the Home Office can get it for you,' Hazelwood said tartly. 'Or are you telling me yours is a strictly nine-to-five department?'

CHAPTER 3

The first police car, a four-wheel-drive Range Rover, arrived at The Firs approximately seven minutes after Harriet had made a 999 call. The two officers belonged to the York rural subdivision based in Selby and had been patrolling the A19, rendering assistance to drivers whose vehicles had spun off the road in the adverse weather conditions. They had been followed by a night-duty detective sergeant from Selby and a police doctor, who at 21.13 hours had pronounced life extinct on all three victims, purely for the record.

There had been a twenty-minute delay before the scene-of-the-crime officer and his team put in an appearance, marginally ahead of two ambulances from York District Hospital. Meantime, the night-duty sergeant, having first contacted the Detective Chief Inspector in charge of the Criminal Investigation Department of A Division, had taken a statement from Harriet. She had stuck to the story Hazelwood had outlined to her and had not attempted to embroider it. The detective sergeant hadn't asked for any clarification; instead he had made another phone call and had then announced that he was driving her into York in order to see his governor, Detective Chief Inspector Oldfield. He'd also informed Harriet that one of the uniformed officers would be following them in the Vauxhall Cavalier.

Oldfield was in his mid-forties, no taller than five feet eight and was beginning to spread in all the wrong places. His ready smile made him appear slow on the uptake, which actually made him a dangerous adversary. First impressions were frequently wrong but Harriet was sure in this instance her more careful assessment would stand the test of time.

'Sorry to have kept you waiting, Mrs Ashton,' he said without offering an explanation. 'I hope my DS has been looking after you. Can I get you another cup of tea?'

'No, thank you, one's enough for me. What I would like is a room for the night.'

'That's already been arranged; the Dean Court Hotel has been warned to expect you.'

'When?' Harriet asked.

'Well, I do have one or two questions to ask you concerning your statement. But it won't take long.'

I bet, Harriet thought.

'I propose to tape this interview if you've no objections, Mrs Ashton. It will save a lot of time.'

'I'm easy.'

'Good.' Oldfield switched on the recorder, announced the time and identified those present, then said, 'Let's see, your home address is 84 Rylett Close, Chiswick?'

'That's right. '

'And you are employed by Household Services?'

'That's not strictly correct,' Harriet told him. 'It's true I'm on their books but I work for myself. The agency rang me late this morning to ask if I would look after Mr Jukes until they could find a permanent housekeeper and I said yes.'

'Just like that?'

'Why not? My husband is away on business. I think you'll find I told your detective sergeant this.'

Oldfield went through the motions of reading her statement, then looked up. 'Yes, so you did. May I ask what Mr Ashton does for a living?'

'Peter is a consultant, specialising in information technology,' Harriet told him, which she thought wasn't so very far off the mark.

'What did Household Services tell you about Mr Jukes?'

'Not a lot. They said he had multiple sclerosis and his daughter had been rushed to hospital. I gathered the agency knew him quite well and that was good enough for me.'

'It was?' Oldfield said, and raised his eyebrows as if astonished by her lack of curiosity.

'I charge one hundred and twenty-five pounds a day, Chief

Inspector, and I know the agency only deals with reputable clients. Besides, Mr Jukes was an old man. What did I have to fear from him?'

Oldfield looked at her statement again. It was, she thought, a ploy to keep her on tenterhooks.

'What was your reaction when you looked up at the roof and saw those TV cameras?' he asked presently.

'If Mr Jukes could afford to employ a permanent housekeeper, he had to be a wealthy man. I assumed he had been advised to have them installed as a backup to the burglar alarm.'

'Did you happen to notice if the cameras were working?'

'I didn't pay much attention to them. As I told your detective sergeant, when nobody came to the front door, I went round to the back and found the kitchen window smashed and the door ajar.'

'Knowing the house had probably been burglarised, wasn't it a little foolhardy of you to go inside?'

'In retrospect, I realise it was damned stupid of me,' Harriet said with conviction, 'but I didn't stop to think.'

'The lights were on in the hall and both front rooms,' Oldfield said, paraphrasing her statement, 'so naturally they were the first places you looked. Nobody was in the dining room but you found the body of an old man in what, at one time, had been the study. You then ran upstairs. Why did you do that?'

Harriet had already been asked the same question by Oldfield's detective sergeant and gave him exactly the same answer. 'I was horrified, OK? I wanted to get as far away from that ghastly scene as possible and the staircase happened to be in front of me when I started running. Sure, the agency had told me there were three house guests – a young couple and a man nearer Mr Jukes's age, but, believe me, I didn't deliberately go looking for them.'

'Nevertheless, Mrs Ashton, you did look in every room upstairs.'

'Yes, don't ask me why. It was just instinctive.'

'And then you made a 999 call at 20.55 hours.'

'What?'

'Five minutes to nine.'

'If you say so, Chief Inspector. I didn't look at my wristwatch.'

'The operator who took the call said you sounded remarkably calm.'

27

'Did I? Well, I expect a large brandy and ginger had a lot to do with that.'

'You fixed yourself a stiff drink before contacting the Emergency Services!'

Oldfield was being deliberately provocative. It was evident to Harriet that he believed she had lied to his detective sergeant and was doing his best to needle her, in the hope she would let slip some damaging admission.

'I was shaking like a leaf,' she told him coolly, 'I needed a drink to steady my nerves.'

'They smashed all the TV screens upstairs. Why do you suppose they did that, Mrs Ashton?'

Harriet shrugged her shoulders. 'Why ask me? I'm not a policeman.'

'I thought you might use your imagination.'

She already had. The TV cameras had tracked her from the moment she had arrived at The Firs and that record on video had had to be erased. She had removed all four cassettes from the video recorders and had burned them on the Baxi in the kitchen. She had then gone upstairs again armed with the poker and smashed the screens before wrecking the telephone. Finally, she had removed the cipher input attachment from the secure speech facility and, from the front porch, had hurled it into the hedgerow. It was the only thing Harriet could do without leaving telltale footprints in the snow.

'Don't let the police shake your story' was Hazelwood's way of saying that he didn't want the investigating officers to realise there was an SIS connection until he'd had a word with their Chief Constable. And whether or not they had seen one before, the cipher input attachment would certainly have aroused their curiosity.

'I'm still waiting, Mrs Ashton.'

'For what?'

'To hear what you make of it?'

'Well, maybe the burglars got mad when they found there was nothing worth stealing in the house. Maybe they vented their rage on the TV screens as well as the men they killed.'

It was the impression she had aimed to create. To have simply removed the tapes from the videos would have looked too clinical in view of the damage the intruders had done elsewhere in the house.

'It's an interesting theory,' Oldfield said in a noncommittal voice, and looked at her written statement a third time. 'I don't believe you said what time you arrived at The Firs?'

'I've already told you, I didn't look at my wristwatch.'

'Well, was it an hour before you made the 999 call? Or longer than that?'

'I think half an hour would be more like it.'

'Really?' Oldfield suddenly looked incredibly pleased with himself. 'According to my DS, there was over two inches of snow on the roof of your Vauxhall Cavalier. He said the car resembled a wedding cake.'

'Oh, yes,' Harriet said trying to feign indifference.

'Furthermore, your footprints had almost disappeared. We can prove you spent at least ninety minutes going over the house with a fine-tooth comb before you condescended to inform the police.'

'I see. Am I being accused of something?'

'Impeding the police, knowingly withholding information . . .'

Harriet looked at her wristwatch. 'For the record, the time is now 11.28 p.m. and I am informing DCI Oldfield that I wish to be legally represented before we go any further.'

Oldfield reached out and switched off the recorder. His face darkened and he was about to give her a piece of his mind when the detective sergeant from Selby poked his head round the door of the interview room to inform him the Chief Superintendent of A Division would like a word. Five minutes later, Oldfield returned, looking even more tetchy if that were possible.

'I should have guessed you were a spook, Mrs Ashton,' he said acidly.

The last hour or so had been singularly unpleasant and there had been moments when Harriet had wondered how much longer she could continue to stall the police. But it seemed Victor Hazelwood had finally come through for her.

'So what happens now?' she asked.

'You're free to go.'

'No more questions?'

'I've got hundreds,' Oldfield told her, 'but I wouldn't believe anything you told me. So I'm going to save them up for the liaison officer your people in London are sending us.'

Ashton passed through Immigration and followed the directional signs for the baggage claim area. Whenever possible he travelled light, packing a change of underwear, socks, a clean shirt and a washbag in his carry-on baggage. That way he walked straight through Customs and out into the main concourse, which saved a lot of time. But on this particular trip he'd spent five days in Washington and had needed something more than a clean shirt and a toothbrush. However, he'd travelled business class and his bag was among the first to be unloaded; lifting it from the carousel, he walked through the 'Nothing to Declare' lane and on out into the concourse. He wasn't expecting anyone from Vauxhall Cross to meet him, and to see Frank Warren, Head of the Technical Services Vetting Division, waiting by the last crush barrier, was not the greatest start to the morning. The faint smile on his lips did not reassure Ashton. Whether Frank was on an even keel or worried sick, it was always there, like a nervous affliction.

'What's wrong?' he said, assuming the worst. 'Harriet's OK, isn't she?'

'Yes, she's fine . . . it's just that she's not at home right now.'

'You want to tell me what is going on?'

'I will, soon as we are out of here. My Volvo's across the road in the short-stay car park.'

There was no point in arguing with Frank; he'd no intention of enlightening him until they were safely cocooned in the car and heading into London on the M4 motorway. It was the longest five minutes Ashton had known for quite some time. The next ten, when Frank told him where Harriet was now and what she had found at The Firs, were no less disquieting. Eighteen months ago, she had resigned from MI5 after being injured in a riot on the streets of Berlin. The stone which had fractured her skull had also knocked some of the stuffing out of her and Ashton wondered how she had reacted to the unnerving experience of stumbling upon three men who had been bludgeoned to death with baseball bats.

'Whose bright idea was it to send Harriet up there?' he growled.

'Well, technically speaking, I suppose you would have to say it was Roy Kelso's.'

'I might have guessed.'

'I don't like the man either,' Warren said, 'but the suggestion wasn't entirely motivated by spite. It was to be a short-term commitment, terminating this coming Friday and there was nobody else available at short notice. And of course, in the end it was Victor's decision.' Warren cleared his throat. 'He probably felt he had no choice . . .'

That was true, Ashton thought. When they had been hard up, Victor had tried to keep their heads above water by putting Harriet on a retainer of ten thousand a year. He had justified the retainer on the grounds that in the present financial climate where every government department was required to make Draconian cuts, it was cheaper than employing a full-time housekeeper. He had also made it possible for them to buy 84 Rylett Close on favourable terms when the Treasury had ordered the SIS to sell all but a fraction of the housing stock they had acquired during the Cold War. With the Treasury now asking a number of awkward questions concerning both the retainer and the house, Victor would have found himself under considerable pressure had he failed to justify his actions when the opportunity arose.

'I can understand why Victor had to send my wife,' Ashton told him. 'What I don't like is the fact that he told her to lie to the police, which obviously didn't go down well with the local CID.'

'That's being sorted; we've sent one of our officers up to York with instructions to smooth ruffled feathers.'

' Who's the diplomat?'

'Brian Thomas.'

Ex-Detective Chief Superintendent Brian Thomas, formerly of E District, the London Borough of Camden, now one of the Grade III interviewing officers in the Security Vetting and Technical Services Division. Ashton knew him for a real hard-nose who believed in speaking his mind no matter whose toes he trod on. In his heyday with the Met, he was noted for lighting a fire under lower forms of life rather than winning hearts and minds but he would probably go down well with the CID in York.

'Where did you say Harriet was staying?'

'The Dean Court Hotel; she's been advised that Brian Thomas will be dropping round to see her as soon as he arrives in York.'

'Good. I'll phone her from the house.'

'Actually Victor has a job for you—'

'I'm sure he has,' Ashton said, cutting him short, 'but later. OK?'

'I guess so.'

'Then take the exit to Chiswick.'

Hazelwood opened the ornate cigar box on his desk and helped himself to another Burma cheroot on the principle that a good smoke was less damaging to his health than the degree of stress running Ashton caused him from time to time. That the stress was entirely of his own making was something he preferred to ignore.

Ashton had been admitted to the SIS by the back door. When reading German and Russian at Nottingham, he had been a member of the University Officers' Training Corps which had so excited his taste buds that he had joined 23 Special Air Service Regiment in the Territorial Army after being taken on by British Aerospace as a technical author, when he'd graduated with a good Upper Second. Bored to tears by the work he'd been doing, Ashton had volunteered for a nine-month tour of duty with the regular army's Special Patrol Unit in Northern Ireland, a move that had ultimately cost him his job.

The Falklands War had rescued Ashton from a temporary post teaching Russian to mature students at a night school funded by the local authority. Still a part-time soldier with the SAS, he had volunteered for active duty and had travelled south with the task force. As a supernumerary with D Squadron of 22 SAS, he had helped to destroy eleven Pucarà ground attack aircraft on Pebble Island. Had the army been able to find a niche for Ashton, they would have kept him on but there was no permanent officer cadre in the regular SAS. The other 'teeth arms' were also out because contemporaries in age would have had at least five years' seniority over him. Fortunately the then Deputy Director of the Secret

Intelligence Service had listened to Headquarters Special Forces and had agreed to give Ashton a trial.

After attending the induction course which had started on 6 September 1982, Ashton had spent the next two years at Century House learning the ropes. This had been followed by a long stint at Government Communications Headquarters, Cheltenham, and a brief overseas posting to South West Africa where he had been tasked to assess the extent of Soviet military involvement in Angola. When eventually he had been assigned to the Russian Desk in 1988, Hazelwood had inherited a well-rounded Grade II Intelligence officer. Although there had been no better analyst in the whole of the Eastern Bloc Department, it was in the field that he had really come to the fore. In Hazelwood's eyes, Ashton was the ideal cutting edge for the high-risk strategy he wished to pursue.

Hazelwood was aware that while he owed much of his advancement from Assistant Director to Director General to the results Ashton had achieved, the younger man had received fewer rewards. In fact, if anything, Ashton's career had been blighted and there were times when the DG had a guilty conscience about that. He experienced yet another twinge when his PA buzzed the intercom to announce that Ashton was waiting in her office and would he like to see him now?

Normally adept at constraining his feelings, he greeted Ashton with an apology even as he waved him to a chair. 'I want you to know I would never have sent Harriet if I'd known what she would be walking into.'

'It's all right, Victor,' Ashton assured him. 'I've spoken to her and she's OK. No harm has been done.'

'No grudges?'

'Absolutely none.'

Hazelwood wanted to believe that. Harriet had never been one of his admirers; she was convinced he had used her husband to get where he was today. And when he thought about it, he knew he should have stood up for Peter back in '91 when the Director had decided his protégé had got too close to a lieutenant colonel in the GRU for comfort and had shunted him sideways into the Admin

Wing. Maybe Ashton would never have got together with the delectable Ms Harriet Egan had he not been cross-posted to head the Security Vetting and Technical Services Division. But if that had been a plus point to the move, there had also been a very definite minus. Hazelwood believed Ashton blamed him for what had happened to Harriet in Berlin and had left the SIS on her account, rather than the fact that he had sent him into Russia once too often. Because Ashton was too good a man to lose, the DG had kept in touch with his former protégé, employing him on a freelance basis from time to time. He had also gone out on a limb for him, fixing it so that Ashton could be reinstated. It had been the old guilty conscience syndrome at work.

'Frank Warren indicated you had a job for me,' Ashton said quietly.

Hazelwood crushed the Burma cheroot in the cut-down shell case. 'Yes, it has to do with the incident at The Firs. Harriet's convinced it was an inside job and I'm sure she's right. Somebody immobilised the alarm before the intruders entered the house. We know the system was in working order because Harriet tested it and she said the noise was loud enough to wake the dead. The alarm would certainly have roused the whole of Naburn if she hadn't immediately switched it off. Of course, it's possible our people were less than vigilant and forgot to activate the anti-intruder system but I doubt it.'

Ashton nodded. 'I hear there are a couple unaccounted for – a man called Inigo and a Grade III Intelligence officer.'

'Sharon Cartwright.' Hazelwood plucked three files of varying thickness from his pending tray and placed them in front of Ashton. 'Her security file is on top; the other two concern Lawrence Rossitor and Harvey Yeo.'

'I assume you want me to go through them looking for anything which hints at an adverse character trait?'

'You've got it.' Ashton was not only quick on the uptake, he could read Hazelwood's mind like a book.

'Does Roy Kelso know about this? I mean there's a chance I'll want to reinterview some of the referees and superior officers and he may feel I am trespassing on his estate.'

'You leave Roy to me.'

'I intend to,' Ashton told him, then said, 'What do we have on Inigo?'

'Not a lot. There's an initial assessment from Head of Station, Santiago, and the weekly progress reports from Harvey Yeo. Tell Roger Benton I said you were to see the requisite file.'

'Right.' Ashton tugged at the lobe of his right ear. 'When I spoke to Harriet, she told me that one of the videos showed Cartwright driving away from The Firs in an MG Maestro . . .'

'The licence number is K299 LYZ,' Hazelwood said, anticipating his next question. 'Rossitor hired it from the Hertz agency in Willsden the day before he left for The Firs. The North Yorkshire Police have been informed. Any other questions?'

'I can't think of any offhand.'

'How did you make out in Washington?'

'Everybody was very friendly,' Ashton told him. 'The CIA's Director of Operations liked our ideas on joint targeting and economy of Intelligence resources. The agency is still pretty much focused on Russia; they reckon the communists are making a comeback and Yeltsin's on the way out. The Chechens worry them sick; their worst nightmare is a nuclear civil war. They gave me a lot of data to support this doomsday projection.'

'How do you rate the material?'

'Could be a work of fiction for all I know.' Ashton picked up the security files and started towards the door. 'Every source has been obliterated. Anyway, I turned the stuff over to Head of Station for onward dispatch in the diplomatic bag.'

'Fine. I'll await your assessment with interest.'

'I'm sorry?'

'Of the security files.' Hazelwood paused, then added, 'By close of play this afternoon.'

The police constable walked on past the Theatre Royal, then crossed the road just before Bootham Bar to check out the car park fronting the Art Gallery. The MG Maestro, licence number K299 LYZ, which he had been told to look out for was in the front rank, farthest away from the road. On closer inspection, the constable discovered that at 4.32 yesterday afternoon, a zealous traffic warden had taped a parking ticket to the windscreen.

CHAPTER 4

Every security file could be likened to a combination of a potted biography, a shooting script for *This is Your Life* and an ongoing obituary. The fattest one belonged to Harvey Yeo, the thinnest to Sharon Cartwright, the prime suspect. A Lancashire girl born at Southport, Sharon was twenty-four, had read Spanish and Italian at Somerville College and had applied to join the Diplomatic. Perhaps it was because she had been called back for a viva before being awarded a First that the selection board had decided she wasn't quite up to the standard the Foreign Office was looking for and had steered her towards the Secret Intelligence Service,

Sharon Cartwright had been positively vetted before attending the induction course run by the training school at Amberley Lodge from 7 September to 11 December 1992. Thereafter, she had spent the next two years learning the ropes, first at Century House and then at Vauxhall Cross when the SIS had moved house. A little over two months ago she had been assigned to the South American desk in the Pacific Basin and the Rest of the World Department. A security status which afforded constant access to Top Secret material was subject to quinquennial review. Sharon Cartwright's initial clearance was therefore still good for another thirty-three months.

It was a slim and very mundane document. As head girl at one of the few surviving grammar schools, Sharon had been considered a shining example to her peers as well as the younger element at William Wordsworth. At least that was how the headmistress had seen her. Sharon had made an equally favourable impression with her tutors at Somerville. Ashton ignored what the referees had had to say about her because she had nominated them and they were unlikely to rubbish her. On the other hand, mature, practical, no financial problems, extremely bright, good sense of humour, loyal to the nth degree, enjoys a drink now and again but never to excess, were but a few of the eulogies she had received from her superiors in the SIS. In Ashton's opinion, Sharon Cartwright was just too good to be true.

Harvey Yeo was the most interesting character of the three Intelligence officers. Aged fifty-seven at the time of his death, he had married a widow of independent means in 1988. Except at weekends, the couple had led separate lives. From Monday to Friday, Yeo stayed at the bungalow in Ruislip which he had inherited from his parents; Saturdays and Sundays were spent at his wife's place in Codford St Mary, a small village between Salisbury and Warminster.

Like Ashton, Yeo had entered the SIS via the back door, but in different circumstances in that, at the time, he'd been employed by Shell as a production supervisor at their Punta Cardon refinery in Venezuela. Between 1965, when he had been taken on officially, and 1984, when he had returned to the UK for good, Yeo had completed no less than five tours in Latin America, two of them back to back. He had been the resident SIS man in Bolivia, Uruguay, Peru twice, and Belize, where he had established a network of agents in neighbouring Guatemala to give early warning of an impending attack on the former Crown Colony. That had been his finest hour though his timely warning, while acting Head of Station in Montevideo, that the Argentines were preparing to invade the Falklands, had run it a close second.

For the past eleven years, Yeo had run the South American desk with no hope of advancement beyond Grade I Intelligence officer. There was nothing in his file to indicate whether he harboured any feelings of bitterness about this.

Lawrence Rossitor was a Grade II analyst, specialising in counter-intelligence. Before joining the Pacific Basin and Rest of the World Department, he had spent six years in what was now called the European Department, which had included a foreshortened tour with the British Embassy in Bonn. Born in Edinburgh on 30 May 1962, he had married the girl he'd met at Glasgow University six months after completing the induction course. He had fathered two sons in quick succession and within five years he had been sued for divorce on the grounds of an irretrievable breakdown of the marriage. The family house in Sidcup had been sold, his ex-wife had returned to Glasgow with the children to live in a rented apartment near her parents, and he had moved into a grim flat with a shared bathroom in Kennington. He was short of money and was finding it hard to make ends meet.

Of the three Intelligence officers, Rossitor was the only one who was vulnerable. Show a wad of money to a man who was steadily going broke, convince him nobody would ever know about the bribe, and if he were desperate enough, there was a chance he might be tempted to accept it. A single moment of weakness that in the end had cost Rossitor his life? Ashton couldn't swallow it; lifting the receiver, he called Roger Benton and asked if he could spare him a few minutes.

When promoted to Assistant Director, Roger Benton only had the Pacific Basin to worry about. In the wake of the first cost-cutting exercise occasioned by the end of the Cold War, he had also acquired the Rest of the World, a development which had not filled him with joy. He was not an ambitious man and had no desire to hold down a high-profile appointment. In fact, Benton wanted nothing more than to soldier on until he reached the compulsory retirement age of sixty. Unfortunately, even today there were still fourteen years to go and he now presided over a very large and distinctly untidy organisation, which like an active volcano, could suddenly erupt with little or no forewarning.

Benton thanked God the Falklands War had occurred when the Rest of the World had existed as a separate department. His worst nightmare was the fear that something very similar might occur in his fiefdom before he retired. In view of what had happened the last time their paths crossed, he regarded Ashton as the living embodiment of the Four Horsemen of the Apocalypse.

'Second time today,' he said with a nervous laugh. 'I am honoured. What can I do for you on this occasion, Peter?' A hopeful expression made a brief appearance. 'Or have you just dropped by to return the Inigo file?'

'Afraid not,' Ashton said cheerfully. 'I'd like to hang on to it for a bit longer.'

'Be my guest,' Benton told him with a bonhomie that sounded contrived.

'Harvey Yeo was in charge of the South American Desk. Correct?'

'I thought everyone knew that, Peter.'

'Maybe, but not too many people are aware that you reckon Inigo is a complete waste of time and money.'

'I may not have shouted my opinion from the rooftops but I certainly mentioned my reservations to Victor Hazelwood and you can't go higher than the Director General.'

'If you had such a low opinion of Inigo, why did you fall in with Yeo's suggestion that he should debrief him in depth?'

'Because he practically went down on his knees and begged me. I got the impression that Harvey believed Inigo represented his last chance to make a name for himself and leave The Firm in a blaze of glory.' A faint, supercilious smile touched the corners of Benton's mouth. 'I agreed to his request because he had a very able deputy and I was sure he wouldn't be missed.'

'And Larry Rossitor – what was his role?'

'He was cast as the professional sceptic.'

'Really? Well, I haven't seen any evidence in the weekly reports Harvey Yeo submitted that Rossitor was doing the job you gave him.'

'We used a separate channel of communication.'

'Like what?' Ashton said in a corrosive voice.

'He would phone me before a copy of the latest debrief appeared in my in-tray.'

'Sharon Cartwright,' Ashton said abruptly, 'what about her? The girl must have been with your department for all of three weeks when she was sent up to The Firs. Whose bright idea was it to include her instead of somebody with more experience?'

'Harvey Yeo's. He wanted Sharon on the team because her Spanish is excellent and he thought she could learn a great deal about techniques of interrogation from him.'

'Did they have something going between them?'

'What, Harvey and Sharon?' Benton chortled. 'Do me a favour, Peter,' he spluttered. 'Harvey was old enough to be her father and what could she possibly have seen in him? Besides, I've never encountered anyone with a more dormant libido.'

'How about Larry Rossitor? What's he been up to since his wife left him?'

'Living like a monk, it was all he could afford to do. I thought a stint at The Firs would enable him to save a bit on the old household expenses. At least he didn't have to pay for his food up there.'

Ashton made no comment. What concerned him was how the three Intelligence officers had organised themselves and functioned as a team when Rossitor couldn't speak a word of Spanish.

'That was never a problem,' Benton assured him and launched into a lengthy explanation.

From what he said, Ashton gathered that each session with Inigo had been recorded and subsequently transcribed on a word processor by Sharon Cartwright. Two draft copies had then been run off: one had gone to Harvey Yeo, who needed to satisfy himself that Sharon had translated the interrogation correctly, while the other had been passed to Rossitor for him to peruse and dissect. Before submitting his comments to London, Rossitor had discussed them with the older man.

'I bet that made for a friendly atmosphere,' Ashton observed laconically.

'You're wrong, Peter, they didn't quarrel. Harvey was very laid back and I can't remember a time when he lost his temper. In his own mind he knew he was right and if you disagreed with him, that was your problem, not his. However, in this case, Harvey was slowly coming round to my view.'

'Pity it wasn't unanimous.'

'What?'

'Think about it, Roger. Three people are dead, Inigo and Sharon are missing; somebody must have thought your bum source was too damned valuable to be left in our hands.'

'I suppose there's no chance it could have been a burglary that went horribly wrong?' Benton said hopefully, then shook his head. 'We should be so lucky.'

'Somebody let the intruders into the house.'

'Well, it wasn't one of my people; I'd stake my reputation on it.'

'You don't know them well enough to be sure of that,' Ashton told him.

'I've had enough of your innuendoes,' Benton said, wagging a finger at him. 'You come into my office inferring I take little or no interest in my subordinates—'

'I inferred nothing of the kind.' Ashton stood up and moved towards the door. 'Believe me, I am not criticising you, Roger. Your knowledge of Cartwright, Rossitor and Yeo is founded on what you see of them during normal office hours and what they voluntarily tell you about their private lives. The same applies to every other assistant director.'

'I don't care what you say,' Benton told him in a loud voice as he left his office. 'I know them all like the back of my hand.'

Ashton walked past the bank of lifts and used the staircase to reach his office on the floor below because it was quicker than pressing the call button and then waiting for a car to arrive. As he unlocked his door and walked into the room, the telephone uttered a plaintive summons; answering it, he found he had ex-Detective Chief Superintendent Brian Thomas on the line.

'Thank God,' Thomas said with feeling. 'You don't know how many times I've rung your number.'

'Well, now your prayers have been answered.'

'And maybe yours too. The Maestro which Sharon took has been found in a car park near the centre of York.'

'That's interesting.'

'It gets better. A traffic warden slapped a parking ticket on the vehicle at 4.32 after the meter had run out. He told the police he'd seen the Maestro arrive shortly after half-two and get this, the driver was a man in his early twenties.'

Ashton didn't like it. One of the TV cameras at The Firs had caught Sharon Cartwright driving off in the MG Maestro shortly after two o'clock. In the following twenty minutes or so, the vehicle had changed hands between Naburn and York. 'Any word on Sharon?' he asked.

'Not a cheep. However, she left her Cellnet in one of the bedrooms. Thanks to British Telecom, we have a list of the regional and national calls which she made. There was one London number Sharon rang a dozen times while she was up here. 0181-636-3911. Sound familiar to you?'

'Yes, it does.'

'Thought it might.' Thomas cleared his throat, then said, 'The interesting thing is that all the calls were made between 18.32 and 19.24 hours.'

'When you might expect the subscriber to be at home,' Ashton said thoughtfully.

'That would be my interpretation,' Thomas agreed.

'Got anything else for me?'

'No, I'll be in touch soon as I have.'

'Right. Do you have any idea where Harriet is now?'

'On her way home to you. She reckoned to be at her parents' house in Lincoln by three and leave within the hour.'

Ashton thanked him and put the phone down, then went over to the safe and took out a small hardcover notebook which listed the home numbers of key personnel. The name of the subscriber on 0181-636-3911 was Jill Sheridan, Assistant Director in charge of the Middle East Department.

There was, Ashton thought, no one quite like Jill Sheridan. Completely ruthless, selfish and ambitious, she always had an eye to the main chance. He no longer harboured any feelings of bitterness towards her but it was a fact that a little over six years ago, they had been engaged, and she had put their marriage on hold when the opportunity to run Intelligence operations in the United Arab Emirates had arisen.

At the time, Ashton had been naïve enough to believe she only intended to postpone the wedding day. He had also persuaded himself that Jill was not being unreasonable in wanting to realise the full potential of her language qualifications. Her father had been an executive with the Qatar General Petroleum Corporation and she had spent most of her childhood and adolescence in the Persian Gulf. Arabic had been her second tongue. Persian or Farsi was an additional language she had acquired at the School of Oriental and African Studies.

But the great career move had seemingly foundered twenty-one months later on the rock of male prejudice. In Arabia, it was a man's world and a woman was definitely a second-class citizen. Unable to do her job property, Jill had asked for a transfer and had been posted back to London to run the Persian Desk. As a result, her peers had wrongly concluded that she was no longer in the fast lane and would be passed over for promotion.

Jill Sheridan was however a born survivor and Hazelwood's predecessor had seen her in a very different light. To the astonishment of the top table, she had been given the Mid East Department when the slot had become vacant and had thereby become the youngest assistant director in the SIS. If that wasn't enough, she had rapidly dropped the man to whom she had not long been married, when his past had begun to catch up with him and her own security status had been under threat as a result.

Ashton returned the notebook to the safe, closed the locking bars and spun the combination dial. Normally, he tried to give Roy Kelso a wide berth. In addition to his snide and thoroughly unpleasant manner, the head of the Admin Wing was conscious of being the longest serving assistant director and expected to be treated with the deference usually accorded to the Director General. But only Kelso could supply him with the information he needed and beggars couldn't be choosers.

'You want Sharon Cartwright's address in London?' Kelso said, and folded his arms. 'May one enquire why?'

'She was phoning Jill Sheridan at least three times a week from Naburn.'

'Was she indeed?'

'So what do you make of it, Roy?'

'I think it strange that Jill Sheridan should be on such friendly terms with a very junior officer.'

From his tone of voice, it was evident to Ashton that Kelso suspected the two women were involved in a lesbian relationship. A lingering doubt that maybe he was doing him an injustice was dispelled when Kelso announced that he intended to ask the Security Vetting and Technical Services Division to look into the matter.

'I don't think Victor would like that,' Ashton told him.

'What the hell . . . ?'

'Think about it, Roy. Sharon Cartwright works for Roger Benton and Inigo is his source. Now, why should Jill Sheridan bother with one of the desk officers in the Pacific Basin and the Rest of the

World Department? That's the real question we should be asking ourselves at this stage.'

'You may have a point.' Kelso pursed his lips. 'If memory serves me right, Sharon Cartwright has a flat in Highgate not far from the tube station.'

'Do you think we could be a little more precise, Roy?'

Kelso buzzed his PA on the intercom and asked her to find out. In less than a minute, she came back with the answer that Sharon Cartwright occupied the penthouse flat at 288 Priory Way.

There was just one thing more Ashton needed. Before leaving Vauxhall Cross, he stopped by Technical Services and signed for a bunch of skeleton keys.

The stride was purposeful, the click clack of heels unmistakable. Hazelwood knew who the footsteps belonged to and wasn't surprised when Jill Sheridan tapped on his door and asked it he could spare her a few minutes of his time. It was, he thought, typical that she should close the door behind her and draw up a chair before he barely had time to nod. As usual, she looked immaculate. Today, she was wearing a green button-through thigh-length tunic, with black piping around the collar and cuffs. As usual, it didn't seem to bother her that an already short matching skirt became even shorter when she crossed her legs.

'I believe there is something you should know about Sharon Cartwright,' Jill told him. 'To put it bluntly, she has been making a nuisance of herself. I think she must have phoned me at least a dozen times from The Firs.'

Hazelwood took a Burma cheroot from the ornate cigar box on his desk.

'For what reason?' he asked.

'Ostensibly because she wanted to know if there had been any letters for her.'

'Am I missing something, Jill? I mean, how could you possibly be expected to know that?'

'I have a key to her flat in Priory Way.' Jill smiled. 'No need to look so alarmed, Victor, there is a perfectly innocent explanation. I got to know Sharon when she was attached to my department for six months as part of her initial training. I didn't see so much of her after she joined Roger Benton but we used to bump into one another at the local supermarket. And, of course, I invited her to dinner a couple of times.'

'You make it sound like a good deed,' Hazelwood told her.

'I never thought of it like that but I suppose it was in a way. Sharon Cartwright is a very introspective young woman; she doesn't make friends easily and I felt sorry for her. Anyway, I played matchmaker and introduced her to a couple of eligible bachelors but nothing came of my efforts.'

'One thing you haven't told me, Jill, is why she gave you the keys to her flat.'

The answer was, Jill told him, very simple. Sharon had been a last-minute choice to make up the interrogation team and had received less than two hours' notice. She had rushed back to Highgate, packed a suitcase and then returned to Vauxhall Cross. Had she been alerted earlier on, Sharon would have undoubtedly arranged for her mail to be held at the post office until further notice.

'She asked me if I would do her an enormous favour,' Jill continued.

'And you said, name it.'

'Something like that, Victor. Sharon's flat in Priory Way is not very far off my route, and stopping by to pick up her letters on alternate days was no great chore.'

Hazelwood struck a match and lit the cheroot. 'Now tell me the real reason why she kept pestering you.'

'Sharon wants a transfer to the Mid East Department. Claims she is not getting job satisfaction in her present appointment, says the work is deadly dull.'

'What possible use could she be to you when Spanish is her first language?'

'Don't think I didn't point that out to her when she first raised the subject.'

'When was that?'

'Almost nine weeks ago.'

'And you didn't mention the fact she was unhappy to Roger?'

'And ruin her career? You know what Roger is like: he expects complete loyalty from his subordinates. Can you imagine the sort of confidential report he would give Sharon if he learned she had gone behind his back and asked for a transfer?'

'So why are you telling me now, Jill?'

'Because you informed us this morning that the girl is missing. Because sooner or later, British Telecom will produce a list of the phone numbers Sharon has called. Because I thought it would save a lot of time and energy if you were aware of the situation.'

'Well, thank you for being so frank with me,' Hazelwood said drily.

When it came to covering one's back, he thought Jill Sheridan was in a class of her own.

Beyond the confines of the inner city, London was a collection of small villages which had been sucked into the maw of the capital with the population explosion in the late nineteenth century. Highgate was one such example, though Priory Way, near the foot of the hill, only dated back to the early 1900s. Like all the other houses in the road, number 288 was a three-storey, semidetached. Built in the days when few people owned a motorcar, it lacked a garage. Some of the more enterprising landlords and owner-occupiers had solved the parking problem by concreting the front garden. The house where Sharon Cartwright lived had no such facility. The privet hedge either side of the front gate looked as if it hadn't been trimmed in years and, although the snow hadn't entirely thawed, Ashton could see that the flower bed in the centre of the tiny lawn was mostly weed. The path was so uneven that, here and there, tufts of grass had taken root in the cracked tiles. Between the solid-looking door and the stained glass window to the right of it, there were three call buttons mounted on a plywood panel. Sharon Cartwright, he noted, headed the list of tenants.

There was no need to use the set of skeleton keys to gain admittance. The last person to enter the house had failed to close the door properly and it swung back noiselessly when Ashton placed a hand on the mortice lock. He stepped into a narrow hall, the staircase to the floors above directly to his front. From somewhere in the ground-floor flat, rap music was coming through loud and clear on a radio, CD or ghetto blaster. He wondered what the hell a young, middle-class, gainfully employed girl like Sharon Cartwright was doing in such a place. The rap was a good deal less intrusive on the first landing; by the time he reached the so-called penthouse flat, it was no more than a minor irritant.

Ashton took out the bunch of keys he'd signed for, went through the masters tagged for Yale locks and opened the door at the third attempt. Aided by the light on the landing, he found the switch inside the hall and put it on. He closed one door behind him, then opened the door to his front and walked into trouble the moment he stepped into the living room. The fist came out of nowhere and crunched into the right side of his jaw. Before he could recover, the assailant pinioned his arms so that a second intruder could use him as a punch bag. It was all over in a matter of seconds: two short arm jabs to the stomach, two more to the head and a knee into the groin lelt him unconscious on the floor.

CHAPTER 5

Everything ached – his groin, stomach, jaw and cheekbone. He could only breathe freely through his mouth and his vision wasn't too good either. It was some moments before it dawned on Ashton that the room was in darkness and there was nothing wrong with his eyesight. He was lying on his left side in the recovery position, his head pointing towards the hall. Getting his bearings was easy enough, getting to his feet was a lot more difficult, and he had to roll over on to his hands and knees before he finally managed to stand upright.

Like a blind man feeling his way in unfamiliar surroundings, he groped for the nearest light switch. Common sense told him it ought to be close by the door, but the builder who had converted 288 Priory Way, had had other ideas. Unable to locate the light switch, he went out into the hall and put on the one by the front door. With that light in the background to guide him, he had no difficulty in finding the switch in the living room.

What at one time must have been a very large bedroom had been converted into a living room with a dining alcove at the far end, which had just enough space to accommodate an oval table, four ladder-back chairs and a cheap-looking sideboard. The lounge area was furnished with a two-seater couch and two easy chairs arranged in an open-sided square, facing the gas fire. There was also a combined bookcase and drop-leaf desk which the burglars had taken apart, scattering the contents of the pigeon holes over the floor. They had done the same thing with the sideboard, removing the centre drawer and upending it on to the fitted carpet.

The kitchen next to the dining alcove had been left untouched, which was more than could be said for the bedroom. The drawers in the dressing table had been tipped out on to the divan bed to join the pile of clothes taken from the wardrobe and tallboy. If it were possible to judge a person's character by the clothes they wore, Sharon Cartwright was something of a split personality. Among the smart business suits, Country Casuals pick-and-mix, tailored slacks, sweaters, blouses, skirts and court shoes, there was a pair of leather trousers, as smooth as black satin, and a deep red blouse with a plunging neckline that would not have looked out of place in a sex shop. There was also a broad leather belt with a steel buckle and attachments, plus a pair of sandals with four-inch heels.

Ashton went on through to the en suite bathroom and confronted the image in the mirror. His nose was swollen and had bled from the right nostril, staining his shirt front and trenchcoat. The left cheekbone was puffed, the eye already closing, and there was the beginning of a lump on the opposing jaw.

He picked up the face flannel draped over the bath, wetted it under the tap and wiped the blood from his chin, shirt front and trenchcoat. There was only a partially used tube of TCP ointment and a tin of Band-Aids in the medicine cabinet above the washbasin. Remembering what Harriet used when she cleansed her face with cream, he went next door and found a bag of cotton wool balls among the jumble on the bed. Breaking off a piece, he plugged the injured nostril, then returned to the living room, switching off the lights as he went.

Ashton started towards the front door, heard the slight grating sound of a key going into the lock and just had time to plunge the hall into darkness, before the newcomer entered the flat. A slim hand groped for the light switch and he could smell the scent she had dabbed behind her ears.

'Good evening, Sharon,' he said, and grabbed the wrist, then, twisting the arm behind her back, he kicked the door shut and simultaneously put the light on with his free hand. Jill Sheridan gave a strangled gasp and cried out in fear.

'Jill?' Ashton said in a bewildered voice. 'What on earth are you doing here?'

She jerked her hand free, turned about and leaned against the wall, breathing heavily, the colour gone from her face. 'Jesus, Peter, you frightened the life out of me.'

'I'm sorry.'

'So you should be.' Jill stared at him. 'My God, what happened to you?'

'There were a couple of intruders on the premises. They didn't like being disturbed.'

'Let's go inside and see if I can't clean you up a little.'

'I already have.'

'You could fool me.'

'Anyway, I'm not hurting.'

'Still the same old Peter, ever the stoic.' Jill Sheridan walked on past him into the living room and put the light on. 'Well, they certainly did this place over,' she observed calmly.

'A simple burglary, is that how you see it?'

'Don't you? Take a good look round and then tell me where the TV and video are?'

'You sound as if you know this flat intimately?'

'I've been here a few times,' Jill said, then added, 'to collect Sharon's mail.'

'How obliging of you.'

'If you are thinking what I think you are, you'd better talk to Victor, he knows all about the arrangement.'

'Since when?'

'Since late this afternoon.' She gazed at the letters and the papers on the floor by the drop-leaf desk. 'Is the rest of the flat like this?'

'There was no break-in,' Ashton told her. 'They didn't have to force an entry.'

'How did you get in?'

'I borrowed a set of skeleton keys.'

'No doubt they were similarly equipped. Criminals are getting very sophisticated these days.'

'There's a definite connection between what happened up at Naburn and this fake burglary. It's silly to pretend otherwise.'

'Have you lost anything, Peter?'

Ashton patted his jacket. 'The bastards have taken my damned wallet.'

'Well, there you are. It was a simple burglary and you got

51

mugged. Let's get out of here. We'll go to my place, I'll patch you up and then run you home.'

'There's no need, I've got a season ticket for the Underground.'

'Have you had a good look at yourself in the mirror? Get on the train with a battered face like yours and people will treat you like a leper.'

'Harriet should be home by now.'

'And you don't want her to get the wrong idea if she should happen to see us together?' Jill said, mocking him. 'Don't tell me Harriet doesn't trust you.'

'I thought you wanted out of here.'

'Are you coming with me?'

'It seems I don't have much choice. I've just discovered they took my season ticket while they were at it.'

'It's an ill wind,' Jill said archly.

The tenant on the ground floor was still into rap and could have been playing the same track for all Ashton knew. Nobody saw them leave the house and they didn't encounter anybody on the street as they walked down the hill to where Jill had been obliged to leave her car.

Considering she had only been married for eighteen months, Ashton thought Jill had done pretty well out of her ex. She had kept the four-bedroom house overlooking Waterlow Park at the top of Highgate Hill, which must have set her husband back all of four hundred thousand. That must have hurt good old Henry even if he was rolling in money. But the bitterest blow would have been the loss of his pride and joy, the top-of-the-range Porsche 928 GTS. This had been included in the settlement because, as Jill pointed out to the Intelligence officer from Security Vetting who'd interviewed her after the divorce, she wasn't claiming maintenance.

Although there was an awful lot of power under the bonnet, Jill Sheridan wasn't intimidated by the 5.4 litre engine. The Porsche was facing the wrong way but despite the fact there were vehicles parked on both sides of the road, she executed a three-point turn at speed. Into second, foot down, up into third; she handled the manual gearbox with all the dexterity and decisiveness of a grand prix driver.

'I'm impressed,' Ashton told her.

Jill deliberately chose to misunderstand him and glanced pointedly at her lap. She had undone the bottom two buttons of her coat to give herself freedom of movement and the hip-length tunic underneath was halfway up her thighs.

'Why so excited, Peter? You've seen my legs before.'

Ashton let it ride. He'd learned from experience to look for an ulterior motive in everything Jill did or said and he knew damned well she wasn't being skittish because she fancied him. At the intersection with Archway Road, she made a left turn, then worked her way across to Highgate High Street and into Bisham Gardens.

The house overlooking the park was in darkness. As they walked down the front path a sensor triggered a powerful security light. Shielding his eyes against the glare, Ashton looked up at the roofline and saw the property was protected by a Sentinel burglar alarm.

'I don't believe in leaving anything to chance,' Jill said, as if reading his thoughts.

But no place was impregnable against a determined burglar, and whoever had broken into the house had known how to neutralise the alarm soon after effecting an entry through the French windows at the back. Leaving Jill to contemplate the mess, Ashton checked out the rooms upstairs. The likelihood that the intruders were still in the house was extremely remote, but he wasn't about to take anything on trust. It was only when he returned to the drawing room that he noticed one of the burglars had had the foresight to bring an electric drill with him and had opened up the wall safe behind the Palmer landscape.

'What did you keep in there, Jill?'

'A string of pearls, a diamond and sapphire ring, a few brooches – nothing over two thousand pounds.' Her eyes narrowed angrily. 'The alarm is wailing away like a banshee and what happens? Nothing – suddenly all the residents have gone stone deaf. So much for Neighbourhood Watch!'

'What's the time delay between you opening the front door and the alarm going off?'

'Twenty seconds – but I know where the control unit is hidden.'

'And nobody else does? No one has seen you switch the system off? A friend you'd invited for dinner? Like Sharon Cartwright, for instance?'

'I should have guessed you would eventually drag her name into it. You see a connection where there is only a coincidence. Break-ins are practically an everyday occurrence in this area where there are rich pickings to be had.'

'So I assume you are going to report this latest burglary to the police?'

'Soon as you leave,' Jill assured him. 'I'd rather they didn't see you. One look at your battered face and we'd never hear the last of their questions.'

'Can you lend me the money for the train fare?'

'I think I can do better than that.' Jill opened her handbag, took out a small, red leather purse and gave him twenty pounds. 'Get a taxi; better still there's a minicab office at the bottom of Archway.'

'Thanks.'

'Your face!' Jill snapped her fingers. 'Wait here a minute. Henry left a pair of sunglasses behind when he moved out.'

Ashton pointed out that in the middle of winter he was going to look a mite obvious in dark glasses and Jill told him he would excite even more curiosity without them. They were both right. With or without the Polaroids, people gave him a wide berth, including the dispatcher at the minicab office who claimed every vehicle was booked solid for the next two hours. In the end, Ashton took the long way home, Northern Line to the Embankment, then the District to Ravenscourt Park. Instead of the stiff drink and touching concern which he had envisaged, Harriet wanted to know why he hadn't phoned to let her know where he was.

Morning prayers were attended by Heads of Departments and started promptly at 8.30 under the chairmanship of the Director General. As the officer responsible for Operations and General Duties, Ashton was two rungs down the promotion ladder from an assistant director. His presence was therefore not required at the daily meeting which was just as well, because it had already broken up by the time he arrived at Vauxhall Cross. He was late into the office for a number of reasons: having decided to drive in to work, he had been inordinately delayed by roadworks. He could also point to the fact the traffic in the vicinity of Westminster Bridge and Parliament Square had been gridlocked for the better part of twenty minutes. But in truth, he had left Rylett Close much later than usual and that was entirely down to Harriet.

Last night's cold snap had thawed by the early hours of the morning with Harriet making the first move, snuggling up to him as the first grey streak of daylight appeared through a chink in the curtains. When the alarm had rung, she had leaned across him and shut it off. 'Be a laggard for once in your life,' she had whispered, and had continued to fondle him. And nine-month-old Edward, who usually demanded to be fed at crack of dawn, had co-operated by sleeping on until a quarter to eight.

Ashton was still basking in the afterglow of Harriet when he walked into the office. Then the phone rang and Victor's PA informed him that his presence was required soonest and he came back to earth with a bump. Hazelwood was on his first cheroot of the morning but the mellowing effect this usually had on him was missing.

'What was the last thing I said to you yesterday afternoon?' he demanded; then added, 'Didn't I tell you I wanted to hear your assessment of the security files pertaining to Yeo, Rossitor and Cartwright by close of play?'

'Yes.'

'So why did you ignore my instructions?'

'I had an interesting phone call from Brian Thomas which I believed offered a much more promising line of inquiry.'

'You should have kept me informed.'

'I'm sorry, Victor. It won't happen again.'

'I should hope not, I don't like getting my information second-hand at morning prayers, especially from someone like Jill Sheridan.'

'She told you about the two burglaries?'

'And what happened to you.' Hazelwood aimed his cheroot at the cut-down shell case on his desk and flicked it, spilling most of the ash on to the blotter. 'I must say you're not looking exactly on top of the world.'

It was something of an understatement. Ashton had a lump on

his jaw, his nose was swollen and one cheekbone was the colour of an overripe banana.

'I'll survive, Victor.'

'You'd be of no use to me if you didn't.'

'Thanks.'

'I know what Jill would have me believe. Now I'd like to hear what you make of the two burglaries.'

'They didn't break into Sharon Cartwright's flat, I believe they had the key to the front door. She might have given it to them voluntarily but I have a nasty feeling they made her hand it over. I think they did Jill's house in daylight because an alarm going off in the middle of the afternoon might not be taken quite so seriously by the neighbours, especially as the security system hasn't been up and running for long. It's quite evident they knew where the control unit for the burglar alarm was located and it's odds on they got that information from Sharon. Same goes for the master switch governing the anti-intruder system at The Firs.'

'Harriet reckoned it was an inside job,' Hazelwood said reflectively. 'But Sharon Cartwright? Did you find anything in her security file which might have caused us some concern if we had looked at the reports with a harder eye?'

Ashton shook his head. 'She came across as pure as driven snow. No character defects whatever. She was very open with the Intelligence officer who interviewed her, admitted to getting drunk once when up at Oxford. This was at the same party where she was introduced to pot. Having sampled both vices, she decided enough was enough.'

'What about personal relationships?' Hazelwood asked.

'Sharon is not inexperienced,' Ashton told him. 'She first had sex while in the fifth form at William Wordsworth Grammar. According to Sharon this was shortly after her sixteenth birthday, which is not quite the image the Head conveyed. At university, she had a steady boyfriend. He was at Queen's College reading law and there was some talk of their getting married but in the end they went their separate ways. When interviewed in connection with her security clearance, she was dating two men: one was a merchant banker with Kleinwort Benson, the other was a commodity broker. Nothing serious – just good friends.'

'She still looks good on paper?'

'Yeah, a real Goody Two-Shoes.'

'You sound doubtful,' Hazelwood said, prompting him.

'There were two or three items in her wardrobe that made me wonder if she was quite so squeaky clean – a pair of leather slacks that gleamed like black satin, a tarty-looking blouse and a wide leather belt with a steel buckle and four bracelets.'

'Bracelets?'

'Handcuffs; the victim's wrists could either be manacled in front of the body or behind the back.'

'Jesus.' Hazelwood stubbed out the Burma cheroot in the brass shell case.

'You don't think anything funny was going on between her and Jill Sheridan, do you?'

'Not in that sense. Ambition is the only reason why Jill cultivated her.'

'What exactly do you mean by that?'

'Her long-term aim is to be the first woman to head the SIS. Right now, however, her sights are set a little lower. The post of Deputy DG became vacant when you were elevated to the peerage and as yet nobody has been nominated to fill your old appointment. Jill wants the job and I think she can probably count on the support of a number of people outside The Firm.'

'Like who?'

'I hear Robin Urquhart, the senior Deputy Under Secretary at the Foreign and Commonwealth Office, is a fan of hers. It's said he regards Jill as the brightest star in our particular galaxy.'

'The man must be senile.'

Ashton didn't care for Jill either but unlike Hazelwood he freely acknowledged that she was head and shoulders above the other Heads of Departments. She had a good brain and had demonstrated on more than one occasion that she could act decisively in a crisis.

'You're prejudiced where Jill is concerned, Victor, and she knows it. Proving she is unquestionably the best is her defence mechanism. She has to be the fount of all knowledge, not only as regards her own Mid East Department but also, in this instance, the Pacific

Basin and the Rest of the World Department. Sharon Cartwright was her source of information.'

'I suppose one should be grateful there was nothing more sinister about their relationship,' Hazelwood said plaintively. 'All the same, what Jill has done goes against the grain. It's positively Machiavellian.'

Ashton wondered how Victor would feel if it turned out that Jill Sheridan had recruited a whole network of informers within The Firm, which was not wholly impossible. She was the only ranking woman in the SIS and undoubtedly served as a role model for every feminist among the clerical assistants, typists, personal assistants and junior desk officers, a number of whom would be prepared to help her in any way they could.

'Sharon Cartwright passes everything Inigo tells his interrogators to Jill because Sharon wants a transfer to the Mid East Department.' Hazelwood opened the cigar box and helped himself to another cheroot. 'Then she betrays Jill to the opposition.'

'Whoever they are,' Ashton said.

'Quite. Question is, what the hell were those burglars looking for?'

'You'd have to ask Jill that.'

'Don't think I won't. But the really big question is how did they know Inigo was squirrelled away at The Firs?' Hazelwood struck a match and lit the cheroot. 'Any idea how you are going to solve that conundrum, Peter?'

'I'd have to talk to every person who had anything to do with Inigo from the moment he stepped off the plane at Heathrow. In addition to a list of names, I need to know where he was initially held and for how long, who decided the interrogation should be conducted up at Naburn and what were the travel arrangements.'

'You'd better see Roger Benton, he has all the answers.'

'I think it would be a good idea if you spoke to him first and smoothed the way.'

Hazelwood buzzed his PA, asked her to give his compliments to Mr Benton and would he kindly spare him a few minutes. 'Satisfied?' he asked, gazing speculatively at Ashton.

'I will be when you tell me the real identity of Inigo.'

In the ensuing silence, it was obvious what was going through Victor's mind. Never tell a man more than he needed to know; never give him access to classified material that had no direct bearing on the task in hand. This was the basic tenet of security; had it been observed in the past, the likes of Philby, Burgess and Maclean, Blunt and Prime would not have been in a position to inflict such grave damage on the nation.

'His real name is Raúl Garcia Menendez,' Hazelwood said eventually. 'He's a Cuban out of Florida.'

'And who are the police looking for?'

'Raymond George Messenger. The Embassy in Santiago issued him with a British passport in that name.'

Thomas waved a hand in front of his face to clear the air. In his opinion it wasn't necessary to be a smoker to get lung cancer. All you had to do was to sit in a small room with half a dozen addicts from the CID squad of A Division, North Yorkshire Police. A pall of blue-grey smoke virtually fogged out the 28-inch TV screen, making it difficult to view the videos that had been impounded from The Firs. Detective Chief Inspector Oldfield however appeared to be thoroughly at home in the pungent atmosphere. He sat next to Thomas, hunched up, arms resting on his thighs, a cigarette burning down between the nicotine-stained fingers of his right hand.

'Stop,' he suddenly announced in a stentorian voice that made Thomas jump. 'Freeze it right there.' Then added, 'Too late, back track.'

A blue Ford Transit van appeared in the gap in the hedgerow fronting the house. The date/time group appeared in the top left-hand corner of the picture.

'See that,' Oldfield continued, 'Tuesday, 24 January, the day Jukes, Rossitor and Yeo were murdered. That's not the first time we've had that van on camera.'

'You're right, guv,' one of the detectives said. 'I went past the house around the same time on the Monday.'

'So it did.' Oldfield stubbed out his cigarette in a glass ashtray that was already near to overflowing. 'OK, let's eject the cassette, put the one for Monday on again and run the tape through until the

Transit is in the frame. There are two cameras sweeping the north side of the house. Maybe one of them got an oblique shot of the number plate.'

'There's something else we should maybe look at again,' Thomas said hesitantly.

'And what's that, Brian?'

'I may be wrong but I think you'll find the Transit appeared about a minute after Sharon Cartwright left The Firs in the MG Maestro. Same thing happened on Monday, the twenty-third.'

'Are you saying there is a connection?' Oldfield asked quickly.

'I wouldn't rule it out,' Thomas said.

CHAPTER 6

Even though the ground had been prepared for him, Ashton knew things would be difficult. For all that Roger Benton had opted out of the promotion stakes, and was supposedly content to soldier on in his present grade, no one was more prickly than the Head of the Pacific Basin and Rest of the World Department if he thought his bailiwick was being unfairly criticised. In his considered opinion, the incident at Naburn called for an internal investigation; that Hazelwood should have taken the matter out of his hands and entrusted it to Ashton was nothing less than disgraceful.

'I ask you,' he said angrily, 'what kind of message does Victor think he's sending my people? Is he implying I might be tempted to suppress evidence which reflected adversely on my department?'

'It's no good asking me,' Ashton told him. 'I can't tell you what goes on in Victor's mind. I assume I was given the job because he considered the investigation fell within my remit. OK?'

'No, it isn't.'

'Well, I'm afraid you will just have to live with it, Roger.'

'So it would seem. Where do you want to begin?'

'From the moment Raúl Garcia Menendez arrived at Heathrow.'

'That was Monday, 2 January, on British Airways flight BA 244 from Santiago via São Paulo. The plane was eight minutes behind schedule and landed at 08.48 . . .'

Benton deliberately rattled off the facts at machine-gun speed, knowing that even with his own brand of shorthand, Ashton would be unable to keep up with him. He regarded it as a personal victory when Ashton asked him to slow down.

'Anything to oblige,' he said cheerfully. 'Well now, Raúl Menendez was met by Harvey Yeo with a limousine and a chauffeur called Eric Daniels from the Motor Transport and General Stores

Section. Crawford, the warrant officer on loan from the SAS, was to have been the third member of the reception committee. Unfortunately, he was involved in a multiple pile-up on the A3 soon after leaving the training school at Amberley Lodge.'

'What time was this?'

'Approximately 04.00 hours; it was very foggy and there was black ice on the road. Crawford ended up in hospital with a fractured ankle and mild concussion.'

The Commandant of the training school had only learned of the accident some three hours after the event. By the time Roger Benton heard the news from a panic-stricken Harvey Yeo, the British Airways flight from Santiago had been fifty-one minutes from Heathrow.

'Crawford was using a pool car belonging to the training school. Had everything gone to plan, he would have met up with Harvey Yeo and Daniels at Vauxhall Cross. All three would then have gone on to Heathrow, collected Raúl Garcia Menendez and conveyed him to Amberley Lodge.'

'He was going to be debriefed at the training school?'

'That was the general idea. It was my intention to get Menendez out of London and thanks to all the cutbacks imposed by the Treasury, we weren't exactly spoiled for choice. Anyway, it was easy enough to rustle up another car to replace the one Crawford had smashed up and Frank Warren persuaded his opposite number in the Foreign and Commonwealth Security Department to lend us one of his interview rooms. This was for a couple of days, while we made alternative arrangements.'

Every government ministry had its own security organisation. The department which looked after members of the Diplomatic Service was located in Matthew Parker Street, a quiet backwater two minutes away from Parliament Square. Ashton knew the place well and had always thought the four-storey, Edwardian-style house fronted by impressive wrought-iton gates deserved a better name than number 4 Central Buildings.

'Did you find a replacement for Crawford?'

Benton nodded. 'I detailed Larry Rossitor for the job. Although he doesn't have the special skills which Crawford has, I've always found him alert and dependable. In short, I believed he wouldn't freeze in an emergency. As for Daniels, well, he'd attended the advanced driving course run by the military police and knew what to do in the event of an ambush.' Benton suddenly stopped as if conscious of committing a *faux pas*. 'Not that we were expecting any trouble,' he added quickly, with a nervous braying laugh.

'Was Sharon Cartwright involved at this stage?' Ashton asked.

'No.'

'Did she know about Menendez, the man you codenamed Inigo?' Benton hesitated. 'She didn't hear about him from me but it's possible Harvey Yeo may have said something.'

Ashton didn't pursue the matter. As far as he was concerned, Sharon Cartwright had had prior knowledge of Raúl Garcia Menendez before she joined the interrogation team. 'Where was Menendez held overnight?' he asked.

'Paddington Green.'

'The police station?'

'Can you think of anything more secure?'

Ashton couldn't. Paddington Green was the nearest thing to a fortress.

'How did you manage to fix that?'

'I saw Brian Thomas and he called in a few markers. Our ex-Detective Chief Superintendent seems to have more "brothers" in the Met than you'd find in a masonic lodge.'

Daniels had driven Menendez to the police station when Yeo had decided to call it a day at 6 p.m. By then, the Cuban had really been suffering from jet lag and had been unable to keep his eyes open. Daniels had collected Menendez from Paddington Green the following morning, and had returned him at the end of the day.

'Let's talk about The Firs,' Ashton said when Benton eventually paused for breath. 'Whose idea was it to use that place?'

'I suppose you'd have to say it was mine. I had sat in on a couple of the sessions held at Central Buildings and had come to the conclusion the man was a blow-hard. I thought he was stretching a thin story a long, long way. Head of Station, Santiago, was also beginning to have his doubts.'

'But not Harvey Yeo?'

'No, as I told you before, he practically went down on his knees and begged me to let him continue with the debrief. I agreed because we had to do something with the man. Since we had outstayed our welcome at both Paddington Green and number 4 Central Buildings, we needed a safe house outside London and The Firs was available.'

'Why not Amberley Lodge as you had originally planned?'

'On reflection, I decided it would be a mistake to send him there.'

'Because of the nature of his information?' Ashton suggested.

'Exactly,' Benton said, tight-lipped.

Menendez had claimed he was a walking encyclopaedia on the drug scene. According to him, there wasn't a cartel he hadn't met and done business with.

In the immediate post Cold War era, MI5, the Security Service, had been desperate to find a new role and had fastened on to the international drug cartels. The SIS too was anxious to find a new major threat to the nation which would capture the imagination of the politicians, all too many of whom believed the world had become a much safer place following the demise of the old Soviet Union. It was doubtful if Menendez could fill the bill; furthermore, whatever he did have to offer fell within the remit of MI5.

'So Menendez was transferred to The Firs on Wednesday, 4 January. Right?'

'That's correct.'

'What were the travel arrangements?'

'They went by car: Harvey Yeo, Sharon Cartwright and Menendez in a Ford Grenada, driven by Eric Daniels. Larry Rossitor followed behind in an MG Maestro he'd hired as a runabout for the whole team while they were up at Naburn. Shortly after they arrived at The Firs, Rossitor ran Daniels into York so that he could catch a train back to London.'

'And that's it?'

'Yes.'

'Two questions, Roger. When was Sharon Cartwright told she would be joining the interrogation team?'

'Tuesday afternoon about four. The next morning, she, Harvey Yeo and Daniels rendezvoused at Vauxhall Cross before collecting Menendez from Paddington Green.'

Jill Sheridan claimed Sharon had told her that she had been a last-minute choice to make up the interrogation team and had received less than two hours' notice. One of them had lied, probably Jill, because she had wanted to pre-empt a potentially dangerous situation and needed a convincing reason to explain why she had the keys to the penthouse flat at 228 Priory Way. But you would never catch Jill out. Even if Sharon Cartwright walked through the door tomorrow and was given a clean bill of health by Security Vetting, she would support Jill's version of the truth. When you were angling for a transfer to the Mid East Department, you didn't shop the assistant director who was running the show.

'And what was your second question?' Benton asked.

'Why was the Ford Grenada left at The Firs?'

'It was a sop to Harvey's ego. The Maestro was all right for the likes of Rossitor and Sharon Cartwright but he wanted a vehicle commensurate with his status. Roy Kelso said he could spare the car but not the driver. OK?'

'It is with me,' Ashton told him. 'Let's hope the Treasury doesn't find out.'

'Is there anything else I can tell you?'

Ashton shook his head. The only person left who could say what had happened during those first three days Menendez had spent in England was Eric Daniels. Everyone else was either dead or missing. When you were conducting an internal investigation which involved dealing with superior officers, it was sometimes necessary to walk on eggshells. After thanking Benton for his help, Ashton went in search of Roy Kelso in order to get his permission to interview Daniels.

Eric Daniels had joined the SIS as a driver in 1979 after serving twelve years in the Royal Military Police, where he had risen to the rank of sergeant. He stood five feet nine and tipped the scales at a hundred and sixty-five pounds which meant he'd only gained a couple of pounds or so since leaving the army. He had a full head of light brown hair and there was hardly a line on his moon-shaped face. He was however beginning to acquire a double chin.

In his time with The Firm, he had completed three overseas tours of duty, spending almost four years in Bonn, followed by three in Rome with a foreshortened spell of twenty-one months in Athens. That the former Head of Station, Athens, was alive today was due in no small measure to Eric Daniels.

An active service unit of the Provisional IRA had attempted to ambush the SIS man on the way to the International Airport and, as was not infrequently the case, the terrorists had opened fire too soon. Daniels had kept his head and had executed a hundred-and-eighty-degree turn at speed. Conversant with the tactical drill evolved by the British military police, the IRA active service unit had anticipated his move and had put out a back stop to counter it. Observing the gunman standing in the middle of the road, Daniels had yelled at his passenger to get down, then whipped the gear lever into second, flattened the accelerator and aimed the Ford Orion straight at him. Engine shrieking in torment, the speedometer hovering on sixty, he'd crunched into the gunman and knocked him clean over the roof of the Ford Orion.

Now Ashton found Daniels in the underground garage, waxing the Ford Grenada.

'We haven't met,' he said, introducing himself, 'but I've heard a lot about you.' One of the things he'd learned from Kelso was the fact that the identity of the Cuban had been withheld from Daniels.

'Same goes for me,' Daniels told him. 'What can I do for you?'

'I'm hoping you can fill in some gaps.'

'Is this to do with the guy they call Inigo?'

'Yes. What did you make of him?'

Daniels looked around the garage. A couple of drivers were taking a rest-break in the tiny glass-fronted office next to the lifts. Nearer at hand, in the adjoining bay, a mechanic was servicing the Daimler Jag provided for the Director General.

'We'd better sit in the car,' he said; 'more private.'

Ashton opened the front near-side door and got in; leaving the duster and tin of wax polish on the bonnet, Daniels walked round the Ford Grenada and joined him, then switched on the car radio.

'That should discourage any would-be eavesdroppers,' he said. 'Now where were we?'

'You were going to tell me about Inigo,' Ashton said.

'Have you seen a photograph of him?'

'Only a passport head and shoulders, which probably didn't do him any favours.'

'He's what you would call good-looking,' Daniels said after a moment's reflection. 'Slim, quite tall, jet-black hair, neat moustache, a ready smile. I don't think he would have much difficulty pulling any bird he fancied. Personally, I didn't like him; he was too smooth and cocky for me.'

'How was he, when you first met him? Nervous? Excited? Calm? Or what?'

'Inigo was smirking, like he was pleased with himself.'

'He wasn't looking over his shoulder then?'

'He was completely relaxed, Mr Ashton. What more can I say?'

'Let's forget Inigo for a moment and turn to Mr Yeo. What instructions did he give you?'

'None, other than he wanted to go to 4 Central Buildings.' Suddenly the penny dropped. 'Oh, I get it,' Daniels said angrily, 'you want to know if I was keeping an eye out to make sure we weren't being followed.'

'I'm aware of your reputation and how many commendations you have received,' Ashton told him, 'but it's a question that has to be asked.'

'No one tailed us into London from Heathrow; believe me, I checked the wing and rear mirrors enough times to bet my shirt on it. Same applies when I was running Inigo backwards and forwards between Matthew Parker Street and Paddington Green.'

'And you noticed nothing untoward on the way up to Naburn?'

'Damn right I didn't,' Daniels said, still aggrieved.

'So tell me about the journey – who sat where, what they talked about, anything which comes to mind, no matter how irrelevant and trivial it may seem to you.'

'Mr Yeo sat next to me, he claimed riding in the back made him feel sick. Inigo was behind him on the near side, Miss Cartwright was in rear of me.'

'What do you think of Sharon?'

'It's not for me to say.'

'Yes it is. I need all the help I can get and I'd appreciate it if you

67

were completely frank. And whatever you do tell me, it won't go any farther. I can promise you that.'

'I think she took a shine to Inigo,' Daniels said slowly.

Although they had conversed in Spanish, a language completely alien to Daniels, their tone of voice had gradually become more friendly, even intimate. He had noticed the change soon after Yeo had fallen asleep.

'Up till then, they had been fairly businesslike and Sharon Cartwright hadn't had much to say for herself. She came into her own when Mr Yeo started snoring. Before very long, she and Inigo were all palsy walsy, sharing a little joke, that kind of thing.'

Even though Daniels couldn't understand a word they were saying, their voices had got lower and lower. There had been some muffled laughter from Sharon Cartwright.

'I heard her say, "Naughty, naughty" in English and she gave him a playful slap on the wrist. He then said something in Spanish and laughed out loud when she answered him in the same tongue. Of course I couldn't see what they were up to but it's a pound to a penny he had his hand on her knee. And she didn't really mind either; matter of fact, I reckon she was all for it.'

They had gone all quiet after she had admonished Inigo and he'd thought that, like Harvey Yeo, they must have dozed off. Then he'd heard a faint drumming noise and changed his mind.

'At first, I couldn't make out what it was, then it dawned on me she was tapping her foot. Not a regular beat, you understand – just every now and again as if she couldn't help it. Didn't take me long to put two and two together and realise Don Juan was having a quick grope under her skirt.'

'Oh, come on, they'd only just met!'

'Yeah, I found it hard to believe too, but Inigo had a way with him, enough to make quite a few women lose their heads.'

'Even someone like Sharon Cartwright?'

'I know what you're thinking – she's intelligent, poised and seems very level-headed. But I can't shake this gut feeling she has this reckless streak and enjoys living on the edge.' Daniels patted his chest. 'Look, I'm a nobody. Right? I'm not a psychologist, just a driver, but I'm telling you now that getting laid by Inigo behind the backs of Mr Yeo and Mr Rossitor would be a real high for Sharon Cartwright. I mean it'd break every rule in the book and would lead to her instant dismissal if she was rumbled. But that would have been part of the attraction.'

'It's a thought,' Ashton said in a noncommittal voice.

'Yeah, well, like I said, I'm only a driver.' Daniels switched off the car radio and got out. 'Been nice talking to you,' he said.

'And you.'

Ashton walked over to the lifts and pressed the call button. When he looked back, Daniels had his head down and was busy polishing the Ford Grenada.

What about Sharon Cartwright then? Was she Miss Goody Two-Shoes who, when interviewed by the Intelligence officer responsible for security vetting, had managed to look ashamed after confessing the first time she'd had sex was shortly after her sixteenth birthday? Was the young woman who'd demurely admitted to smoking pot and getting drunk at a party while up at Oxford the real Sharon Cartwright? Or was the kinky twenty-four-year-old with a taste for leatherwear, high-heeled sandals, wrist locks and a penchant for living dangerously the true version?

If Sharon had been having it off with Raúl Garcia Menendez, she would have been open to blackmail and the Cuban could have ended up controlling her like a puppet. Apply sufficient pressure and she would be running errands for him, making phone calls, contacting his friends, when his life was supposedly in danger. It didn't add up, at least not so far as he was concerned, but maybe Hazelwood could make something of it.

Ashton heard a set of doors open behind him, stepped into a vacant car and pressed the button for the top floor.

A few hours ago, the cancer ward had been the smoke-filled CID squad room; now it was the equally nicotine-polluted office of Detective Chief Inspector Oldfield. One more day with A Division and instead of experiencing it second-hand, Thomas reckoned he might just as well take up smoking again.

'Thought you might be interested to see the autopsy reports on our three murder victims,' Oldfield said, lighting a cigarette from the stub of the one he'd been smoking when Thomas entered his office. 'The pathologists believe Angus, or Gus Jukes as he was better known, was the last one to be killed. I don't see how they reached that conclusion when the medical evidence indicates all three men died within a time span of ten to fifteen minutes.'

Thomas picked up the reports and went through the motions of reading them, confident that the DCI would give him an accurate résumé of the contents.

'Of course Jukes was suffering from multiple sclerosis and was confined to his bed, so the quacks probably figured the intruders had decided they could safely leave him till last. The bastards who did it broke into The Firs with the deliberate intention of killing everybody, with the exception of Raymond George Messenger.'

'Is that so?'

'It's in the reports.' Oldfield removed the cigarette from his lips and spilled ash into the wastebin. 'I presume Messenger isn't an alias?'

'It's the name in his passport.'

'There's a frank answer.'

'My brief is to afford you every assistance.'

'So long as national security is not endangered.'

'You said it, not me.' Thomas scratched an itch under his chin. 'I see the pathologist who performed the post-mortem on Rossitor found a number of splinters embedded in the skull.'

'Read on, you'll find they dug a few out of Yeo too.'

'Wooden blunt instrument – a cricket or baseball bat. What's your favourite?' Thomas asked him.

'A baseball bat, you can swing it easier.'

'You got any characters in this neck of the woods who go around killing people with baseball bats?'

'No. But the West Yorkshire Police have one unsolved case involving such a murder weapon and they've been used in a number of robberies.'

Thomas handed the autopsy reports to Oldfield. Except for minor points of detail, the pathologists hadn't really told the police anything they hadn't already surmised. Rossitor had sustained a compound fracture of the left arm when he'd evidently tried to ward off the blows aimed at his head and Yeo had had both wrists broken in the mêlée.

'Forensic did the best they could with the number plates on the Ford Transit,' Oldfield said, changing tack. 'It's definitely a J registration but the numbers which follow it could be 893, 398, 393 or 898. The 3 could be an 8; that's why we've got this variation.'

'Tough.'

'It gets worse,' Oldfield said morosely. 'Of the group of letters, we can only identify the middle one with any certainty and that's a W. Depending on what letter follows it, the damned vehicle could have come from Brighton, Bristol, Cardiff, Chelmsford, Coventry, Dudley, Leeds, Liverpool, Manchester, Oxford, Sheffield, Swansea or Worcester. God knows what the licensing centre at Swansea is going to produce but we could be looking at a print-out a yard long. Of course, we are not holding our breath waiting on the Driver and Vehicle Licensing Agency. My officers are out and about now in Naburn with pictures of the Ford Transit taken from videos.'

'Let's hope you get lucky.'

'We could do with something better than passport photos of Messenger and Sharon Cartwright.'

'They're already on the way,' Thomas assured him. 'Should arrive any time now, by Special Delivery.'

'Thanks.' Oldfield slowly exhaled, watched the smoke drift towards the ceiling.

'Was there anything going on between those two?' he asked casually.

'Not that I know of. What prompted the question?'

'Forensic went through the laundry baskets and found a pair of satin pyjamas belonging to her. There were traces of semen in the pyjama bottoms. DNA tests show it hadn't been ejaculated by either Yeo or Rossitor.'

CHAPTER 7

On most mornings in most households, breakfast is not the happiest event of the day. On the law of averages, at least one member of the family is bound to feel out of sorts and the meal will either be eaten in complete silence or else the response to any attempt at making conversation will be a series of grunts. The uncommunicative person is invariably the male, and while Ashton hadn't got out of bed on the wrong side that morning, the only feedback Harriet was getting from him was the occasional long-drawn-out yawn. Good at tenpin bowling, she retaliated by lobbing her napkin ring into the bowl of cornflakes Ashton was eating.

'What the heck did you want to do that for?' he asked bemused.

'To get your attention.'

'I was thinking,' Ashton told her, and removed the ring from his cereal.

'You mean you're not grumpy because Edward is teething and you were kept awake most of the night?' Harriet said in mock surprise.

'Our son didn't disturb me. I couldn't sleep because I had too many other things on my mind.'

'Such as?'

'Such as what really happened at The Firs that last afternoon. The killers were into that house so damned fast.'

'The control room wasn't manned,' Harriet said. 'I've a feeling it never was from the moment they arrived at the safe house. How many hours a day would they have spent debriefing Menendez? Six? Eight? More than eight?'

'Eight would be more like it. Probably spread over three sessions – say half-eight to twelve in the morning, two to four in the afternoon and five to seven before dinner.'

73

'Well then?'

Harriet was right. There was no way the control room could have been manned round the clock. Although Harvey Yeo would have done most of the questioning, he had specifically asked Sharon Cartwright to be on the team on the grounds that her Spanish was excellent, and the experience would be good for her. That being the case, it was reasonable to presume that she had been present at most of the sessions. Since Sharon had also been responsible for transcribing the audio record of each one in English, she would have had very little free time. Larry Rossitor would not have been so hard-pressed. He couldn't speak Spanish; by trade he was an Intelligence analyst and his job had been to assess the information Menendez had disclosed to his interrogators. He could probably have put in an eight-hour shift in the control room but it was difficult to see how the other sixteen could have been covered. Ashton was very clear about one thing: from what Eric Daniels had told him, he couldn't see Harvey Yeo putting himself on the duty officer rota. That would have been beneath his dignity.

'They just went through the motions of having a duty officer,' Ashton said, drawing the only possible conclusion.

And whenever you adopted a policy of simply going through the motions, people became very lax. The cameras might have been sweeping the grounds when the killers arrived, but no one had been monitoring the screens in the control room and this meant another safeguard must have been regularly circumvented.

'I had a word with Security Vetting and Technical Services Division yesterday afternoon. Among the defensive measures they installed at The Firs was an electronic central-locking system. When that was in operation, the only way you could get back into the house was to smile sweetly into the camera and press the doorbell. The duty officer in the control room would switch off the alarm temporarily and spring the lock.'

'The system was down,' Harriet told him. 'They were using a key to get in.'

'You guess.'

'No, there was a key rack in the hall and one was missing.'

'Sharon Cartwright took the key when she left the house around four o'clock and subsequently handed it over to the killers?'

'That's the way I see it, Peter.'

'And when the killers let themselves into the house, they had fifteen seconds in which to neutralise the alarm before it started wailing. And they knew where the master switch was located because Sharon had told them?'

'Exactly,' Harriet said emphatically. 'Of course, whether she did so voluntarily is another matter.'

The videos showed that Sharon Cartwright had left the house on Monday, 23 January, at 14.00 hours and again the following afternoon at the same time, a matter of a few hours before the killers had broken into The Firs. On both occasions, a blue Ford Transit had cruised by the house within a minute of her departure.

'I believe she was kidnapped,' Ashton said. 'Somewhere along the road between Naburn and the outskirts of York, the van driver overtook Sharon and waved her down. She was then overpowered and bundled into the Transit. As soon as the Ford had moved off, one of her kidnappers drove the Maestro into York and abandoned it near the Theatre Royal.'

'And what happened on the Monday was a dress rehearsal?'

'No, I think they'd intended to lift her but there had been too many people about and they had been forced to postpone it for twenty-four hours.'

'Suppose conditions had been equally unfavourable on the Tuesday? What would they have done then?'

'Search me. I don't think even Menendez could have blackmailed her into making a third consecutive trip to York.'

'How do you know she wasn't a willing accomplice?'

'Sharon had nothing to gain and everything to lose. She would have been a fugitive for the rest of her life.'

Treachery was not one of Sharon Cartwright's defects. She was kinky, reckless and probably incapable of forming a lasting relationship. She had been attracted to the Cuban and had happily gone down on her back to accommodate him, and maybe her stomach too, according to what Brian Thomas said the forensic scientists of the North Yorkshire Police had found. The risks she had taken had been truly horrendous, but Daniels had been undoubtedly right when he had ventured the opinion that this had been the major attraction for Sharon Cartwright. And then, Menendez had turned the screw and suddenly she was no longer a free agent. It wasn't difficult to understand why Sharon Cartwright had behaved the way she had, but Menendez was an altogether different conundrum.

'Menendez is the real villain of the piece,' Ashton said, voicing his thoughts. 'Three people are dead because of him and nothing he did makes any kind of sense to me. There wasn't a damned thing he told Harvey Yeo that was worth dying for; I know, because I've read every debrief. Yet, a little over twenty-four hours later, the killers have turned Sharon's flat upside down and broken into Jill Sheridan's house, looking for God knows what.'

'Seems to me there's only one thing you can do,' Harriet said.

'And what might that be?'

'Find out just who Raúl Garcia Menendez really is.'

Ashton mulled it over. He could go to MI5 and ask their anti drug section if they'd heard of the Cuban. Farther afield, the Miami Field Office of the FBI might have come across him. And if Menendez was as big as he liked to make out, his name would surely be known to the Drug Enforcement Agency? But first, he would have to clear it with Hazelwood.

'I think you've just pointed me in the right direction,' he said.

'Well, I'm glad something came out of this animated conversation we're having.'

'What was it you wanted to tell me before we got started on Menendez?'

'It'll keep,' Harriet told him.

'Will it?'

'Well it will, for at least six months. I happen to be pregnant.'

It was not the first time Brian Thomas had been inside a mortuary and he hadn't spent thirty-five years in the Met without seeing his share of the dead, many of whom had been horribly mangled. But familiarity had not dulled his senses and the clinical smell of a mortuary always got to him and made his stomach churn. The younger the deceased, the more he felt the waste of a life cut short.

He and Detective Chief Inspector Oldfield had driven down to

Nottingham because the body of a young woman had been re-covered from the River Trent at the Beeston lock on the south-western outskirts of the city. A Division of the North Yorkshire Constabulary had been advised of the discovery because the deceased resembled the description of Sharon Cartwright which, at Oldfield's request, had been widely circulated throughout the East Midlands.

'Recognise her?' Oldfield asked.

'Yes.' Thomas cleared his throat and tried again. 'Yes, that's Sharon Cartwright.'

She had been hooded and shot twice in the back of the head. Purely on the diameter of the entry wounds, the Detective Chief Inspector in charge of the Scene-of-the-Crime Department was of the opinion that the murder weapon had been a small-calibre pistol. The thumbs and fingers of both hands were noticeably swollen, which led the police doctor to believe that her hands had been tied behind her back for some considerable time. From the burn marks on her body, it was evident that Sharon Cartwright had been system-atically tortured. The scene-of-the-crime officer was sure more than one man had been involved.

'The bastards used this woman like an ashtray,' he said, 'kept stubbing out their cigarettes on her. It looks as if they scorched her buttocks with a naked flame.'

'What about a post-mortem?' Oldfield asked.

'It's scheduled for two o'clock this afternoon.'

Thomas left them to it and went outside to get a breath of fresh air. He thought a number of people at Vauxhall Cross would have cause to revise their opinion of Sharon Cartwright. True, she had been a little too free with her favours and there was reason to believe her sexual proclivities had been pretty far out but when push came to shove, she'd had courage in abundance. He could only begin to guess what agonies Sharon must have suffered before she told her torturers what they wanted to know about the anti-intruder system at The Firs and how to neutralise it before the alarm was triggered.

'Bastards,' Thomas snarled in a rare display of rage. 'Fucking bastards.'

'We'll get them, Brian, you can depend on that.'

Thomas flinched involuntarily, then turned slowly about to face Oldfield.

'I didn't hear you sneak up on me,' he said in a wooden voice.

'I'm sorry, I didn't mean to startle you.'

'That's OK.' Thomas faced his front again, stood there listening to the distant hum of traffic on Maid Marian Way down the hill from the General Hospital. 'Why did they drive ninety miles to put her in the river when the Ouse was on the doorstep?'

'They were playing safe. Rivers have a habit of giving up their bodies. You don't need me to tell you that, Brian.'

Damned right he didn't; he'd seen a few fished out of the Thames, caught in a lock upstream. The killers had put Sharon into a body bag, lashed a couple of breeze blocks to weight it down and then discovered it was a lot heavier than they had allowed for. Instead of the body bag landing in mid-stream when they'd heaved it into the river, it had ended up in the shallows, where it had been spotted yesterday afternoon by an elderly man out walking his dog.

'Are you going to tell the press what they did to her? I mean, somewhere out there, somebody knows who did this – a wife, girlfriend, a close relative. Maybe we can shame them into coming forward.'

'I don't think we can spell it out,' Oldfield said. 'There's the next of kin to consider.'

'And if we get their permission?'

'We'd need to have it in writing.'

Thomas firmly believed that if there was one man who could make the parents see why it was necessary, it was the Director General.

'Consider it done,' he said.

Ashton had first met Clifford Peachey back in 1991 when the MI5 man had been one of the leading lights of Kl. The men and women of this section had been known as the Kremlin Watchers because it had been their task to ferret out the KGB and GRU officers in the Soviet Embassy, Trade Delegation and Consular Service. Peachey had looked typecast for the job and still did. He was a small man with sharp, pointed features which reminded Ashton of a rodent.

His grey hair was cut short back and sides, even though it was beginning to get a little thin on top. Clifford Peachey had started out as an interrogator and had earned himself a reputation second only to that of the great Jim Skardon who, in the 1950s, had broken a whole string of communist agents including Klaus Fuchs, the atom spy. Changing jobs for the third time, he was now Head of the newly created Counter Narcotics Intelligence Team. The first question he put to Ashton, as they shook hands, had absolutely nothing to do with the drug scene.

'What's the Nelson touch in aid of, Peter?'

'What?'

'The black patch over your eye.'

'It's less obvious than wearing sunglasses in the middle of winter.' Ashton raised the patch and showed him his bad eye.

'That's a beauty. Who did it? Harriet?'

'Who else?'

'So how is she keeping these days?' Peachey enquired in his usual avuncular, if somewhat proprietary manner.

'Blooming,' Ashton said tersely.

In the four years Harriet had spent at Gower Street before her secondment to the SIS, she had got to know all the Kremlin Watchers very well, especially Clifford Peachey whom she regarded as a good friend. The affection she had for him had been more than reciprocated; Peachey had taken Harriet under his wing, and in the passage of time had seen himself as her guardian. In his inimitable fashion, the MI5 man had made it clear that he didn't think Ashton was good enough for her.

'Blooming,' Peachey repeated. 'And what about Edward?'

'He's teething, keeps us awake at nights.'

'Like Señor Raúl Garcia Menendez, perhaps?'

'You've heard of him?' Ashton said eagerly.

'Not before Victor Hazelwood rang me to say you were on the way here to pick my brains.'

'Is that another way of saying that I'm wasting my time and yours?'

'Not at all. Nobody called Menendez has come to our notice but names can't mean a great deal in the drug world. It could be we have him carded under an alias. What can you tell me about him?'

'Only what he told Head of Station, Santiago, when he asked for political asylum.'

'It's possible his story contained more than a grain of truth,' Peachey observed mildly.

'Well, OK, Menendez is forty-two years old and was born in Havana. Says he doesn't remember much of his childhood, because his parents fled Cuba hours before Fidel Castro and his ragtag and bobtail army entered the capital. An uncle on his mother's side left it too late and went before a firing squad. Apparently, his execution was shown on the newsreels of the day. This would be sometime in January 1959.'

Peachey switched on his desk-top Amstrad computer.

'Do you happen to know his name?'

'Yes, but that part of his story has already been checked out by the Pacific Basin and Rest of the World Department.'

'It won't do any harm to compare notes and see if we've got something you haven't.'

'Why not? His name was Leon Valdes. He was Chief of Police, Pinar del Río.'

Peachey tapped in the information, his fingers hitting the keyboard with all the dexterity of a sixty-words-a-minute touch-typist. Then he punched up the codeword ordering a search and sat back waiting for the data to appear on the screen.

'We don't appear to have any more on Leon Valdes than you do,' he said presently.

'I'm not surprised. Roger Benton probably got his information from the same source.'

'Leon was the eldest of four brothers,' Peachey said, reading from the visual display unit. 'The other three, Arnaldo, Humberto and Rafael, were quicker off the mark and escaped to Florida. Humberto later took part in the abortive Bay of Pigs invasion and was one of the eighty-odd men killed in action between 17 and 20 April 1961. He was then aged twenty-six.'

'We don't have that on file,' Ashton said. 'How did you acquire it?'

'From two sources, the FBI and the Drug Enforcement Agency.'

Peachey took out a pipe and filled the bowl with Dunhill Standard Mixture from a tin he kept in the top right-hand drawer of his desk, then struck a match. 'Arnaldo Valdes is not exactly your model citizen,' he said between puffs. 'See for yourself.'

The printer started chattering and didn't stop until it had produced a two-page listing of his activities from the time he had first come to the notice of the Miami Police Department and the FBI. In a career spanning thirty years, there were few crimes Arnaldo had not committed. From living off the immoral earnings of his girl-friend, whom he had persuaded to turn the occasional trick to swell their joint income, he had ended up running a minimum of two hundred call girls. Prostitution had financed his initial bulk purchase of cocaine and the foot soldiers he had needed to eliminate any business rival who tried to move in on his territory. By 1984, that meant the whole of West Palm Beach. Along the way he had acquired a chain of liquor stores, a casino, four hotels, the odd condominium and a controlling interest in one of the offshore banks in the Bahamas. These legitimate businesses enabled him to launder the millions of dollars earned on the street.

Now aged sixty-two, Arnaldo was currently serving twenty years for second-degree murder and would not be eligible for parole until November 2002. The family business however continued to prosper under younger brother, Rafael, a corporate lawyer and highly respected member of the community. At least, the Drug Enforce-ment Agency, the FBI and the West Palm Beach PD were convinced Rafael Valdes was running the show; proving it, as they freely admitted, was a different proposition.

Peachey ripped off another page and passed it across the desk to Ashton.

'This is a computer image of Rafael Valdes. See any family resemblance to your man?'

'Only if I indulge in wishful thinking.'

'Victor told me that Menendez claimed to have done business with all the major drug barons.'

'That's his story,' Ashton said.

'But he never once mentioned the Valdes brothers?'

'Correct.'

'What the hell was he doing way down there in Santiago? He was practically falling off the end of the world.'

'Menendez was buying two million dollars of pure one hundred per cent cocaine on behalf of Roscoe Quibell, a singularly murderous Afro-American with a penchant for disembowelling his enemies. The deal was for the Colombians to deliver the cocaine by air via the Dominican Republic using a twin-engine Beechcraft Baron.'

'For two million dollars? That's hardly good business.'

'There were other buyers,' Ashton told him. 'Menendez was taking less than five per cent of the consignment. To avoid refuelling on the temporary landing ground, the plane had been fitted with auxiliary tanks which enabled the pilot to make the round trip to the Dominican Republic. The airstrip had been laid out on the edge of the Everglade National Park, approximately fifteen miles southwest of Holmstead.'

'Let me guess,' Peachey said. 'The Colombians failed to deliver?'

'Not according to Menendez. The plane flew in under the radar screen and arrived on schedule. The turnaround was also completed in double-quick time; it was only much later that Menendez discovered the cocaine was sixty per cent sugar.'

'What about the other buyers? Did the Colombians pull a fast one on them as well?'

'Menendez didn't stop to find out, told us he had no desire to end up tied to a tree with his intestines hanging out. South America had seemed a good idea at the time to him, but Roscoe Quibell's foot soldiers proved harder to shake off than he'd bargained for.'

'You don't believe his story?'

'I don't think anybody at Vauxhall Cross does. The deal never went down because Menendez absconded with the money and it was probably a lot more than two million dollars.'

'I take it there is a Roscoe Quibell?'

'Yes. Roger Benton got Head of Station, Washington, to check him out with the FBI and virtually every Law Enforcement Agency in Florida.'

Roscoe Quibell existed all right, and was everything Menendez had said he was. But the curious thing was that neither the FBI nor the Drug Enforcement Agency displayed much interest in him. They were even less interested in hearing what the Cuban had to say for himself.

'Did Menendez say how he got started in the drug trade?'

'Yes, he was running a liquor store in West Palm Beach and came to the conclusion there was an easier way of making a living. So he sold up, moved down to Fort Lauderdale, found himself a supplier and started pushing drugs in the high schools. That's when Roscoe Quibell caught up with him and suggested they went into business together. The Afro made him an offer he couldn't refuse if he wanted to stay healthy.'

'The liquor store was in West Palm Beach?' Peachey said.

'You don't have to spell it out for me,' Ashton told him. 'I know what you're thinking.'

The Valdes brothers owned a chain of liquor stores in the same area and Menendez was allegedly related to them on his mother's side. For Roscoe Quibell, read Rafael Valdes, the corporate lawyer who was overseeing the business while elder brother languished in jail. Menendez had helped himself to a slice of the family's bankroll and the uncles hadn't liked it at all.

'So what do you think, Peter?'

'That's easy. I don't believe the SIS should get involved. This whole business falls within the remit of MI5; we should turn over everything we have on Menendez to you and back off.'

'Is that what you are going to recommend to Victor?'

'Yes.'

'Will he accept your advice?'

'No chance,' Ashton said. 'We've lost three Intelligence officers and he won't rest until somebody has paid for that.'

The satellite link was good, so good that the Caller might have been in the next room instead of several thousand miles away in a different time zone. Right now in London, it was five minutes to six in the evening; here in Savannah, Georgia, it was almost midday.

The Caller from London said, 'You will be happy to know we have been able to locate the merchandise you wanted.'

'How much is it going to cost us?' the Broker asked.

'The amount you said I could go to – five million dollars,' the Caller told him, and hung up.

The Broker put the phone down. He just knew Rafael Valdes would be pleased to hear his money was safe.

CHAPTER 8

It was the first time Ashton had attended morning prayers. Although it was not unknown for a Grade I Intelligence officer to sit in, there was a feeling among heads of departments that any assistant director who needed his senior desk officer to be present wasn't really up to his job. Since, in the absence of a Deputy Director General, he was answerable only to Victor Hazelwood, his presence in the conference room was viewed with considerable suspicion.

Hazelwood sat at the head of the table with Rowan Garfield, the Head of the European Department, and Jill Sheridan on his left. Roger Benton was seated immediately to his right with the Head of the Asian Department; Roy Kelso had taken the chair normally occupied by the Deputy DG at the far end of the table, opposite Victor Hazelwood. Ashton shared a separate table with the PA who was responsible for recording the minutes of the meeting.

Monday was for catching up on developments that had happened over the weekend. As Ashton knew from personal experience, had anything of significance occurred, Saturday and Sunday would have gone by the board. The officers of Garfield's Russian Desk were worried about the continuing war in Chechnya and feared it might spill over into the neighbouring republics, but so far they had no evidence of troop movements to suggest this was likely to happen in the near future. Head of the Asian Department confessed there had been no further news of the two British hostages kidnapped some three weeks ago by Kashmiri separatists and doubted if there was much more the Indian Army could do before the weather improved with the coming of spring.

Jill Sheridan spoke of a buzz going the rounds of the coffee shops in Tehran that the Ayatollahs were preparing a very nasty surprise for the American capitalist hyenas. The means of retribution were ten times more destructive than any nuclear, biological or chemical weapon yet devised by man, and best of all, it would be years before the Yankee imperialists realised how much damage they had suffered. Jill had little faith in the source who had supplied the information. Based on his previous record, he was graded D5, which indicated the man himself was less than reliable and the information was probably untrue. The Americans had heard similar rumours and regarded it as wishful thinking on the part of the Iranians.

Roger Benton had nothing to report other than the purely negative fact that there had been no new developments since the last meeting on Friday. The murder of three of their colleagues had shaken members of his department to the core and morale had understandably plummeted. With almost Churchillian fervour, Benson had then assured everyone around the table that his people would soon bounce back.

Suddenly Roy Kelso's moment of glory had come. All the other assistant directors had had their say and now the spotlight was on him. It was a comparatively new experience for the longest serving head of department. Before the move to Vauxhall Cross, there had been insufficient office space in the tower block on Westminster Bridge Road for the whole SIS to be accommodated under one roof. Consequently, the Admin Wing had been shunted off to Benbow House over in Southwark where Kelso had been out of sight and largely out of mind. In those days, he had not been required to attend morning prayers, not least on the grounds that the Administrative Wing had little to contribute, though no one was tactless enough to say this to his face. With the whole organisation now concentrated in one location, there was no longer any excuse to keep him at arm's length and he had become a regular face at morning prayers. This morning was one of those rare occasions when he had something worthwhile to impart.

'It's all yours, Roy,' Hazelwood said in a voice lacking enthusiasm.

'Thank you, Victor. Well, as you already know, I went up to Southport over the weekend to see the parents of Sharon Cartwright. They're a very pleasant couple and are obviously well off, if their house is anything to go by. The property is in a very desirable neighbourhood and they must have an acre of land at the back of the house . . .'

Suddenly conscious that Ashton was watching her, Jill Sheridan stopped doodling on her notepad and returned his gaze. Raising one eyebrow, she nodded in Hazelwood's direction as if to say, Why doesn't he tell Roy to stop waffling and get to the point?

'I explained why we believed the police shouldn't hold anything back from the media.' Kelso rested both elbows on the table and pressed his palms together to form a church steeple. 'To make absolutely sure they appreciated what was involved, I left the prepared statement with them over Saturday night. When I returned the following morning, they had already signed the certificate stating they had no objections.'

'Dear God,' Benton said in disgust. 'What must the Cartwrights think of us? We're like a pack of bloody hyenas.'

'The press release will read as follows,' Kelso said unperturbed. ' "While held captive, the deceased was systematically tortured by her kidnappers. A total of seventeen burns were found on her body – four on the inside of each thigh . . ." '

Ashton found himself admiring Jill Sheridan's composure. Like the other assistant directors, this was the first time she'd heard what had been done to Sharon. And if her peer group were shocked, her horror was compounded by the knowledge that she was partly responsible for what had happened.

' "Finally, there were scorch marks on the buttocks which, in the opinion of the pathologist, had been inflicted with a blowtorch." '

Outwardly, Jill still appeared to be very cool and collected, but the white knuckles of the clenched right hand betrayed her.

'This is all very well,' Benton said, raising his voice in protest, 'but how is the police spokesman going to present it to the press? Will he still maintain this was a burglary that went terribly wrong?'

'Basically.'

'Basically? What does that mean, Roy?'

'It means the spokesman will say the police believe the burglars had been watching The Firs for some time and abducted Sharon Cartwright in order to learn how to bypass the security system.'

'It's a thin story and it won't hold up. We should have leaned on

Detective Chief Inspector Oldfield and persuaded him to treat Sharon's murder as a separate crime and leave the subsequent investigation to the Nottinghamshire Constabulary.'

'That was never an option, Roger,' Hazelwood told him. 'The North Yorkshire Force had already circulated her description to neighbouring constabularies. Too many people knew Oldfield was looking for Sharon Cartwright; any fancy footwork he then did at our behest would smack of a cover-up, and believe me, word of it would get out.'

'It will anyway. Some smart investigative journalist is bound to discover Sharon's London address, and what's he going to think when one of the neighbours tells him her flat was broken into?'

'We'll deal with that problem when it arises.'

'I think we should prepare a contingency plan now, Victor, rather than later.' Benton turned his head in Jill Sheridan's direction. 'Don't you agree?' he asked.

'I don't see it has anything to do with me.'

'Don't be ridiculous, Jill. Your house and Sharon's flat are both covered by the same police station in Archway Road. Any journalist worth his salt knows who to ring in the Met when he's looking for information. First thing he is going to ask is how many other properties were broken into that day and you will be in dead trouble if yours is the only other one which was burgled.'

'Who's going to tell him I'm an officer in the Secret Intelligence Service?'

'You will,' Benton told her triumphantly. 'This journalist won't come knocking on your door, asking for an interview. He'll watch the house and tag you all the way to Vauxhall Cross—'

'You've made your point, Roger,' Hazelwood said, cutting him short. 'If it looks as though we are unable to contain the situation, Peter will hold a special briefing for the chairman and editors of all the national newspapers.'

Ashton blinked, wondered if he'd heard Victor correctly. It wasn't the first time he'd had to field a fast ball and it wouldn't be the last one to come his way either. The job description of his appointment contained the all-embracing heading of General Duties, which he supposed was flexible enough to include public relations.

He was still trying to picture himself addressing an audience of hard-nosed newspapermen when Hazelwood brought the meeting to a close. Adhering to the instructions he'd received from Victor on Sunday evening, Ashton hung back and did not attempt to tag on behind the heads of departments as they filed out of the conference room.

'So what's your opinion of the ice maiden?' Hazelwood asked when they were alone.

'I don't think it would take much to convince Jill that she is responsible for what happened to Sharon Cartwright.'

'Then go to it, push her over the edge. Find out what Sharon really told her.'

'What inducement can I offer Jill?'

'Inducement?' Hazelwood echoed. 'I hope you are not suggesting I should offer the lady a reward?'

'Jill is ambitious; she is not going to admit to anything which could damage her career.'

'In return for her co-operation, she'll expect to keep her job. Is that what you are telling me, Peter?'

'She might settle for that.'

'Might?' Hazelwood reached inside his jacket and took out a leather cigar case, only to find it was empty. 'I need a damned smoke,' he said, and walked out of the conference room. Ashton followed him into the corridor and on past the PA's office into the DG's. Opening the wooden box on his desk, Hazelwood helped himself to a Burma cheroot and lit it, drawing the smoke down into his lungs with obvious relish. 'What else is she likely to ask for?'

'A guarantee in writing that no detrimental remarks will appear in her annual confidential report while you are running the firm.'

'She can piss off.'

'In that case, we won't get anything from her.'

'You won't know that until you've tried,' Hazelwood growled.

Jill Sheridan presided over the second largest department in the SIS. It was organised on the same lines as the other three operational entities but on an establishment larger than the Asian, and the Pacific Basin and Rest of the World Department put together. The bottom strata consisted of the nonclassified typing pool and the translators who read the editorials of every newspaper printed in the Arab world, as well as the principal articles appearing in trade journals and magazines. The cipher operators, code breakers and archivists comprised the middle layer and worked in the restricted access area. Desk officers and analysts, Special Intelligence, formed the crust on top. All told, Jill directed the activities of a hundred and thirty-seven men and women and did so extremely well.

'My door is always open,' she liked to tell subordinates who felt aggrieved about anything. When Ashton dropped by, Jill was alone and seemingly engrossed in a file that lay open on the desk in front of her.

'Come in, Peter,' she said without looking up, and before he could knock. 'Better close the door behind you.'

'You must be psychic.'

'No. We lived together once and I haven't forgotten the sound of your footsteps.'

Jill never made small talk at the office even when attending the staff Christmas party. There was always a hidden purpose behind the most casual of observations and he told himself it was unlikely she intended to use their former relationship to her advantage.

'You've got a good memory,' he said.

'I was also expecting you.'

'Really?'

'Well, Roy Kelso's performance at morning prayers was staged entirely for my benefit, wasn't it? I also thought Roger Benton deserved an Oscar for best supporting actor.'

'Now you're being silly. It was anything but an act. The police want to shock members of the public into coming forward with information and Kelso was given the job of obtaining the Cartwrights' permission to publicise what had been done to their daughter by the kidnappers. Roy isn't used to being in the limelight and he was simply revelling in the experience, that's all.'

'You always did have a glib tongue, Peter.'

'Why don't you hear me out?'

'Who said I wasn't listening?'

'Then keep an open mind about Roger Benton. You know what

he's like, anything for a quiet life. He's worried the media will discover that all four murder victims are either members of, or connected with, the SIS. And if that should happen, Roger would find himself in the firing line, which is the last place he wants to be. That's the reason why he looked to you for support.'

'I see. And what exactly were you doing at morning prayers? Correct me if I'm wrong, but I don't recall seeing your smiling face at the daily conference before. I'm especially puzzled because you contributed absolutely nothing to the proceedings.' Jill leaned over the side of her swivel chair, picked up the handbag she'd left on the floor and took out a packet of cigarillos and a book of matches. 'I did however notice that you spent the entire time gazing at me. I don't think it was out of admiration. Matter of fact, I know you were trying to intimidate me and it didn't work.'

'Have you listened to yourself, Jill?'

'Suppose you get to the point?'

Ashton did just that. He would have preferred a more subtle approach but Hazelwood had declined to give him anything to barter with, which left him no alternative but to go for the jugular.

'You recruited Sharon Cartwright with a promise to back her request for a transfer to your department. In return, she kept you appraised of everything Menendez told Harvey Yeo and a few things only she had learned.'

'You're twisting the facts,' Jill told him coolly. 'As I've already explained to Victor, Sharon was making a nuisance of herself—'

'Save your breath,' Ashton said tersely. Making a partial admission was a tactic Jill had used before when she'd found herself skating on thin ice. 'It's a stone-cold certainty Sharon did more than phone you; she put everything she personally had learned from Menendez in a letter to you. That's why your house was broken into.'

'And Sharon's flat?'

'Same reason.'

'Nonsense. It was a straightforward burglary. I don't know if there was anything of value in Sharon's flat but I had a string of pearls and a sapphire and diamond ring stolen. The pearls were insured for eleven hundred and seventy-five, the ring for one thousand, nine hundred and fifty.'

'And you've submitted a claim on the policy?'

'Of course I have; we're talking about a loss in excess of three thousand pounds—' Jill suddenly broke off, her eyes narrowing. Leaning forward, she crushed the cigarillo in a glass ashtray. 'How very dim of me,' she said angrily. 'It's taken a long time for the penny to drop but now I see what you're getting at. You are inferring there was no robbery as such, that my insurance claim is simply a smokescreen . . .'

Ashton thought it was a class act but then Jill had always been able to work herself up into a fine temper when she put her mind to it. She also had the ability to convince herself she was being completely truthful when telling a blatant lie.

'Understand this,' Jill continued, 'I did not recruit Sharon Cartwright and there was no secret communication. Do I make myself clear?'

'Perfectly.'

'Good. I hope I've heard the last of this nonsense.'

Jill renewed her interest in the file which still lay open on the desk. If there was a ruder and more humiliating way of being dismissed, Ashton had yet to encounter it. He walked over to the door and opened it, then turned about.

'A friendly word of advice,' he said. 'Stay alert, change your routine and watch your back.'

'Are you trying to be funny?' Jill asked without looking up.

'No, I'm telling you what they did to Sharon Cartwright. If she did write you a letter, it's possible they may come after you.'

Last time they had talked, the Broker had been in Savannah and the Caller in London. Now, seventy-two hours later, they were face to face in the Broker's house on East State at Wright Square in the Historic District. To be precise, they were in the conservatory on the east side of the house, which was not overlooked by the neighbouring property. The Caller was Frederic Norden, which sounded like a good WASP name except his bloodline made him anything but an Anglo-Saxon Protestant. His grandfather had left Düsseldorf in 1913 to avoid serving in the Kaiser's army, while his mother was of Spanish extraction. He was forty-six years old and had served with special forces in the Vietnam War where he had been actively involved in the Waste Disposal Programme, the assassination of suspected Vietcong activists. Following his discharge from the army, Norden had specialised in electronic surveillance, industrial espionage and enforcement, a euphemism for assault with a deadly weapon. What made him popular with Rafael Valdes was the fact that he didn't have a criminal record.

'You finished the job in good time,' the Broker observed. 'Mr Valdes said to tell you he's impressed.'

'We aim to please,' Norden said in a flat monotone.

'May I inspect the merchandise?'

'Sure.' Norden picked up the executive briefcase he'd left by his chair and placed it on the wicker table before unlocking it with a key attached to his belt by a fine link chain. Raising the lid, he opened the velvet drawstring bag inside the briefcase, and tipped out more diamonds than could be held in the palm of one hand.

'There you are,' he said, 'all five million dollars' worth.'

'I'm sure you're right but I have to have them verified against our schedule.'

'How long's that going to take?'

'No time at all,' the Broker assured him. 'The man who originally purchased them on behalf of Mr Valdes is waiting in the next room.'

'Then call him in and get on with it.'

The Broker hesitated. He would have been happier if the check could have been carried out in private but he sensed Norden would never agree to that and he wasn't inclined to make an issue of it. Bowing to the inevitable, he pressed the bell under the table to summon the man in the next room, then went over to the drinks cabinet and looked out a bottle of Jack Daniel's.

'First today,' he said. 'Care to join me?'

'No, thanks.'

The Broker poured a stiff one into a Waterford cut-glass tumbler and promised himself that come what may, he would make it last. The check was going to take some time and he didn't want Norden to get the impression he was a lush. More importantly, he was anxious that Mr Valdes shouldn't hear about his drinking habits from the hatchet man facing him across the table. Unfortunately, his good intentions fell by the wayside and he needed a top-up before the check was completed. By then, he was having to choose his words with care for fear he wouldn't be able to get his tongue around them.

'Are you satisfied now?' Norden asked when they were alone once more.

'Absolutely.' The Broker reached inside his jacket, took out a thin envelope and gave it to Norden. 'I think you will also find everything is in order.'

Norden ripped the envelope open and extracted the flimsy inside.

'What the hell's this?' he demanded angrily.

'A bank statement representing the balance of your fee,' the Broker told him calmly. 'It shows you have one hundred thousand dollars in your current account with the Standard World Wide Charter Bank of the Bahamas.'

'Which happens to be controlled by the Valdes brothers.'

'Is that a problem?' the Broker asked.

'It is when the statement doesn't show an account number. How the hell can I transfer the money without one?'

'Mr Valdes will give you the number in person, when you see him tomorrow.'

'What?'

'I'm going to give you a phone number; commit it to memory and make the call tonight at seven.'

'Who the fuck do you think you're talking to?'

'A man who will do as he's told.' The Broker paused, then said, 'The number is 404-656-0005. Now repeat it back.'

'404-656-0005,' Norden said through gritted teeth.

Intelligent, courteous, modest, honourable were qualities people instinctively associated with Robin Urquhart, the senior of four Deputy Under Secretaries at the Foreign and Commonwealth Office. Anyone who'd got a Double First in Modern Languages, Politics, Philosophy and History at Cambridge, obviously had a brain but in addition to his academic qualifications, Urquhart brought plenty of common sense to his chosen career. It was said of him that he knew the first name of every clerk, typist and messenger in the building, which in fact was no exaggeration. He was popular with the lower administrative grade, because he treated them the same as he did his peers. Most people with similar achievements would have gone through life quietly letting it be known they had got a Double First; he did not and was genuinely embarrassed when taxed about it. Urquhart was considered honourable on two counts: his word was known to be his bond and he was loyal to his crippled wife, Rosalind, whom close friends and mutual acquaintances considered unworthy of his devotion. Rosalind was county; Urquhart was the lower-middle-class boy made good, thanks to his parents who had scrimped and saved to send him to Winchester. He had met Rosalind while in charge of the British Consulate in Berlin and she had come out to spend three weeks with her elder brother, a major in the Royal Green Jackets, whose regiment had formed part of the garrison. Three weeks had become eleven months after Rosalind had got herself a secretarial job with the Berlin Infantry Brigade.

For sixteen years, Rosalind had been a model wife and had done much to further her husband's career. Things had started to go wrong with their marriage shortly after Urquhart had been appointed to the European Community Policy Division in London. Within a year, Rosalind had left their rented house in Hyde Park Gardens and had moved in with a junior, but well-heeled, partner in the biggest firm of commercial lawyers in the City.

From childhood, Rosalind had ridden to hounds with the Belvoir Hunt in Leicestershire. Thanks to the influence of her lover, she had subsequently joined the Withersfield Hunt. One frosty morning in November 1989, she had put her horse at a six-foot-high hedgerow by a ditch and the animal had balked. Rosalind had been thrown and, landing awkwardly, had broken two vertebrae, leaving her paralysed from the waist down. The lover had disappeared while she was still in Stoke Mandeville Hospital.

Urquhart had taken her back, which in the eyes of friends and acquaintances made him a saint. Rosalind now resided in a detached four-bedroom house in the better part of Islington which Urquhart had purchased and had adapted to suit her special needs. These also happened to include a live-in nurse. As he was the first to admit, without her private income to fall back on, they could never have managed, a fact of life he was not allowed to forget.

He had met Jill Sheridan two years ago when she had been promoted to head the Mid East Department, and had been very much taken with her. He regarded her as the brightest of all the assistant directors in the SIS and was convinced she possessed all the qualities to run The Service at some future date. He also found her extremely attractive and had been absurdly jealous of her husband; when they had split up, he'd been delighted, which was even more absurd, because there was nothing between Jill and himself and never would be. But sometimes in his lonely and sexless life, he would fantasise about Jill Sheridan.

When she had phoned him late in the afternoon, to ask if he could spare her a few minutes of his time that evening to discuss a personal problem, Urquhart had promptly agreed to meet her. Choosing a discreet venue had exercised them a bit, but eventually they had settled for the Villa Belmente in Camden.

Jill Sheridan had arrived at the trattoria before him and had secured a table for two beyond the bar. Leaving his raincoat with the hat-check girl, Urquhart hastened to join her. A waiter, responding to a raised finger, beat him to it.

'I think a large gin and tonic is called for,' she said, then smiled at him. 'Am I correct, Robin?' she asked.

'Fancy you remembering,' he said, and sat down on her right.

'Well, you graced two of our dinner parties before the divorce.'

'Yes. Are you still living in Bisham Gardens?' he said, making small talk while they waited for the waiter to bring the gin and tonic.

'I'm thinking of moving,' Jill told him.

'Oh, why's that? House too big for you?'

'I was burgled nearly a week ago. Well, last Wednesday, to be accurate.'

'I'm sorry to hear that.'

'They stole a string of pearls and rather a nice ring.'

'Valuable?'

'Together they were worth in excess of three thousand.' She lowered her voice. 'Some people think they took something else beside the jewellery.'

Urquhart leaned a little closer to hear what she was saying and somehow his knees accidentally brushed against her right thigh. He had read about the triple murder in the newspapers but hadn't known that two of the victims had been SIS. And, until this moment, he'd had no idea that Sharon Cartwright had been a member of the ill-fated interrogation team led by Harvey Yeo.

'I made the great mistake of looking after her when she was a probationer. A bright enough girl, Robin, but somewhat immature and definitely unstable.' Jill sighed. 'I should have distanced myself from her before she came to live in Highgate and then none of this would have happened. No – that's a terrible thing to say. What must you think of me?'

She looked vulnerable and worried out of her mind. He recalled Jill telling him over the phone that she badly needed some good advice and there was no one else she could turn to. It made him feel protective and gratified that such an attractive and self-reliant young woman should want to confide in him.

'I like to think I'm a good friend,' he said, warming to her. 'But first, I have to know what is troubling you before I can help.'

It was as if a dam had suddenly burst. Where formerly Jill had been hesitant, the words now came tumbling out in a slightly breathless voice.

'I tried to stop Sharon phoning me from Naburn but she wouldn't listen. She hated the job she was doing and wanted a transfer to my department.'

The police, he learned, had found Sharon's Cellnet in one of the bedrooms at The Firs. Thanks to British Telecom, they knew when and how many times she had called Jill.

They are saying the source confided in her and she kept that information from Harvey Yeo and sent it to me instead.'

'Why would anyone think that?'

'Because somebody broke into Sharon's flat the same day my house was burgled. The accusation is that the burglar was looking for a letter she allegedly wrote to me.'

'And there was no letter.'

'Of course there wasn't. You surely don't think I would have held on to it if she had written to me, do you, Robin?'

Urquhart reproached himself. He should have known better than to ask.

'Forgive me, it was a foolish question.'

'Well, I'm glad you believe me; everybody else wants me to prove there was no letter.'

It seemed to him that Jill was being asked to prove a negative, which was an impossibility. She was under investigation and the way things were going, she feared Hazelwood would have to call for her resignation.

'It's not Victor who's got it in for me, it's his investigating officer, Peter Ashton. We were engaged at one time and I broke it off. He's held a grudge against me ever since.'

Jill did not have to spell it out for him. He could quite see that Ashton was an embittered man and would seize this opportunity to get his own back. All he had to do was to poison Hazelwood's mind against her, which in the circumstances, wouldn't be difficult.

'It's going to be all right, Jill,' he said and gave her knee an encouraging pat. 'We will fix Mr Ashton.'

'But Peter will know who made the complaint and that will only make things worse than they already are.'

She sounded thoroughly alarmed and was fidgeting with the tablecloth. Urquhart glanced down at her lap and saw she was wearing a thigh-length green tunic.

'Rest assured, it will be done very discreetly,' he said, and made to give her another encouraging pat but this time, his hand came to rest lightly on her thigh.

'We've had years of practice at the Foreign Office doing that sort of thing.'

The girl who walked into the Isle of Dogs police station in West Ferry Road, was wearing a thin T-shirt under an anorak, faded jeans and Doc Martens. Her long, unkempt, blonde hair was soaking wet like her clothes. The duty sergeant thought she was no more than twenty, if that.

'Raining outside, is it?' he asked cheerfully.

'I've come about my boyfriend,' the girl told him in a listless voice. 'Says he's going to top himself.'

'Why would he want to do that?'

'It's on account of what's in the *Evening Standard* about that girl they fished out of the river.'

Suddenly the duty sergeant was all ears.

CHAPTER 9

Breakfast in the Ashton household was a noisy affair. Edward, having eaten all he wanted, had demanded to be lifted down from his high chair and was now sitting on the floor banging an upturned saucepan with a wooden tenderizer that was unlikely to be used on a piece of fillet steak again. On Radio 2, 'I Want to Hold Your Hand' was trying to compete with the racket but was losing out. Harriet was busy rearranging yesterday's cutlery and crockery in the dishwasher to make room for the breakfast things and was talking to herself. At least, Ashton assumed, she wasn't trying to communicate with him. In the circumstances, it was nothing short of a miracle that he eventually heard the muted trill of the Mozart secure speech facility in the sitting room.

'Duty officer, Pacific Basin,' a clipped voice informed him when he lifted the receiver. 'I was about to hang up.'

'Pity you didn't,' Ashton said. 'We're still having breakfast in this house. What did you say your name was?'

'I'm the duty officer.'

'You've got a first name, haven't you?'

There was no reply. Ashton guessed the duty officer was a comparative newcomer and was trying to decide whether he would be committing a breach of security if he disclosed his name. Not only was the Mozart crypto-protected, the code was changed every seven days, making it impossible for an outsider to eavesdrop on their conversation.

'It's not a state secret, is it?'

'No.' The duty officer cleared his throat. 'Actually, it's Barry.'

'Well, I'm glad we've got that sorted out, Barry. Now, what can I do for you?'

'The police have detained a man in connection with the murder of Sharon Cartwright. He's at Paddington Green now, helping them with their inquiries. Mr Benton thinks the DG will want you to be present.'

'He thinks,' Ashton repeated. 'Meaning it's not definite yet?'

'I'm sure the Director will contact you shortly.'

'OK, Barry. What can you tell me about this suspect?'

'I think it would be better coming from the DG.'

Ashton told him he was probably right and hung up. Moments after he had replaced the handset, the phone rang again. A wheezing sound on the line told Ashton that Victor was enjoying his first Burma cheroot of the day, which meant he was calling from the study, the only room in the house where his wife, Alice, permitted him to smoke.

'I assume Roger Benton's duty officer has spoken to you?' Hazelwood said, dispensing with the usual pleasantries.

'Yes, he said you would tell me about the man the police have in custody.'

'His name's Fox,' Hazelwood said, 'Ronnie Fox. His girlfriend walked into the Isle of Dogs police station last night and turned him in.'

Oldfield's press briefing had been attended by reporters from the northern editions of the national dailies, including a stringer for Associated Newspapers, acting for the London *Evening Standard*. Consequently, the statement detailing the injuries that had been inflicted on Sharon Cartwright had first appeared in the early edition of that paper.

'Fox was picked up in the small hours of this morning,' Hazelwood continued. 'Oldfield is on the way down from York to question him. It's possible he and Brian Thomas have already arrived at Paddington Green.'

'Brian Thomas is going to be there?'

'Haven't I just told you so?' Hazelwood said, a touch irritably.

'I'm sorry,' Ashton said, 'I must be very slow this morning. Why are we doubling up?'

'Because I would like to compare notes with him. All right?'

'Yes, of course.'

'Then please get there as soon as you can. I'm counting on you to ensure we're not denied a ringside seat.'

If there were any question of ex-Detective Chief Superintendent Brian Thomas being shown the door by fellow police officers, Ashton couldn't see why they should take any notice of him. He was about to make that point when Hazelwood severed the link.

Ashton returned to the kitchen to finish the slice of toast he'd been eating when the phone had rung.

'Got to fly,' he told Harriet.

'Don't take the car,' she said. 'I need it today.'

'You can have it.'

'That's big of you.'

'I'm a generous man,' he said and kissed her firmly on the mouth.

It had been raining during the night and the dark clouds suggested there was more to come. Leaving Rylett Close, he cut through the recreation grounds and caught a District Line train from Ravenscourt Park. At Hammersmith, he changed on to the Metropolitan, then walked the rest of the way from the Underground station at Edgware Road.

Oldfield and Thomas had caught the first train out of York and, as Hazelwood had surmised, they had already established themselves at Paddington Green by the time he arrived at the police station. So had Clifford Peachey, which was something Victor had not anticipated. Ashton didn't have to ask the MI5 man what he was doing there.

'This is where all the IRA suspects and dangerous criminals are detained,' Peachey informed him. 'Terrorists are our bread and butter, so are the drug barons now. That's why we keep a liaison officer here round the clock.'

'It also explains how the Security Service was able to obtain preferential treatment,' Thomas said.

'Preferential treatment?' Ashton echoed, and looked to Clifford Peachey for an explanation.

'It means I will be present in the interview room.'

'While we are on the outside, looking in through a one-way window,' Thomas added.

'You will be able to hear every word that's said,' Peachey told him curtly.

'But we can't put any questions directly to Fox and you can. That's the difference.'

'You must be Chief Inspector Oldfield,' Ashton said, turning to a middle-aged plain-clothes officer who was beginning to spread in all the wrong places. 'My name's Peter Ashton.'

'Glad to meet you.'

'I wouldn't want you to get the impression that we are always at loggerheads with MI5.'

'This is a police investigation,' Oldfield reminded them. 'MI5 and the SIS are only here on sufferance. I'll be interrogating Ronnie Fox, assisted by a detective sergeant from the Isle of Dogs. Any questions you have I'll put to the suspect.'

There was, Ashton thought, nothing like establishing the ground rules.

'We'll need to hear what Fox has got to say for himself first,' he said.

'No problem,' Oldfield assured him. 'I'll call a break every two hours or so. That will give you an opportunity to discuss any points you would like me to raise with him.'

'Fine. What do the police already know about Ronnie Fox? Does he have any previous convictions?'

'Not since he was a juvenile. He had five convictions for TDA before he was sixteen.'

'What's TDA?'

'Taking and driving away,' Oldfield said. 'He was a joyrider, knew how to hot-wire a car before he reached puberty.'

Fox was still mad about cars and, while they couldn't prove it, the Met's Criminal Intelligence Branch had him in the frame as the getaway driver in two particularly audacious bank robberies committed in the late eighties. Around the Isle of Dogs, he also enjoyed a reputation for being a hard man. To Ashton, he did not sound like someone who would contemplate suicide.

'He's a minicab driver,' Oldfield continued, 'works nights for the Fleetspeed company. Detectives from the Organised Crime Squad had Fox under surveillance on and off for close on six weeks between October and December last year. They got nothing; all his fares were legitimate. He didn't pick up any known criminals.'

'Did Organised Crime tell you how long he's been employed as a minicab driver?'

'Four years.'

'And before that?'

'A series of dead-end jobs – labourer on various building sites all over London, shelf-stacker in a supermarket. Then he joined the merchant navy soon after his nineteenth birthday and was a cabin steward on the Peninsula and Orient Line.'

Fox had quit the sea twenty-one months later to become a chauffeur to an elderly widow with more money than sense. Within a year the lady had sacked him, allegedly for being insolent to her. Rumour had it that she had caught him dipping into her purse once too often but had been too embarrassed to report it to the police. He had then joined the army, enlisting in the Royal Corps of Transport.

'Did a couple of emergency tours in Northern Ireland,' Oldfield said, consulting his notebook. 'Bought himself out of the army eighteen months before his due date of release. Conduct rated as good.'

'That means he must have collected a regimental entry for some military offence,' Ashton said.

'If he did, the National Identification Bureau hasn't recorded it.' Oldfield put his notebook away and made a great show of consulting his wristwatch. 'Now, if you've no more questions, we'll get this show on the road.'

'What about his solicitor? Has he arrived?'

'There isn't one; Fox reckons he doesn't need to be legally represented.'

'Cocky.'

'I'm told he's all of that,' Oldfield said.

Ashton saw that for himself when Fox walked into the interview room and sat down at the table facing Oldfield and the detective sergeant from the Isle of Dogs. There was an annoying smirk on his mouth when the DS formally introduced Oldfield.

'Fancies himself, doesn't he?' Thomas observed.

'How old is he?'

'Thirty-one and still single. If I were in his shoes, I don't think I would be in a hurry to get married either. He can get all the nooky he wants without giving up his freedom.'

Ashton thought a lot of women might be smitten by Ronnie Fox. He was a couple of inches under six feet and had the kind of physique which announced to all and sundry that here was a man who liked to keep himself in good shape. When he wasn't smirking, he had an appealing face, but the slate-grey eyes under the blond thatch told Ashton he had a mean streak.

'Got a lot of girlfriends, has he?'

'A bloody great harem by all accounts,' Thomas said morosely.

'The latest being the one who turned him in?'

'No, I'd say the flavour of the month is a redhead called Edwina. When the snatch squad lifted Fox, he was in bed with her over in Poplar High Street, a fair way from Debbie's place.'

'This Debbie,' Ashton said, feeling his way, 'is she the girl who walked into the police station?'

'That's the one.'

'Let me guess,' Ashton said wearily, 'Debbie told the police where they should look for him.'

'You've got it.'

'And Fox is going to say that she made the story up out of jealousy.'

'I'd bet a month's salary on it.'

'What about Debbie?' Ashton said. 'Is she going to retract her statement?'

'I don't know, I left my crystal ball at home.'

'We're going to end up with egg on our faces,' Ashton said gloomily. He didn't hear Thomas contradicting him.

Jekyll Island, Georgia, was not an island but a peninsula and the once-famous exclusive club was now a hotel. In 1886, two smart realtors from Georgia had journeyed to New York to sell a concept to the old and not so old money. Jekyll Island, they said, was everything a man could desire when planning a family vacation. The land was a hunter's paradise, the sea teemed with fish, the climate was superb, and complete privacy would be guaranteed, which made it an idyllic place to relax and enjoy life with their own kind. The realtors pitched their sales talk to the Vanderbilts, the Rockefellers and bankers like J. P. Morgan. And for good measure they invited some of their prospective investors to come down and see for themselves what the island was like. Then to make sure the place was everything it was supposed to be, the realtors had imported game birds and deer from the mainland before the first guests had arrived.

The hard sell had been successful and had attracted more than enough capital to build what amounted to a huge, sprawling clapboard family hotel, complete with an observation turret, grand dining room, smoking room, ladies' drawing room, library and games room. Lawns had been laid, a landing dock constructed and, directly in rear of the club, accommodation had been built for the servants and their families which had included a school for their children. To escape the sweltering heat of New York in summer, club members, with their retinue of servants, had moved to Jekyll Island where they would spend three or four months on vacation.

Changing fashions had started the club's decline; the stock market crash in October 1929 had virtually killed it off. Ownership had changed several times thereafter with the result that buildings had been allowed to fall into disrepair until eventually the servants' quarters and school had had to be demolished. During World War Two, the club had been taken over by the military and the interior modified to suit their requirements. Then, after years of neglect, the club had been acquired by the Radisson Resort Hotels Corporation and lovingly restored.

It was not the kind of location Norden would have chosen for a meeting. The Jekyll Island Club was a little too exclusive for his liking; for privacy he preferred a bustling city where there was safety in numbers and he was just an anonymous face in the crowd. But Rafael Valdes had suggested they met at Jekyll Island and Norden had known better than to disagree with him. So he had left his office in Jacksonville, Florida, crossed the state line into Georgia on Interstate 95 and continued on north to pick up US 17, then State 520. Fifty-five miles and seventy minutes after setting off, he pulled up outside the club.

A slim blond-haired man appeared from nowhere to open the

front offside door of the Honda before Norden could do it for himself. The stranger looked to be in his late twenties, had sharp pointed features, thin lips and watchful pale blue eyes.

'Mr Valdes is waiting for you on the boat,' he said in a surprisingly high-pitched voice. 'You want to come this way?'

A concrete path skirted the croquet lawn and led straight to the landing dock. Moored alongside was the boat belonging to Rafael Valdes, a large cabin cruiser powered by twin V8 engines. Norden had been told that the Cuban-born lawyer had named the craft *Maria* in honour of his daughter.

The engine rumbled into life the moment Norden stepped aboard; as he went below, the blond man helped the second bodyguard to cast off and the boat pulled away from the jetty.

Valdes clearly believed in dressing the part, in sneakers, white slacks and a thin, dark blue rollneck sweater under a blazer with gold, Staybrite buttons. He wore a yachting cap at a jaunty angle. The effect was rather comical but Norden suppressed his amusement. It was said of the Valdes brothers that you laughed with them, not at them.

'I hear from our mutual acquaintance in Savannah that you are unhappy with the bank statement,' Valdes said, and pointed to the opposing bench seat. 'So why don't you sit over there and tell me what's eating you?'

'I don't have a beef, Mr Valdes, I just want the number of my account.'

'That's why you're here, isn't it?'

'I hope so.'

Norden licked his lips. Including the helmsman, there were three bodyguards on board and they were heading out into the Atlantic Ocean at something approaching twenty knots. If Valdes had a mind to, his goons could put a bullet through Norden's body and nobody would hear a goddamned thing. And what could be easier than put his body over the side, weighted down with chains? Come to that, why bother to shoot him first? That would have been Arnaldo's way, but Norden persuaded himself that younger brother, Rafael, was a tad more civilised.

'There's also my expenses over and above the fee.' Norden took out a thin envelope. 'I have an itemised list here; perhaps you'd care to run your eye over it?'

Valdes ignored the suggestion. 'Tell me, Mr Norden,' he said, 'have I seen the last of my nephew?'

'Raúl Menendez won't bother you again.'

'Can you guarantee he won't be found?'

'It would be a million to one shot if he was.'

Menendez had been buried in a landfill site used by Bradford City Corporation. With a couple of helpers Norden had scooped out a pit some two feet deep in the confident expectation that within twenty-four hours the shallow grave in the snow would be buried under several tons of garbage.

'And what of the others? The people who were questioning my nephew?'

'They're all dead,' Norden informed him.

'Good. Now, tell me how you found nephew Raúl Garcia?'

'I'm not sure where to begin.'

'Take it from when the party returned to the States.'

Valdes had sent a diamond merchant to Amsterdam to purchase five million dollars' worth of precious stones. The necessary capital had been transferred from the Standard World Wide Charter Bank of the Bahamas. In addition, he had provided two bodyguards, one of whom had been Raúl Garcia Menendez. Choosing him had been a big mistake but Menendez was family and Valdes had evidently decided he could be trusted. And while they had been in Holland, Menendez had justified the trust placed in him. It was only after their KLM flight had landed at John F. Kennedy that he'd made his move. At some stage during the flight, he'd convinced the diamond merchant that, as a frequent traveller, his face was undoubtedly known to US Customs. It would therefore be safer if they swapped their carry-on baggage and he took the stones through.

'Your nephew and the bodyguard were waved on after presenting their declaration forms but surprise, surprise the diamond merchant is stopped and subjected to a body search.'

'Why did Customs pick him out?'

'They were tipped off by one of Raúl's accomplices and Immigration were asked to look out for him and inform Customs.'

'That's your guess.'

'No, I got it from the man himself.' Norden grinned. 'Your nephew was very co-operative; he was only too happy to answer my questions when we caught up with him. Anyway, when they reached the main concourse, Menendez told the bodyguard to watch their bags while he made a phone call to report what had happened.'

It hadn't been his intention to have the bodyguard killed but the accomplice who had plunged the hypodermic into the back of his thigh had loaded it with enough Sodium Pentathol to drop an elephant in its tracks.

'Your nephew acted concerned, yelled for somebody to please call the paramedics, then slipped away in the resultant confusion. He took a cab to La Guardia Airport where he caught the first available flight. The destination was unimportant; he just wanted to get the hell out of New York.'

Valdes had tried to deal with the situation himself but had been hamstrung by US Customs, who were determined to prosecute him for illegally importing diamonds to the value of five million dollars. By the time Valdes had backed off and hired Norden to run his nephew to ground, Menendez had clocked up over forty thousand air miles crisscrossing the States before heading down to Chile.

'I broke into his house at West Palm Beach and put together a list of credit cards from the statements he'd received. With a little hacking, it was then possible to trace his movements. I also figured that sooner or later he would touch base with either the latest woman or some member of the Menendez family to find out what was happening.'

With this in mind, Norden had traced every member of the Menendez family and put them under electronic surveillance.

'At one time or another, he talked to nearly all the people we'd bugged.'

'We?'

'My associates,' Norden said laconically. 'Anyway, his elder sister in Fort Lauderdale received more phone calls than anyone else.'

The last time he had phoned, Menendez had asked her if she had received his present. She had assumed he meant the cute little box and wanted to know what the keys were for, and he had told her that was his business.

'He'd rented a safety box somewhere,' Valdes said slowly.

'Yeah. He'd wanted a secure hiding place for the diamonds but he couldn't risk an Embassy security officer finding the keys on him. See, by then Raúl had realised he was leaving a trail we could follow and were closing in on him. So he decided to seek refuge with the British Embassy in Santiago. The Brits aren't completely stupid; they would recognise the keys to a safety deposit when they saw a pair and would know Menendez for what he was and show him to the door.'

After the Embassy had taken him in, the only way out of Chile for Menendez was a British Airways flight to Heathrow. Leaving the local hired help to keep an eye an the diplomats in Santiago's Avenida el Bosque Norte, Norden had taken off for London to arrange a reception committee.

'I travelled on a Canadian passport, checked into a quiet hotel in South Kensington and established contact with the hired help back in Santiago. I also called on a private investigator I'd done business with before and told him what I needed.'

Specifically, Norden had wanted three good man to shadow whatever vehicle collected Menendez from Heathrow. The total flight time from Santiago to Heathrow was approximately thirteen hours which was therefore the maximum advance warning he could expect to receive. Playing it safe, Norden had stipulated the surveillance team was to be available at eight hours' notice.

'The private investigator recommended we used motorcyclists on the grounds they wouldn't get boxed in by traffic and could pass themselves off as couriers. I was happy to take his advice and we had no problem tracking the official car into London. The Brits made it easy for me because they didn't accord Menendez the VIP treatment and brought him off the plane with the other passengers. It was only after they had taken Menendez to Matthew Parker Street that I learned British Intelligence were interested in him. This made things a little more complicated.'

That was something of an understatement. They'd had to trail Menendez back and forth between the Foreign Office Security Department in Matthew Parker Street and Paddington Green, which meant there had been a real danger they would be spotted. From his first-hand experience of Intelligence operations, Norden had known that Menendez would soon be transferred to a safe house, possibly outside London.

'It was touch and go,' Norden confessed. 'We couldn't work the biker routine if they moved him out of the capital and I knew we would get precious little warning. So each morning I had one driver in a car parked near Paddington Green police station, waiting for the bikers to call him on their mobile phones if British Intelligence took a different route. The guys on the motorbikes had to stay with the target vehicle until our standby driver caught up with them, which he did thirty miles up the M1 motorway.'

It had taken Norden much longer to close on the quarry in the Ford Orion he'd rented from Avis. Thereafter it had been an uphill task all the way. One look at the safe house outside Naburn and it had been apparent there would be no speedy resolution. The Firs had looked well protected and almost impossible to keep under surveillance without being spotted by the occupants. Cracking the problem had taken all of three weeks but most of the delay had been attributable to Valdes, who'd decided to keep a tight rein on the operation once he'd heard about the situation. But in the end, the Cuban lawyer had come through and provided the necessary support.

'The weather almost did for us,' Norden continued. 'The snow may have covered our tracks at The Firs but the journey to Bradford was a nightmare.'

'But mostly you had good luck,' Valdes observed. 'Especially with the woman.'

'Sharon Cartwright: yeah, she couldn't stop talking,' Norden said with heavy irony. 'Told me all I needed to know about the security system and a lot more besides. Found a letter on her addressed to Ms Jill Sheridan. Turned out she was a hotshot in British Intelligence and wasn't entitled to the reports Sharon Cartwright was sending her.'

'Did my nephew tell the Cartwright girl about the diamonds?'

'She didn't know he had been to Amsterdam.'

'You're quite sure about that?'

'Sharon Cartwright was interrogated with the utmost hostility,

Mr Valdes. Believe me, she didn't hold anything back.'

'Good.' Valdes snapped his fingers. 'Now let me see your expenses.'

'Sure.' Norden gave him the envelope containing the itemised list. 'I think you'll find everything in order.'

'I'm sure it is.' Valdes ripped the envelope open, took out the invoice, and barely gave the figures a cursory glance. 'Your checking account number with the Standard World Wide Charter Bank of the Bahamas is 0453296 FN.'

'OK, 0453296 FN,' Norden said, and made a note of it in his pocket diary.

'Your expenses will be added to the current balance plus a retainer of fifty thousand dollars.'

'Retainer?'

'Your job isn't finished yet,' Valdes told him.

By three o'clock, it was blindingly apparent that Ronnie Fox was not going to crack. The police had nothing on him and he knew it. The interview had reached the point where Oldfield was ready to quit when he called a halt for the fourth time.

'We're getting nowhere,' he told Ashton and Thomas when he joined them in the corridor. 'We can't place him at the scene of the crime, his prints aren't on the MG Maestro and the girlfriend who turned him in has retracted her statement. Says she was just getting her own back.'

'What do the Met reckon?' Ashton asked.

'They are going to charge her with wasting police time.'

They were talking at cross-purposes. Ashton had wanted to know if the Met were equally willing to let Fox walk.

'I want the address of his fixed abode,' he told Oldfield. 'Same goes for his latest girlfriend. Then I want you to go back in there with Clifford Peachey and grill him for another four hours.'

'Who do you think is running this investigation?'

'Well, we all know you are,' Thomas said, chipping in, 'but judging by the way you are conducting it, you could do with some help.'

'We're getting het up over nothing,' Ashton said. 'If Fox could hear us now, his smirk would stretch from ear to ear.'

'You're right,' Oldfield agreed reluctantly. 'Why do you need four more hours?'

'Because I'm banking that soon after Fox walks out of Paddington Green, he'll make a phone call, and I'm going to eavesdrop on the conversation.'

'You're going to plant a few bugs,' Oldfield said accusingly.

'It's best you don't know.'

'What if he has a Cellnet?'

'I know a man who has a scanner,' Ashton said cheerfully.

CHAPTER 10

The man with the scanner was Terry Hicks of the Security Vetting and Technical Services Division. Widely regarded as the king of electronic warfare and countermeasures, he had, at the height of the Cold War, helped to build the plastic dome inside the British Embassy, Moscow. Shaped like an igloo with a hinged door, it was completely soundproof and therefore ideal for Top Secret briefings; unfortunately after thirty minutes in the cocoon, people tended to emerge looking like wet dishcloths.

The downside to Hicks was that he had an uncanny knack for rubbing people up the wrong way. Kelso referred to him as 'that cocky, insolent little oik of a technician'; his opinion of the Assistant Director in charge of the Admin Wing was unprintable. When the post of Operations and General Duties had been established in 1994, the electronics wizard and his assistants had been placed under Ashton's direction, a sea change that had met with Kelso's wholehearted approval.

However, in the field of electronic countermeasures or ECM for short, Hicks was still very much a part of Frank Warren's fiefdom. In the ECM role, it was Hicks's job to spring clean the more sensitive embassies. 'Spring clean' was in-house jargon for debugging, while 'sensitive' was a euphemism for those embassies most likely to be targeted by potential foes and friends alike. Since the tour programme for 1995 had already been finalised before Operations and General Duties had come into being, Hicks had remained answerable to Frank Warren for electronic countermeasures.

The dual chain of command worked because the division of responsibilities had been mutually agreed between Ashton and Frank Warren, which would have made it extremely difficult for Hicks to play one man off against the other, had he felt so inclined.

Used to dealing with two masters, Hicks had made no comment when Ashton had phoned his office from Paddington Green to tell him what he wanted. At that stage, Ashton had no reason to suspect Hicks was unhappy with the task he'd given him; this only became evident when he arrived at Vauxhall Cross and sought him out.

'These phone taps you want,' Hicks said pensively, 'I hope they're kosher.'

'Kosher?'

'Got the Home Secretary's chop on them. I mean anything goes when you're playing away from home but things aren't so free and easy on your own turf.'

Ashton could understand why he was worried. The days when somebody like Peter Wright of MI5 could run around London, happily bugging all and sundry, were long gone. Unlike in the seventies, the high-priced help were no longer prepared to close ranks and form a protective shield; nowadays, if you failed to do things by the book, they would throw you to the lions without a second thought.

'Let me set your mind at rest,' Ashton said, poker-faced. 'What I'm asking you to do is not strictly legal.'

'That's a relief,' Hicks said in an equally droll voice. 'For a moment I thought you were going to tell me it was downright crooked.'

'All right, Terry, we've had our little joke, now let's hear how far along we are.'

'I passed the information you gave me to a friend in British Telecom, and you're right, Ronnie Fox does have a Cellnet. Question is, has he got it with him now?'

'Fox was pulled out of Edwina's bed in the early hours of this morning. Chances are he left it in her flat.'

'I was coming to that lady; she's a hairdresser, lives above the shop in Poplar High Street. Edwina isn't listed in the directory but according to the rental charges on the phone bill for the shop, there are two instruments on the same line.'

'And one of them is likely to be in the flat,' Ashton said.

'That's what I figured. Debbie, the girlfriend on the Isle of Dogs, isn't on the phone.'

Ashton wasn't surprised. Debbie was twenty-one, divorced, unemployed and had two small children by different fathers, a boy aged four and a girl of eighteen months. According to the detective sergeant from the Isle of Dogs, the Child Support Agency had tried to nail Fox for maintenance on the grounds he was the father of the little girl. Fox had denied it, a subsequent blood test had taken him out of the frame and he had walked away laughing. It had been no laughing matter for Debbie: two days after the CSA had conceded defeat, she had been hobbling around with a split lip and a bruise on her cheekbone. Her neighbours on either side had reckoned there were a lot more bruises on her ribs and stomach judging by the way she'd been holding herself.

'When do you expect to have everything set up?' Ashton asked.

'The scanner on the roof is already locked in,' Hicks told him.

'What about the implants?'

'I plan to leave an Ultimate Infinity Receiver with Edwina. It looks exactly like a plug. I'll also take the larger version with me in case she's using adaptors in the power points. The Infinity Receiver will be in the hairdressing salon but as soon as I dial her number and hang up, it won't matter which phone she uses. Upstairs or downstairs we'll hear every word that's said on her line.'

Once given the opportunity to hold forth on his favourite topic, there was no stopping Terry Hicks. He had two state-of-the-art gadgets he intended to deploy against Ronnie Fox, sophisticated bugs which were virtually undetectable.

'Terrific,' Ashton told him, 'but you haven't answered my original question. As of now, we've got less than three hours to play with and I want to know if you will be ready on time.'

'We should be.'

'Oh yeah? Why is it I get this feeling you haven't started yet?'

'I'm waiting until it's dark.'

'Look out of the window, Terry, it already is.'

'I suppose I'd better get cracking then.'

'Would you like me to lend a hand?'

Hicks shuddered at the memory of what had happened the last time they'd paired off. No plan was ever foolproof and what should have been an easy lunchtime job had come within a hair's breadth of total disaster when the husband had returned home unexpectedly, It had been nobody's fault; it so happened Ashton had been watching the wrong party and had been unable to warn him. Trapped inside the apartment, he'd managed to catch the man unawares with a sucker punch. Trouble was, he couldn't be sure that his victim hadn't caught a glimpse of him and things had been a little dicky for a while. Fortunately, they had been playing away from home and it was a lot easier to hide a foul-up when you were six thousand miles from London.

'No offence,' Hicks said, 'but I think it's best I use my own technicians on this one.'

'Fine. I'll be in my office; contact me on the direct line when you're up and running. The area code's the same as the one for the switchboard but the last four digits are 0028. OK?'

'No problem.'

'Well, don't let me hold you up,' Ashton said cheerfully.

The telephone did just that as Hicks was about to leave. Answering it, he gave a grunt then passed the handset to Ashton.

'For you,' he said, 'Mr Hazelwood's PA.'

Victor, it transpired, wished to see him and would he please make himself available as soon as possible?

In the Civil Service, offices were furnished on a scale deemed appropriate for the seniority of the occupant, a practice that was also observed by the SIS and MI5. A junior Grade III Intelligence officer was therefore only entitled to a steel desk with sliding drawers and a tubular steel chair with a padded seat and backrest. On the other hand, the Director General was provided with a large oak desk complete with brass handles on all the drawers, a matching bookcase, a comfortable swivel chair and three leather armchairs for visitors. In addition, there was either an Axminster or Wilton carpet on the floor and a somewhat old-fashioned hatstand instead of a hook on the back of the door. Finally, undersecretaries and their equivalent were offered a choice of paintings from a list of original watercolours and oils held by the Property Services Agency.

Hazelwood could have had a Canaletto, a Turner, a Utrillo or any one of a dozen other famous artists, but his taste definitely verged on the jingoistic. He had, in fact, chosen a signed print of Terence Cuneo's *The Bridge at Arnhem*, a picture showing a battered-looking corvette on a storm-tossed Atlantic, entitled *Convoy Escort*, and *Enemy Coast Ahead*, which depicted a vic of three Wellington bombers on a moonlit night approaching a smudge of land on the horizon. Both the latter paintings bore only the initials of the artist.

Hazelwood was standing with his back to the door and in the middle of the room where he could admire all three pictures simultaneously.

'They arrived this morning,' he said without turning round. 'What do you think of them?'

'They're you to a T,' Ashton told him.

'I'm glad you approve.' Hazelwood returned to his desk and sat down, then automatically opened the ornate cigar box and took out a Burma cheroot.

'There was a JIC meeting this morning,' he said and paused.

Ashton got the impression that Victor was allowing him time to make some sort of comment but he couldn't see why. There was nothing earth-shattering about his statement. The Joint Intelligence Committee always met every Tuesday under the chairmanship of the Deputy Cabinet Secretary and was attended by the Directors General of the SIS, MI5 and Government Communication Headquarters, plus the Chief of the Defence Intelligence Staff.

'As we broke up, the Deputy Cabinet Secretary took me aside. He said he could understand our determination to exact retribution but wouldn't it be better to leave the murder investigation to the police instead of launching our own parallel witch-hunt.'

'Witch-hunt?'

Hazelwood struck a match and lit the cheroot. 'That's what he said.'

'Sounds as if Jill Sheridan has been complaining to her friends.'

'Quite. What exactly did you say to her?'

Hazelwood wasn't joking. If Harriet had been present, she would have said it was no more than what she would have expected of Victor. In her opinion, when the going got tough he was the first to duck below the parapet.

'Are you serious?' Ashton asked.

'Am I smiling?' Hazelwood countered.

'You seem to have a convenient memory, Director,' Ashton told him in a cold rage. 'I warned you Jill would not admit to anything which might damage her career unless I could offer her some sort of inducement. You wouldn't hear of it and maintained I wouldn't know that she wouldn't co-operate until I tried. So I tried.'

'And did what?'

'I accused Jill of recruiting Sharon Cartwright with a promise to back her request for a transfer to the Mid East Department. I said that in return, Sharon kept her informed of everything Menendez told Harvey Yeo and a few things only she could have learned. Jill denied everything and insisted the burglars who'd broken into her house had been after her jewellery only.'

'And you left it at that?'

'No, I advised Jill to stay alert in case the killers came after her.'

'Unwise, smacks of harassment.'

'If that's what Ms Sheridan inferred then she must have something to hide.'

'Could even be taken as a veiled threat,' Hazelwood continued, preoccupied with his own thoughts.

'I was hoping to get through to her.'

'Well, it didn't work and the mistake was all mine. I should have taken more account of your previous relationship and got someone else to interview Jill.'

'You want me to give the lady a wide berth in future?'

'Yes.'

'That's fine by me,' Ashton said. 'I never was keen on the idea anyway.'

'Best thing you can do is concentrate on Mr Ronnie Fox.'

'I'll need to watch my step. The police are already pretty fed up with Brian Thomas breathing down their necks and he was one of their own not so very long ago. If we're not careful, we'll have the Home Secretary down on us like a ton of bricks.'

'You let me worry about that.' Hazelwood left the cheroot to burn out in the cut-down shell case, oblivious of the smoke which drifted in front of his face. 'I hear the police are going to release Fox.'

Ashton nodded. He supposed Thomas must have phoned him

soon after he'd left Paddington Green. Or else Victor had got the news from Clifford Peachey.

'I also hear you intend to bug him?'

No two ways about it, the source of his information had to be the ex-Detective Chief Superintendent. Furthermore, Victor didn't sound too pleased. 'You don't approve?' Ashton observed.

'I like to be consulted before you initiate such an operation,' Hazelwood told him.

'Point taken, Director.'

'You're being a little formal, aren't you, Peter?'

'I suppose I am but I'm not too clear where I stand any more. When Operations and General Duties was established, you told me I was your personal troubleshooter.'

Ashton could have said there was a time when he knew instinctively what Victor wanted from him and could bank on his support, no matter what.

'It comes as a shock when you discover the Deputy Cabinet Secretary is one of Jill's allies.'

It seemed incredible that Hazelwood should feel threatened by the most junior of all his assistant directors. You could go no higher than Director General in the SIS; when you reached that dizzy pinnacle, the only thing to look forward to was a knighthood. In days of old before Prime Minister Major decided to make honours and awards more democratic, Hazelwood would have automatically been made a Knight Commander of the Bath on appointment to DG, and his wife would have become Lady Alice. Nowadays, you had to earn the KCB which, in Victor's case, meant the Permanent Undersecretary of State at the Foreign and Commonwealth Office had to recommend him. And it was an even chance that the chairman of the Joint Intelligence Committee would be consulted. Was his heart set on a knighthood and he could see it slipping away from him? Was that why Victor was on edge? Or was it simply that he wasn't up to the job? That he had grown weary of resisting the savage cuts the Treasury would dearly love to impose and was just plain irritable as a result?

'You believe Fox will make a phone call the moment he is released from Paddington Green?'

'I think it's likely,' Ashton said.

'And by that time you will have him under electronic surveillance?'

'If all goes well.'

'What happens if Fox uses a pay phone?'

'We lose out.' Ashton smiled. 'But we have to get lucky sometime. I'm also going to borrow a couple of drivers from the Motor Transport section. One will cover the offices of Fleetspeed in Poplar High Street, the other will watch Fox's home address.'

Hazelwood grunted, seemingly unimpressed. 'Are there any other avenues you can explore?'

'Yes. Fox was in the army a few years back. I've a hunch he left under a bit of a cloud.'

'So what are you doing about it?'

'I'm going to ask the Armed Forces Desk to obtain his documents.'

Given the name, initials and service number of a soldier, the appropriate Records Office would have no difficulty in finding the Record of Service, medical documents, squadron and regimental conduct sheets. However, all the SIS could tell the army about Fox was his date and place of birth and that he'd enlisted in the Royal Corps of Transport sometime in 1986 when aged twenty-two. Locating his documents on the basis of that information was not an impossible task for the Records Office. It would just take them a little longer to produce the relevant papers.

It was easy enough to locate the ladies' hairdressing salon on Poplar High Street. There was a great big sign above the shop window which proclaimed it was EDWINA's and it was sandwiched between a newsagents and a minimarket owned by K. P. Roy of Bombay, Calcutta and London. The minimarket was a family-run business and was the only shop still open at this hour in the precinct. Hicks walked on past Edwina's, turned left into a side street a hundred yards beyond the salon and wheeled left again into an unlit alleyway that ran parallel with Poplar High Street. A hundred yards was a hundred and twenty full-length paces. He counted them off silently, while simultaneously noting how many back gates he passed.

The flat above the newsagent's was in darkness. Although the curtains were drawn next door but one, Hicks could see the lights were on in the upstairs back room of K. P. Roy's minimarket. Edwina didn't even have a net in the window and her place was lit up like a gin palace. The other hazard confronting Hicks was the back gate of her establishment, which hung askew and would scrape the concrete yard when he pushed it open. He raised the latch, lifted the gate bodily and rammed it hard against the rotting post to provide the necessary ground clearance as he swung it back. Some idiot had left the dustbin in the way and he caught it a glancing blow, dislodging the lid, which wasn't on properly. It landed on the concrete with a clatter, loud enough in his imagination to wake the heaviest sleeper. Mouth bone dry, Hicks waited for someone to call out and ask what he was doing in the yard, but there was no reaction. He closed the gate quietly behind him, then tiptoed across the yard.

The pencil thin flashlight he carried showed that the back door to the hairdressing salon was secured by a Yale lock. He took out a bunch of skeleton keys and tried four of them before he found one that fitted. The room he entered was no bigger than a walk-in cupboard. Adjustable racks on either side of the passageway were used to store towels, caps, coveralls, shampoos, tints, dyes, combs, rollers and spare blow-dryers. The inner door facing him had a mortice lock; probing it with a steel rod 3 mm in diameter, he discovered the key was still in the door on the reverse side. With infinite care, he pushed the key out of the door, hoping the radio or music centre he could hear upstairs would drown out the noise it made landing on the floor.

There was not a lock in London he couldn't open; all it took was time, patience and steady nerves. Ashton had said he had until seven o'clock to complete the task, so time wasn't a problem. It was however difficult to be patient when the tension was getting to him and none of the damned keys would fit. He wondered if he had got the set Ashton had borrowed nearly a week ago. It would be like him to use brute force when a light touch was required. Could be Ashton had well and truly buggered the vital key, in which case the job wouldn't get done. One more time, Hicks promised himself, just one more time to make absolutely sure he wasn't at fault. It turned out to be a wise decision. Much to his surprise, on this occasion, the first skeleton key he tried slid home and unlocked the door.

The glare from the streetlights meant he could dispense with the pencil flash. To his left were two complete units consisting of a large wall mirror, a washbasin above a fitted cupboard, a pedestal, a leather upholstered armchair and what Hicks thought of as a bone dome hair-dryer. Two bench seats arranged in an inverted letter L and a low round table covered in women's magazines constituted the reception area. The office was a desk, an appointments diary and an answerphone hidden out of sight behind a multicoloured plastic curtain. A couple of hot air blowers was the only form of heating in the salon, which explained why there were adaptors in every power point.

Hicks decided to replace the adaptor nearest the answerphone with the larger version of the Ultimate Infinity Receiver, a job that took him all of three seconds to complete. 'Easy as falling off a log,' he whispered to himself, then nearly jumped out of his skin when the BT Response 300 suddenly came to life. Reacting quickly, he activated the answering machine, and turned the volume down while the phone was still ringing. Answer it, Edwina, he pleaded silently, answer the bloody thing before the tape cuts in and the caller hears your pre-recorded message. Then there was a faint click as she lifted the receiver and he immediately relaxed.

A man said, 'Have you missed me?'

'Ronnie?'

'Who else is bonking you?'

'Cheeky sod.'

Hicks glanced at his wristwatch: 18.23 and Fox out on the street thirty-seven minutes early. Situation normal, all fucked up. When did anything go according to plan?

'Where are you calling from?' Edwina asked.

'A payphone in Edgware Road. I told you they would have to let me go.'

'Yeah.'

'How did you make out with the filth? They give you a hard time?'

'You mean apart from smashing down the door to my flat with a sledgehammer and putting me in bad odour with the neighbours? The Roys haven't stopped complaining. Anybody would think it was my fault the police woke their baby. Bad news travels fast. I don't know how many women cancelled their appointments. It's been a bloody awful day.'

'Never mind that, did you call Willie?'

'What for? He's not a carpenter, couldn't replace my door, could he?' Edwina paused and Hicks could envisage her frowning. 'Are you coming round?' she asked in a nervy voice.

'Later,' Fox told her. 'Got to earn some dosh first.'

'You going minicabbing?'

'I'll see you shortly,' Fox said and hung up. There was a telltale click as Edwina put the phone down.

Hicks rewound the tape and hoped to God that any messages subsequently left on the answering machine would overrun the conversation he'd recorded. He readjusted the volume, moving the control back to its original position. Switching the machine off was the tricky bit because the BT Response 300 emitted a loud peep and he had no idea where the extension in the flat was located. It would be nice to think it wasn't in the sitting room and the time it had taken her to answer the phone suggested this could be the case. On the other hand, she could have been dozing or, alternatively, she might have turned the sound down on the radio, music centre or TV first. Mentally crossing his fingers that she wouldn't hear the peep, he touched the appropriate button.

He retrieved the key to the mortice lock, pushed it home, then stepped into the storeroom and closed the door behind him. Inserting a pair of thin tweezers into the keyhole, he attempted to lock the door but there was nothing for the claws to get a grip on and he gave it up as a bad job. Since nothing in the salon had been disturbed, he reckoned there was a good chance that Edwina would conclude she had forgotten to lock the inner door.

Hicks went on through and let himself out into the yard and a persistent drizzle that had obviously started while he was in the salon. Faced with a totally smooth surface without so much as a letterbox to hang on to, closing the door wasn't the easiest thing to do in the world. He shoved a skeleton key into the Yale and turned it until the lug had retracted into the housing, then exerting an upward pressure to hold the key in place, he drew the door flush with the jamb and allowed the lock to engage. After that performance, opening and closing the wooden gate was child's play.

Hicks walked along the alleyway, turned right, then crossed Poplar High Street and made his way to the Dockland Light Railway station where he'd left his van in Stoneyard Lane. Dipping his right hand into the pocket of his anorak, he took out the Cellnet and punched up Ashton's direct-dial office number which enabled him to bypass the switchboard at Vauxhall Cross.

CHAPTER 11

Assistant directors, their deputies and a few privileged Grade I Intelligence officers occupied north-facing offices with a river view from the National Westminster towerblock to the Houses of Parliament. Even on a wet and windy evening the vista could be exciting to the eye. Five months ago, Ashton had enjoyed a similar outlook from his office on the fourth floor. He was still on the same floor, but in one of those internal reorganisations which all government ministries indulge in from time to time he had been moved across the corridor. Instead of the river, he now had a view of the railtracks from Vauxhall to Queenstown Road, Battersea. If you were a train spotter, there was a lot to be said for his twelve by nine shoebox. If you weren't a railway buff, that was just too bad because the skyline of the London Borough of Lambeth was not exactly uplifting.

At least Ashton did not feel uplifted, especially as everybody else on the fourth floor had gone home long ago. Turning away from the window, he returned to his desk and sat down. The PVS 5400 hand-held radio which he had drawn from the General Stores Section was manufactured by Plessey Military Communications. Intended primarily for the Infantry, the transceiver had a maximum range of four kilometres. The two drivers he'd asked for were in position and had established radio contact, though how long this would last was problematical. Both Eric Daniels, the former RMP sergeant who was keeping Fox's one-bedroom flat under observation, and the second driver, whose task was to watch the Fleetspeed office in Poplar High Street, were already at the outer limit of the hand-held radio. If, through force of circumstance, they moved out of voice range, both men would then have to rely on their cellular communications, which would slow things up and make it difficult to react to a rapidly changing situation.

A communication blackout would be about par for the night. Fox had been released at least thirty-seven minutes earlier than planned, when he had rung Edwina at 18.23 hours from a pay phone in the Edgware Road, and it was now 19.55. For God's sake, how long was it going to take him to reach his place on Billingsgate Road? All Fox had to do was to board a Circle Line train at Edgware Road, get out at Tower Hill and transfer to the Docklands Light Railway. Even allowing for an off-peak service on the Underground, he should have showed up a good half-hour ago. Maybe he had lied to the current number one girlfriend? Maybe Daniels was catnapping?

Ashton depressed the transmit button on the hand-held radio. 'One, this is zero,' he said crisply. 'How do you hear me?'

'One, loud and clear, over.'

'One, Roger, send sitrep.'

'One, nothing to report,' Daniels told him, then said, 'Correction. I assume you know Bluebell is in my location with Minor?'

Bluebell was the appointment code for an electrical and mechanical engineer, Minor indicated an assistant. The fact that Hicks and one of his technicians were still in the vicinity was news to Ashton. As he reached for the Cellnet, Callsign Two came up on the air to inform him that there had definitely been no sign of Fox at the minicab firm. Acknowledging the message, Ashton told both outstations to maintain listening watch, then punched up Hicks on the mobile phone.

'All right, Terry,' he said, 'suppose you tell me what you are playing at. Why are you and your assistant still in the area?'

'I've got it wrong, haven't I?' Hicks said, doing his best to sound rueful. 'You didn't mean for us to stick around in case Daniels needed help. Right?'

Ashton mulled it over and decided it might be advantageous to leave the technicians in place. There was no telling what Fox might get up to and the additional manpower could prove useful if he had the pair of them under tight control. In words of one syllable Ashton left Hicks in no doubt that he would be hung up to dry if he moved so much as an inch without his permission.

Ashton wondered if he should call Harriet again. He had already warned her that he was going to be late and she had asked him how late was late, a question he had been unable to answer. And nothing had changed since then. The simplest decisions were often the hardest to consider and he was still trying to make up his mind when he heard footsteps in the corridor. He assumed it was the duty officer and called out, 'Working,' to let him know there was no point in carrying out the nightly security check of his office just yet.

'I can see you are,' Thomas said from the doorway.

Ashton looked up. 'I thought you must have gone home when they let Fox go.'

'No. I persuaded Oldfield to have a farewell drink with me before he departed for York. I wouldn't say we parted the best of friends but at least we were on speaking terms. I said some pretty harsh things to him this morning.'

'I shouldn't let it bother you,' Ashton told him. 'Oldfield was pretty stroppy too.'

'Had a right to be, we were taking over his investigation.'

'Is that why he didn't continue the interview until 19.00 hours as we'd asked?'

'No, you'd have to lay that at Peachey's door. He told Oldfield point-blank they were getting nowhere and he was all for calling it a day. This was said out in the corridor, not in Fox's hearing.'

'That's just as well.'

'The detective sergeant from H District supported your friend from MI5, even went so far as to suggest that with the lack of evidence we had against him, Fox could sue the Met for wrongful arrest. Oldfield didn't need a lot of convincing. I mean, Fox was so damned cool he even had me believing he had been put on the spot by a jealous girlfriend.'

'So what time was he released?'

'Must have been a few minutes before six.'

The time was now five past eight. In the two hours and ten minutes that he had been at liberty, Fox could have journeyed to the outermost suburb and back again. Provided, of course, he wasn't skint.

'How much did Fox have on him?' Ashton asked.

'Moneywise? Under four pounds in loose change.'

'Are you sure?'

'Dammit, I was there when he signed for his property. You have to remember Fox was yanked out of bed before the crack of dawn. His clothes were thrown at him and he was told he had two minutes in which to get dressed. They didn't give him time to put his socks on, never mind look around for his wallet. He had to finish dressing at the police station.'

What could a man do with less than four pounds in his pocket? Not a lot, except ride the Underground, doubling back on his tracks to make sure he wasn't being followed. For over two hours? What did it take to satisfy Fox that he was clean? Maybe he'd rung another friend and got himself picked up? That would explain how two hours had slid past without anyone catching sight of him.

There was never a more welcome sound than Daniels clearing his throat before announcing his call sign.

'I think we've got something,' he said. 'One drowned rat in jacket and trousers, shirt open at the neck, has just appeared in view. Looks soaked to the skin and sorry for himself . . . Turning into Mandela Court . . . walking past the lockups . . . Got to be Fox, fits his description. Subject now entering block of flats and no longer in sight.'

Ashton told Daniels to keep him informed of developments, checked with Callsign Two that he'd heard the transmission and then called Hicks on the mobile to ascertain whether he had sighted their quarry.

'Not from where I'm parked.'

'What about your mate?'

'He's even farther away.'

'OK. Go tell him what's happened, then return to your own van.'

Above all, Hicks was to keep the line open. Ashton made that very clear to him. If Fox did leave his one-bedroom flat, every second would count and he didn't want to waste precious time tapping out Hicks's mobile number.

'Planning to shadow Ronnie Fox?' Thomas shook his head. 'You've got to be a hell of an optimist. He didn't put a foot wrong when Organised Crime had him under surveillance for seven weeks, and they're the experts. A tenner says he will spot our people inside five minutes.'

The faint background mush on the hand-held radio suddenly cut out and Daniels came through loud and clear to report that Fox had reappeared.

'Changed his clothing . . . now wearing a dark anorak and jeans . . . He's opening one of the lockups on the forecourt . . . raising the up-and-over door . . .'

Daniels stopped talking but continued to hold the transmit button on send. In the ensuing silence, Ashton could hear him breathing quickly in and out like a man who had just completed a fifty-yard dash. There was no mistaking his excitement when he came up on the air again to report that Fox had just reversed out of his garage and was moving off.

'Making a right turn on Billingsgate, heading towards the old West India Dock.'

Ashton glanced at his wristwatch. In the five minutes that had elapsed since Daniels had first spotted him, Fox had changed out of his wet clothes and was on the move again. By any standard, that was pretty good going. Still listening to the running commentary from Daniels, he picked up the Cellnet and asked Hicks if Fox had used the phone while he was in the flat.

'Definitely not,' Hicks told him.

'The bug is OK? I mean, it hasn't caught a cold or anything like that?'

'It's as fit as a fiddle.'

Fox had passed under the Docklands Light Railway and made a right into Aspen Way. When he turned left into Casper Lane, Ashton was sure he was heading for the minicab office in Poplar High Street.

'You got a car handy?' he asked Thomas.

'Yeah, a Honda Accord; it's in the basement garage.'

'Good. Do you know any senior officers in Special Branch? Someone who would be prepared to do you a favour?'

'That would depend on the favour,' Thomas said cautiously.

'It would entail deflecting a query from a member of the public with a small white lie.'

'Oh yeah? I know your white lies, they're big enough to get a person hanged.'

'I just want him to confirm that I really am one of his detective sergeants.' Ashton smiled. 'Don't look so alarmed, there's every chance the party will take my word for it.'

'Are you going to tell me what the hell is going on?'

'Yes, just as soon as I know myself.'

Daniels broke in again, his voice fluctuating, normal one moment, practically inaudible the next, a sign that he was operating partially beyond the maximum range of the set. By getting him to repeat every word twice, Ashton learned that Fox had entered the minicab office, having left his vehicle in Woodstock Terrace approximately twenty yards beyond it. He gathered Callsign Two was parked directly across the street from the office and facing west while Daniels was on the other side of the road, pointing in the opposite direction.

Ashton found both locations in a copy of Nicholson's *London Streetfinder*, then ordered Hicks to proceed to Woodstock Terrace and told him how to get there.

'What about my mate?' Hicks asked.

'Tell the guy to go on home, we don't need him.' Ashton put the phone down and faced Thomas. 'Now would be a good time to ask that favour of your friend in Special Branch,' he said.

'I will, soon as I know what's going down.'

'Well, the way I see it, Edwina wasn't the only person Fox rang from a pay phone. I don't pretend to know who he called after speaking to her but I'm betting he told this anonymous joker to order a minicab from Fleetspeed and to ask for him by name.'

'A bit far-fetched, isn't it?'

'I don't agree. It's how he fooled the Organised Crime Squad when they were following him around. Anyway, after Fox has departed, I'm going to have a word with the dispatcher and find out who the fare is.'

'I can think of a dozen reasons why you'll probably draw a blank.'

'So can I,' Ashton told him, 'and all of them amount to an excuse for doing nothing, which isn't my style.'

'I guess I'd better call my friend,' Thomas said. 'Mind if I use your phone?'

'Don't touch the mobile, I need to keep that line open to Hicks. Use the other phone. Dial 9 first and you'll bypass the switchboard.'

Ashton left him to it, went over to the combination safe and opened it up. Among the aids he had acquired from the Security Vetting and Technical Services Division was a fake warrant card good enough to deceive any law enforcement officer up to and including the Commissioner in charge of the Metropolitan Police Force.

Hicks came through on the Cellnet to say he was in position, while Thomas was still buttering up his friend in Special Branch. To add to the confusion, Daniels attempted to pass a message which was reduced to pure gobbledegook by factors outside his control. The communication failure convinced Ashton that moving to within voice range was more important than anything Special Branch might be prepared to do for him. Signalling Thomas to wrap it up, he grabbed the hand-held radio and Cellnet phone and started off down the corridor. An angry Brian Thomas caught up with him at the bank of lifts.

'What the hell are you playing at? You ask me to set things up with Special Branch and then bugger off while I'm talking to Commander Isherwood.'

'I'm sorry.' Ashton stepped into the lift and pressed the button for the basement.

'You're sorry!' Thomas echoed. 'Listen, I had to ring Isherwood at home, which didn't go down too well with Mrs Isherwood because she had organised a dinner party and they were right in the middle of it. And Paul didn't sound best pleased either, probably because his wife had given him an earful . . .'

Like you're giving me now, Ashton thought.

'But I've known Paul since he was a detective constable and we're old friends, so his feathers didn't stay ruffled for long . . .'

'Good.'

'And I'm getting him used to the idea of my saving your bacon when you take off like a scolded cat.'

'Because I've lost contact with everybody except Hicks and I don't want to be caught flat-footed if Fox takes off before we are in voice range.'

The doors opened at the basement level. Ashton stepped out of the lift and walked towards the only Honda Accord in the garage. Thomas continued to give him a piece of his mind as they crossed Westminster Bridge and sped up the Embankment. Radio contact was re-established before they reached Cannon Street station. A few minutes later, Daniels reported that their quarry had just left the minicab office and was proceeding on foot towards Woodstock Terrace.

The Fleetspeed Minicabs office was just beyond the recreation ground. It was, Ashton calculated, only a matter of a hundred yards from the ladies' hairdressing salon which went some way to explaining how Fox had come to meet Edwina. By the time he and Thomas had arrived on the scene, Fox was heading towards Whitechapel on the Commercial Road with Hicks, Callsign Two and Daniels in tow.

The surveillance detail had been put together in a hurry and had never worked as a team before. With the exception of Daniels, their special driving skills had not been tested for real. If that wasn't bad enough, they had no common means of communication; worse still, Ashton knew he would be unable to contact Callsigns One and Two if they were more than four kilometres from his position. Consequently, he had stipulated that they should not attempt to ring the changes. In accordance with his instructions Hicks had led off, followed by Callsign Two, with Daniels, the most experienced driver, bringing up in the rear. Each man in turn would shadow Fox for a maximum distance of three miles and then break off. Ashton had laid down two exceptions to this ruling: if Fox behaved in a way which suggested that he suspected he was being followed, then whoever was in the lead at the time would immediately abort. The other variation applied only to Daniels: as the last man in the team, he could use his discretion whether to break off at the three-mile point.

'Do you want me to come with you?' Thomas asked.

'No, this was my idea. If anything goes wrong, I should be the one to catch the flak.'

'Well, good luck.'

'Thanks.'

Ashton got out of the Honda. Poplar High Street on a wet and windy night at the end of January, when winter was really beginning to bite, was not the locale to lift the spirit. The pavements were deserted because most sensible people were indoors watching TV or doing whatever happened to be their thing. On such a night, even the fish and chip shop two doors along from Fleetspeed Minicabs wasn't doing much in the way of business that Ashton could see.

Fleetspeed occupied long, narrow premises which Ashton surmised must have been a drugstore at one time, an assumption based on a faded poster on the back wall that asked him if he had Macleaned his teeth today. The furniture consisted of three easy chairs arranged round a low table, scarred with cigarette burns, and a half-moon-shape cocktail bar that looked as if it had been cobbled together by a singularly untalented DIY enthusiast. Tucked into the corner of the shop, the cocktail bar served as an office for the dispatcher, a thin-faced man whose approaching baldness was badly disguised by a few strands of greasy hair slicked across his scalp. The dispatcher was watching a football match on a portable TV, the solitary driver was plugged into a Walkman and had his nose in a paperback. He did not look up when Ashton flashed his warrant card at the dispatcher and introduced himself.

'Detective Sergeant Ashton,' he said. 'You want to turn the volume down on the TV?'

The dispatcher muttered an obscenity under his breath and reluctantly complied.

'That do you?' he said belligerently.

'Yes. You have a driver called Ronnie Fox . . .'

'Who?'

Ashton leaned over the counter, put his face close to the dispatcher's.

'Look at me,' he said softly. 'You've really no idea how unpleasant I can get when a piece of low-life crap like you tries it on with me. Now let's start again. Ronnie Fox left this office ten, maybe fifteen minutes ago and he wasn't going home. I want you to produce your log and show me the name and address of his fare.'

The dispatcher placed his clipboard upside down on the counter so that Ashton could see it, then pointed to the last entry with a nicotine-stained finger.

'There you are, Mr Philip Easter, 34 Trinity Square, London EC3. Said he wanted to go to Heathrow.'

'He specifically asked for Fox?'

'Yep.'

'He's picked up Easter on a previous occasion?'

'Must have done.'

'Right. Let's have a look at your *London Residential Directory*.'

The dispatcher produced a dog-eared copy that was two years out of date. Easter was not a common surname and the only subscriber with the right initial lived in Spitalfields. There was however a V. P. Easter of Trinity Place in the correct postal district. Ashton made a note of both phone numbers and returned the directory, then cautioned the dispatcher to keep his mouth shut.

'No friendly warning to Fox. Got it?'

'I'm way ahead of you,' the dispatcher told him. 'And just for the record, I wouldn't tell that bugger anything.'

Ashton jerked a thumb over his shoulder.

'What about pally over there?'

'As far as he's concerned, you dropped in to ask the way to Macrow Walk.'

'That's the style.'

Thomas had the car radio on and was rapidly going through the pre-set frequencies to find something to his taste. *Evening Session* on Radio 1, *The Best of Country Music* on 2 and the London Mozart Players on 3 apparently did not appeal to him. The lecture on Radio 4 merely caused a puzzled frown.

'Try making a U-turn,' Ashton told him, 'then head up the Commercial Road.'

'What have you got?'

'The name and address of the fare – maybe.'

Ashton was right to strike a cautious note. Mr P. Easter of Spitalfields was at home and most definitely had no intention of going to Heathrow, while V. P. Easter turned out to be a very fiery woman who assumed he was making a nuisance call and threatened to have the police on him.

'I told you he was smart,' Thomas said with gloomy satisfaction. Ashton made a third phonecall on the mobile and learned that Hicks had peeled off at Aldgate and was on his way back to Vauxhall Cross. So far so good, he thought, and switched to the hand-held radio. When both callsigns answered almost simultaneously, he didn't have to wait any time at all to have his worst fears confirmed.

'We've lost him,' Daniels said laconically.

'So where are you now?' Ashton asked.

'Primrose Street, north of Liverpool Street station.'

'It will take us about five minutes to get there,' Thomas informed him quietly.

Ashton made no comment. What difference did it make whether it was five minutes or half an hour? Getting there quickly wouldn't lessen the sour taste in his mouth. Maybe he had done his best to anticipate every eventuality but clearly his best had not been good enough.

He saw no reason to change his opinion when Daniels explained what had happened. From Aldgate, Fox had turned into Middlesex Street and headed towards Liverpool Street station before branching off at Bishopsgate. He had then left the main road and started to quarter the back streets.

'My partner thought Fox must have rumbled him,' Daniels continued, 'so he broke off contact and I took over. I cruised every street bounded by Bishopsgate, Great Eastern Street and City Road but could find no sign of him.'

'The fare must have been waiting for Fox at an rv they'd previously agreed,' Ashton said, thinking aloud.

'This was during a phone call he made soon after being released from Paddington Green?' Thomas queried.

'Yes.'

'Well, I wouldn't quarrel with that assumption but where does it get us?'

'Daniels and his mate have been searching for the wrong car. We should be hunting for the one the fare used, to get to the rv.'

Thomas snorted in disgust. 'And just how do we go about that?' he snapped.

'We look for a vehicle with a warm engine,' Ashton told him. 'Jesus Christ,' Thomas growled, 'you never give up, do you?'

CHAPTER 12

If anything, the area search had proved a little too successful. In the back streets enclosed by Bishopsgate, Great Eastern, City Road and London Wall, they had found no fewer than four vehicles with engines that were still faintly warm to the touch. Three of them had been parked near Liverpool Street station, the fourth had been left at Finsbury Square. From bitter experience, Ashton had learned that trying to second-guess Fox was a fruitless exercise. He had three vehicles to play with and four possible targets which to all intents and purposes was a no-win equation. Furthermore, he couldn't be certain that Fox had simply used the area to run a check to make sure nobody was following him before going on to a rendezvous farther away.

In the end, Ashton had decided to stand everybody down and fax the four registration numbers to the Driver and Vehicle Licensing Centre, Swansea. It hadn't helped to be told by Thomas that he had done the sensible thing. The fact was he'd failed, and that was down to bad planning, a lack of foresight and inadequate resources. Returning to Vauxhall Cross, Ashton had collected the radios from the two drivers and locked all three sets in his office safe overnight. Daniels had offered to drive him home but he'd been in a hair shirt mood and had walked across Westminster Bridge to catch the District Line train to Ravenscourt Park. On a day when everything had gone wrong and Ashton was beginning to wish he had never got out of bed that morning, using the Underground had been one more bad move. There had been a signals failure between South Kensington and Gloucester Road which had caused a forty-five minute delay; then a sad middle-aged man had thrown himself under the train as they pulled into Earls Court.

It had gone midnight by the time he'd finally arrived at

Ravenscourt Park. The gates to the recreation ground had been locked hours ago and he'd had to walk the long way round to Rylett Close. Harriet had left a note for him in the kitchen. His supper, she had written, was in the oven and needed to be warmed up. She wanted him to know that it had started out as a shepherd's pie but had already been reheated so many times it now resembled a piece of asphalt. Unless he was desperately hungry, she advised him to empty the dish into the wastebin.

Ashton took her advice, disposed of the burnt offering and dined off Jacobs' cream crackers with a stiff whisky and soda. He thought about looking in on Edward but his son was a notoriously light sleeper, and Ashton was probably in enough trouble with Harriet as it was. He undressed in the dark, draped his jacket around the back of the upright chair and left the rest of his clothes on the seat; then gently drawing the sheets and blankets aside, he slipped into bed.

'A bad day, huh?' Harriet said quietly.

'Some people had it worse,' he said, thinking of the unhappy man who'd thrown himself on to the live rail and the horrified train driver who had been unable to stop in time.

Harriet turned over on to her right side and hugged him close with her left arm around his shoulder.

'Don't let it get you down, there's always tomorrow.'

'I'll try to remember that.'

'Meantime, tonight can only get better,' she murmured and began to stroke his thighs with her free hand.

As in so many other instances, Harriet was proved right. Come the morning, Ashton was less inclined to blame himself entirely for the abortive operation. The restoration of his self-esteem was completed shortly after he arrived at the office when Hicks tapped on the door and walked in with a huge smile on his face.

'I think you'll want to hear this,' he said, and placed a cassette on the desk.

'Fox used his mobile and the scanner picked up the call?'

'You got it. Cocky bastard rang his mate while he was driving to the minicab office.'

'The mobile must have been in his car all the time.'

Hicks nodded. 'Sure as hell wasn't in his flat or Edwina's.'

Ashton opened the bottom drawer of his desk and took out an old battery-powered Sony recorder and inserted the cassette.

'One of these days I must get an up-to-date model,' he said, and depressed the play button.

A man with a deep voice said, 'Hello, 3893.'

Fox did not identify himself, merely said, 'Hi, Jeff, it's me again.'

'As if I didn't know,' Jeff growled.

'I'm on my way; call the Fleetspeed office now and book a minicab to Heathrow. Ask for me.'

'Yeah.'

'Soon as you've done that, head for the rendezvous we chose. OK?'

'No, it's not OK. I don't see why we've got to meet.'

'Because I'm in deep shit, that's why. And I'm looking to your Canadian friend to get me out of it.'

'Impossible. He's no longer in this country.'

'So what? You've got a telephone and a fax machine and you know where to find him.' Fox paused as if to catch his breath, then said, 'Now stop fucking me about and ring Fleetspeed.'

The tape ran on, silent except for a faint hissing noise.

'That's all there is,' Hicks said.

Ashton stopped the recorder and pressed the rewind. He hoped it wasn't wishful thinking on his part but to his ears Fox had sounded rattled as well as angry. He hadn't used the phone in the flat to call Jeff because he didn't believe in taking chances. He'd felt comfortable with the Cellnet because he could tell that nobody had broken into the car. Why hadn't Fox rung 'Jeff' from a pay phone as he'd done previously? Could it be he was arrogant, or impatient to set wheels in motion?

'Refresh my memory,' Ashton said. 'When he spoke to Edwina, he asked her if she had contacted Willie?'

'That's what Fox said.'

'Be nice to know the name of his lawyer.'

'Can't help you there, squire,' Hicks said cheerfully.

'Never thought you could, Terry.' Ashton extracted the cassette from the Sony. 'Is this the only tape?' he asked.

'No, I made a copy.'

'Good. I'll hang on to this one. You've done a good job of eavesdropping on Fox but it isn't over yet. Keep the scanner locked on to his mobile and let me know the moment you have another intercept.'

Ashton put the recorder away, picked up the cassette and moved towards the door, gently steering Hicks in the direction of the corridor.

'Same goes for the two implants,' he added and made his way to the Security Vetting and Technical Services Division.

Morning prayers were still in session, which meant Kelso wasn't around to throw a spanner in the works. After tipping his hat to Frank Warren, who was in charge of the division, Ashton sought out Brian Thomas. He found him working through an in-tray that had been filled to overflowing during his absence in York. Two of the dossiers on his desk were the security files pertaining to members of the armed forces.

'We're looking for a replacement for Warrant Officer Crawford,' Thomas said before Ashton even thought of asking.

'I didn't know Crawford was due to be relieved.'

'Oh yes, his secondment to us ends on 1 October, and 22 SAS have sent us a couple of names. We've one from the Royal Marines who think it's time the corps was represented. They've nominated a high-flyer who's currently serving with the Special Boat Squadron. A very interesting guy; took part in the Falklands campaign when he was a nineteen-year-old Marine, then did a couple of emergency tours of Northern Ireland. In 1990, he was selected for an exchange posting to the US Marine Corps and served with their 1st Marine Division in the Gulf War in the rank of sergeant. The commandant of the training school thinks he's tailor-made for the job.'

Thomas moved the relevant security file to his pending tray.

'Have you seen Victor Hazelwood this morning?' he asked casually.

'Morning prayers haven't finished yet.'

'Ah, well, Roy Kelso wanted to know what I was doing here.'

'So what did you tell him?'

'The truth. I said there was nothing more I could usefully contribute to the investigation and that Oldfield had made it pretty evident that I was getting in his hair. He promised to keep us informed of any developments and, after discussing the matter with you, we agreed my presence was no longer required in York.'

It was an accurate summation of their discussion and had undoubtedly been delivered by Thomas in his inimitable, forthright, no-nonsense manner. Ashton could imagine how Kelso must have relished repeating it word for word at the morning conference, could imagine too how Victor must have felt to learn of the development second-hand.

'Is Frank Warren *au fait* with all this?'

Thomas looked genuinely astonished. 'No. He never asked me why I wasn't in York.'

'Then I think you should brief him.'

'Anything else?'

'Yes. What about those four registration numbers?'

'I faxed them to Swansea last night.'

'And when are we likely to get an answer?'

'Three, maybe four days' time.'

'I'd like it by the end of the morning.'

Thomas snorted. 'You'll be lucky.'

'We've got a lead, Brian,' Ashton said, and told him about the phone call the scanner had intercepted. 'I want the Driver and Vehicle Licensing Centre to pull their fingers out because one of those four cars is owned by a man called Jeff!'

His name was Iqbal Khan. He was thirty-seven and had arrived in Bradford from Karachi when six years old. Following the death of his father in July '94, Iqbal Khan had become the sole proprietor of a newsagent and tobacconist on Mill Street off the Leeds Road. A married man with three daughters aged fourteen, twelve and seven, he was the kind of conscientious, responsible citizen to gladden the heart of someone like Detective Chief Inspector Oldfield. While he had been questioning Fox yesterday, Iqbal Khan had walked into Bradford Central. Although much of his statement had been hearsay, the CID officers of the West Yorkshire Metropolitan Police had been sufficiently impressed to refer him to their opposite number in York, who had then arranged to collect him from his home that morning.

Although first impressions were frequently wrong, Oldfield prided himself on being a good judge of character. Soon after meeting Iqbal Khan, he came to the conclusion that the Pakistani took himself very seriously, lacked a sense of humour and was a touch pompous, though well-meaning. Whatever else he was, Iqbal Khan was highly intelligent and articulate with it, as Oldfield rapidly discovered when he asked him to repeat his story.

'It is not a story, Chief Inspector. I did not make it up to spite the Hosein brothers.'

'I'm sure you didn't.'

'Although I have good reason to make trouble for them.'

'Oh? Why's that?'

'They are Islam fundamentalists, extreme Shi'i Muslims. They would like to see every woman in purdah and believe young girls are corrupted by Western education. They told my eldest daughter, Rana, that she is a harlot because she dresses like the English girls at her school. They also threatened to cane her on her legs unless she conformed. Now she wears trousers and the hijab, or headscarf as you would call it.'

'You could have them for intimidation, Mr Khan.'

'No, I couldn't. Rana would deny it. If you can believe it, my daughter says she is grateful to the Hoseins for making her see the error of her ways. They are very powerful and have many followers.'

'Who? The Hosein brothers?'

Khan appeared surprised he should ask. Although the police could not prove it, everybody knew that Nizamodeen and Ayab Hosein had created and organised the Islamic Self-defence Force. Whenever an Asian was beaten up by a gang of skinheads, the self-defence force would take reprisals.

'Two for every one of ours, that is their motto, Chief Inspector. Like the Children of God, they look to Iran for inspiration and their hatred of the British and Americans is just as intense as any Iranian Ayatollah's. To Nizamodeen and Ayab, I am an imperialist lackey because most of my customers are from the indigenous population. In other words, Chief Inspector, they are white.'

'You are the target for a lot of verbal abuse?' Oldfield suggested.

'No. They are just saying that I am an unbeliever and the young people are encouraged to picket my shop. They do not use insulting language but they parade up and down the pavement carrying placards and these intimidate my customers in increasing numbers. It is very bad for business.'

Oldfield could see that Iqbal Khan would have a grudge against Nizamodeen and Ayab Hosein. Whether he had deliberately set out to make trouble for them was however a different matter.

'What do the Hoseins do for a living?' he asked.

'They have their own printing business. They must have been doing quite well because suddenly they had a blue-coloured Ford Transit a fortnight ago. Of course, the van was second-hand but even so it would have set them back a pretty penny.'

'You personally have seen this vehicle?'

'Yes, and so have other members of my family.'

'Close enough to see the numberplate?'

Khan shook his head. 'We were always too far away.'

Oldfield learned that the Hoseins lived in an old terraced house in Weavers Avenue, a parallel road at the rear of Mill Street. From the flat above his premises, Khan had a diagonal view of the Hoseins' back garden and the wooden shed they used as a print shop. Like many residents in the neighbourhood, the brothers had ripped out the hedgerow at the bottom of their garden. This had given them access to the dead-end lane between Mill Street and Weavers Avenue.

'They have a car port next to the print shop,' Khan told him. 'And they use the lane as if it were a metalled road instead of a cinder track. The Hoseins did much damage to the surface when they were running about in an old Mini van but the Ford Transit really cut up the lane.'

'When did they get rid of the Mini?'

'That's just it, Chief Inspector, they didn't. We did not see the vehicle for nearly a fortnight and thought they must have part exchanged it for the blue Transit. Then last Friday the Mini re-appeared and the Ford vanished. At first, I told myself the Hoseins must have borrowed the van for a few days because they had a lot of business. But then I read this story in the Bradford *Telegraph & Argus* about the girl who had been murdered and how the police were looking for a dark blue Transit van.'

Thinking about it, Khan had recalled that the Hoseins had been particularly busy the day Sharon Cartwright had been abducted. They had left the print shop shortly before noon and had returned approximately three hours later.

'My mother saw them—'

'Your mother?' Oldfield said, interrupting him.

'Yes, she lives with us. Well, she saw the Hoseins remove a rolled-up carpet from the van and carry it into the shed. The carpet was bulky and appeared to be heavy. There was an infidel with them.' Khan allowed himself a brief smile. 'My mother is a devout Muslim. To her, all the English are infidels.'

No two ways about it, there was a family feud between the Khans and the Hoseins. It was something to bear in mind when considering how much reliance could be placed on Iqbal's account. Sharon Cartwright could have been bundled up inside the carpet roll; alternatively, Iqbal may have invented the incident to get his own back on the Hosein brothers.

'They drove off in the van again as it was getting dark. This would be about four o'clock in the afternoon; I remember the time because it had started snowing. They were gone several hours; my mother heard them return when the *Nine O'Clock News* was on BBC 1.'

'She heard their vehicle above the television?'

'My mother doesn't speak English. She was in her bedroom, which overlooks the lane at the back.'

Keeping watch like a sentry, Oldfield thought.

'Did she actually see the Hoseins?'

'No. It was very dark and snowing heavily.' Khan took out a handkerchief and blew his nose. 'Please excuse me, Chief Inspector, I am recovering from a bad cold.'

'I'm glad you're getting better.'

'Did I tell you that they backed the van up to the print shop?'

'No. Was that unusual?'

'Normally they drove straight in but that day they reversed – twice, as if they had something to hide.'

146

An afterthought or, as was more likely, a piece of embroidery? It was the kind of statement calculated to make a police officer sit up and take notice. That being so, Oldfield resolved to take it with the proverbial pinch of salt.

'The last time you saw the Ford Transit was on Friday, 27 January. Correct?'

'No, that is not what I told you, Chief Inspector. I said the Ford had vanished and the Mini van was back again. The last time we saw the Transit was on a Thursday afternoon.'

For 'we' read 'granny', the sentinel of Mill Street. Neighbourhood Watch had nothing on her.

'Any idea what time this was?' Oldfield asked.

'Ten minutes to four. It was beginning to get dark when they left.'

'How many were there in the vehicle?'

'Only the Hoseins.'

Definitely granny, and she must have been keeping an operations log, noting the time of every incident.

'What happened on the Wednesday? Did the brothers use the vehicle that day?'

'No, it stayed where it was from morning to night.'

Oldfield didn't question it. Had the vehicle moved so much as an inch, one of the Khans would have made a note of the occurrence.

'I think that is all I can tell you, Chief Inspector.'

Khan sounded apologetic, as if somehow he had been less than vigilant. Sensing this, Oldfield tried to set his mind at rest.

'You've been extremely helpful,' he told him. 'I only wish there were more like you out there.'

It was a message he repeated more than once before the civilian driver arrived to convey Iqbal Khan back to Bradford. After the Pakistani had departed, Oldfield looked out the post-mortem on Sharon Cartwright and read it again. According to the pathologist, death had occurred some thirty-six hours before the body had been dumped in the River Trent. The young woman had disappeared on Tuesday afternoon; two days later her corpse had been spotted by a man out walking his dog. Sharon Cartwright had therefore been shot only a few hours after she had been abducted.

It was equally certain the killers had attempted to dispose of her body during Wednesday night and the early hours of Thursday morning. And that was the problem because if the Hoseins had been involved, Khan had told him the Ford Transit had not been taken out on Wednesday. Perhaps his mother had been mistaken? Hell, nobody was infallible. Or was he guilty of wishful thinking? Whatever, he would consult his opposite number in Bradford and convince him they should obtain a search warrant and pay the Hoseins a visit. It would have to be done quietly, of course. No using a sledgehammer on the front door in the middle of the night, otherwise they would have a race riot on their hands.

Brian Thomas had left the Metropolitan Police on retirement in 1983. One by one his contemporaries had followed suit with the result that twelve years later nobody who had joined the Force at roughly the same time as he had was still serving. There were however a considerable number of officers in high-profile appointments who had served under him in days gone by and who owed not a little of their success to him. When it came to asking the Driver and Vehicle Licensing Centre to give priority to their request for information, Thomas had known the right people at the top of the tree who would be prepared to help him by exerting pressure on Swansea.

Shortly after two o'clock, the Licensing Agency had responded with the names and addresses of the registered keepers which, despite what he had said to Thomas, was a lot earlier than Ashton had really expected. Since the registered keeper was not necessarily the legal owner, Swansea had gone one better and sent facsimiles of the relevant driving licences which showed the first or Christian name of the holder. In view of the reaction the last time he had set an operation in motion without consulting Victor, Ashton thought he'd better walk the print-out from Swansea upstairs and tell him what he had in mind.

Hazelwood was surrounded by files like an editor in a publishing house with unsolicited scripts. The inevitable Burma cheroot gathered ash in the cut-down brass shell case on the desk. The pile of documents in the pending tray was considerably higher than the other two combined.

'And what can I do for you?' he asked without looking up from the open dossier in front of him.

'It's OK,' Ashton told him, 'I'll come back when you're not so busy.'

'Tell me now, only keep it short.'

Ashton did just that, explaining in a few brief sentences about the intercept and the information it had subsequently drawn from Swansea.

'The man Fox spoke to is Jeffrey Irwin. His home address is 41 Karen Road, West Hampstead, and he is the owner of a BMW 520, licence number BYF 1.'

'That's a peculiar registration.'

'It's pre-war, London north-west. He probably paid a lot of money for it.'

'How do you know you've got the right man?'

'I can't be a hundred per cent sure, Victor, but Irwin is the only one of the four who has the right Christian name.'

'OK, what's your next step?'

'Find out all I can about Mr Irwin, maybe put him under electronic surveillance.'

'No bugging, Peter.'

'Right – no bugging.'

'And once you have established what Mr Irwin does for a living, turn everything over to Clifford Peachey.'

'Peachey? Look, I know MI5 has found a new role for itself in combating the international drug cartels but we don't seriously believe that Menendez was dealing in Coke, do we?'

'You've got hold of the wrong end of the stick,' Hazelwood told him calmly. 'Clifford Peachey is to become Deputy Director.'

Ashton wondered what Jill Sheridan had made of that when she had heard the news. She'd had her eye on that particular chair; now she could forget it for the next three years or so. Into every life a little rain must fall; she had just got drenched in a monsoon.

'Why are you so surprised? There is a precedent for this, Peter.'

'Yes?'

'Sir Dick Goldsmith White. He was head of MI5 in 1953 and three years later became our Director General.'

'That was before I was even born.'

'What are you trying to do, Peter? Make me feel old?'

'There's no chance of that. When does Clifford take over?'

'On Monday officially, but of course he will have to be fully briefed before that, starting the day after tomorrow. That's why I am sorting out which files should go straight to him.'

'May I ask a question?'

'By all means.'

'When you said I was to turn everything over to Peachey, does that include the entire case file on the Naburn incident and its various ramifications?'

'In a word – yes.'

'Do I continue to work on it?'

'No. If Clifford feels further action is required, Roger Benton will have to find the necessary manpower from within his own resources.'

Clever, Ashton thought, very clever. If the spotlight should fall on Jill Sheridan again, there would be little she could do about it. He was no longer involved and while Urquhart might support her cause at the Foreign and Commonwealth Office, she would know that good old Robin would become a mite suspicious if she complained about Clifford Peachey.

CHAPTER 13

The office which Norden rented in Ponte Vedra Beach under the alias of John Novaks was located on Ocean View, a run-down side street off Atlantic Boulevard. From his point of view, half the attraction of Ponte Vedra Beach lay in the fact it was only twenty-three miles from his place in downtown Jacksonville. The other plus point was that for all the local population numbered twenty-five hundred, the inhabitants tended to mind their own business, which was pretty unusual in a small town. Those few people who were inquisitive enough to ask Norden what he did for a living were told that he was a sales promoter, an explanation that was accepted unquestioningly.

The Seascape Center was a somewhat grandiose name for a slim, three-storey office block where over half the total floor space was invariably unoccupied. The four hundred square feet which Norden had leased on the second floor was one of the smaller units; nevertheless the desk, three-drawer filing cabinet and swivel chair were lost in it. There were only two items of office equipment – an answerphone and fax machine. A remote interrogator enabled him to retrieve any message left on the answerphone without going near the office, whereas the fax machine demanded his personal attention. This meant routinely checking the office twice a week to see if there was anything for him. This morning, when retrieving the messages on the answerphone, he had heard the Englishman's voice and knew before driving out to Ponte Vedra Beach that there was a fax waiting for him.

Finding a parking space outside the Seascape Center was never a problem; locking the Honda, Norden walked into the building and rode the escalator up to the second floor. The office known to the janitor as Novaks Promotions Incorporated was the end room on the right with a view of the wasteland in rear of the Seascape Center. Of the twelve units between the moving staircase and the one he rented, only three other premises were leased. However, nobody was around when Norden let himself into his office. The psychiatrist with a drink problem rarely held a consultation before noon, the attorney-at-law was on vacation, and according to the sign on the door, the realtor was out with a client viewing property.

There was nothing in the fax Irwin had sent him that would have made the janitor or any of the office cleaners suspicious, had they seen it. To an outsider, the text suggested a business deal that had gone sour. It read, 'Fox is unhappy about his position regarding the contract and wants to renegotiate it. Unless you are prepared to give him the Brazilian franchise he will consider taking his business elsewhere. I do not regard this as an idle threat . . .'

In veiled terms, Irwin was telling him that Fox was in trouble and wanted a one-way ticket to Rio de Janeiro with enough folding money in his pocket to keep the wolf from the door. Once there, all he had to do to avoid extradition, was to marry some local girl and get her pregnant. If they failed to meet his demands, Fox would go instead to the police and get the best deal he could for himself. In British parlance, this meant he would sing like a canary, spill his guts, grass them up. And Irwin had assured him Fox would never snitch on them no matter what, which just went to show what a load of crap that had been.

Norden broke open a packet of Marlboro and lit one. What could Fox do to him? He didn't know his real name, his home address or anything of his background. To Fox he was Frank Norris, a Canadian currently living in New York City. No, Irwin was the only one he could really hurt. At the very least, Fox could link the private investigator to Menendez and that could make life difficult for him personally.

Norden slowly exhaled, watched the cigarette smoke drift towards the ceiling. He hadn't exactly picked Irwin out of the *Yellow Pages*; they had done business before, back in 1991 to be precise. The nineteen-year-old stepdaughter of one of Jacksonville's most prominent citizens had taken an extended vacation in Europe and had written that she had found the man she wanted to spend the rest of her life with and wouldn't be coming home. The girl had been an heiress in her own right with an eight-figure bank balance and stepfather had figured the lover boy had to be after her money, something he had been determined to prevent. Norden hadn't asked the man why he had chosen him instead of going to a big agency. That had become clear to Norden when the stepfather had indicated that no measures were too extreme if he succeeded in breaking up the relationship,

There had been a London postmark on the last letter she had written to her mother, which had meant Norden hiring an English associate to help him run her to ground. He had asked a friend in Pinkertons if he could recommend somebody the agency had used and had been given a list plus a contact in Scotland Yard who would be prepared to run his eye over the names. Jeff Irwin had been the first of three PIs who'd been highly recommended and Norden hadn't bothered to look any farther.

Using the information the family had provided, it had taken Irwin just over a week to discover where the lovebirds were residing. The subsequent negotiations with the boyfriend had taken over three times as long. One look at the photographs of the heiress which Irwin had taken surreptitiously and there had been no doubt in his mind that money had been the principal attraction for the boyfriend. The girl was plain, had thick ankles, thick legs, broad hips and a small bust. The stepfather had authorised him to offer the boyfriend ten thousand pounds per annum for the next five years if he would dump her, but he had known a goldmine when he saw one.

It was only after the negotiations had become deadlocked that Norden had learned just how ruthless Irwin could be. For the sum of five grand up front plus five more on completion, the Englishman had guaranteed he could resolve the problem. Three days after Irwin had received the down payment, the boyfriend had telephoned the distraught girl and informed her that it was all over between them. During the intervening seventy-two hours, the man had been quietly lifted from the house while his meal ticket had been out and had been taken to a derelict warehouse in the Docklands. The abductors had stripped him from the waist down, lit a wood fire and boiled a kettle of water. They had produced two thousand in cash and had advised him to grab the money and disappear; and had then tipped some of the boiling water over his thighs. They had also splashed a few drops on to his testicles to let him know what to expect if he declined to co-operate. The boyfriend had seen the light and the unhappy heiress had been collected by her stepfather.

End of story: well, not quite the end, because Norden had used Irwin again and this time they'd got kind of pally. Maybe not so friendly that the Englishman was aware of his real identity but he certainly did know far too much about Mr John Novaks of Ocean View, Ponte Vedra Beach, Florida. Norden stubbed out his cigarette; no question about it, he couldn't afford to sit back and let Irwin catch the flak. In block capitals he printed: 'WITH REFERENCE TO YOURS OF JANUARY 31. BRAZILIAN FRANCHISE IS NOT AN OPTION. STRONGLY RECOMMEND WE TERMIN-ATE CONTRACT. ASSUME MY PRESENCE NOT REQUIRED IN THIS CONNECTION? AM WILLING TO DEFRAY ANY EXPENSES INVOLVED.'

After reading it twice, he faxed the reply to Irwin.

It didn't take Ashton as long as he'd thought it would to discover what Jeffrey Irwin did for a living. Although he was ex-directory, Irwin had given his subscriber's number when Fox had called him. Since the Driver and Vehicle Licensing Centre had provided his home address, Ashton had simply looked up the area code for West Hampstead and put a call through to his residence in Karen Road. He'd found himself connected to an answer machine and had immediately recognised Irwin from the deep voice the scanner had picked up and recorded. He'd listened to Irwin apologising for the fact that nobody was at home right now but if the caller would care to leave a name and contact number, he would phone back as soon as he returned. Irwin had also suggested he could be reached on 0171-446-9581 if it was urgent. One more phone call spiced with a liberal amount of blarney and Ashton had learned that Irwin was a private investigator and security consultant. *Yellow Pages* had then informed Ashton that the man's office was in Finchley Road.

Primed with that information, he looked in on Brian Thomas

again. Although his in-tray was a good deal lower than it had been earlier in the day, the former hard-nose of E District greeted him with the martyred expression of a man who just knew he was about to be imposed upon.

'Let me guess,' he said with infinite weariness, 'you want me to plug into the old boy network again. Right?'

'Yes. This is a follow-up on Jeffrey Irwin.'

'Why don't you try paying off a few debts first? I get my friends to persuade the DVLC to accord us priority and what do we give them in exchange? A great big zero. We didn't tell them about the telephone conversation the scanner picked up, never mind the fact we've identified the man Fox spoke to.'

'We will as soon as we know a little more about Irwin. OK?'

'It has to be, you've got the ear of the Director and I haven't.'

'Irwin is a private detective,' Ashton said calmly as if Thomas had been all sweetness and light. 'His business address is 987 Finchley Road, West Hampstead.'

'So?'

'Well, I imagine the local CID must have heard of him. I mean, there he is, an amateur operating on their patch; they're bound to have sussed him out.'

Thomas opened the top drawer of his desk and took out a well-thumbed copy of *The Police and Constabulary Almanac* and opened it at the section devoted to the Metropolitan Police.

'Finchley Road falls within S District,' he said, and frowned, 'and there we have a problem because I don't know any of the officers listed on page 29.'

'Use whoever it is you consult when you're clearing a guy for constant access to Top Secret material. Pretend the candidate has nominated Irwin as a referee and you'd like to know if he is a sterling character or not. Make a big production of it, tell him you think it odd that a member of the armed forces should have nominated a complete outsider to vouch for him.'

'And exactly who is this member of the armed forces?'

'Use the name of that Marine whose security file you were looking at this morning.'

'I know I've said it before, but you never give up, do you?'

'Would you be happier if I got one of the other vetting officers to do this?'

'Hell no,' Thomas growled, 'with your game plan it should be a doddle.'

Ashton hoped he was right. It was, he believed, one way of fishing for information without arousing suspicion because it so happened that Scotland Yard was involved in the vetting process. The personal details of civil servants, members of the diplomatic service, armed forces, GCHQ, MI5 and the SIS who required a security clearance were sent to Department C4, the National Identification Bureau, to check whether or not the applicant had a criminal record. As the security vetting inquiries progressed, it was not unusual for the case officer to go back to Scotland Yard with additional queries. However, at no stage was the security file itself sent to the police. There was therefore no way they could discover if Irwin had been nominated as a referee, short of asking him.

The Major belonged to the Middle East Division of the Russian Intelligence Service which had risen from the ashes of the old KGB's First Chief Directorate. Two days ago he had been serving with the Russian Embassy in Tehran where he had ostensibly been employed as the Third Secretary, Commerce. Now he had been summoned to an office on the top floor of the Council of Ministers building within the walls of the Kremlin. Located on the south-west side of the building and almost under the great dome, the office was currently occupied by Pavel Trilisser, special adviser on Foreign Affairs to President Yeltsin.

The Major had been warned not to be fooled by Trilisser's lean, aesthetic-looking appearance. Strangers encountering Trilisser at a social function might take him for a member of the Academy of Sciences, a high-ranking judge or a distinguished physicist, but the Major should remember that he was dealing with a man who, in 1987, had been the youngest Lieutenant General ever to be appointed Deputy Head of the Foreign Intelligence Service. Treacherous was the adjective his superior officer had used when describing the dominant characteristic of President Yeltsin's special adviser.

'Please sit down, Nikolai Grigoryevich,' Trilisser said, and pointed to the upright chair in front of his desk. 'Cigarette?' The Major blinked, taken back by the unexpected use of the patronymic. It was as if the General regarded him with some affection as he might the son of an old friend.

'I don't smoke, sir,' he said weakly.

'Neither do I, one keeps them for visitors who do.'

Nikolai Grigoryevich lowered his gaze. He thought Pavel Trilisser had the bluest eyes he had ever seen and they seemed to burn with the intensity of an oxyacetylene torch. The faint smile on the General's lips did nothing to soften a manner that had all the warmth of an iceberg.

'I understand you are the author of the reports which have so alarmed our President?'

'I hope . . .' His mouth suddenly bone dry, Nikolai Grigoryevich licked his lips and tried again. 'I hope you don't think I made them up, sir?'

'I have read suspense novels that were less sensational.'

'I only reported what I was told by the source.'

'Ah yes, the man you so originally codenamed Scheherazade.' Trilisser became even more vitriolic. 'And who might he be? A waiter in a coffee house perhaps? Or some lowly clerk in their Ministry of Internal Affairs?'

'My source was a banker, sir.'

'How long ago was this? When Mohammad Reza Pahlavi was getting piles from sitting on the Peacock Throne?'

'His name is Shahpour Bazargan,' Nikolai Grigoryevich said, his eyes still downcast. 'He was opposed to the Shah and was a prominent member of the Iran Liberation Movement. Ayatollah Khomeini was ready to make Bazargan his Minister of Finance when the Shah was deposed and went into exile, but the clerics wouldn't have him. He was too Westernised for their liking.'

'What's the point of all this?' Trilisser demanded impatiently. 'Are you trying to lecture me on Iranian politics?'

What Nikolai Grigoryevich was trying to do was to establish the credibility of his source. He wanted the President's special adviser to understand that Bazargan was a high-grade informant, a man who had been close to the centre of power for the last sixteen years. It was however difficult to get this message across in the face of such hostility from the former KGB General, but he ploughed doggedly on and was finally rewarded.

'All right, I'm convinced,' Trilisser told him. 'Bazargan is a valuable acquisition. How much did his information cost us?'

'Nothing. He is dying of leukaemia, money is of little use to him.'

'What about his family? Doesn't he wish to provide for them?'

'Shahpour Bazargan is fifty-eight years old; both his parents are dead and he has never married. There is an older sister but I understand they hate the sight of one another. The fact is he is motivated by patriotism.'

'Is that the opinion shared by your superiors in the Middle East Division?'

'Yes.' On reflection, Nikolai Grigoryevich decided he had been a little too assertive and sought to modify what he'd just said. 'Well, nobody disagreed with my assessment,' he added hastily.

'You don't think revenge has anything to do with it?'

'Revenge?' Nikolai Grigoryevich echoed blankly.

'We have to assume there was a time when he was not without ambition. As you have already told me, Bazargan was a leader of the Iran Liberation Movement but the Ayatollahs did not care for his outlook. In their eyes, he was not a true follower of Islam and they denied him the power he craved.'

'He is trying to save his country—'

'By betraying it,' Trilisser said before he could finish. 'Every source is a traitor, Nikolai Grigoryevich. It is important to keep that always in mind.'

'Bazargan was convinced that what the Ayatollahs were planning would prove catastrophic for Iran. It would take years to accomplish and it was by no means certain that they would be successful.'

'Yes, yes, I have read your reports. What President Yeltsin can't understand is why Bazargan should have approached us instead of the Americans or even the British. After all, those two countries have the most to lose.'

The United States had made no move to restore normal diplomatic relations with Tehran. American interests in Iran were looked after by the Poles. As for the British, it was common knowledge that everybody entering and leaving their Embassy was photographed by the secret police. The same applied to the private houses occupied by members of the diplomatic staff. Pavel Trilisser could hardly fail to know all this so what was he trying to do? Catch him out? It would be imprudent to make this point to the President's special adviser.

'Bazargan felt safe coming to us with the information,' Nikolai Grigoryevich said. 'Relations between Moscow and Tehran have never been better.'

'I'm sure that's right on a personal level.'

Unsure what to make of the observation, Nikolai Grigoryevich nodded in agreement. It seemed the safest thing to do in the circumstances.

'Thank you, Nikolai Grigoryevich,' Trilisser said abruptly. 'You have been most helpful.'

'Sir?'

'You are free to go. Enjoy your stay in Moscow.'

Even then Trilisser was obliged to stand up before Nikolai Grigoryevich realised the interview was over. Try as he might, the young Major could not disguise his sense of relief as he backed out of the office. When the door closed behind him, Trilisser went over to the window and stood there gazing at the lights showing in the Kremlin Theatre. Moscow, six o'clock on a bitterly cold night in February; he wondered in whose arms Nikolai Grigoryevich would find comfort on such an evening, when Shahpour Bazargan was so far away. The two men were lovers, there was not the slightest doubt about that in his mind. Relations between Moscow and Tehran had never been better, had they? After the way Moscow had dealt with their fellow Muslims in Chechnya? Who did Nikolai Grigoryevich think he was fooling?

Trilisser returned to his desk and sat down. What he could not decide was how much reliance could be placed on the Iranian's story. What was it Bazargan had allegedly told his gallant major? The attack on the US dollar could destabilise the Russian economy? Well, there was a good joke if ever he heard one. With the economy and the rouble already in free fall, how much worse could it possibly get? And this so-called Cuban involvement he had spoken of; where had that ageing, moribund, revolutionary Fidel Castro found the muscle to take on the United States? If he went to the Americans with such a tale, they would fall about laughing.

Should he therefore advise Yeltsin to ignore the reports he'd received from his Intelligence chiefs? Trilisser frowned; he could not afford to make a third mistake. His career in the KGB had suffered a major setback when the hardliners had turned against Gorbachev in August 1991. A number of Yeltsin's supporters had been convinced that he had waited until it was evident that the coup was going to fail before he arrested his own chief and sent word to the Minister of the Interior, Boris Pugo, to surrender himself to the paratroopers of the Ryazan Division. In October '93, he had been a party to a conspiracy to overthrow Yeltsin and had only saved his own skin by the timely execution of his personal second in command. His betrayal of Prime Minister Rutskoi had also helped to remove whatever doubts the President might have had concerning his loyalty and had led to his present appointment.

It was essential he took steps to cover himself against every eventuality. He would use the back door approach and pass the information to the British. They liked to believe they enjoyed a special relationship with the Americans. That also was a good joke.

Ashton walked home through the park, the collar of his trenchcoat turned up. The meteorologists had forecast a wet and windy day and they'd got it right. They always did when predicting adverse conditions; if they said the outlook was for sunshine and occasional showers you could bet the sky would be overcast from morning to night and it wouldn't stop raining. He went on past the seesaw, sandpit, paddling pool and swings; leaving the park, Ashton took the quick cut below the railway embankment which led him past the Royal Masonic Hospital, across Goldhawk Road and into Rylett Close.

There was no sign of the Vauxhall Cavalier outside number 84. Somebody who obviously didn't live in the close had left a rather swish-looking Ford Mondeo in the space he had always regarded as theirs. He wondered where Harriet had parked their car but wasn't curious enough to go looking for it in the rain. Soon as their finances improved, he would have the front garden concreted over to provide a hard standing for the Vauxhall. He pushed the gate open, walked up the path and let himself into the semidetached house.

'I'm home,' he announced rather unnecessarily as Harriet met him in the hall.

'What do you think of it?' she asked with a huge smile.

'Think of what?'

'Our new car.'

'Are we talking about that Ford Mondeo out there?'

'Yes. Don't you like it?'

'That's not the point. It's an M registration; what makes you think we can afford a car that's less than a year old?'

There was a lot more he could have said. Among other things he wanted to know what gave her the right to enter into a hire purchase agreement without consulting him. Fortunately the telephone rang before he could say something they would both come to regret. Answering it, Ashton found he had Brian Thomas on the line.

'Are you sitting down?' Thomas enquired.

'No.'

'Then prepare yourself for a shock. Jeff Irwin was a detective sergeant; he left the Met in 1989 to set himself up as a private investigator and security consultant. There was some talk at the time that he had been taking the odd backhander but nobody could prove it.'

CHAPTER 14

Irwin reached inside the breast pocket of his jacket, took out the fax he'd received from Novaks yesterday evening and unfolded it. He didn't need to refresh his memory, the text was burned into his mind and the implications of the coded message were brutally clear. Last night, his first instinct had been to put the fax through the office shredder but on reflection he knew that Ronnie Fox would have to see it in black and white before he accepted that Novaks wanted him dead.

Novaks had to be barking mad if he seriously expected Irwin to go out and hire a hit man to resolve the problem. As for himself, he had been pretty stupid. Novaks had paid him to recruit a team for what he had been led to believe was a routine surveillance job, which in the event had been anything but straightforward. He should have called the whole thing off after the target had been conveyed to 4 Central Buildings, Matthew Parker Street. Towards the end of his career in the Met, he had worked in Special Branch and knew that this was the address of the Foreign and Commonwealth Office security department.

It hadn't taken an Einstein to conclude that the Secret Intelligence Service was probably involved. But the money had been too good to walk away from, and Novaks had persuaded him to keep the surveillance going while he sought further instructions. By the time John Novaks heard from his client, the target had been residing at The Firs in Naburn for the better part of a fortnight and the team, with the exception of Fox, had been paid off. Irwin looked at the fax again and decided his first instinct had been right after all. Showing it to Fox was just about the most dangerous thing he could do. If anything was calculated to push Fox over the edge, it was the Canadian's refusal to throw him a lifeline and the implicit threat to his life. Accompanied by his slimeball lawyer, he would go to the police and get the best deal he could, something he'd threatened to do the night before last.

Novaks was sitting pretty: what Fox knew about him could be written on the back of a postage stamp. No, the man who had most to fear was himself; if Fox opened his mouth, he would be looking at a ten stretch. And he wouldn't be able to cut a deal because when you looked at the bottom line, what did he really know about Novaks? Even money that was an alias, probably one of many. In fact, his whole identity had undoubtedly been manufactured layer upon layer, a tradecraft he could have acquired in Vietnam while serving with Special Forces. So Irwin knew Novaks' fax and telephone number, but how long would it take to wipe out that trace? Maybe, just maybe, that was something he could not accomplish overnight.

Irwin left his desk, went over to the shredder and switched on the power, then fed the sheet of A4 into the slot. He felt the machine snatch at the paper and pluck it from his grasp like a hungry, caged animal. In seconds, the fax was sliced into threads no thicker than strands of hair and woven together to resemble candyfloss.

Fox wouldn't be quite so easy to dispose of but to every problem there was a solution and he was beginning to see one. His partner, Kathy, wouldn't like it because it would cost them a great deal of money but in the end she would see they had no choice. Passport, loose change, folding money for a plane ticket to Miami from Paris; at a rough guess, Irwin reckoned the necessary arrangements would set them back a cool seven and a half grand. There should be no excessive withdrawals of cash if they were to avoid drawing attention to themselves. Fortunately, they had eight current accounts dotted all over north London – two with the Midland Bank at the Kilburn and Acton branches, with Barclays in Islington and Wembley, one with the Trustee Savings Bank in Cricklewood, the Nat West in Maida Vale and Lloyds in Finchley Road and Bayswater. There was also a safety deposit box containing five thousand in blank traveller's cheques with Morgan Price in Knightsbridge. They would split the banks between them, withdrawing no more than three hundred and twenty-odd pounds from each branch. Kathy could take the Midland and Barclays; he would visit the others and access the deposit box held by Morgan Price.

Fox would need French francs and US dollars for taxis and incidentals, and the best place to get them with the least fuss were from the Bureaux de Change at the Heathrow Terminals. Time enough for that when they had the cash in hand. First thing he had to do was convince Fox that the deal was on. No face-to-face meeting yet; a phone call on the mobile would do for now. He would get Kathy to do it; the wrong number routine which would alert Fox to return the call from a pay phone would sound genuine coming from her. Life had taught Irwin never to take anything for granted. On Monday, the police had interrogated Ronnie for over ten hours before releasing him, which had given the spooks ample time to bug his flat and the one belonging to his latest girlfriend. He had warned Fox about this when they'd met the same night and had told him not to do anything clever, like getting some electronics buff to sniff out the bugs. That would surely send out all the wrong signals.

Ashton picked up the phone for the fourth time since arriving at the office and, as had happened on the three previous occasions, found himself talking to Hazelwood's Personal Assistant. Morning prayers had lasted longer than usual because Victor was holding a dress rehearsal for the presentation of the briefing Clifford Peachey would receive when he arrived tomorrow. According to the draft programme, the dress rehearsal should have finished half an hour ago. The Director's stalwart PA was however apparently unaware of this and refused to put him through.

'What do you mean, he's busy?' Ashton said. 'Are you saying this very detailed timetable which the Chief Archivist put in my hot little hand this morning is already out of kilter?'

'Mr Hazelwood left instructions that he is not to be disturbed.'

Ashton felt his hackles rise. He had rung Victor at home last night to brief him about Irwin and had been asked if it couldn't wait until morning. Now he was beginning to get the distinct impression that the DG was determined to avoid him. Showing considerable constraint, Ashton politely enquired if she had informed the Director that he would like to see him?

'Of course I have.'

Ashton looked at the timetable again. The draft programme indicated that Heads of Departments would show Peachey around their respective fiefdoms after he had received a general briefing in the conference room but nowhere did it say that Hazelwood intended to rehearse the walkabout. Puzzled to know what was going on, Ashton asked her if the timetable had been amended.

'Absolutely not. Mr Garfield is with him.'

Rowan Garfield: no wonder there was a hiatus. The Head of the European Department could talk the hind leg off a donkey.

'Rest assured,' the PA told him, 'I'll buzz you the moment the Director is free.'

Ashton thanked her and hung up. Had anyone been present to take him up on it, he would have wagered ten pounds that Victor would be engaged all morning. Within five minutes he would have lost the bet.

For a man who had allegedly been on the go since the moment he'd walked into the office, Hazelwood seemed remarkably laid back. Last night's tetchiness had been replaced by an air of well-being as if he had breakfasted off champagne and orange juice.

'Your friend in Moscow has been making amicable noises again,' he said.

'What friend?'

'Pavel Trilisser.'

Ashton grunted. Pavel Trilisser was no friend of his and never would be. Two years ago, the former KGB General had banged him up in Moscow's Lefortovo Prison where he had been kept in solitary confinement for seventy-eight days. Although the men who had interrogated him had never resorted to violence, they had been very good at applying psychological pressure and he hadn't been allowed much sleep. Shortly after that episode, Trilisser had moved into the Kremlin to become President Yeltsin's special adviser on foreign affairs, in the course of which he had established an unofficial channel of communication with the British Embassy. In Ashton's opinion, no good had come of it so far.

'What's he offering us this time, Victor?'

'We don't know yet. The marker which Trilisser must have put out during the hours of darkness was only spotted at 08.00 hours Moscow time this morning.'

The marker was some everyday object which was left in a prearranged location. It told the case officer that his source wanted to meet him that evening at a given time at a fixed rendezvous.

'Now why do you want to brief me about Irwin?' Hazelwood asked, rapidly changing the subject. 'I thought I told you yesterday to turn everything over to Clifford Peachey.'

'You did, but Irwin used to be a detective sergeant in the Met and I figured that changed things. Besides, Clifford isn't officially in the chair until Monday and I don't think we should spring this on him before then.'

'I've told you – no illegal bugging.'

'Suppose we put Irwin under physical surveillance?'

'For how long, Peter? A few days, a week or medium to long term? And will we be watching Irwin during daylight hours only, or round the clock in eight-hour shifts each involving a team of at least three operators?' Hazelwood shook his head. 'We don't have the people power.'

'Well, if we are not going to act on this information, I don't see how we can sit on it.'

'So what do you suggest we do?'

'We brief the Met and let them get on with it,' Ashton told him.

'Why should they work their socks off for us?'

'They'll be doing it for themselves, Victor. We'll just be the sleeping partners getting what we want for next to nothing. Officially, Irwin left the Force to set up in business because he hadn't been promoted. However, his peers reckon he had been on the take and had got out before the bribery and corruption squad decided to investigate his private affairs. Now when the police hear the tape of that telephone conversation between Fox and Irwin which was captured by our scanner, they'll be very interested indeed. They'll want to know how an ex-detective sergeant residing in West Hampstead is on friendly terms with a villain like Ronnie Fox who lives miles away in a council flat on the Isle of Dogs.'

'Who are you going to approach at the Yard?'

'I thought we'd leave that to Brian Thomas. Of course, I'll go with him.' Ashton smiled. 'Just to make sure the Met is suitably grateful,' he added.

'You'd better go ahead and do it then.'

No hesitation, no prevarication; Hazelwood was his old self again – crisp, decisive and in control. For the past week or so, he had seemed riddled with self-doubt, now suddenly all that was behind him. Ashton wondered if the change had anything to do with Clifford Peachey. Maybe the fact that he'd had to function without a Deputy Director for nearly a year had finally got him down. Whatever the cause and effect, Ashton was glad his old guide and mentor was back on an even keel.

Ashton made his way down to the fourth floor where he found Hicks lurking in the corridor near his office.

'Waiting for me?' he asked.

'The scanner's picked up another conversation,' Hicks said, and followed him into the office. 'Doesn't make a lot of sense to me but maybe you can make something of it.'

Ashton opened the bottom drawer of his desk and took out the battered Sony recorder. Inserting the cassette Hicks had produced, he depressed the play button.

Fox did not give his phone number, merely said, 'Hi.'

The caller was a woman. She said, 'I'm sorry about the short notice but I've got to cancel my appointment for this afternoon. Can you fit me in sometime on Friday?'

'I think you've got the wrong number.'

'Oh? I thought I'd dialled 9841.'

'No, this is 9814.'

'I'm sorry.'

'That's OK,' Fox told her, and switched off.

'What do you make of it?' Hicks asked. 'Do you think it was a genuine mistake? I mean, Fox sounded dead puzzled to me.'

'He's a good actor.'

'Yeah, but—'

'I know the lady,' Ashton said. 'I spoke to her yesterday; she works for Irwin. What you heard was a coded message.'

'Saying what?'

'If I knew that I'd be a happy man.' Ashton rewound the cassette and ejected it. 'I take it this is a spare copy?'

'Yeah.'

'Good. This, and the other cassette, should go down well at the Yard. As long as it doesn't remind anybody of that old saying.'

'What old saying?'

'Beware of the Greeks who bring gifts.'

'But you're not a Greek,' Hicks said, who was inclined to be pedantic.

Fox walked into the Polyphoto booth in New Oxford Street, drew the curtain across the entrance and removed his anorak, dropping it on to the floor. After reading the operating instructions next to the coin box he sat down on the metal seat and adjusted the height until his head and shoulders were reflected in the mirror facing him. Leaning forward, he fed two one-pound coins into the pay slot and straightened up, his face composed, the derisive smile that was usually present wiped from his mouth. Despite being prepared for it, the first automatic flash made him blink. After the third and last take, he picked up his anorak and put it on before leaving the booth to wait outside while the prints were being developed.

Fifteen minutes after the wrong number routine, he had returned the call from a pay phone in Poplar High Street and learned that the Canadian had given Irwin the old thumbs-up. Tomorrow, or the day after at the latest, he would be on his way, money in his pocket, a new passport and a different name. All he had to do until then was stay loose, which was why he'd crisscrossed the town using the Docklands Light Railway, the Underground and the buses to make sure nobody was following him before he got his picture taken.

The damp strip of prints dropped into the box; picking the photos up between finger and thumb, Fox waved them about until they were dry enough to fold in three and slip into the pocket of his anorak. Dodging the traffic, he crossed the road, boarded a bus for Marble Arch and alighted outside Bond Street station. Although he had never met Kathy, he had spoken to her several times on the telephone and knew what she would be wearing. He had also been told where and when to meet her in Selfridges.

* * *

Commander Paul Isherwood was more than just a name to Ashton. The Special Branch officer had been an up-and-coming detective sergeant when Brian Thomas had been the Chief Superintendent in charge of E District's CID. He was also the man whose dinner party Ashton had been responsible for interrupting, much to Mrs Isherwood's annoyance, the night Ronnie Fox had walked out of Paddington Green. Isherwood was in his mid-forties, had sandy-coloured hair cut short back and sides, and a strong, not unattractive face. Broad across the shoulders, he had the muscular frame of an athlete who went to great lengths to keep himself in shape. In his younger days, he had in fact been a rugby player of some distinction and as an attacking full back had been regularly selected to play for Harlequins Second XV. According to Thomas, he had been noted for the ferocity of his tackling. Players who were hit by Isherwood didn't get up again in a hurry. After shaking hands with him, Ashton could well believe it.

'So you're the one whose bacon I was asked to save,' Isherwood observed.

'Yes, well, as the saying goes one good turn deserves another.'

'We think you will be interested to hear these tapes, Paul,' Thomas said in explanation.

'Have your lot been doing some illicit phone tapping, Brian?' Isherwood said with a faint smile that touched the corners of his mouth.

'They were picked up by a scanner,' Thomas told him woodenly. 'I'm a little out of date so I don't know if that constitutes an offence or not.'

'You haven't changed, Brian. You were always ready to cut the odd corner if it helped to get a result.'

'I'm the one who cut the odd corner,' Ashton said.

'Then why don't you tell me what this is all about?'

Ashton did so in a few brief sentences, linking Irwin to the multiple killings in Naburn in the sure knowledge that there was no reason to withhold any information on security grounds. Isherwood held the requisite PV clearance on two counts: he was in charge of B Division, the Special Branch, and as a Commander in the

Metropolitan Police, he was the equivalent of an Assistant Chief Constable. Any doubts Isherwood might have entertained when Ashton finished briefing him were dispelled after he had listened to the cassettes.

'Irwin's Canadian friend,' he said abruptly; 'any idea who he is?'

Ashton shook his head. 'It might be possible to identify him through his fax number,' he said diffidently.

'Assuming he has one, Mr Ashton. We'd also have to know Irwin's fax number.'

Ashton didn't think that was a Herculean task for Special Branch. He had given them Irwin's business address and with the backing of the Home Secretary, they could persuade British Telecom to disclose the number. Regardless of the fact that it was privileged information, they could also prevail upon BT to provide a list of the recipient numbers he'd faxed in the last few weeks. In addition to the number, the fax would reveal the name and location of the recipient.

'You're presuming of course that Irwin contacted the mysterious Canadian?'

'Let's say I'm hoping he did.'

'And in exchange for the information you've given me, you'd like to extract the necessary data from BT.'

'I think it would be in your interest to do so as much as ours,' Ashton said coolly. 'Could be his itemised phone bills would yield the Serious Crime Squad a few dividends. I don't believe Fox was the only criminal Irwin recruited on behalf of the Canadian, and the odds are it wasn't the first time he'd been down that particular road for other clients. I would think Irwin regards it as a lucrative sideline to his legitimate business.'

'And he used to be a detective sergeant.' Isherwood made it sound like a requiem.

'So I was informed,' Thomas said, chipping in.

'This would be from one of your contacts at the Yard, would it, Brian?'

Ashton thought the ex-Detective Chief Superintendent was not alone in having a friend on the inside. Somebody must have tipped Irwin off that a former girlfriend had just blown the whistle on Fox and he'd put a couple of frighteners on to her. There could be no other explanation for Debbie's subsequent retraction of her statement. Proving it was however another matter.

'Are the North Yorkshire Police aware of this latest development?' Isherwood asked.

'Not yet,' Ashton told him. 'We thought it would save time in the long run if Scotland Yard heard the intercepts first.'

'It took you long enough to hand them over to us. Fox tells Irwin he's in deep shit and expects his Canadian friend to bale him out. That's significant information but you people sat on it and played detective, something you're not trained for.'

'In other words, the SIS should have left it to the professionals?' Thomas suggested.

'Yes.'

'Come off it, Paul. If we had done that, where would the Met be now? Nowhere. It was the professionals of D and H Districts between them who let Fox walk away without putting a tail on him. Or if they did, he lost them pretty damned quick. And it was these same professionals who failed to stake out his pad in Mandela Court and Edwina's hairdressing salon.'

The faint smile appeared again on Isherwood's mouth.

'Same old Brian,' he said with good-humoured affection and turned to Ashton. 'I remember him going for the Commissioner when the great man said that, apart from being a law unto itself, the CID was also riddled with corruption. Brian really blew his stack that time.'

'I can imagine,' Ashton said.

'So is your scanner still locked on to Fox?' Isherwood suddenly asked.

'Yes, but I've a hunch he won't be using his Cellnet to contact Irwin in future.'

'You're guessing that was the coded message behind the wrong number routine?'

'Yes.'

'Any idea who the woman is?'

'We think her name is Kathy,' Thomas said. 'Irwin met the lady when her house in West Hampstead was burgled and he was a detective constable working out of Rosslyn Hill. She fancied him, he took a shine to her and they started having nooky while her husband was at the office. Finally they ditched their respective spouses and set up home together in Karen Road. End of story.'

'It is for you, Brian,' Isherwood said, and got to his feet.

The audience was over, a message conveyed so directly that neither man could have any doubts on that score. Less than two minutes later, Ashton and Thomas found themselves out on the street.

'Think we'll hear anything from the Serious Crime Squad or whoever takes this on?' Ashton asked.

'We'd better,' Thomas growled. His tone suggested that he would lead Isherwood a dog's life if they didn't.

The Golden Nugget was on Georgiijevski Street, a mere thirty metres from the Bolshoi in Theatre Square. Six months ago, the casino had been known as the Scheherazade when it had been part of a chain of restaurants, bars and whore houses owned by Babushkin *Mafiozniki*. It had been acquired by the L'Ublino syndicate whose negotiating tactics had included the liberal use of RPG 7 rocket launchers against the more vulnerable establishments belonging to their commercial rivals.

Apart from the name nothing else had changed. The clientele were still mainly drawn from the local nouveaux riche, the commodity brokers, currency speculators and dubious entrepreneurs whose business activities would have landed them in jail in any other country. The casino was, however, close enough to the plush Metropole Hotel to draw the odd Westerner who wanted to sample Moscow's night life without getting mugged in the process. On the other hand, once safely inside the Golden Nugget they were invariably taken to the cleaners on the roulette tables which the previous management had imported from Las Vegas in the confident expectation that with the benefit of a double zero, the house could scarcely lose.

Tim Rochelle had no intention of losing anything, though his dignity suffered a dent when one of the goons on the door insisted on conducting a body search before he would allow him into the casino. Leaving his overcoat with the hat-check girl in the vestibule, Rochelle walked on through the gaming room and perched himself on one of the high stools at the bar. He had joined the British Embassy in Moscow on Wednesday, 7 September 1994, and was officially the Second Secretary, Cultural Affairs; in reality he was a member of the SIS cell. He had been in the post for just three weeks when Head of Station had introduced him to his Russian contact. Except they hadn't actually shaken hands. The SIS chief had taken Barbara and himself to Gorky Park for coffee and ice cream at the rinkside café in order that Head of Station could point out Vasili Ivanovich Sokolov.

'That's the man you'll be dealing with,' he said. 'And rest assured, Tim, his minder is pointing you out to him at this very moment.'

At the time, he'd thought the whole cloak-and-dagger bit would not have seemed out of place in a farce directed by Brian Rix. It looked as if the curtain was now about to go up on act two because there was no sign of Sokolov in the gaming room, on the dance floor or at one of the tables in the alcove which passed for an intimate restaurant.

Rochelle ordered a whisky and soda and studiously ignored the come hither looks he was getting from a voluptuous brunette at the other end of the bar. He didn't know too much about fashion but the dark grey business suit she was wearing hadn't been run up in Moscow. Haute couture imported from France, if the quality and cut were anything to go by. One thing Rochelle did know: he couldn't afford to buy his wife, Barbara, such an outfit. A fashion buyer stopping off for a quick drink on the way home? Or maybe she was here to meet a business associate for dinner? And why not? He'd been told the restaurant served good food and the liquor hadn't been distilled in some back-street garage.

The scent was overpowering and he knew without looking round that the brunette had left her seat at the bar and perched herself next to him. She was no different to the croupiers in their strapless evening gowns who were available for other games when the Golden Nugget closed for the night, provided your wallet was fat enough.

'Have you got a light?' she asked in English with an odd mid-Atlantic accent.

'I'm afraid I don't smoke,' he said apologetically, then mentally cursed the bartender who gave him a book of matches.

'That's what I call service.' Somehow she managed to swivel round on the bar stool so that both her knees were pressing against his leg. She was holding the cigarette in her left hand; as he fumbled with the matches, the other hand came to rest on his thigh before wandering up with a light caressing touch. It was not a wholly unpleasant sensation, which made him feel guilty as hell.

'What is that you are drinking?' she asked.

'A whisky and soda,' Rochelle told her.

'I'll have the same,' Sokolov said behind him.

'Who invited you to join the party?' the girl demanded.

Sokolov abandoned English in favour of his mother tongue. Although Rochelle had passed a Grade I interpreters' examination, some of the more choice expressions hadn't appeared in any of the textbooks he had read. The girl gave as good as she got, called Rochelle a poxy fairy and hoped his lover gave him Aids.

'Ignore her,' Sokolov told him, 'she is trash.'

Thoroughly shaken by the incident, Rochelle downed his whisky in one go and ordered another.

'Allow me to pay for it,' Sokolov said, and laid a hundred-dollar bill on the bar, then gave him a friendly nudge in the ribs. 'Watch the barman,' he added, 'see how he reacts.'

A terrified scream from one of the croupiers in the gaming room was not the sort of reaction either man had anticipated. There was silence for a split second, then a hubbub of confused voices which suddenly died away following a harsh word of command. Rochelle looked around and gazed blankly at a forest of raised arms. A hold-up: half a dozen masked gunmen armed with Kalashnikovs and semiautomatic pistols; one of them coming towards him.

Rochelle stepped down from the bar stool and slowly raised his hands. Sokolov followed his example but only after grabbing the hundred-dollar bill, which was still lying on the bar. It was the biggest mistake the Russian could have made. Without the slightest hesitation the gunman shot him in the head, drilling a neat round hole directly above his nose and blowing out the back of his skull.

Anxious to pacify Sokolov's killer, Rochelle reached for the wallet in the breast pocket of his jacket and realised in that same instant that he too was sending out the wrong signal. Reacting swiftly, he raised his hands even higher and stretched his lips in a sickly smile to show that he meant no harm – but to no avail. As the Makarov pistol swung in his direction, Rochelle tried to sidestep out of the way and was hit twice in the upper body. The double impact literally knocked him off his feet and suddenly there was nothing but pain and darkness.

CHAPTER 15

The Jaguar XJ6 was Rowan Garfield's pride and joy. He had bought the second-hand 1992 model at the beginning of December last year as a Christmas present to himself and in his opinion it had to be the bargain of the year at £18,750. Up to now, he hadn't had an opportunity to see what the Jag could do but at three o'clock in the morning there was very little traffic on the roads and he could really put his foot down. Ten minutes after the duty officer at Vauxhall Cross had phoned him, Garfield had left his house in Churt, picked up the A3 at Hindhead and headed into town, pushing the speedometer beyond the hundred mark whenever it was safe to do so.

It was the one occasion he felt justified in exceeding the speed limit in a built-up area. Head of Station, Moscow, had given his message a signals precedence of Emergency, which meant it took priority over all communications other than one designated Flash. Since joining the SIS, Garfield could only recall two Flash signals. The first had been from the Governor of the Falklands on 2 April 1982 announcing that the Argentinians had landed in Stanley while the second had been sent by Head of Station Kuwait, half an hour after T72 tanks of the Iraqi Republican Guard had crossed the border and were motoring down the north–south super highway to the city. For that matter, it wasn't every day that an Emergency transmission was received by Vauxhall Cross.

While the Emergency communication didn't signify an act of war, it was indicative of a potentially dangerous situation. The signal the duty officer had received had been in the nature of a contact report. It had simply stated that Tim Rochelle had been shot and further details would follow shortly. The way Garfield saw it, that alone provided him with sufficient reason to ignore the thirty-mile-an-hour restriction as he swept through Wandsworth and on up the Albert Embankment. As Head of the European Department, Garfield was also conscious that he should have all the facts at his fingertips before Victor Hazelwood appeared on the scene. It was always going to be a race against time because Willow Walk in Hampstead was a damned sight closer to Vauxhall Cross than the house in Churt. To give himself a sporting chance of arriving ahead of the Director, he'd hinted that the duty officer should wait twenty minutes before informing Victor.

As he approached the art deco building, Garfield automatically signalled he was turning left even though the road was clear behind him. Shifting into third, he went down the incline leading to the basement garage, announcing his arrival with a light pap on the horn. The entrance to the parking area was sealed off by a steel trellis guaranteed to stop any intruder vehicle dead in its tracks. When he switched off the headlights, an armed police officer wearing a flak jacket appeared from the gatehouse to check his ID. After scrutinising the official pass bearing Garfield's photograph, the officer turned about and signalled to his companion inside the garage to raise the electrically operated trellis. Garfield drove inside, parked the Jaguar in the space allocated to him and took the lift up to the communication centre on the third floor where the duty officer was also located.

Two further communications had been received from Moscow since he'd left home, the second of which ran to eight paragraphs and repeated much of the information contained in the earlier transmissions. One of Garfield's attributes was his ability to speed read and instantly memorise the contents of any paper set before him. It was a talent that had served him well in the past and did so again when Hazelwood arrived just as he was halfway through the penultimate paragraph of the second communication. The fact that Victor suggested they should discuss the matter in his office gave him time to mentally digest the rest of the signal in the lift on their way up to the top floor.

Hazelwood waved him to take a chair, sat down at his desk and immediately helped himself to a Burma cheroot from the ornate cigar box. Garfield hoped in vain that he wouldn't light it.

'The duty officer informed me that Tim Rochelle had been shot,' Hazelwood said after slowly exhaling. 'Unfortunately that was the limit of his information. Do we know how he is?'

'Yes. According to the latest signal from Head of Station, Rochelle is in a critical but stable condition. He was rushed to the First General Hospital on International Avenue behind the Ukraina Hotel, It wasn't the nearest hospital but a number of other people were badly wounded and the First General is better equipped to cope with a major incident. Anyway, Tim was wheeled into the operating theatre a few minutes after the ambulance delivered him to Casualty. He had been hit twice: one bullet went into the stomach low down and right of centre, the other smashed the left hip and travelled downwards to exit on the inside of the thigh a couple of inches above the kneecap. Unfortunately, it appears the leg might have to be amputated.'

'I'd say it was more than unfortunate,' Hazelwood said pensively. 'How is Barbara taking it?'

Garfield shook his head in admiration. Rochelle hadn't even been engaged when Victor had been in charge of the Russian Desk. In fact he'd moved two rungs up the ladder to Deputy Director by the time the young woman had entered Tim's life. True he'd met her briefly just before Rochelle had left for Moscow when she and Tim were being briefed by the Foreign and Commonwealth Office but his predecessor, Sir Stuart Dunglass, would have forgotten her name in a trice.

'I don't know,' Garfield confessed. 'Head of Station didn't mention her in any of his signals. I imagine one of the wives will be with Barbara, lending her moral support.'

'Soon as we've finished, phone the Embassy and find out how she is.'

'Right.'

'Was Tim deliberately targeted or was he simply in the wrong place at the wrong time?'

The answer to that question was in the last signal but Garfield knew Victor wanted to hear it from him.

'Tim was caught up in an episode of gang warfare.'

The militia couldn't say which *Mafiozniki* gang had been involved but they favoured the former owners of the Golden Nugget. Nobody knew for sure how the gunmen had got past the two guards outside the casino without creating a major disturbance. However, since both men had disappeared, it was assumed they had been bought off with a fat wad of US dollars which, at the current rate of exchange with the rouble, would probably keep them in clover for months.

'All told there were six gunmen,' Garfield continued. 'A couple of them forced the manager of the casino to open the safe in his office before calmly executing him in cold blood. Naturally the other gunmen robbed all the patrons, relieving them of their hard currency, jewellery and Rolex watches. They weren't interested in roubles, but then I don't imagine there was an awful lot about. I understand you can't buy chips at the Golden Nugget with roubles. It's hard currency or nothing.'

There were grounds for thinking robbery was not the principal motive. Two men, apparently chosen at random, were pistol whipped until they collapsed unconscious, and the gangsters had thrown two hand grenades into the crowded gaming room as they left.

'That's why there were so many casualties.'

'Callous bastards,' Hazelwood growled.

'Well, the whole idea was to terrorise people so that they will be scared to go near the place. They want to close the Golden Nugget down. At least that's the current thinking.'

'What time was the robbery?'

'Approximately 18.30 hours Moscow time. Head of Station was not aware of the incident until it was reported on the ten o'clock news. However, it was gone midnight before the duty officer at the Embassy discovered which hospital Tim had been taken to.'

Moscow was three hours ahead of Greenwich Mean Time yet the date/time group of the first signal from Head of Station showed that it had been originated at 01.30 hours GMT. When the different time zones were taken into account, it meant there had been a delay of nearly four and a half hours before London had been informed of the incident. Garfield couldn't explain it and was relieved when Hazelwood didn't ask him to.

'Am I right in thinking Sokolov is still running errands for Pavel Trilisser?'

'You are,' Garfield told him.

'Do we know if he kept the rendezvous with Tim Rochelle?'

'There is no mention of Sokolov in any of the signals we've received.'

'Get on to Head of Station, Moscow . . .' Hazelwood paused to crush his cheroot in the cut-down shell case, something he often did when he wanted to give special emphasis to a point. 'Tell him to find out pretty damned quick. Tell him I personally want to know the answer.'

'I'll get a signal off right away,' Garfield said, anxious to escape from the smoke-laden atmosphere.

'Use voice, call him over the satellite link.'

'Now?'

'Yes, now.' Hazelwood pushed his chair back and stood up. 'The sooner we know why Trilisser wanted to establish contact the better.'

Garfield followed Hazelwood out of his office and walked with him towards the bank of lifts.

'That could take a little time, Victor. I mean, whoever we appoint as the case officer won't know Sokolov by sight, assuming our Russian friend is still available.'

'Ashton knows him,' Hazelwood said. 'They met in Warsaw a year ago.'

Garfield closed his eyes. Dear God, not Ashton. He might get things done but there was usually blood on the carpet before he'd finished.

Nizamodeen and Ayab Hosein plus their wives and four children lived with their ageing parents, a cousin, two widowed aunts and the maternal grandmother in an old terraced house on Weavers Avenue, a parallel road in rear of Mill Street. Oldfield had wanted to obtain a search warrant and turn the place over but the West Yorkshire Metropolitan Police wouldn't hear of it even though he didn't propose to call on the Hoseins in the middle of the night armed with a sledgehammer to break down their front door. In their opinion, the information Iqbal Khan had given Oldfield just wasn't strong enough to go the whole hog. So twenty-four hours later than he would have wished, they had settled for the ultra softly,

softly approach. One police car, the Detective Inspector from Bradford Central, the Community Relations officer, an Asian woman police constable and himself. The velvet glove treatment also meant they arrived at a respectable hour in the morning and knocked politely on the door.

The man who opened the door to them was about five feet seven, had a round, pockmarked face and double chin. Oldfield reckoned he weighed something in the region of a hundred and seventy pounds, most of it flab.

'Mr Nizamodeen?' the DI enquired.

'No, I'm Ayab; you wish to see my older brother.'

'And you as well, sir.' Oldfield produced his warrant card and identified himself. 'You may have seen in the newspapers that we are anxious to trace the movements of a J registered dark blue Ford Transit?'

'Oh, yes indeed, Chief Inspector,' Ayab said happily. 'My brother and I have such a vehicle.'

'May we come in, Mr Hosein?'

'But of course. Please to forgive me, I am forgetting my manners.'

Ayab Hosein backed off down the hall, opened a door on the right, then called out to his brother Nizamodeen to come and join them in the parlour. The older brother was as different as chalk from cheese. He was almost five inches taller than Ayab and was at least ten pounds lighter. A pencil-thin moustache adorned his upper lip and nature had given him a lazy right eye. Although more reserved than his younger brother, he was equally polite and seemed disappointed when nobody wanted tea and sweetmeats. Oldfield found it hard to credit that these same Hosein brothers had threatened Iqbal Khan's daughter Rana with a caning because she dressed like the English girls at her school.

'These gentlemen wish to hear about our delivery van,' Ayab informed his brother.

'It is not yet our van,' Nizamodeen said. 'We are still negotiating the price with Mr Bhutto. He wants too much money.'

'But you have been using the vehicle?'

'We have his permission,' Ayab said. 'My brother can show you the letter he wrote to us from Pakistan, Chief Inspector.'

'When are you expecting Mr Bhutto to return to this country?' Oldfield asked.

'Mr Bhutto will not be coming back,' Nizamodeen told him. 'He has gone home for good.'

'Then I think I'd better see this letter.'

Nizamodeen left the room to return a few minutes later with a sheet of lined notepaper that looked as if it had been torn out of a child's exercise book. Oldfield took one look at the script and passed it to the Community Relations officer who in turn consulted the Asian WPC.

'It's written in Pashto,' she said.

'What does it say?' Oldfield asked her.

'I think it gives Mr Hosein permission to use the van, sir.'

'Are you sure of that?'

'Are you saying that my brother and I are liars, Chief Inspector?' Ayab demanded angrily.

'Of course I'm not.' Oldfield cleared his throat. 'Where is the vehicle now, Mr Hosein?'

'It's kept in a garage on Laisterdyke Lane near the railway line.'

'I'd like to see it.'

Neither of the Hosein brothers seemed the least bit perturbed by his request. Ayab however insisted on coming along despite the fact that his older brother had volunteered to show them where the garage was. To solve the transport problem, the WPC stayed behind at the house while Oldfield travelled with Ayab Hosein in the Mini van.

The garage was a lockup under the railway arches which Mr Bhutto had rented when he was still in England. It was secured by a formidable-looking padlock to which Nizamodeen possessed a key. Except that he didn't need one on this occasion because somebody had cut through the hasp with a hacksaw. There was of course no sign of the dark blue Ford Transit which caused the Hosein brothers no end of distress.

'All right, that's enough of the weeping and wailing,' Oldfield said in his blunt fashion. 'Now tell me the last time you saw the damned vehicle.'

'Last Friday,' Nizamodeen said promptly.

'More like the previous Wednesday,' Ayab said.

'That would be 25 January?'

'Yes.'

'OK. Who has the vehicle registration document?'

'We did, it was kept in the vehicle along with the insurance certiticate.'

Oldfield had addressed the question to Nizamodeen but younger brother had stepped in and answered it.

'And the registration number?'

'The registration number,' Ayab repeated frowning.

'Yes. Don't tell me you've forgotten it already?'

'The number is J988VWS.'

'Thank you,' Oldfield said with false civility.

He would run the number past the Driver and Vehicle Licensing Centre, Swansea, and if there was just one tiny discrepancy he would be back with a search warrant.

Ashton opened the top drawer of his desk, took out the glossy brochure on the Ford Mondeo and read it again for the umpteenth time since Harriet had sprung it on him the night before last. No one at Vauxhall Cross could fail to know what had happened to Tim Rochelle and he felt guilty in the circumstances about taking another peek at the literature Harriet had obtained from the local Ford dealer. Ashton felt he ought to be doing something more productive but Kelso had beaten him to it and obtained Rochelle's PV file from the Security Vetting and Technical Services Division. Roy hated to be caught out and he had obviously done a little private research so that he could answer any questions which might arise during morning prayers.

The Ford Mondeo was under a year old and had been the agency's demonstration model but it had less than five thousand on the clock and was in immaculate condition. Stapled on the back cover was a financial statement which Harriet had prepared. It showed the asking price for the Ford Mondeo which had been reduced by £1,500 (after what must have been some pretty fierce haggling) and the clearly overinflated trade-in value of the Vauxhall Cavalier.

When Harriet made up her mind to do something, there was no

stopping her. As part of her hard sell campaign, she had persuaded the dealer to let her take the Mondeo home for the night so that she could go to work on him, having left the Vauxhall as security. The Ford was now back with the dealer but not for long; the financial statement she had prepared for his benefit proved conclusively that they could afford a new car. He reached for the phone, intending to call Harriet and tell her to go ahead and clinch the deal but was interrupted before he could lift the receiver.

'Busy, Peter?'

He looked up expecting to see a mocking smile on Jill Sheridan's lips and instead found one that was oddly hesitant.

'Can you spare me a few minutes?' she asked and then closed the door behind her before he could think of an excuse to put her off.

The Sony recorder was lying in the pending tray where, somewhat gratuitously, he had left it yesterday evening after reloading with a fresh cassette. While Jill still had her back to him, he switched on the Sony and quickly covered it with the glossy brochure.

'Be my guest,' he murmured and glanced at the programme for the Deputy Director which the chief clerk had left on his desk. 'Aren't you supposed to be briefing Clifford Peachey about now?'

'Morning prayers overran,' she told him. 'At the moment he's with Rowan Garfield getting the lowdown on the European Department. The point is, Victor announced that among other responsibilities Clifford Peachey would be handling the Naburn business from now on.'

'Yes?'

'Well, I wasn't being exactly honest with you the other day when you asked me about Sharon Cartwright.'

Jill took a deep breath, the kind of thing people did when they felt stressed out and couldn't think how else to unwind. If it was just an act, Ashton thought it was the finest performance he had ever witnessed.

'The fact is, Sharon was passing information to me, things she had learned from Menendez which Harvey Yeo and Larry Rossitor didn't know about.'

'What did she tell you?'

'I'm coming to that, Peter.'

'Well, get a move on,' Ashton said in a hostile voice. 'I haven't got all day.'

'Please, this isn't easy for me. I have to do it my own way. Sharon had me worried sick. You wouldn't believe what she was up to.'

'You're wrong, I most certainly would.'

'As a security precaution, Menendez was locked in his room at night but she got hold of a spare key somehow and would let him out when everybody else was asleep. He was bonking her, for God's sake, and what I found really incredible was her demeanour. I mean, she was quite open about it.'

'That was part of the attraction for Sharon,' Ashton told her. 'She got a thrill out of living dangerously. Of course I'm being wise after the event. She kept that trait well hidden from us all.'

'You know what scared me to death, Peter? The strong possibility that if Sharon was caught, she would claim I had put her up to it. With a threat like that hanging over me, do you wonder I was unable to confide in you?'

'You just muzzled me instead. I don't know what story you pitched to Robin Urquhart but I caught a lot of brickbats.'

'I'm sorry. I should never have done that to you of all people, but I was in a blind panic. I could see my whole career in ruins, everything I'd worked for destroyed overnight.'

'All right, I believe you, Jill, you didn't tell Sharon to get herself laid by Menendez.'

'I never asked her to keep me informed either.'

There was a limit to the amount of bullshit Ashton could stomach and he'd just about had a bellyful.

'Don't go overdoing it,' he warned Jill. 'If you mean to confide in me, you'd better start now.'

'OK. Well, first of all, Sharon told me they didn't really need an interpreter because Menendez was fluent in English. He deliberately gave the impression that his command of our language was limited in order to revert to Spanish whenever he was forced into a corner.'

'And Harvey Yeo never twigged?'

'No. Sharon reckoned he saw Menendez as his last chance of glory. He wanted to finish his career on a high note and was eager to believe everything the Cuban told him.'

'What else?'

'Sharon said Menendez was an out-and-out liar. I gather he admitted as much when they were enjoying a cigarette together after he had shafted her. Seems our Cuban-American friend thought Harvey was a big joke.'

Ashton had a mental picture of Sharon Cartwright and Raúl Menendez lying in each other's arms making sly jokes in whispers about a man who was worth ten of them. Then he recalled what Sharon's kidnappers had done to her and his anger focused solely on the Cuban.

'She claimed Menendez more or less admitted to her that he had only been on the fringes of the drugs scene and was inventing most of the stuff he was feeding Harvey Yeo.'

'Roger Benton suspected as much but somebody wanted Menendez badly enough to have four people murdered on his account.'

'Well, for what it's worth, Peter, I think he had stolen something really valuable.'

'Such as?'

'Diamonds.'

'Diamonds!' Ashton echoed.

'Yes, diamonds. Sharon had told him point-blank that she didn't believe he had fled to Chile because his life was in danger. In her book he was a con man pure and simple, who'd taken the British Government for a ride. She obviously injured his pride because Menendez lost his temper and boasted about the diamonds he'd salted away. They were supposed to be worth millions of dollars.'

'When did Sharon tell you this?'

'The day before she was kidnapped and the others murdered. She rang me at home on the Monday evening to say she had put everything in a letter which I could expect to receive the following morning. It duly arrived in the first post.'

'And?'

'Well, naturally I read the letter before I burned it.'

'So, what did Sharon say in her letter?'

'Very little that she hadn't told me on the phone.'

Extracting information from Jill was like getting blood out of a stone. After questioning her relentlesly, Ashton learned that Menendez hadn't said how he had obtained the diamonds or what he had done with them before fleeing to Santiago.

'Didn't you tell her to go to work on Menendez and dig a little deeper?'

'Certainly not. I've already made it clear that I never asked her to keep me informed.' Jill stood up and smoothed her skirt. 'I've gone out of my way to be helpful but I'm not about to put my hand up for something I didn't do.'

'Right.'

'And when you repeat the gist of our conversation to Clifford Peachey I suggest you stick to the truth,' she said, and started towards the door.

'And what is the truth, Jill?' he asked.

'Sharon's letter arrived the day after the murders. I burned it in a panic because I realised the contents could be misconstrued. It was silly of me to withhold the information until now but we all have our failings and I am only human.'

'What about all those phone calls you had?'

'As I've already told Victor, she was pestering me about a transfer to the Mid East Department.'

'Nice one, Jill.'

'I think so too,' Jill said, and walked out of the office.

Ashton waited until he could no longer hear her footsteps in the corridor before he removed the glossy brochure and stopped the recorder. After rewinding the cassette, he played it back. The quality was lousy, their conversation virtually inaudible even on full volume. It was not however a total disaster; in the hands of an expert like Hicks, the recording could be enhanced until it was possible to hear what had passed between them. Ashton wasn't sure what he was going to do with the finished product yet, but when one was dealing with Jill Sheridan, it was only prudent to have an ace up one's sleeve.

CHAPTER 16

J988 WVS was the registration number of a 1991 Peugeot 405, the registered keeper of which was a Mr Raymond Ellington of 29 Nightingale Avenue, Bristol. On the strength of that information from the Driver and Vehicle Licensing Agency, Swansea, Oldfield had no difficulty in persuading the West Yorkshire Metropolitan Police to obtain a search warrant. It was however made clear to him that the search would be conducted by CID officers from Bradford Central and that he would be present merely as an observer.

There was no velvet glove this time round. Although the Community Relations officer and the same Asian WPC were involved, the DI from Bradford Central now had the scene-of-the-crime officer and his team, a sniffer dog and handler, plus one sergeant and eight police constables to back him up. Two additional uniformed officers had been posted in the earthen lane between Mill Street and Weavers Avenue to watch the back of the house occupied by the Hosein family. The sergeant and eight constables were responsible for crowd control, which was a euphemistic way of saying it was their job to deal with a riot should one occur. For the present, their protective clothing was tucked out of sight in their patrol van. Also hidden away was a fourteen-pound sledgehammer.

It was Ayab Hosein who again answered the door. Unlike the previous occasion, he definitely wasn't pleased to see them and became downright angry when the DI confronted him with the search warrant.

'What is this nonsense?' he shouted at Oldfield. 'I demand an explanation, Chief Inspector.'

'You deliberately misled us,' Oldfield told him calmly. 'The number you gave me is on a Peugeot 405 in the Bristol area.'

'This is police harassment,' Ayab screamed, 'and racially motivated into the bargain. I can tell you the Chief Constable will be hearing from our solicitor.'

'Are you going to let us in, Mr Hosein?' the DI enquired politely.

'I do not want that pye-dog in the house.'

'My dog is not a pariah,' the handler said indignantly, 'he's a pure-bred German shepherd.'

The DI sighed. 'I know that, constable, but take him round to the lane at the back of the house.'

The compromise did little to calm things down. Ayab was still in a highly excitable state and continued to shout the odds about police brutality as they trooped down the hall into the kitchen, where Nizamodeen Hosein attempted to bar their way. The four Hosein women who happened to be present all started yelling at once at the top of their voices. Ayab pushed Oldfield aside, grabbed a mobile phone that was lying on the Welsh dresser and yelled at everybody to shut up.

'I am going to phone our lawyer,' he shouted. 'Mr Jinnah will soon tell these policemen where they get off.'

'I hope you are calling your lawyer, sir,' the DI warned him, 'because if a crowd suddenly gathers outside this house, I'll have you for inciting a riot.'

'You hear that, Chief Inspector? He is threatening me.'

'Why don't you call Mr Jinnah?' Oldfield said, and opened the back door.

The garden was approximately sixty feet long by thirty wide and was separated from the neighbouring properties by tall overgrown privet hedges. There were no flowerbeds and as a keen gardener, it pained Oldfield to see that the lawn had never received a final cut at the end of the growing season. As a result, the lawn was uneven and disfigured by clumbs of couch grass. The wooden shed the brothers used as a print shop was at the bottom of the garden right on the boundary line with the lane. The car port which Iqbal Khan had spoken of was a very amateurish and unsightly affair. It consisted of six timber posts sunk in the ground with wood cross-ties to which half a dozen sheets of corrugated iron had been nailed three abreast. Each panel was six feet long; an average-size family car therefore protruded by as much as a yard. The so-called hard standing had been made out of clinker from the kitchen boiler.

The handler and his sniffer dog were waiting for them in the lane. Ayab came running, still talking to his lawyer, the mobile phone pressed against the left side of his chubby face.

'Mr Jinnah says you are not to do anything until he arrives,' he announced breathlessly.

'I'll give your solicitor exactly ten minutes,' the DI informed him, 'then you either unlock the shed or I'll have one of my officers break down the door.'

Ayab switched off the phone and retracted the aerial before exploding. If the police damaged their print shop, he would take the officer in charge to court and sue him for thousands of pounds. He had a lot more to say on the subject before Nizamodeen intervened and told him to shut up. It was the first time Oldfield had seen the older brother assert his authority.

After that, nothing more was said by the Hoseins. Oldfield lit a much-needed cigarette and made inconsequential small talk with the scene-of-the-crime officer. When five minutes had gone by, the DI made a great show of consulting his wristwatch and gave the impression that he was just longing for an excuse to break into the shed. To his even more obvious disappointment, Mr Jinnah, a thin man with hawklike features and the glittering eyes of a predator, arrived two minutes before the ultimatum was due to expire.

The lawyer wanted to see their search warrant, then asked on what grounds they had obtained it. When Oldfield told him the police had reason to believe that Sharon Cartwright had been held against her will in the print shop, Jinnah dismissed the assertion as complete nonsense.

'Utterly preposterous, Chief Inspector.'

'You may well be right, sir,' Oldfield told him, 'but the information came from a responsible member of the public and we are duty-bound to follow it up.'

'Iqbal Khan.' Ayab took a deep breath. 'I tell you, Chief Inspector, that man is a troublemaker.'

Not from where I'm standing, Oldfield thought.

'I think you should advise your client to unlock the shed, Mr

Jinnah,' the DI said. 'If this standoff continues, he will be only making things worse for himself.'

It transpired Nizamodeen had the keys; while the lawyer was still explaining the facts of life to the younger brother, Nizamodeen stepped forward and opened the door. Although no expert on the printing business, Oldfield had never seen a tidier-looking workshop. There was a complete absence of litter on the bench, the letters of the alphabet had been put away in the drawers underneath, neatly arranged in trays according to the typeface, and the old-fashioned manually operated rotary press was spotlessly clean. There was no sign of the roll of carpet Iqbal Khan had mentioned in his statement; there was however a peculiar aroma which reminded Oldfield of aniseed. He wondered how the German shepherd would react to the smell, wondered too if it would put him off the scent. They would know soon enough because the handler had been given a piece of the satin pyjamas belonging to Sharon Cartwright which had been found in the linen basket at The Firs.

Oldfield watched the handler remove the square of satin from the hermetically sealed plastic envelope with a pair of tweezers and hold it out to the Alsatian. If the Hosein brothers thought they had done enough to neutralise the threat posed by the sniffer dog, they were sadly mistaken. The moment he entered the shed, the German shepherd became very excited. At first it seemed to Oldfield that the dog was simply chasing its tail but then he began scrabbling at the floor, lying on his belly to reach under the workbench with his front paws.

'Looks to me as if this contraption has been moved,' the handler said. 'It ought to be near the window instead of at the back of the shed.'

'I think you're right,' the DI told him. 'Get Fang out of there and we'll put the SOCO team in.'

The handler considered his charge had been slighted and felt duty-bound to stick up for him.

'The dog's name is Bruce, sir,' he said in a sharp voice.

Harassed by Ayab Hosein, who was threatening to sue the police authority should their property be damaged, the scene-of-the-crime team moved in, picked up the workbench and set it down again in the middle of the shed. Although there was nothing to show that the floorboards had been lifted at any time, they used a claw to draw the rusty nails and removed the panels one by one. Part of the earth underneath had been dug over, then flattened with a spade in an effort to make the coffin-size area blend in with the rest of the impacted soil.

'Do you think they originally intended to bury Sharon Cartwright under the shed?' the DI asked.

'Too risky.' Oldfield lit another cigarette, drew the smoke down on to his lungs and slowly exhaled. 'I've a hunch they laid Sharon in a shallow trench until they were ready to dispose of her. She certainly wasn't tortured in this place.'

'Another hunch?'

'There were seventeen burns on her body and there were also scorch marks on her buttocks which the pathologist reckoned had been inflicted with a blowtorch. OK, there were indications that she had been gagged with some implement but it would have been removed every time they wanted an answer from her.' Oldfield tapped the wooden frame. 'This shed is hardly soundproof and she must have been in great pain.'

Like archaeologists on a dig, the crime team set to with garden trowels, carefully filling dozens of plastic bags. The shed rested on a foundation of breeze blocks. Soon after they started digging, it became apparent that one breeze block had been removed.

'We all know where that one finished up,' Oldfield said grimly.

The shallow trench which the team finally excavated was only marginally bigger than a coffin. In it they found the remains of what appeared to be a soft-nose bullet, a minute piece of cloth and traces of blood. But the really solid piece of evidence was a .22 calibre rimmed cartridge case which had been ejected from a semiautomatic handgun. It gave Oldfield considerable pleasure to inform Mr Jinnah that his clients had a lot of explaining to do.

The sight of Clifford Peachey seated at the desk while Victor Hazelwood occupied one of the two chairs provided for visitors seemed incongruous to Ashton. Peachey was always neatly attired and looked every inch the senior servant. Hazelwood was a large, untidy man. Although nowadays his suits were made by Gieves & Hawkes, he treated them so badly that one could be forgiven for thinking he had bought them at a church jumble sale. Peachey too was a smoker but as far as Ashton knew, he wasn't in the habit of dropping hot ash on his ties and shirt fronts. Hazelwood had never worn a Van Heusen or an Austin Reed shirt until it was going threadbare; usually he managed to set fire to them long before that. The whole morning and the early part of the afternoon had been taken up by the assistant directors who had briefed Peachey about their respective departments. By the time Ashton came on song, the MI5 officer was practically punch-drunk.

'Operations and General Duties,' he mused. 'That's a pretty all-embracing remit.'

'Has to be,' Hazelwood told him before Ashton could open his mouth. 'Peter is our troubleshooter – by that I mean yours and mine.'

'And at the moment, he's investigating the Naburn incident?'

'I'm about to relieve him of that chore. I want Peter to be readily available in case I have to send him to Moscow.'

Ashton felt superfluous and not a little annoyed that both Peachey and Hazelwood were talking about him as though he weren't present. He also wasn't too happy that Victor was toying with the idea of sending him to Moscow, a city he had visited at least once too often.

'So how far has the investigation progressed now?'

Ashton waited for Hazelwood to answer, then realised he was expected to deal with the question.

'We've stepped back a pace and left the police to get on with it.'

'I assume they've undertaken to keep us informed?'

'Yes. They know we have an interest in the two separate lines of inquiry they are persuing.'

Ashton told him about the relationship between Fox, Irwin and the unknown Canadian, and the steps he hoped Special Branch were taking to identify the latter's fax number.

'Who did you see at Special Branch?' Peachey asked.

'Commander Paul Isherwood. The meeting was arranged by Brian Thomas, who knew him when God was a boy.'

'Ah yes, I met Thomas at Paddington Green.'

And didn't take to him, Ashton thought.

'What about Menendez? Any word on him?'

'No. I think he's dead and buried some place where we're unlikely to find him.'

'He wouldn't be the first drugs dealer that's happened to,' Peachey observed.

'Menendez wasn't involved in the drugs scene; he'd stolen several million dollars' worth of diamonds.'

'Who told you that?' Hazelwood asked sharply.

'Jill Sheridan; she came to see me while Clifford was being briefed about the European Department. She got it from Sharon Cartwright the night before they were all murdered.'

Peachey tapped out his pipe in an ashtray he'd apparently brought with him from the Gower Street headquarters of MI5.

'Why didn't she tell you this before now?' he asked.

Ashton told it the way Jill had and left Peachey to draw his own conclusions. He wasn't being chivalrous; it was simply that everybody knew there had been a time when he and Jill had been lovers. If he'd given his version, Peachey might feel he was prejudiced against her.

'Did Sharon Cartwright explain how she had learned about the diamonds Menendez claimed to have acquired?'

'Yes. She said they were in bed when he told her.'

'Perhaps Menendez was merely trying to impress her?'

'I'm sure he was but I don't believe he was lying about the stones. And I'll tell you something else: there was no way the man whose diamonds he stole could claim for them on his insurance.'

'And that's about it, Clifford,' Hazelwood said, and got to his feet. 'From now on it's Roger Benton's job to monitor the investigation.' He paused, then added, 'Under your direction, of course.'

'Thank you, Victor – and you too, Peter,' Peachey smiled. 'What you've told me has been most illuminating.'

Ashton followed Hazelwood out of the room and along the corridor to his office. Although Victor hadn't said he wanted to have a word with him, there was one particular matter which Ashton refused to leave hanging in the air.

'Were you serious about sending me to Moscow?' he asked, after closing the door behind him.

'Sokolov is dead,' Hazelwood said tersely. 'I expect you've already heard he wasn't the only casualty?'

'There is a buzz going the rounds. I presume someone from the Embassy has been to see Tim Rochelle in hospital?'

'Yes, but we didn't get that from Tim. He's in no fit state to answer any questions – keeps slipping in and out of consciousness.'

'Is he going to pull through?'

'The latest word from Moscow is that the surgeons are happy with the way Tim's recovering from the operation. Contrary to their earlier prognosis they're also hopeful that his left leg can be saved.'

'That is good news.'

'Yes, it is.' Opening the cigar box, Hazelwood took out a cheroot and savoured the aroma, then suddenly put it back. 'I'm trying to cut it down,' he said.

'Good idea.'

'Alice has been on to me to give up smoking altogether.'

Hazelwood was stalling him for some reason and he was damned if he would let him get away with that.

'Who told us Sokolov was dead?' he asked bluntly.

'Head of Station heard it on the 9.00 a.m. newscast. The anchorman described Sokolov as a member of the Foreign Affairs Advisory Team with special responsibility for Anglo-Russian relations. He was said to be irreplaceable. The statement was undoubtedly authorised by Pavel Trilisser.'

'And you think he was sending us a coded message?'

'I know he was,' Hazelwood said forcefully. 'Trilisser is serving notice that he won't be reopening the covert link with the Embassy. He's under the illusion that he can cut himself off from us. Needless to say the sooner Trilisser is disabused of that notion the better.'

'And just how do you propose to bring him to his senses?'

'You're his *bête noire*, Peter. You have the same effect on him as an enema.'

Ashton recalled the seventy-eight days he had spent in solitary confinement in the Lefortovo Prison courtesy of Pavel Trilisser. He also had a vivid memory of the shoot-out in Deep Shelter Four, one of six bunkers sited around the periphery of Moscow, which he'd been lucky to survive.

'I'll let you into a secret, Victor, the terror is mutual. If I frighten Trilisser, he scares the shit out of me.'

'There won't be any unpleasantness,' Hazelwood said airily. 'If you do have to go to Moscow, it will be a quick in-and-out job.'

Ashton wondered where he had heard that one before.

Fox left the Piccadilly Line train at South Harrow, walked down the steps and, passing through the booking hall, joined the queue at the bus stop outside the station. Approximately four minutes later, two buses arrived in tandem. Ignoring the 114, he boarded the 140 to Hayes and Harlington, only to alight at the very next stop. When the bus moved off again, he crossed Northolt Road and turned into Corbins Lane. Although he had never been to South Harrow before, it was obvious to him that Kathy Irwin knew the suburb pretty well; she had told him what landmarks to look out for and there was no way she could have acquired that information from reading a street map. He walked on past St Paul's Church, turned left at the T junction and there, two hundred yards farther on, was the cemetery. The Tithe Farm where he was to meet her was only a short distance away.

A nasty feeling that he and Kathy were going to look conspicuous was dispelled the moment he walked into the saloon bar. At 2.30 on a Friday afternoon, there were still a reasonable number of late lunchers or early weekenders on the premises for the two of them to pass unnoticed in the crowd. However, a woman on her own in a pub was always conspicuous; to avoid drawing attention to herself while she was waiting for him, Kathy Irwin had tagged on to a group at the bar and was conversing animatedly with a woman in her mid-forties and a man who looked old and bent enough to be drawing the old age pension. She was, he had to admit, a fine actress; catching sight of him, she waved a hand and signalled to come and join her. To get involved with two complete strangers was the last thing Fox wanted but there wasn't much he could do about it.

In the event, Kathy did most of the talking, leaving him to say yes or no as the occasion demanded. After he'd had a quick beer, she announced it was time they were making tracks, and almost before he knew it, they were out of the pub and walking towards the Ford Escort she'd left in the car park behind the Tithe Farm.

'Yours?' he asked.

Kathy shook her head. 'It belongs to Mr Hertz, I rented it this morning.' She unzipped the large shoulder bag she was carrying, took out the car keys and, unlocking the Ford, got in behind the wheel.

'I hope you're clean, Ronnie,' she said, and gave him the shoulder bag to hold while she started the engine.

'You don't have to worry about me, girl. I've got eyes in the back of my head.'

Nobody had been on his tail when he'd boarded a number 23 bus in Poplar, after leaving Edwina's flat where he had spent the night. And he'd waited long enough at Aldgate East for a District Line train to Ealing Broadway to have outed any plain-clothes officer who might be shadowing him. He'd also run another check when he'd switched to the Piccadilly Line at Ealing Common, the penultimate station on that section of the District Line. There was nowhere anybody could hang about on that exposed platform and not be noticed. Five other people had alighted at Ealing Common and all of them had left the station. More importantly, he had been the only passenger to board the Piccadilly Line to Rayners Lane. Of the eight passengers who'd got out at South Harrow, none had joined him at the bus queue. The final walkabout through Corbins Lane, which had been Kathy's idea, had convinced him that he wasn't under surveillance.

'How about you, Kathy?' he asked.

'You don't have to worry about me,' she told him with a faint smile, 'I've got eyes in the back of my head.'

Smart arse, he thought, and cocky with it.

'So what have you got for me?'

'Take a look, the goodies are in my shoulder bag.'

The first of the goodies was an old-fashioned UK passport, number N386623E that was due for renewal in March 1996. It had been issued to Mr Charles Barclay born on 13 August 1963 at Ilford, but the laminated photograph on page 3 embossed with the Home Office stamp was Fox's.

'Neat,' he said.

'I'd call it a work of art. I hope you can forge Mr Barclay's signature.'

'Shouldn't be difficult. When did Mr Barclay lose his passport?'

'Mr Barclay died three months ago; his common-law wife was happy with the three hundred pounds she got for it.'

There were two white envelopes in the shoulder bag: one contained five hundred French francs in various denominations while the other yielded 875 US dollars.

'Loose change,' Kathy Irwin said laconically.

'Can't have too much of that. Whose is the leather wallet?'

'Yours.'

The wallet had a used look about it which was complimented by a number of dog-eared business cards. There were of course no credit cards of any description, but there were ten fifty-pound notes and another five hundred pounds in twenties.

'There's also five thousand in blank traveller's cheques,' Kathy told him.

'This must be my lucky day,' he said.

'It gets better. My going away present to you is a suitcase with enough clothes to last you for a few days.'

'Anything else?'

'You're booked on British Airways flight BA322 to Paris, departing 17.25 hours tonight from Terminal 4. The ticket will be waiting for you at the airline desk and they know you'll be paying cash.'

No hotel reservation had been made for him in Paris but this wasn't the tourist season and she didn't imagine he'd have any difficulty in finding somewhere. The same applied to the onward flight to Miami by Air France.

'You're dumping me,' Fox said, voicing a growing suspicion. 'You're planning to leave me high and dry in Florida.'

'I've already told you, the Canadian will see you right.'

'How can I be sure of that? What if he doesn't come near me? You want to tell me what to do then? I don't even know where to begin looking for the bastard.'

'The bastard is a private investigator,' Irwin's woman told him coolly. 'He calls himself John Novaks. He has an office in Ponte Vedra Beach not far from Jacksonville, Florida. The fax address places it on Ocean View. OK?'

'You know something?' Fox said. 'I'm feeling better already.'

The Thank God It's Friday attitude prevalent throughout Whitehall had its fair share of adherents in Vauxhall Cross. One of them happened to be Terry Hicks, who was usually out of the building on the stroke of five, if not before. On this particular Friday however some prick of conscience had made him seek out Ashton when he would normally have been heading for the exit.

'Can you spare me a minute?' he asked from the corridor, transferring his weight from one foot to the other like a man dying to take a leak when there wasn't a vacant urinal.

'Take as long as you like,' Ashton told him.

'It's about Fox.'

'He's not really my pigeon now.'

'Yeah. Well, I'd sooner deal with you. I've only said hello to the new man.'

The new man on the case was Clifford Peachey and Hicks feared the Deputy DG would be likely to detain him well beyond five with a load of questions.

'I know how it is, Terry,' Ashton said drily.

'I doubt you know that Fox called the Fleetspeed office from his flat yesterday afternoon and told the dispatcher he wouldn't be doing any minicabbing that evening. Then he rang Edwina and said they were going up West for a special night out. Subsequently he phoned the Riverside Restaurant and booked a table for two at eight. Finally, he rings Fleetspeed from Edwina's flat and asks for a minicab to pick them up from the salon.'

'And that was the first time Fox used either phone since he was released from Paddington Green?'

'Yeah. What do you make of it?'

'I think Fox suspects both phones have been bugged and is being cute because he is getting ready to leave.'

Like me, Ashton thought, except Fox wouldn't be going to Moscow.

CHAPTER 17

It had been a bad night in Bradford. The rioting by gangs of Asian youths had started in Weavers Avenue shortly after dusk when vehicles belonging to the scene-of-the-crime officer and his team had been stoned. The sergeant and eight constables who had remained in the area after the Hoseins had been conveyed to Bradford Central had attempted to disperse the mob, only to find themselves suddenly outnumbered by eight to one. Unable to contain the situation until reinforcements arrived, they had been forced to make an undignified withdrawal after three of their number had been injured.

Like a bush fire fanned by the wind, the riot had then spread into the neighbouring streets. Cars had been hijacked and torched, a motorist who had stopped at the traffic lights had been dragged from his car and beaten up, while in another affray two white youths aged sixteen and seventeen had been stabbed. On Mill Street the newsagent's and tobacconist's owned by Iqbal Khan had been fire-bombed. The firemen who had responded to the 999 call had been repeatedly attacked and had needed police protection before they could tackle the blaze effectively. By the time order had been restored Iqbal Khan's shop and flat above had been reduced to a burned-out shell.

Oldfield had lost the only witnesses he had. Completely demoralised by what had happened to his family, Iqbal Khan had insisted on making a second statement retracting everything he had said in the first. His mother had not seen the Hoseins carrying a rolled-up carpet into their print shop and her memory wasn't all that good, especially as regards dates and times. She was an old lady and sometimes her mind wandered and she made things up in order to gain attention. Oldfield thought Khan would probably obey a summons to appear in court but he would have to be treated as a hostile witness to get any evidence out of him and that was unlikely to go down well with the jury.

Oldfield was left with the forensic evidence, which was pretty good, but maybe not quite damning enough to be absolutely certain of obtaining a conviction. Of the three items, the strongest was the .22 cartridge case; the fact that the metal jacket wasn't discoloured was proof that it hadn't been lying in the earth very long. All that the scientists had been able to tell him about the blood spoor was that the sample was type O, which matched Sharon Cartwright's blood group and a large proportion of the UK population. A whole series of tests were still being carried out on the fibres and it could be that these tiny fragments would settle the issue, but he couldn't bank on it.

Good as the circumstantial evidence was, Oldfield doubted if it was yet strong enough to shift the burden of proof from the prosecution to the defence during the trial. The blue Ford Transit had apparently disappeared without trace and the chances of finding the murder weapon seemed extremely remote. His only hope of finding either one lay in turning Nizamodeen or Ayab Hosein. The interrogation of the brothers had reached such an impasse that the West Yorkshire CID were quite happy for him to assume the lead role in what would be the last attempt to break them down.

The question which exercised Oldfield was who was the more likely to crack – Ayab or Nizamodeen. Ayab was the more excitable of the two, full of bluster and threatening to take the Chief Constable and assorted police officers to court one moment, all smarmy the next, professing his admiration for the British way of life and eager to co-operate with the authorities. But even when he was supposedly being helpful, Ayab went round and round in circles, telling his interrogators absolutely nothing. Contrary to his appearance and manner, Ayab was a tough nut and particularly enjoyed provoking the CID officers at Bradford Central.

Although Nizamodeen was no pushover, Oldfield believed he was not as bright as his younger brother and was more open to persuasion. Furthermore, it was Mr Jinnah himself, and not one of his junior partners whom he'd summoned to Bradford Central, who was always present when Nizamodeen was questioned. To Oldfield that suggested the wily old lawyer considered the older brother was the more vulnerable.

Mr Jinnah had spent over twelve hours at the police station with his clients, returning home at three o'clock in the morning. He was therefore less than enthusiastic when he had been roused four hours later and informed that the police were going to question the brothers again. He had complained that, as a matter of policy, the police were depriving the Hoseins of sleep in the hope that one of them would eventually make a damaging admission. It was an accusation he had repeated even more vehemently when he learned that Nizamodeen was the one whom Oldfield intended to question. He was in full voice when Oldfield switched on the tape recorder in the interview room and identified those present for the record.

'Listen to me, Chief Inspector,' he said. 'You should either charge my client or release him without further ado.'

'I don't think we can do that just yet, Mr Jinnah.' Oldfield turned to Nizamodeen. 'I'm going to tell you what actually happened on Tuesday, 24 January. But first of all, you should understand that I don't believe you personally murdered Sharon Cartwright . . .'

Mr Jinnah clapped his hands. 'Splendid. At least we are agreed on something. May I assume you are now prepared to release both Ayab and Nizamodeen?'

'You did however assist your brother and others to kidnap Sharon Cartwright,' Oldfield continued relentlessly. 'You were filmed driving past the house where she was staying on Monday the twenty-third and again the following day . . .'

'You have photographs to support this allegation, Chief Inspector?'

Oldfield refused to be thrown out of his stride and ploughed doggedly on. He wasn't saying Nizamodeen had tortured Sharon Cartwright but he had been present when the burns had been inflicted. Where and when this had been done to her was un-important; what really mattered to him was the last few minutes of her life.

'She was conveyed to Weavers Avenue in the back of the Transit van rolled up in a carpet.' Oldfield pointed an accusing finger at Nizamodeen. 'You helped to carry the lady into your print shop and placed her in the shallow trench which you and your brother dug . . .'

'I really must protest at this line of questioning,' Jinnah said in a shrill voice.

'Noted,' Oldfield snapped, then continued in the same vein. 'The carpet was removed and she was left there lying face down in the earth, head in a gunny sack, bound hand and foot. I don't suppose it occurred to you that she only had seconds to live and it must have been quite a shock when the sahib produced the semiautomatic and stood over her?'

Elder brother was rattled and couldn't look him in the eyes. Fear had suddenly drained the saliva from his mouth and he was beginning to sweat. Oldfield aligned the index finger on top of the first finger, curled the other two into the palm of his right hand and held them in place with his thumb. Then he aimed the pistol at the Pakistani.

'He was as close to Sharon as I am to you when he shot her in the head – pow, pow, pow.'

'This is absolutely disgraceful, Chief Inspector—'

'Except the "pistol" didn't make a sound like that. It was more of a hollow cough because the weapon was fitted with a silencer. Right?'

'This must stop! I will not allow you to browbeat my client—'

'What I want from you, Nizamodeen, old son, is the name of the white man who did it. I mean, why do you want to protect him? What's he done for you? Or are you keeping quiet because little brother told you to keep your mouth shut?'

'No . . . No.'

'So you are capable of making your own decisions?'

'I always have,' Nizamodeen said in a sullen voice.

'Then presumably you are quite happy to spend the next twenty years of your life in prison?'

'I'm . . .' Nizamodeen swallowed and tried again. 'I'm not going to prison—'

'You don't have to say anything,' Jinnah shrieked at him. 'This interview is terminated—'

'The hell it is, Mr Jinnah.'

'I know nothing,' Hosein said.

Oldfield closed his eyes. So near and yet so far. Nizamodeen had been on the point of blurting out the truth but in his eagerness, he had pushed him too hard and had blown it.

'I repeat, Chief Inspector, I cannot allow this to go on. Mr Hosein has been very co-operative but there is nothing more he can tell you. We have reached a point where you must either charge my client or release him from arrest.'

'How right you are,' Oldfield said wearily. He pursed his lips. 'She was hooded but not gagged. I wonder why?'

'She had forced it out of her mouth,' Nizamodeen said and froze.

A warm and beautiful smile appeared on Oldfield's face.

'Bingo,' he said and beamed at Mr Jinnah. 'I do believe we've hit the fucking jackpot.'

It was the fifth time Ashton had been to Moscow. In 1991 he had got his local travel agent to book him a trip to Leningrad and Moscow with forty-odd tourists who unwittingly had provided the necessary cover for a covert operation. A year later, when Head of the Security Vetting and Technical Services Division, he had visited the British Embassy on Maurice Thorez Embankment to carry out the annual inspection. Soon after this had been completed, he'd returned to Moscow at his own expense and without authorisation, using a forged passport and Russian identity card which he'd stolen from Frank Warren's safe at Benbow House. He had done this for the best of motives; unlike the Head of the European Department, he had been unable to distance himself from a Russian informant whose activities had placed her in great danger. Ashton had got her out of Russia because his philosophy was that you didn't walk away from someone in trouble.

In '93, with the active co-operation of the UK-based company, he had gone to Moscow as the sales representative of Stilson Manufacturing and had caught the backlash from the attempted coup by Vice President Aleksander Rutskoi to overthrow President Yeltsin which had been bloodily defeated. In retrospect there had been nothing surprising about that; every visit he'd ever made to the Russian capital had resulted in bloodshed. There was no earthly reason why this pattern should continue, but few people at Vauxhall Cross had been prepared to wager on it.

For the first time ever a ranking officer from the Embassy met Ashton at Sheremetyevo Airport and conveyed him to the villa on Maurice Thorez Embankment. Head of Station, Moscow, had leaned on the Commercial Counsellor to detail one of his attachés for the task in what he probably regarded as a clever move on his part. To his way of thinking, the ruse protected the identity of the SIS officers on the diplomatic staff and helped to create the impression that Ashton was a businessman. The ploy might well have been successful but for the fact that Ashton's face was definitely known to the Russian Intelligence Service.

He did not of course make this point to the Third Secretary, Commerce, who had drawn the short straw. Although the junior diplomat put a brave front on it, and was extremely pleasant, Ashton could tell that nursemaiding a visiting fireman from London wasn't his idea of a fun way to spend a Saturday evening. Ashton could think of any number of better things to do on a Saturday evening and Harriet had had a whole mouthful to say on the subject when she'd learned where he was going.

Head of Station, Moscow, was a new face whom Ashton hadn't met before. He had seen George Elphinstone's name in the Blue List and knew something of his career. A fluent Arabist, he had been the number two man in Cairo until 1992 when he had attended the two-year Russian language course run by the combined services at Beaconsfield. It seemed that they were unlikely to get better acquainted, at least not immediately. The Ambassador was hosting an important dinner party for Yeltsin's inner cabinet that evening and Elphinstone was required to be present.

'Is Pavel Trilisser one of the guests?' Ashton asked.

'No, he wasn't invited and the Russians didn't suggest he should be. I take it you know where to look for him?'

'Rowan Garfield briefed me yesterday evening. I was told Pavel Trilisser had recently acquired a house on the Moscow Heights near the Lemonosov University; he also has a dacha at Solnechnogorsk, forty miles out on the St Petersburg Highway.'

'I think you'll find there is a third abode,' Elphinstone told him.

'It's a sort of *pied-à-terre* next to his office in the Kremlin. We only heard about it the other day.'

'Right. What's the latest on Tim Rochelle? I believe you saw him yesterday?'

'Only for a few minutes while his wife, Barbara, was with him. He's making a good recovery but he's definitely not up to receiving visitors yet. Of course, I don't know what your plans are but I very much doubt if the hospital authorities will allow anyone other than Barbara to see him before Monday.'

'Point taken. What can you tell me about the layout of the Golden Nugget?'

Elphinstone wanted him to understand that of course he had never visited the establishment and he therefore had to rely on what he'd heard about the place from the younger set. By that, Head of Station meant the diplomatic wireless people, archivists, and lesser mortals like the support staffs of the Military, Naval and Air Force Attachés. According to these senior NCOs the roulette tables occupied something like eighty per cent of the available floor space, which meant the restaurant and bar were pretty cramped. The dance floor, they said, was decidedly intimate.

Nobody had ascertained exactly where Tim Rochelle had been when the gunmen had shot him down. Knowing something of the financial straitjacket which the Treasury had imposed on the SIS, there was not the slightest chance that Rochelle would have been reimbursed had he taken a turn at one of the roulette tables. The same applied to the restaurant, and he could scarcely have waited for Sokolov on the dance floor. That left the bar.

'Where are you staying?' Elphinstone asked.

'Roy Kelso arranged for Frazer McNeil to book me into the Intourist Hotel on Gorky Street.'

Frazer McNeil was a small firm up in Derbyshire which turned out printed circuit boards. It was one of several companies which were prepared to assist the SIS whenever it was necessary to provide a legend for a field agent.

'I hear the Intourist is very comfortable.'

'That's good.'

It also happened to be one of the cheapest, which had been the principal attraction for Kelso, ever mindful of the need to husband the limited resources of the Admin Wing. The hotel was, however, conveniently located for what Ashton had in mind.

'What's the state of your contingency fund?' he asked. 'In hard currency terms?'

'Don't tell me London didn't give you any cash for expenses?'

'I'm not broke but I may want to lay my hands on some extra for operational reasons.'

'I've got fifteen hundred pounds in the office safe.'

'No US dollars?'

'I'm afraid not.'

'Pity. The Russians seem to prefer greenbacks.'

'Is there anything else we can do for you?' Elphinstone asked, a touch acidly.

'No, I think we've covered just about everything.' Ashton glanced at his wristwatch. 'I've kept you long enough as it is.'

Head of Station didn't contradict him. The Third Secretary, Commerce, was also glad to see the back of Ashton and disappeared virtually in a cloud of blue smoke after he had dropped him off at the Intourist.

The whole business of checking into a hotel had improved out of all recognition since the last time he'd been in Moscow. Two years ago the desk clerk would have taken anything up to half an hour to allocate a room and you were better off carrying your own bags rather than waiting for a bellboy to do it. On this occasion Ashton was actually asked whether he preferred a smoking as opposed to a nonsmoking room and was swiftly conducted to what the management described as a de luxe single on the eighth floor overlooking Gorky Street.

Fortunately some things hadn't changed. The telephone directory showed that Katya Malinovskaya's security agency was still in business at number 124 Gorky Street. Few offices were open for business at 6.30 on a Saturday night but Katya had always been a grafter, which meant weekends and normal working hours didn't apply to her. Lifting the phone, Ashton rang the security agency, spoke to Katya Malinovskaya and made an appointment to see her forthwith.

* * *

Number 124 Gorky Street was a grey anonymous building at the top of an incline approximately four hundred yards from the Boulevard Ring which used to be Marx Prospekt when the Communists had been in power. The large square windows either side of the entrance had each acquired a pair of bottle-green curtains in the last two years and the tiles on the passageway fronting the half-dozen shops and offices on the ground floor had been relaid. In '93 the security agency had been sandwiched between a bookshop and an arts and crafts emporium; since then it had swallowed the adjoining premises, visual evidence that crime was a growth industry.

Katya Malinovskaya was an attractive brown-haired woman whose striking features could have earned her a reasonable living as a fashion model. But Katya had always been more than a pretty lady. As a direct result of the reforms initiated by Mikhail Gorbachev she had been chosen to represent the more acceptable face of the KGB's Second Chief Directorate. The fact that Katya was highly photogenic was not the only reason why she had been thrust into the limelight. Until a near-fatal knife wound in the back had put paid to her career, she had been one of the rising stars in the Criminal Investigation Division which had grown out of the former Twelfth Department.

Katya had used the skills she had acquired during her service when she had gone into much the same line of business on her own account. She specialised in protecting valuables, property and people; with the breakdown of law and order, her agency was in great demand by the nouveaux riches. She was thirty-one years old; success had given her a taste for the good things in life and her waistline had suffered accordingly. However, apart from being a few pounds heavier, Ashton didn't think Katya had changed all that much in the past two years.

'Remember me?' he said in fluent Russian when they shook hands.

'But of course. As I recall you were employed by Stilson Manufacturing when you put some business my way in '93. I believe you told me they made industrial tools, dies and all kinds of precision instruments.'

'You've got a marvellous memory.'

'Not really. I keep records of all my clients. I looked you up after you had phoned me from the Intourist Hotel.'

'You're giving your trade secrets away.'

'I don't think so. Who are you working for now, Mr Ashton?'

'Frazer McNeil, a small firm which is hoping to market some of their printed circuit boards over here.'

'What you know about engineering could be written on the back of a postage stamp. I know what happened the last time you were here in Moscow, so please don't waste my time with a cover story which doesn't stand up. I used to be with the KGB's Second Chief Directorate. Remember?'

'How about the FCO?'

'And what do they make?'

'Trouble,' Ashton told her.

'Well, that's my business too. Please take your coat off and make yourself comfortable.'

Ashton did so with alacrity. There was ten degrees of frost outside; in the office the climate was subtropical and humid with it.

'There was a major incident at the Golden Nugget the other night,' he began.

Ashton didn't get any further. The smile on Katya's lips rapidly disappeared and she raised her hand to silence him.

'I don't want to know about it.'

'One of our reps was badly wounded—'

'I'm sorry to hear that but it's nothing to do with me.'

'He had gone there to meet Sokolov . . .'

'Now we're talking politics and *Mafiozniki*. That's a lethal cocktail.'

'It damn nearly was for our man.'

'I don't know what you expected of me, Mr Ashton, but I'm not interested in your problem.'

'They were probably standing at the bar – Sokolov and our man . . .'

'You can save your breath.'

'Whatever pleases you.' Ashton reached inside his jacket and took out a leather wallet. In the end everything came down to money with Katya and he knew that to support her current life style, she couldn't afford to be too choosy what she did to finance it. He took out a thin wad of fifty-pound notes and very slowly began to lay them down one by one face up on her desk.

'This is by way of a retainer,' he said, and noted the speculative look in her eyes.

'How many times do I have to tell you that I'm not interested?' she asked in a voice that was singularly unconvincing.

'I want you to find that barman and ask him what Sokolov and the Englishman were doing just before they were shot. Get him to tell you what they said, what he heard and whether anyone approached the Englishman while he was waiting for Sokolov. OK?'

'I'm not sure.'

'There's five hundred pounds there; get the job done right and you can double it.'

'Make it another thousand.'

'Done.'

Kelso was going to have a fit; so was Elphinstone because Ashton didn't have the extra thousand she had demanded and good old Head of Station, Moscow, would have to find it.

'How do I get in touch with you?' Katya asked.

'You can leave a message with the desk clerk at the Intourist if I'm not in.' Ashton picked up his raglan and started towards the door, then turned about. 'Oh, and one thing more,' he said, 'don't go using your imagination. If you draw a blank, say so. I'm not in the market for fiction.'

Norden had been in a foul mood from the moment he'd dialled the office in the Seascape Center, activated the remote interrogator and heard Irwin's voice on the answer machine. He wished he'd destroyed all trace of John Novaks when he'd first thought of it. But no, he'd decided to put that on hold until he learned what Irwin had done about Fox. That meant the phone and fax numbers at the Ponte Vedra Beach office had to be kept on line, otherwise there was no way Irwin could get in touch with him. His temper wasn't improved when he found there wasn't a parking space to be had outside the Seascape Center and he was forced to leave the Honda on the wasteland behind the building. There was worse to come.

'Don't often see you on a Saturday, Mr Novaks,' the janitor said when he walked into the building. 'Guess you must have heard the news.'

'What news?'

'The Center was burgled last night; figured you were here to check your office like the other folks.'

Norden walked on to the moving staircase.

'Anybody call the police?' he asked over his shoulder.

'I did. They've been and gone.'

'Did you let them into my office?'

'Yeah, but I was with them the whole time. They didn't take a thing.'

Norden stepped off the escalator and picked up the continuation on the other side of the central pillar. Alighting at the second floor, he noticed that even the psychiatrist with the drink problem was in this morning.

The fax from Irwin was brutally short. It read: 'Termination of contract is not an option in this country. Our former associate now on his way to US via Paris to seek interview with you. Will be staying at the Fontainebleau Hilton, Miami Beach, under the name of Charles Barclay. Will arrive Monday, 6 February, at the latest.'

Fox knew the address of Novaks Promotions Incorporated in Ponte Vedra Beach and he had Irwin to thank for that. The god-damned son of a bitch had shovelled Fox out of the UK just as fast as he could. He'd fixed the guy up with a false passport and given him a wad of folding money, or had he? Norden read the fax a second time and knew he was right. Irwin had only booked him as far as Paris; from there on Fox had to make his own arrangements and he sure as hell couldn't use a credit card.

If Monday was the latest Fox would arrive in Miami what was the earliest? This afternoon? It wasn't impossible; he had already been on his way to Paris when Irwin had sent that damned fax. One thing was very clear: if he didn't confront Fox head on, the Brit would eventually show up at the Seascape Center, and even if he was long gone before then, Fox still had a story to tell which could interest the FBI.

First thing he had to do was check with the Fontainebleau and ascertain when they were expecting Charles Barclay. Then he would be able to call the airlines, starting with Air France, and pitch them a yarn about how his company was expecting a Mr Charles Barclay who was flying from Paris. Once he had something more definite to go on, he could start planning a suitable welcome for Fox.

He wondered what the officers from the Ponte Vedra Beach PD had made of the fax, assuming they'd read it? Not a lot, hopefully. They wouldn't know what to look for between the lines but they might just remember the fax if Fox ever showed up and started asking questions.

CHAPTER 18

Sunday had been bloody; nothing much to do and all day to do it in. To kill time, Ashton had rented a self-drive Lada through the concierge and had gone out to the Moscow Heights, otherwise known as the Lenin Hills. After quartering the area around the university he had eventually found Pavel Trilisser's house but had seen no sign of life apart from the militiamen on guard outside the gates. Some attitudes hadn't changed with *Perestroika*: the militiaman had treated him with the greatest suspicion when he'd asked if Trilisser was at home. The Russian had been surly and hostile, so much so that Ashton had sensed he was just looking for an excuse to butt stroke him about the head with his AK47 assault rifle.

Following that encounter, Ashton had crossed the Moscow River, picked up the Garden Ring road and headed out of town on the St Petersburg Highway. Beyond Sheremetyevo Airport on the outskirts of the city, the road cleaved through mile after mile of birch forests interspersed by the odd lake. There was little to distinguish one village from another and it was difficult to see what had drawn so many Muscovites to the Solnechnogorsk region. Spotting a sign in the grass verge, he swung off the highway on to a track that had meandered through the birch forest in the general direction of the lakes before doubling back on itself. Dozens of minor tracks radiated outwards from the main circuit, each one ending in a clearing large enough for three, sometimes four, dachas. In the majority of cases, the name of the owner was displayed on a sign planted ankle-high in the ground.

Ashton had spent the better part of two hours checking out every clearing but had been unable to locate the dacha allegedly owned by Pavel Trilisser. In the end he had come to the conclusion that the former KGB General was one of the self-effacing minority who preferred to remain incognito. It had also been apparent that most of the owners had decided to stay in the city rather than spend the weekend in the country.

No messages had been waiting for him when he returned to the hotel and, so far, today looked as if it were going to be equally frustrating. He couldn't phone the Embassy to ask how Rochelle was because all incoming calls to the villa on the civil network were assumed to be monitored by the ESK, the Russian internal security espionage service.

He couldn't get to Pavel Trilisser because it appeared that President Yeltsin's special adviser on foreign affairs had shut himself in the Kremlin. Breakfast over, he returned to his room on the eighth floor just in time to catch the phone before the caller hung up.

'At last,' Katya Malinovskaya said impatiently.

'I could say the same,' Ashton told her.

'Save your breath and listen to me instead. Do you have a car?'

'Yes, a Lada. I rented it yesterday.'

'Good. You will find one of my assistants waiting for you in the lobby. His name is Sasha; he's all in black – tight-fitting jeans, rollneck sweater, hip-length leather jacket, fur hat. Sasha looks very young and he is no taller than your shoulder and weighs about seventy kilos. He also has red hair.'

'I think I'll recognise him,' Ashton said drily.

'Forget the jokes. Just follow Sasha's directions and bring plenty of money. This is going to cost you.'

'Now, listen to me–' Ashton said, but she had already put the phone down.

There was no mistaking Sasha. However, although Ashton spotted him the moment he stepped out of the lift, he did not approach Katya's assistant until he was satisfied the Russian was alone.

'I think you're waiting for me,' he said.

'Mr Ashton, yes?' Sasha beamed at him and dipped his head. 'I take you to Katya. You have car?'

Sasha, he rapidly discovered, was keen to practise his limited English which Ashton found was something of an unnecessary handicap when it came to giving directions. They went down

Pushkin Street, made a left turn on the Boulevard Ring, then headed for the Mira Prospekt, passing the all too familiar Lubyanka on the way.

Katya Malinovskaya owned a villa five miles out of town on the road to Zagorsk. Even so, Ashton thought it was still too close for comfort to the notorious Babushkin District, the home territory of one of the most ruthless *Mafiozniki* gangs in Moscow. The villa had been built in a clearing hacked out of the forest. Comparatively modern, it was a typical example of the country retreats the Communist Party élite had enjoyed in the good old bad days before Boris Yeltsin had turned everything on its head. The wrought-iron railings which surrounded the property had warned the hoi polloi off when Leonid Brezhnev had been running the show in the 1970s; two decades later, they had no deterrent effect whatsoever as the wrecked front gates bore silent witness.

Two years ago, Katya Malinovskaya had been running about in a top-of-the-range Porsche 911 coupé; today the status symbol was a red Mercedes-Benz SL600. Except the past tense might have been more appropriate because the last word in luxury was no longer in the pristine condition it had been when she had taken delivery. The whole bodywork from headlights to rear bumper was a mass of jagged holes.

'Is very bad business,' Sasha announced judiciously. 'They came in the night – rat-a-tat, rat-a-tat-tat.'

'That's some calling card,' Ashton said.

'What does that mean?'

'Forget what I said, it's not important.' Ashton got out of the car to confront a very angry Katya Malinovskaya.

'Are you OK?' he asked.

'Look what they have done to my Mercedes . . .'

'Yeah. I know it's a hell of a thing but are you OK?'

'This is your doing,' Katya said furiously.

'My doing? How do you work that out?'

'I warned you politics and the *Mafiozniki* is a lethal combination. They broke into the house, dragged me out of bed and forced me to watch while they machine-gunned my car. "Next time we do this to you," they said. I had to stand there in my pyjamas and bare feet. It was a bitterly cold night and I damn nearly froze to death.'

'Why did they come after you? I mean, how did those people know you were looking for the bartender at the Golden Nugget?'

'The police told them – that's how.'

Katya had telephoned one of her former colleagues in the Criminal Investigation Division and had asked him to do her a favour by supplying the names and addresses of those members of staff who'd been present when the casino had been raided. He'd told Katya she would have to be a little more specific because he wasn't on the case and the investigating team wouldn't disclose a list of witnesses without due cause. With great reluctance she had then told him she was really only interested in tracing the barman.

'It was the only way I was going to obtain his name and address. Of course by the time I arrived at his flat in the Vladykino District late yesterday afternoon he'd already vanished.'

'And was that down to your friend?'

'No, I still trust him; it had to be one of the officers on the case.'

'Yeah? So how did this anonymous officer know it was you who'd asked for the information? Face it; either your former colleague is very indiscreet or else he betrayed you.'

'You're wrong.'

'If that's what you want to believe.'

'You're wrong, Mr Ashton, because he did more than give me a name and address. He also told me that the gunman who killed Sokolov shoved a hundred-dollar bill into his mouth after he was dead.'

'You mean Sokolov wasn't robbed like the other victims?'

'Who knows? The police didn't find his purse.'

Ashton asked the question which he could see Katya was dying for him to raise.

'So if his purse was stolen, why did the gunmen return a hundred-dollar bill?'

'Perhaps because it was counterfeit and was of no use to him.'

The Golden Nugget was strictly hard currency and everybody who worked there from the hat-check girl to the waiters would know what to look out for. Ashton couldn't believe that Sokolov had meant to offer a fake one-hundred-dollar bill to one of the staff. No way could the Russian have been that stupid.

'What are you going to do about my car, Mr Ashton?'

'What?'

'It's a total write-off.'

'Well, I hope you're insured because Her Majesty's Government isn't going to pay for a replacement.'

'You bastard.'

'But I know a man who will.'

'You want to tell me the name of this benefactor?'

'Pavel Trilisser.'

'Is that another English-type joke?'

'Get a message to Pavel Trilisser; tell him it's time he and I sat down and talked about funny money. Do that and believe me he'll find the cash for a new Merc.'

'You're mad. How do you think I can relay a message to President Yeltsin's special adviser?'

'Easy. Major General Gurov is still the Chief of Police, and he is the man who thrust you into the limelight when he wanted to change the image of the KGB. Gurov probably still has a soft spot for you. Besides, I hear he loathes Pavel Trilisser.'

Katya gave it some thought, then nodded to herself as if she had reached a decision.

'What about the thousand pounds that's already outstanding?' she asked.

'It's yours soon as I hear from Pavel Trilisser. OK?'

'It will have to be.'

'Good, I'm glad we see eye to eye.' Ashton smiled. 'Now can I offer anyone a lift into town?'

Katya Malinovskaya told him in no uncertain terms what he could do with his offer.

The folder containing the army documents of 54844434 Driver R. Fox, Royal Corps of Transport, was delivered to Brian Thomas by the chief clerk of the Admin Wing along with the first post of the day. Attached to the folder was an internal memo which Ashton had written on Friday evening before leaving the office. In it, he explained, due to reorganisation of the armed forces, and the absorption of the administrative and support services by the newly formed Adjutant General Corps and the Royal Army Logistical Corps, it had taken the army longer than usual to identify the correct Ronald Fox and locate his documents. Having read the entries on Fox's Regimental Conduct sheet, Ashton wondered if the effort had been worth it.

Thomas could see what he meant. Fox had been tried by District Court Martial at Catterick for striking a superior officer, a corporal in charge of the unit fire picket. He had been found guilty as charged and sentenced to eighty-four days' detention. Ashton hadn't thought it would be of much interest to Oldfield but felt the information should be passed on if only because he had more or less promised to keep him informed. Unfortunately, he had been unable to contact Oldfield on Friday.

'So good old muggins here has got to do it,' Thomas said aloud.

The truth was he had been on the point of ringing Oldfield anyway. The Yorkshireman had agreed to keep him up to date about the investigation and he hadn't heard from Oldfield since they had parted company six days ago. Reaching for the phone, he punched up the number for A Division in York and led the switchboard operator to believe that he was still a serving Detective Chief Superintendent. It was a harmless deception he occasionally resorted to whenever he needed to bypass the minions and go straight to the top. And as it had so often done in the past, it worked a treat. Although the information he had on Fox was pretty thin, Thomas knew how to inflate it out of all proportion without actually telling a pack of lies in the process.

'So how are things progressing on your front?' he asked with seeming indifference.

'I was about to ring you,' Oldfield told him and sounded embarrassed as hell.

Thomas left the excuse hanging in the air. He could have made any number of sarcastic responses but total silence was the most effective of them all. It made the other party feel particularly guilty and eager to atone. Half a minute was all it took before Oldfield was chattering away at machine-gun speed, telling him about Iqbal Khan and the Hosein brothers and what had been found at their house on Weavers Avenue in Bradford. He related the peaks and troughs of the case against the Hoseins, which had looked good one moment, lousy the next, especially when the star witness, Iqbal Khan, suddenly became as talkative as a Trappist monk.

'Jolly him along, he'll come round,' Thomas said airily, and provoked an explosion.

'You people in London aren't living on the same planet. It may have escaped your notice but there was a bloody great riot in Bradford on Friday night.'

'I saw it on TV.'

'Did the news reporter tell you that Iqbal Khan and his family were burned out of house and home? Are you aware that his business has gone up in smoke and that he and his wife have lost all their possessions? I tell you this, he knows what will happen to his wife and family if he doesn't keep his mouth firmly shut. And it's very evident to me that he will never testify in court.'

Despite this setback, Oldfield thought he'd cracked it after Nizamodeen Hosein had inadvertently disclosed a minor point of detail that only somebody who had been present when Sharon Cartwright had been shot could have known. Unfortunately the Pakistani had then clammed up and refused to answer any further questions.

'Nizamodeen pretended he'd misunderstood what I'd said and maintained we'd been talking at cross-purposes. I couldn't see the magistrate agreeing to a remand in custody and it had begun to look as if I would have to let him go.'

Forensic and the minute piece of cloth the SOCO team had found in the shallow trench under the print shop had saved the day for Oldfield. DNA tests had shown that the smears of blood and brain tissue matched the samples taken from the victim.

'That gave me enough to get both Hoseins remanded in custody.'

'So you reckon you've got the pair of them bang to rights?'

'I'd be a lot happier if we could find that damned Ford Transit,' Oldfield told him. 'Bloody thing seems to have vanished from the face of the earth. I'd also be a sight more confident if I could show a motive but the Hoseins won't help me there. They've suddenly become deaf and dumb on the advice of their lawyer, the slippery

Mr Jinnah. I don't understand why they are willing to protect the man you people call Raymond Messenger. The brothers deny all knowledge of him.'

'Well, they would. They probably had a hand in killing him.'

Oldfield snorted. 'Like hell they did. Three people were murdered at The Firs; forensic and the SOCO team went over every inch of the house and they didn't find any bloodstains belonging to a fourth person. I would hazard an informed guess that your Mr Messenger helped the intruders batter the life out of his erstwhile companions.'

'No, Messenger is buried somewhere in the Bradford area in a place you'd never think of looking.'

'Is that what your crystal ball tells you, Brian?'

'He told Sharon Cartwright that he had hidden a load of diamonds worth several million dollars.'

'Diamonds?' Oldfield repeated in a faraway voice.

'That's what I said.'

There was a protracted silence.

'Are you still there?' Thomas asked.

'It doesn't gell,' Oldfield said slowly.

'What doesn't?'

'The Hoseins are devout Muslims. Matter of fact they are staunch members of a fundamentalist sect.' Oldfield paused, then said, 'Wait a minute, how do you know what Messenger told Sharon Cartwright?'

Thomas was hard-pressed not to give voice to a litany of four-letter words. It had taken a long time for the penny to drop but Oldfield had finally latched on to the slip he'd made when talking of a possible motive for the crime.

'Have you been holding out on us, Brian?'

'No way. The information has only just come to light; Sharon Cartwright put it in a letter to her parents and they finally told us.'

'Really?'

'Yes, really.'

'I'll believe you, Brian, even if thousands wouldn't.'

'You don't know how good that makes me feel,' Thomas said and put the phone down.

He thought it was amazing how Jill Sheridan always landed on her feet. She was the one who actually encouraged Sharon Cartwright to breach every known rule of security, and had subsequently been guilty of withholding information, and now he had been forced to lie in order to protect her. Now he would have to see Kelso and explain why he wanted him to phone the Cartwrights and persuade them to compound the lie. He could imagine what the Admin king would have to say about that. What he needed was some good news to put Kelso in a reasonable frame of mind before getting down to brass tacks. Lifting the phone, he called Paul Isherwood. As sometimes happened, an officious-sounding personal assistant attempted unsuccessfully to head him off after she had ascertained who was calling.

Less than a minute into their conversation he knew why Isherwood had been reluctant to accept his call. His one-time colleague wanted it clearly understood that Special Branch was not to blame: the information had been passed to the Assistant Commissioner in charge of Criminal Investigation who had decided the Serious Crime Squad should look into it and they had been unable to find Fox.

'Are you saying he has disappeared?' Thomas asked incredulously.

'So it would seem. The fact is he hasn't been seen in any of his usual haunts.'

'I see. What about British Telecom? Have they produced a list of the people Irwin has been faxing since the beginning of January?'

'If they have, Serious Crime hasn't informed me, but there's no reason why they should. It's their case.'

'I think you should take an interest, Paul.'

'Don't you presume to tell me what I should do. The days when you could do that are long gone, Brian.'

'I'm sorry, I was completely out of order.'

Thomas wondered how he could retrieve the situation without actually grovelling. In his whole life, he had never crawled to anybody and he wasn't about to start now.

'Look, you've got everything going for you,' he said, in what he hoped was the right note. 'You will make at least Assistant Commissioner of Police before you retire, provided you play your cards right.'

'Are you threatening me?' Isherwood said in an ominous tone.

'No, I'm saying don't make the mistakes I did. You need more than sheer ability to get to the summit. You need friends in the right places and that means being nice to people you may not like . . .'

'You want me to be nice to you, is that it?'

'Oh, for Christ's sake, I'm trying to make you see that you are in danger of making some bad enemies.'

'Like who, for instance?'

'Well, there's our Director, Victor Hazelwood. I wouldn't like to get on the wrong side of him. But Ashton is the man I'd really be leery of. You could say he is Hazelwood's pit bull. And he already has a nasty feeling that he won't hear anything from Serious Crime unless you chase them up. Said as much to me after we left your office on Thursday afternoon.'

'I'm trembling in my boots.'

'Look, all I'm asking is for a few lousy fax numbers.'

'Starting from when?'

'I'd settle for Tuesday, 24 January.'

'All right, I'll talk to British Telecom.'

'Thanks.'

'Save it, this is the last favour I do for you,' Isherwood said, and hung up on him.

Barbara Rochelle was a tall, exceedingly attractive brunette; she was also the youngest wife of the youngest diplomat on the staff of the British Embassy. From what Ashton had heard, she regarded these two factors as something of a curse which he thought was understandable. For every admiring glance she drew from the men, she would receive an equal number of venomous ones from the women. Within minutes of meeting Barbara Rochelle for the first time, he learned that even before Tim had been shot, she had been counting the days to their mid-tour home leave.

Ashton had gone to the Rochelles' apartment in the diplomatic compound to find out how Tim was doing, and had been told by Barbara that he could see for himself if he would care to accompany her to the First General on International Avenue. Ten minutes into the hospital visit, he was beginning to wish he had declined the invitation. His bedside manner wasn't lacking but it was difficult to make small talk when they had so very little in common. He had left the Russian Desk before Tim Rochelle had joined it and he could count the number of times he had bumped into the younger man on the fingers of one hand. Consequently he had virtually no knowledge of Rochelle's interests outside the service. Rochelle had told him how much better he was feeling, which Ashton had found hard to believe considering he still looked at death's door – his eyes lacklustre, the skin waxy, his cheeks sunken. If Head of Station, Moscow, hadn't already set the wheels in motion, Ashton resolved to make it his business to see that Rochelle was casevaced to the UK by air ambulance as soon as he was fit enough to travel.

'Is there something you wanted to ask me, Peter?' Rochelle managed a faint smile. 'I imagine you didn't come here just to enquire after my health?'

'Well, I admit I am curious to know what passed between Sokolov and the barman.'

'Nothing. I'd just ordered another whisky and Sokolov said allow me to pay for it. As I recall he placed a hundred-dollar bill on the bar, then he gave me a friendly nudge in the ribs and said I should watch the barman and see how he reacted.'

No one knew how the barman had reacted but the gunman who'd shot Sokolov had allegedly stuffed the counterfeit bill in his mouth. Ashton thought that if passing a dud note had been the Russian's idea of a joke, then the last laugh had definitely been on him.

Fox opened his eyes, found himself looking up at the ceiling and wondered where he was. London? Paris? Miami? This time on Friday he had been in London buzzing around like a blue-arsed fly; Saturday night and most of Sunday morning he'd spent in Paris, shafting a tart he'd picked up on the Boulevard des Capucines opposite the Place de l'Opéra. Jet-black hair, high cheekbones, sharp features, sallow complexion and a great body; his mind dwelled pleasurably on the things she had done to him and vice versa. It had been a great way of killing time while he waited for the Air France flight to Miami. So this had to be Monday and he was staying at the Fontainebleau Hilton – ocean on one side, waterway across the road from the hotel on the other.

The phone brought him wide awake and made his heart skip a beat. Rolling over to his left side, Fox reached out and lifted the receiver. A nasal voice announced that this was his wake-up call and urged him to have a nice day. The clock radio was showing 8.30; the way he felt it could have been the middle of the night. A few moments after he'd hung up, the phone burred again. This time the caller was Novaks, though he didn't admit to it.

'Remember me, Mr Barclay?' he said. 'My name's Fox, Ronald Fox, realtor.'

'I remember you well,' Fox told him.

'Well, I haven't forgotten the kind of property you're after and I reckon I've found just the place. You got a scratchpad handy?'

'Hang on.' Fox sat up on the edge of the king-size bed and reached for the hotel memo pad and customised Biro on the table. 'OK, I'm ready.'

'The property I have in mind used to be a motel called the Everglades. It's about ten miles west of Dania on State 84.'

'What's the asking price?'

'How high are you prepared to go?' Novaks asked.

'I can raise two million dollars.'

'Are we talking cash, Mr Barclay, or a bank draft?'

'Half and half.'

Novaks wanted to know how much his silence was going to cost him. Now he knew it was a cool two million, half of it in cash. It had taken his breath away.

'I think the owner would be prepared to go along with that. Let me set up a meeting.'

'When for?'

'Eleven o'clock tomorrow morning.'

'Suits me.'

It would give him time to rent a car and look the place over. If it was too isolated, he would find an alternative rendezvous and wait for Novaks to get in touch with him again. There was not the slightest doubt in his mind that the private investigator would want to know why he had failed to show up at the Everglades Motel. He knew far too much for the Canadian to walk away from him.

'OK,' Novaks said, 'here's how you get to the motel.'

Fox took the directions down in a neat, rather childlike hand, then read them back to make sure he had got it right.

CHAPTER 19

Norden could understand why nobody had been able to make a success of the Everglades Motel. Had the original entrepreneur deliberately set out to establish an ongoing tax loss, he could not have done a better job. Situated just twelve miles west of Fort Lauderdale and Dania, it was not the ideal location to entice the passing tourists to stop over. Anybody travelling west to east from Naples on the Gulf of Mexico was more likely to press on to one of the beach resorts rather than spend the night at the motel. Similarly, it would be exceptional for anybody making for the Gulf Coast to stop before they had even reached the Everglades Parkway.

The motel now consisted of seven cabins in varying states of disrepair and an equally dilapidated front office and diner. At one time there had been a dozen guest units but in 1993, Hurricane Alice had demolished five, leaving only the foundations. Seen from above, the motel compound was a small island in a vast ocean of tall saw-grass that extended over 3500 square miles from Lake Okeechobee to the north. The way the complex itself was laid out resembled a figure 9 with the front office and diner located at the bottom of the stem and therefore nearest Route 84.

Although the front office did not enjoy a commanding view of the road, Norden could see a west-bound vehicle while it was still a hundred and fifty yards from the motel. To make sure the Honda could not be seen by the passing traffic, he had parked the car behind the farthermost cabin at the top of the loop.

If you had a boat and somebody to give you a helping hand, you could lose almost anything in the Everglades but he didn't have either. Rafael Valdes had a whole army of soldiers at his beck and call and could have detailed somebody to assist him, like the slim, blond-haired bodyguard he'd encountered that day at the Jeykll

Island Club. He could also have provided a Cessna or some other five-seater plane, which would have been a hell of an improvement on a boat when it came to dumping a load of garbage. But he had decided that the less Valdes knew about this particular problem, the better it would be for him. He had assured Valdes that his nephew Raúl Menendez would never bother him again, but in giving that guarantee, he had reckoned without Fox.

Although the connection was tenuous, Valdes would undoubtedly regard the Brit as a potential threat to his security and would react accordingly. What should have been a Jim Dandy situation was soured for Norden by the very real fear that the Cuban would see him as an even bigger threat. It was this distinct possibility that had convinced him he should go it alone.

He had gotten close to Fox in the days leading up to the assault on The Firs and knew just how his mind worked. The Brit liked to think he was smarter than anyone else, that the man had yet to be born who could steal a march on him, which only showed what an asshole he was. As sure as night followed day, Fox would check out the rendezvous long before they were due to meet at eleven o'clock tomorrow morning. It was the way he operated.

By the same token, Fox would rent a car because a cab driver would ask him too many awkward questions. Norden would give odds of ten to one on that but it would be no sweat if the guy didn't arrive alone. With the hardware he was carrying, the son of a bitch could roll up with a whole goddamned army and still lose out.

The hardware was manufactured by Arms Research Associates, Mannheim Road, Stone Park, Illinois. In military parlance, it was known as the KF-9 Assault Machine Pistol. The weapon had been designed to meet the needs of Special Forces engaged on operations likely to involve close-quarter combat. Chambered for the standard 9 mm parabellum, the machine pistol was extremely light, weighing a mere two and a quarter pounds when empty. With the stock folded, the KF-9 measured exactly eleven and a half inches. On top of that, the cyclic rate of fire was a staggering 800 rounds per minute. The box magazine to feed the hungry weapon came in four different sizes; for this particular job Norden had chosen the largest with a capacity of 108 rounds. From the extensive list of accessories, he had also chosen a noise suppressor.

Norden checked his wristwatch. Fox would want to see the proposed rendezvous in daylight and that meant his vigil would have to continue for a minimum of another five hours before the night drew in. A cigarette would help to while away the time but he was determined not to leave any signatures behind when he left. Before getting out of the car, he had donned a pair of cotton gloves and shoved his feet into a couple of plastic bags which he'd then tied above the ankles. They would find no fingerprints of his in the front office or on the ammunition he'd loaded into the box magazine, which could be matched with the set the Pentagon still had on record from the days when he'd served with Special Forces in 'Nam. And there would be no footprints on the dusty floor of the front office for the police to photograph. Furthermore, they could search the whole compound and make all the plaster casts they liked but they would get no distinctive heel, sole or toe impressions from him. But no matter how carefully you planned a job, an element of luck, good or bad, always entered the equation. Fox might conclude he'd seen all he wanted to of the Everglades from the road and drive on by. There were some things you just couldn't anticipate.

Since Fox had been told exactly what landmarks to look out for, it was reasonable to assume he would slow down as he neared the Everglades, but the Sunbird compact which swung off the highway was doing close on forty when it zipped past the front office, the rear end fishtailing. Although Norden had spotted the vehicle while it was still a hundred and fifty yards from the motel, he'd thought the car was going too fast for the driver to do anything but continue on towards the Everglades Parkway. The agonised screech from the tyres when the driver stamped on the brakes should have alerted Norden but he was slow to react and the vehicle swept on past the office before he could positively identify the man behind the wheel. Yet only a hot-shot driver like Fox could have made what amounted to a ninety-degree turn at speed. Hesitating no longer, Norden opened the door and lumbered out of the office.

The vehicle was stationary somewhere at the tip of the loop, Fox gunning the engine like an Indy driver waiting for the chequered flag. Norden wondered if the Brit suspected he was lying in wait and was trying to spook him out into the open. One thing was certain, any second now Fox would shift into drive, flatten the accelerator and take off.

Norden ran on, his gait made awkward by the plastic bags covering his shoes. Holding the machine pistol across his chest with the left hand, he yanked the cocking handle out of the safety notch so that the KF-9 was ready to fire, then transferred the weapon to his other hand, wrapping his thumb and three fingers around the pistol grip while the index finger took up the slack on the trigger. He heard the rear wheels of the Pontiac Sunbird bite into the dirt and instinctively jumped to the right as the car came round the loop and suddenly appeared in view.

Norden swivelled round to be sure of shooting Fox in the head as the Brit sped past, only to find himself about to blow away one very scared Afro-American. As he squeezed the trigger, he automatically raised the barrel as if to fire a *feu de joie*. The short burst of five to six rounds just cleared the car roof, the noise of the discharge reduced to a hollow cough by the suppressor. The Afro lost control of the Pontiac, which swerved off the dirt track, mounted the grass verge and clipped the pole holding the motel sign aloft. Somehow the driver managed to regain sufficient control of the vehicle to steer it back on to the track. Still in a blind panic, the black man then shot across the undivided highway, provoking an angry blast from the driver of an oncoming Volvo. Burning rubber, the Afro made a left turn and headed in the direction of Miami.

The black son of a bitch had looked straight at him and had seen the gun in his hand. So what was the Afro likely to do about that? Report the incident to the police? Oh yeah, he could just see that happening; the Blacks and the Miami PD were real soul brothers.

There was something else worth thinking about. What had brought the Black to the Everglades Motel? He sure as hell hadn't come to look the place over with a view to buying it. Had he stolen the Pontiac to order and was about to sell it on? Or maybe he was in the market for H and was there to cut a deal? If he'd spotted the Honda, he might have thought it was a setup. Norden smiled to himself; could be the stupid bastard had mistakenly believed he was an undercover law enforcement officer. No, the Afro wouldn't go to the police but all the same he would need to choose a different RV. Right now he couldn't think how he was going to explain the necessity for that to Fox without arousing his suspicion.

Norden had almost reached the Honda when he heard the car. The low note of the engine suggested the vehicle was travelling very slowly as though the driver were looking for something or somebody. He took cover behind the nearest cabin, his back pressed against the wall while he tried to deduce what the intruder's next move might be. As the vehicle went past his position, it suddenly dawned on him that the driver was circling the compound in an anticlockwise direction. Still facing outwards, he sidestepped around the cabin, then sneaked a quick look. It took him no more than a split second to identify Fox as the man behind the wheel of the Chevrolet compact.

The car was just over halfway round the loop and was heading back to the stem of the figure 9 when Norden broke cover. Fox had his head turned the other way, looking at the cabins immediately on his right and was unaware of the danger until Norden opened fire at a range of fifteen yards. The opening burst stitched the nearside door and shattered the window. He knew that at least one round had found the target because Fox drove the car straight into the end but one cabin and stalled the engine. The hood reared up like a startled horse, coolant spewing from the fractured radiator.

Norden didn't hesitate; wrenching the door open, he finished the Brit off with two quick bursts to the head and chest, then calmly walked back to the Honda. He dumped the machine pistol in the trunk, got into the car, stripped off the cotton gloves and removed the plastic bags from around his feet. Later he would dispose of them along with the KF-9 machine pistol but for the time being they were safe enough underneath the adjoining seat. He started the engine, shifted into gear and drove off. Luck was with him all the way; when he reached the highway there were no vehicles to be seen in either direction.

Although he wasn't unpleasant, Elphinstone did not make Ashton feel particularly welcome. The SIS Head of Station seemed to take it as a personal affront that Ashton should have called on Barbara Rochelle without first informing him. That he had then accompanied her to the First General only added to his sense of grievance.

'I'm surprised the hospital authorities allowed you to see Tim,' Elphinstone observed sourly. 'They told us that with the obvious exception of Barbara he wasn't up to receiving visitors.'

'So you told me on Saturday but this is Monday and he's feeling a lot better.'

'I'm glad to hear it.'

'Of course he would make an even faster recovery in the UK.'

'That's already in hand,' Elphinstone told him.

'Good.'

'So where is Barbara now?'

'Still at the hospital.'

'You left her there on her own? What were you thinking of? Moscow is a very dangerous place these days.'

Head of Station was lecturing him as if he'd never been to the city before, which Ashton found a little galling. Barbara Rochelle had driven to the hospital in her own car and had told him she intended to return to the diplomatic compound while it was still daylight.

'I need a thousand pounds from your contingency fund,' he suddenly announced, which stopped Elphinstone in his tracks.

'A thousand pounds?' Elphinstone repeated incredulously, as if he wasn't sure he'd heard Ashton correctly.

'Yes. You told me you had fifteen hundred in the safe.'

'For emergencies.'

'This is an emergency, George.'

Elphinstone looked taken aback. They had met for the first time on Saturday night and he wasn't used to being addressed by his first name on such a brief acquaintance. He was also senior to Ashton and was evidently very conscious of his dignity.

'Has this anything to do with Pavel Trilisser?' he asked, recovering his composure.

'Indirectly.'

'Could we be a little more precise?'

'The money is going to Katya Malinovskaya, provided she brings pressure to bear on Pavel Trilisser and he agrees to see me.'

'I don't think I've heard of the lady.'

It was Elphinstone's way of saying that he wanted to know her pedigree. As concisely as he knew how, Ashton told him about Katya Malinovskaya's career in the KGB and of the various jobs she had done since going freelance.

'Naturally, Katya wasn't aware that SIS was her paymaster. At least not then.'

'But she does now?'

'Katya's not unintelligent; she can put two and two together and come up with the right answer.'

'And presumably money is her sole motivation?'

'What's so unusual about that, George? I mean, how many patriots did you have on the books when you were helping to run the show in Cairo?'

'We didn't throw money at our sources; they knew they would receive a modest reward.'

Money did not necessarily procure good information but an agent needed to feel appreciated, especially if the intelligence he or she provided could only be obtained at great personal risk. That meant you made a fuss of the Joes and gave them a nice present every now and again. If Elphinstone's parsimonious attitude had been shared by the rest of the SIS cell, Ashton thought it was no wonder so little intelligence of real value had come out of Egypt.

'Do I get the thousand pounds?' he asked.

'You want it now?'

'That was the idea.'

'It's a large sum of money to be carrying around on your person. Suppose you are mugged?'

'Why should that worry you, George? If I've signed for the cash, I'm responsible for the loss.'

Elphinstone's lips met in a thin straight line. Without another word, he stood up and went over to the bricked-in safe in the far corner of the room in rear of the desk. Taking care to ensure Ashton couldn't observe the sequence of numbers, he rattled through the combination which released the lock, then yanked the handle down and opened the Chub safe. He removed two packages, closed the safe by spinning the combination dial and returned to his desk. From the centre drawer, he took out a pad of official receipts and filled one out.

'If you'd like to sign there,' he said, pointing to the appropriate space before passing the form to Ashton together with both packets. 'One thousand pounds in twenties.' A faint smile appeared on his mouth. 'Don't spend it all at once.'

'And there I was hoping to have a night out on the tiles with Katya.' Ashton saw the smile rapidly disappear from Elphinstone's lips. 'Just joking,' he added.

Ashton riffled through each packet in turn, then slipped them into the breast pocket of his jacket. The twenty-pound notes were brand-new; worse still, the serial numbers were in sequence. Somebody in the financial branch at Vauxhall Cross had made a crass mistake and he was surprised that Elphinstone had accepted the consignment. The notes would be treated with the gravest suspicion by any agent who received them in payment for services rendered. He doubted if Katya Malinovskaya would be enamoured with them either and she was better placed to shuffle the money around than most people.

'Is there anything else we can do for you?' Elphinstone asked in a tight voice which suggested there'd better not be.

'Yes – keep your fingers crossed that nothing goes wrong.'

'Is that another Ashton-type joke?'

'I hope so, George, I really do.'

Ashton picked up his raglan and left the office. After surrendering his visitor's pass to the Embassy security officer on the ground floor, he walked out into the cold air and made his way back to where he'd parked the car on the Maurice Thorez Embankment. The sun was low down on the horizon and the lights were already burning in the Great Kremlin Palace across the river.

An impatient Katya Malinovskaya was waiting for him in the lobby when he arrived back at the Intourist Hotel. Time was money, she told Ashton, repeating a maxim he'd heard before.

'And you're being well paid for it.'

'You have the money?'

'The question is, have you done your stuff?'

'Of course I have.'

'So where do I meet my friend?'

'I don't know, he will phone and tell you.'

Ashton frowned: that didn't sound like the former KGB General. Pavel Trilisser might have moved on to become President Yeltsin's special adviser on foreign affairs but he was still a secretive man. If he rang the Intourist, he would have to go through the hotel switchboard and there would be a certain amount of chitchat with the operator because he didn't know which room number to ask for. Also the operator would want to know who was calling before connecting him, which would lead to all sorts of complications, including the possibility that a third party might eavesdrop on their conversation.

'Are you telling me he is going to ring this hotel?'

'Your friend is not stupid; he will call you pay phone to pay phone. Now, if you wish to proceed, you had better fetch your money.'

'I don't have to,' Ashton said, and patted his chest. 'You want to see it now?'

'Not here,' Katya said hastily. 'Do you still have the Lada?'

'Yes, it's parked out front.'

'Then let's go.' Katya launched herself from the chair, toted the shoulder bag and striding out made it to the street well ahead of him. 'We will go to the Park Kultury Metro station,' she said when he caught up with her.

'You'll have to show me the way.'

Ashton steered her towards the car, opened the nearside door, then walked round the Lada and got in behind the wheel.

'Now you can give me the money,' Katya told him.

'What about giving me some directions first?'

'Go on down to the Boulevard Ring and turn right.'

Ashton started up, shifted into gear and moved off; then, reaching inside his jacket he gave her one of the packages. Out of the corner of his eye, he watched Katya riffle through the banknotes, her displeasure made obvious by the way the lips pouted. Opening the shoulder bag, she took out a pencil-thin flashlight and proceeded to examine one of the twenty-pound notes plucked at random from the centre of the wad. She looked for the silver thread to the right of Britannia, which on the reverse side appeared as a black line slicing through Michael Faraday's likeness.

'These notes are brand-new,' she complained.

'You have a problem with that?'

'I prefer used ones, they cause less comment.'

'Well, I'm sorry the banknotes don't meet with your approval but they're all I have on me. You'll just have to crumple and scuff them a bit.'

'There's only five hundred pounds here.'

'That's right; you get the rest when I meet Pavel Trilisser.'

The verbal explosion which followed was remarkable for Katya Malinovskaya's vocabulary of obscenities. In addition to some choice expressions in her own language, the diatribe also included every known Anglo-Saxon epithet. It was the second time she had verbally abused him that day and the repeat performance was no less impressive.

'Turn right at the next set of traffic lights,' she said, finally calming down.

Ashton checked the rear-view mirror, drifted across into the nearside lane and filtered right. Shortly thereafter they passed a vaguely familiar monument set in the garden fronting a neoclassical mansion and he suddenly realised they were in the old section of Kalinin Avenue. The new part began beyond a curious building which resembled a Spanish castle, the avenue spreading out until it was almost a hundred yards wide. On the left-hand side of the road, four huge ultra-modern blocks, shaped like open books, housed various government departments. At the bottom of the avenue, Katya instructed him to turn left on to the Gardens Ring.

The evening rush hour was not much heavier than Ashton re-membered from the last time he had been in Moscow. It was however dense enough to make life difficult for one driver.

'We've got company,' he said.

'What?'

'A Volkswagen Passat; it's been on our tail since we left the hotel.'

'That will be Sasha,' Katya informed him.

They went on past the Foreign Ministry, which belonged to the wedding cake school of architecture. Unable to leave the Lada outside the Metro station, Ashton had to turn off the Garden Ring and park up in a sidestreet which led to the onion-domed church of St Nicholas. As he locked the car, Sasha drove past studiously ignoring them.

'He's still on a learning curve,' Katya said with a faint hint of a smile.

There was a bank of six pay phones outside the entrance to the Metro station, two of which were immediately available. Neither apparently suited Katya, who was determined to have the second from the left which was being used by a short balding Russian with a beer belly. She waited impatiently for him to finish, consulting her wristwatch every few seconds. Finally, she unzipped her bag, took out a police badge and ducking under the plastic hood above the pay phone showed it to the fat man. Ashton heard him tell Katya to shove it up her anus, a bad mistake which he compounded by knocking the badge out of her hand before poking a stubby finger into her chest.

It was a very uneven contest; the man was practically blind drunk whereas Katya was stone-cold sober. Grabbing his index finger with her left hand, she twisted it back towards the knuckle, snapping the bone like a matchstick as he danced away from the phone. At the same time, she drew a Makarov semiautomatic from the bag and began to pistol whip him about the face.

'Stop it!' Ashton yelled. 'Enough is enough! Let the poor bastard go.'

'You stay out of this,' she yelled back, and threatened him with the Makarov.

Every citizen in the vicinity looked the other way and walked around them. Nobody attempted to help the man when Katya finally relented and he stumbled away, bleeding copiously from the mouth and nose. In Moscow, with its endemic crime rate, it was prudent not to get involved.

'What's happened to you in the last two years?' Ashton demanded. 'You're not the woman I remember. You went at that man like a homicidal maniac.'

'I don't like drunks and I don't take chances. I know his sort, he could have been carrying a knife.'

The pay phone, which Katya had fought for, suddenly came to life and she ducked under the hood to answer the muted burr. The subsequent exchange was brief and largely one-sided, Katya saying 'yes' twice and 'no' once, before she handed the phone over to Ashton.

'Your friend wants to have a word with you,' she said.

Ashton's conversation with Pavel Trilisser was equally one-sided and there was nothing he could do about it, which was even more annoying. Yeltsin's special adviser made it very clear that he either accepted what was on offer or returned to the UK empty-handed.

'Now, give me the rest of the money,' Katya demanded after he'd put the phone down.

'Pavel Trilisser isn't going to meet me,' Ashton told her. 'He's sending a Nikolai Grigoryevich instead. I am to meet him at seven o'clock in the Ritz Grill on Arbat Street.'

'What's wrong with that?'

Ashton ignored her question. 'How did Trilisser know when to ring that pay phone?' he asked.

'Sasha has a mobile phone. He called your friend when we left the Intourist Hotel. Now give me the other five hundred.'

'I'm withholding half,' Ashton said.

'You're doing what?'

'You failed to arrange a face-to-face meeting.'

'Your mother is a whore,' Katya snarled.

'Don't worry, you'll get the rest before this night is over. All you have to do is watch my back while I'm dining with Nikolai Grigoryevich.'

'I see.' Her eyes narrowed thoughtfully. 'What do you expect me to do if there's trouble?'

'Inform the British Consul,' Ashton told her grimly.

CHAPTER 20

Two years ago there had been very few places to eat out in Moscow apart from the restaurants in hotels. The arrival of McDonald's and the Big Mac had changed all that. Almost overnight, scores of grills, diners, cafeterias and restaurants had mushroomed throughout the central district of the city, most of them providing indifferent food with equally indifferent service. The Ritz Grill on Arbat Street was a prime example of a greasy spoon café with a highfalutin name designed to entice the unsuspecting diner to step inside. The Arbat was a mile long and the only pedestrian precinct in Moscow. The Ritz Grill had stayed in business because it was situated at the halfway point and most people having come that far on foot, couldn't be bothered to turn back and start looking for some other place to eat.

The restaurant was small, crowded and smoke-filled; it was the sort of establishment Ashton would have walked away from, especially when the surly headwaiter informed him that all the tables were taken and he needn't bother to wait. A ten-pound note and a judicious bit of name-dropping changed the headwaiter's attitude and secured a table for two.

From the description Pavel Trilisser had given him, Ashton knew that the man he was waiting for had fair hair, looked much younger than thirty-one, weighed no more than a hundred and forty pounds and was under five feet seven. The former KGB General had also said some people would think Nikolai Grigoryevich was good-looking, although in Russian the word he'd used could also mean pretty. The inflection Trilisser had given it and the way he'd emphasised 'some people' suggested he was hinting that Nikolai Grigoryevich was a homosexual. The thirty-one-year-old Russian was allegedly a career diplomat and that being the case, Ashton didn't see how he could have been retained in the Foreign Service if his superiors suspected he was gay.

A waiter placed a small glass in front of Ashton, filled it from a bottle of Stolichnaya vodka, then handed him a stained menu card before walking off. The Ritz Grill occupied the whole of the ground floor of what had once been a town house at the turn of the century. The first room across the narrow entrance hall had been the front parlour, then a bookshop and was now the bar where Katya Malinovskaya had taken post. Ashton presumed that the back room on that side of the house was the kitchen. On his side of the former house, the dividing wall between the front and back had been demolished to accommodate twenty tables and a stage at the far end of the room.

A notice board outside the restaurant promised live entertainment in the Liverpool mould at 7 and 11 p.m. Fifteen minutes later than scheduled, the first group appeared – four Beatles lookalikes in drainpipe trousers, winkle-picker shoes, sweaters over open-neck shirts and mophead hairstyles. The group had energy and enthusiasm in abundance but not much else; they were more than halfway through their opening number before Ashton realised they were singing 'Eleanor Rigby', Nikolai Grigoryevich was shown to the table by the headwaiter as they started to give a unique rendering of 'Ticket to Ride'.

For a moment Ashton thought the Russian was going to kiss him but in the end he dipped his head and shook hands. The same waiter who'd served Ashton, placed a glass in front of him and filled it to the brim. Etiquette demanded they downed the vodka in one go; the effect was like hitting the fuse of a delayed-action bomb with a hammer.

'Is good, yes?' Nikolai Grigoryevich asked.

'Explosive.'

The waiter reappeared to ask if they had made up their minds what they wanted to eat. Nikolai Grigoryevich went through the menu recommending in halting English that they would start with red cabbage and sour cream soup, then pike for the first main course followed by shashlik, which was the Russian equivalent of a kebab. Ashton found himself supplying the right words for Nikolai

Grigoryevich but since it obviously helped the Russian to relax, he was prepared to continue in the same vein for a bit. But sooner rather than later they would have to use a common language otherwise they would get nowhere.

'Shall we converse in Russian?' he asked after the waiter had left them.

Nikolai Grigoryevich looked alarmed. 'Do you speak Persian?'

'I'm afraid not – my German is pretty good though.'

'Arabic is my other language.'

Jill Sheridan should be here, Ashton thought wryly. She could rattle through an interview in either Arabic or Persian.

'I guess Russian is the favourite.' Ashton leaned forward, elbows on the table. 'But don't worry about it. Who the hell is going to hear what we're saying above this racket?'

Nikolai Grigoryevich visibly relaxed. As if to oblige them, the Beatles lookalikes swung into their version of 'Help!' For those nearest the stage the decibel level was close to being physically painful.

'You're right, Mr Ashton,' he said with a broad smile. 'I doubt even you can hear me.'

'Well, let's see how it goes. I understand you've just returned from Tehran with some important news?'

Nikolai Grigoryevich scowled. 'My superiors in Moscow don't appear to think so.'

'President Yeltsin's special adviser obviously doesn't share their opinion, otherwise you and I wouldn't be here now looking at one another across a narrow table.'

'Pavel Trilisser seemed very sceptical to me.'

'That's the way he is,' Ashton said tersely. 'But I'm different, so let's get on with it.'

'Have you heard of an Iranian banker called Shahpour Bazargan?'

'I can't say I have.'

'That's awkward. I'm not sure where to begin.'

'You can start by telling me who he is and how you came to meet him.'

After a moment's reflection Nikolai Grigoryevich told him that the Iranian banker was fifty-eight years old, had never married and was dying of leukaemia. The only son of a wealthy landowner, he had been educated at the American School in Beirut before going on to Harvard where he had gained a Masters in Business Studies. Bazargan had gone into banking because he'd wanted to play a leading role in the modernisation of Iran.

'This was in 1963,' Nikolai Grigoryevich continued. 'At that time, he thought the Shah could do no wrong. Ten years later he was one of Reza Shah's bitterest opponents.'

Opposition to the Shah and his policies had never been far from the surface of Iranian life and this had become more and more evident as preparations to celebrate the 2500th anniversary of the monarchy in 1971 went ahead. The very unequal distribution of the oil revenue had added to the increasing unrest. But it had been the ruthless activities of SAVAK, the government security agency, in suppressing opposition to the regime that had finally tipped the scales for Shahpour Bazargan.

'He became a leading light in the Iran Liberation Movement and played no small part in toppling the Shah. Ayatollah Khomeini had a very high opinion of Bazargan and would have made him his Minister of Finance but the Islamic Revolutionary Council wouldn't hear of it. Despite what he had done to assist the Liberation Movement, they regarded him as tainted. However, that hasn't stopped Doctor Hedi Namazi, the current Minister of Economic Affairs and Finance, from consulting him.'

Nikolai Grigoryevich had met the banker at the opening of a new steel plant at Esfahan which had been built with technical and material assistance provided by Moscow. As the Third Secretary, Commerce, he had been low down in the pecking order and had been largely ignored by the Iranian officials. Nikolai Grigoryevich didn't know why Shahpour Bazargan had been invited to attend the official opening but he too had received much the same treatment from his own people.

'We both felt out of things; it was this offhand treatment which threw us together.'

'Who made the first move?' Ashton asked.

'Shahpour Bazargan.'

'And when did this ceremony at Esfahan take place?'

'Wednesday, 25 May last year. Six weeks later almost to the day, he invited me to dine with him at his house. Naturally, I informed my superiors and sought their advice before accepting.'

Thereafter, the two men had met at least once a month for dinner. For someone who was supposedly an outsider, Shahpour Bazargan was extremely well informed about the economic difficulties facing Iran. Within a matter of weeks, the Russian came to regard him as a valuable source of information.

'Do you think Bazargan is getting his information from the Minister of Economic Affairs and Finance?'

'We believe so. That's why our Ambassador in Tehran was so alarmed when I told him about this massive attack on the US dollar which the Islamic Revolutionary Council has set in motion.' Nikolai Grigoryevich gave a nervous laugh. 'We'd all feel pretty sick if the almighty greenback went down the sink. After all, it's still the leading currency in the global marketplace.'

'What does this attack involve?'

'Counterfeiting on a truly massive scale. Some financial experts have calculated that up to ten billion dollars' worth of fake bills are already in circulation outside the United States. The Iranians plan to put fifty times that amount into circulation within the first twelve months.'

'There must be a lot of crooked printers out there in the world,' Ashton said.

'You don't need their skills these days when you've got colour copiers with such innovative features as two-sided printing.'

It seemed the Canon CLC 800 was not the only copier on the market which was capable of producing virtually undetectable fake bills. Aware of the threat to their currency, the United States Treasury Department had made a number of changes to the present security features.

'The new hundred-dollar bill will come into circulation in 1996. However, Bazargan claims the Revolutionary Council has already anticipated this. Before the initial print run of the hundred-dollar bills, they will be able to reproduce the new security features, courtesy of the Cubans.'

'What Cubans?'

'Bazargan couldn't say.'

Or wouldn't, Ashton thought. Then again, maybe Doctor Hedi Namazi had developed a bad case of cold feet and had been too scared to pass the relevant information on to the banker. He noticed that Nikolai Grigoryevich had also gone a little green around the gills and with good reason. The four men moving purposefully towards their table were not about to serve them with red cabbage and sour cream.

The plain-clothes man in charge of the squad produced his shield, then all four officers began shouting at the top of their voices. Somebody pulled the plug on the Beatles lookalikes and the live entertainment went *sotto voce*. Two officers yanked Ashton to his feet, cuffed his wrists behind his back and hustled him out of the restaurant into the cold night air and a waiting police van. What was certainly a full minute passed before Nikolai Grigoryevich joined him in the custody wagon. If Ashton's treatment by the police had been less than gentle, it was nothing compared with the way they'd manhandled their fellow countryman who was bleeding profusely from the nose, mouth and a nasty-looking jagged cut on the right cheekbone.

'It's going to be OK,' Ashton told him.

'What are you? A prophet?'

Ashton smiled. The ace up his sleeve was Katya Malinovskaya; she was still owed two hundred and fifty pounds and he was counting on her to report the incident to the British Consul.

'I'm an incurable optimist,' he said.

His confidence was misplaced. The words were hardly out of his mouth when Katya was heaved into the vehicle literally kicking and screaming. Tired of her insults and bad language, a woman police officer who was a good ten pounds heavier than her prisoner drove a fist into Katya's stomach and winded her. Then before Katya had time to recover, the woman shackled her ankles. One of the male officers did the same to Nikolai Grigoryevich but Ashton was privileged, nobody bothered to hobble him.

What the State Police found at the Everglades Motel was completely at variance with the information the Miami PD had received from an anonymous 911 call. Instead of some weirdo running around with plastic bags over his shoes and threatening people with a sub-machine-gun, they had found a dead man behind the wheel of a bullet-riddled Chevrolet compact. The discovery had been made at 16.25 hours; by the time the Medical Examiner and the detectives from Homicide arrived on the scene just over an hour of daylight had remained.

As soon as the ME had pronounced the victim officially dead, the body was photographed from every angle and all personal effects were removed and bagged up. The corpse was then taken to the Samaritan Hospital in Dania to await a post-mortem. A total of seventeen ejected 9 mm cases were found inside the Chevrolet and a further six approximately ten yards from the vehicle. More empty cases were found in the vicinity of the front office and diner. Although no expert from ballistics was present the homicide detectives were convinced that all munitions had been ejected from the same weapon because they could see that the firing pin had hit every percussion cap in exactly the same place. Finally, they noted that the metal pole holding the motel sign aloft had recently been clipped by a vehicle which the paint streaks indicated was dark blue in colour.

Tentative identification of the deceased was made on the strength of a bloodstained UK passport and the British Consul in Miami was informed accordingly.

Rowan Garfield could not recall when, if ever, he and Eileen had taken a bottle of champagne to bed with them. But it had been their twentieth wedding anniversary and while that did not have quite the same significance as a silver wedding, it was still something to celebrate. A lot of marriages they knew of hadn't lasted as long; within their limited circle of friends and acquaintances, he and Eileen could name four couples where the husband or wife had divorced their former partner. To celebrate the occasion, Garfield had taken Eileen to see the *Phantom of the Opera* at Her Majesty's, followed by a late supper at the Café Royal before going on to the Twenty-One Club. The champagne which he had ordered from room service had been waiting for them when they returned to the Dorchester at 2.30 in the morning.

With hindsight, the champagne had been a mistake; they both had had enough to drink and were already pretty high. Eileen had been in a very amorous mood and the sight of his wife emerging from the bathroom in high-heeled sandals and an oyster-coloured satin slip had been particularly tantalising. In all their years together, she had never ceased to surprise him; demure and sexually modest for most of the time she could suddenly shed all her inhibitions and take the lead. No question of going to bed, Eileen had made love to him in the armchair. Unfortunately, too much alcohol meant he had performed less than satisfactorily, much to her disappointment. Worse still, he had then fallen asleep.

So here he was, still in the armchair at a quarter to five in the morning, half undressed, a crick in the neck and a mouth like the bottom of a birdcage. The lights were still on and Eileen was in bed, breathing deeply. Garfield thought it was time he joined her and slowly got to his feet. When the room stopped revolving, he removed the rest of his clothes, tiptoed round to his side of the bed and removed the pair of pyjamas from under the pillow. He put on the jacket easily enough but experienced some difficulty with the bottoms while balancing on one leg like a stork. Taking care not to disturb Eileen, he then drew the bedclothes aside and slipped between the sheets. He was about to congratulate himself when the telephone on the bedside table rang.

'Oh my God,' Eileen moaned, 'what time is it?'

'It's the phone.' Garfield turned over on to his right side, lifted the receiver off the cradle and took it into bed with him, then grunted into the mouthpiece.

A vaguely familiar voice said, 'We've got a problem with one of your patients, Mr Garfield.'

Garfield pinched both eyes between thumb and index finger. Patient? What the hell was this lunatic talking about?

'I'm sorry,' he mumbled, 'I'm still half asleep. What's all this about a patient?'

'The operation hasn't gone as well as we hoped it would, the patient has had a relapse. I know I'm only a houseman, Mr Garfield, but I really do think you should come in and have a look at him.'

Suddenly everything fell into place. For houseman, read duty officer. In accordance with standard operating procedure he had left word that he would be staying the night at the Dorchester. In contacting him through the hotel switchboard operator, the duty officer had naturally used veiled speech.

'I'll be with you in fifteen,' he said, and put the phone down.

'What was all that about?' Eileen asked in a sleepy voice.

'Bloody Ashton,' Garfield told her. 'He's in trouble again and I've got to go into the office.'

He rolled out of bed, stumbled into the bathroom and stood under the shower. The cold water took his breath away; it also sobered him up in double-quick time and the little men inside his skull stopped pounding his head with their hammers.

Fifteen minutes was a wildly optimistic guess but it only took him a fraction over six to get himself dressed and down to the lobby. A minute or so later, thanks to the doorman, he was in a cab heading down Park Lane to Hyde Park Corner. There was very little traffic on the road but, as luck would have it, nearly all the lights were against them and he was practically foaming at the mouth with pent-up frustration by the time they were motoring across Westminster Bridge.

The duty officer knew what happened to a harbinger of bad news and was anxious to offer the Assistant Director of the European Department a few crumbs of comfort. He therefore made the most of the fact that, as yet, he had not informed the DG or his deputy.

'I'll brief them,' Garfield told him, and took the signal from Moscow upstairs to his office.

The date/time group indicated that the signal had been dispatched on Tuesday, 7 February, at 04.53 hours Greenwich Mean Time. Garfield reminded himself that Moscow was three hours ahead of GMT which put the sequence of events into perspective. Still reading the cable, he lifted the receiver off the cradle and tapped out the DG's home number. When Hazelwood answered the phone, he apologised for disturbing him and tried to sound as if he meant it.

'The fact is, Victor, I need to speak to you on the other means. I'm in the office.'

'It's like that, is it?'

Garfield was about to confirm his assumption but Hazelwood had already hung up.

'Typical,' he said aloud, 'bloody typical.'

The other means was the secure speech facility known as Mozart, an improved version of the crypto-protected Brahms. Not for the first time Garfield wondered at the psychology of the person who had dreamed up these codenames. The muted trill from the phone ended speculation and he moved to answer it.

'All right,' Hazelwood said, 'tell me the worst.'

'The Foreign Office has received a signal from the Consul General in Moscow which they passed on to us. It seems Ashton was arrested last night along with a Russian official called Nikolai Grigoryevich Yakushkin.'

'What else?'

'The Russians claim they have evidence that Peter was engaged in espionage.'

'They would say that,' Hazelwood growled.

'Well, the fact is Peter had two hundred and fifty pounds on him in brand-new twenties sequentially numbered.'

'Sounds very much like a plant to me,' Hazelwood said.

'Maybe. The interesting thing is the Russians are being quite conciliatory about the affair. Of course our Consul General was contacted by a comparatively junior official in their Foreign Ministry. The man did stress that nobody wants to do anything which might damage the cordial relations which exist between our two countries.'

'Very interesting. What's your interpretation, Rowan?'

Garfield frowned. The last thing he wanted to do was express an opinion which could make him look pretty stupid if subsequent events showed he had completely misread the situation.

'I think it's possible they don't intend to bring charges against Peter,' he said reluctantly.

'And assuming you are right, what then?'

'I think they might deport him,' Garfield said with even greater reluctance to commit himself.

CHAPTER 21

Thomas pushed his shirtcuff back, made a great show of consulting his wristwatch and then half grunted, half sighed to show his displeasure. Neither gesture had the slightest effect on Isherwood's PA. She had phoned shortly after nine o'clock to ask if he could come to see the Commander whenever it was convenient and he had told her there was no time like the present. He had assumed Isherwood was available and she had said nothing to disabuse him of the notion. It was therefore somewhat annoying to be told on arrival at Scotland Yard that Isherwood was conferring with the Assistant Commissioners in charge of Criminal Investigation and the Special Branch.

'They will only keep the Commander a few minutes,' she had informed him with saccharine sweetness. He had no idea what constituted a few minutes in her little world but more than three-quarters of an hour had gone by since that glib assurance. Thomas promised himself that he would give it another five minutes and then leave. It was the knowledge that he would do no such thing which irritated him most of all. He was about to ask the PA if he might have a look at her newspaper when Isherwood put his head round the door to say he was back. He also wanted to know if there were any messages for him.

'No, but you've got a visitor,' Thomas said before the PA could answer.

Isherwood greeted him with a curt nod, looked enquiringly at his PA and seemed disappointed when she confirmed there weren't any.

'Well, I suppose you'd better come with me, Brian,' he said, and opened the communicating door.

Thomas followed him into the adjoining office and closed the

253

door on the PA. He and Paul Isherwood went back a long way and it saddened him that a rift had occurred in their relationship. He hoped it wouldn't become permanent.

'I think this is what you're after,' Isherwood said, and plucked a slip of paper from the pending tray on his desk. 'It's a list of the numbers Irwin has faxed since 4 January.

'Thanks, Paul.'

'Well, as I said before, this is the last favour I'll do for you.'

'That's understood,' Thomas said meekly.

'There is only one overseas fax number on the list and that's for Novaks Promotions Incorporated in Ponte Vedra Beach.'

'Where's that?'

'Florida, but I wouldn't read too much into that. It could be Irwin was lying when he told Fox that his Canadian friend was no longer in this country.'

'Why would he do that? To protect the Canadian?' Thomas shook his head. 'Sounds a little too noble for me. No, the way we see it, somebody must have traced Menendez to Santiago . . .'

'Who's we?'

'Ashton and me.'

'I'm surprised he's not here. Got better things to do, has he?'

'No, he's . . .' Thomas was about to tell him that Ashton was in Russia but managed to bite it back. Officially he didn't know what had happened in Moscow but the top floor had been in one hell of a flap when he'd arrived at the office and if only half the rumours he'd heard were true, Ashton was in deep trouble. 'No, the fact is Ashton is indisposed,' he said with unconscious irony. 'Anyway, it seems likely that Irwin only entered the picture when it became evident that our Embassy was sending the Cuban-American to the UK. Be interesting to hear what kind of business Irwin had been doing with Novaks Promotions Incorporated. Doesn't sound like a detective agency to me.'

'They don't have to be in the same line of business. Novaks Promotions could be selling something he wants.'

'Is that what Irwin told the Serious Crime Squad?' Thomas asked slyly.

'I wouldn't know.'

'So Irwin is being questioned then?'

'Let me tell you something, Brian,' Isherwood said with barely suppressed anger. 'I've just had a roasting from two Assistant Commissioners, my own chief and the Sherlock Holmes in charge of Criminal Investigation. It seems someone pretty high up on British Telecom has got wind of the fact that I obtained details of Irwin's fax account without proper authorisation and complained to the Home Office. My own boss is hopping mad because he didn't know what I was up to until he heard about it from the Commissioner of Police himself. And Sherlock Holmes' nose is out of joint because I never declared my interest when I handed over the tape of that conversation between Fox and Irwin.'

'Are they saying that somehow you've hindered the Serious Crime Squad?'

'No, they were annoyed because we could have got our wires crossed.'

'And Irwin is proving a tough nut to crack.'

'You didn't hear that from me,' Isherwood said quickly.

'Of course I didn't but you did tell me about his career in the Met and it wasn't difficult to second-guess his reaction to the tape.'

As a detective sergeant, Irwin would have questioned his share of villains and would be familiar with all the tricks of the trade. He had also sat on the other side of the table when officers from Bribery and Corruption had reason to suspect he had been taking backhanders. They hadn't been able to break Irwin then because he had known the right to silence was his best defence; and there was a good chance they would be equally unsuccessful this time around. The police couldn't use the tape recording of his conversation with Fox because it had been obtained illegally. Any lawyer worth his salt would get it thrown out of court on the grounds of inadmissible evidence.

'Is Willie acting for him?' Thomas asked.

'Who?'

'Fox mentioned the name when he rang his girlfriend, Edwina, the night he was released from Paddington Green. We thought this Willie might be his brief.'

'Now I'm with you,' Isherwood said, and snapped his fingers.

'His name is Willis; he's a legal executive and I'm told he has an office of sorts in Poplar. Apparently Willis is as straight as a corkscrew. You need an alibi, he will find somebody to give you one. That's how he earned his nickname of Will-lie Willis.'

Obviously Hicks had misheard the name when he'd eavesdropped on Fox and Edwina. Although the information hardly represented a breakthrough, Thomas felt that at least it answered one of the questions that had been bugging Ashton. There was however one other point that needed to be settled before he left.

'About this firm Novaks Promotions Incorporated—'

'That's all I have for you,' Isherwood said, bluntly dismissing him before he could finish.

'Yes, of course. You've been very helpful . . .'

'It is the last time, Brian.'

'Sure, that's understood.'

There was something very final about the way Isherwood shook hands with him. In a disconsolate mood, Thomas walked to the bank of lifts and pressed the call button. How long had they known one another? Fifteen – sixteen years? And now it was finished. He just hoped the people on the top floor at Vauxhall Cross would do something positive about Novaks Promotions Incorporated.

The doorbell was erratic; occasionally it rang out loud and clear but mostly the wretched thing emitted a low buzzing noise as if the battery had run down. Harriet had lost count of the number of times she had asked Peter to fit a new one but somehow he always had a good excuse for putting it off until tomorrow. She was beginning to realise that in their household DIY literally did mean do it yourself. Meantime the neighbours on either side, and trades-men who called regularly at the house, had learned to rattle the letter slot when they failed to get an answer. This morning however somebody with bone-hard knuckles was trying the woodpecker method of announcing his or her presence.

Of all the people it might have been, Clifford Peachey was the very last person Harriet had expected to see when she opened the door. Her heart started to pound and she felt breathless, the way she had when the police had called at their house in Lincoln barely thirteen months ago to inform her that Peter had been shot. The two officers had been able to tell her very little. 'He's still alive,' one of them had said and then added that it had happened in California at Lake Arrowhead, as if she had been concerned to know this. Now, she was horribly afraid that history was about to repeat itself.

'It's all right,' Peachey said quickly, 'Peter hasn't been injured.'

'Thank God,' Harriet said with heartfelt relief.

'May I come in?'

'Yes, of course.' Harriet stepped aside. 'Do forgive me, I'm not thinking straight.'

'I'm the one who should apologise. I should have phoned to let you know I was coming.'

'That might have been worse, Clifford. I've got a vivid imagination.' Harriet opened the first door on the right and showed him into the sitting room.

'Can I get you a cup of coffee?'

'No, thank you.' Peachey smiled. 'They seem to drink a lot of coffee at Vauxhall Cross and it's practically coming out of my ears.' He waved a hand urging her to sit down before perching himself on the edge of the settee.

'I'm afraid Peter has been arrested by officers of the Counter Espionage Security Service.'

Harriet folded her arms and hugged herself.

'When did this happen?' she asked in a small voice.

'Last night, about nine o'clock Moscow time. The Russians seem almost as embarrassed by what has happened as we are.'

'Oh well, that really does make a difference. My husband is in jail and both sides feel bad about it. I can't tell you what that does for me.'

'You don't understand, Harriet. The men around President Yeltsin are anxious to maintain the present status quo. The last thing they want is a show trial; that's why they are going to deport Peter.'

'When?'

Peachey shifted uncomfortably. 'Not today.'

'Tomorrow?'

'Possibly.'

'Not today, possibly tomorrow,' Harriet said angrily. 'You don't know when they are going to release Peter, do you? Have the Russians even said they intend to deport him?'

'Not in so many words but the Foreign and Commonwealth Office has every reason to believe they will do so.'

'What you mean is some official at the FCO has been looking into his crystal ball.'

'That's unworthy of you, Harriet, and you know it.'

It was a diplomatic way of saying it was a cheap shot and he was disappointed with her. Theirs had been a long association dating back to the days when she had worked in K2, the section which dealt with subversives, and Clifford had always seen himself as her guide and mentor. Perhaps even a father figure.

'Peter didn't want to go to Moscow,' Harriet said, as if she owed him some explanation.

'What exactly did he say?'

The professional interrogator, she thought, quick to pounce on a possible breach of security.

'He didn't.'

'Then how do you know?'

'Peter didn't have to say a word, I could tell what he was thinking.'

Harriet doubted if Clifford believed her for all that he nodded sagely. And he was right not to because intuition had had very little to do with it. Friday had been one of those days when nothing went right. Edward had been fretful with teething problems and she'd had a bad case of morning sickness that had lasted well into the afternoon, which was a symptom she hadn't experienced this early during her first pregnancy. Then the washing machine had thrown a wobbler and had stopped in the middle of the eco cycle full of water, with the result that she had been unable to open the door.

She had tried four repair firms without success before Domestic Appliance Servicing had said they could fit her in towards the end of the day. The repair man who'd finally turned up at two minutes to five had been a real know-all. His discovery that the blockage in the pump had been caused by a five-pence coin had earned a lecture on the need to make sure nothing had been left in the pockets before the jeans were put in the wash. Then to cap everything Peter had stayed on at the office until dinner had been well and truly ruined, which had sparked off a blazing row.

Hostilities had ceased in bed. For some time they had lain there in the dark, together yet apart; then Peter had tentatively reached out to hold her and she had responded with a fervour that had surprised them both. And afterwards, when she had felt thoroughly satiated and ready to fall asleep, he had talked of the job Hazelwood was sending him to do in Moscow. He had made light of it but he was going in there to bait Pavel Trilisser and she knew that underneath the wry comments, Peter was apprehensive.

'It's going to be all right, Harriet,' Peachey told her quietly.

'I hope for all your sakes it will be.'

'What do you mean?'

'Peter has a problem; he's totally loyal to Victor Hazelwood. But I'm not. Victor likes to think he makes things happen, that he's a risk-taker whereas, in fact, he is simply reckless. Naturally, he doesn't put himself in the firing line; that's what foot soldiers like Peter are there for.'

'We'll get him back.'

'You'd better,' Harriet said grimly, 'because if anything happens to my husband, you'll find out just what a deep throat I've got.'

Barely forty-eight hours after meeting him for the first time, George Elphinstone had decided that Ashton was not the sort of acquaintance with whom he'd like to keep in touch. In a career that spanned twenty-five years, he could not recall anyone who had caused quite so much trouble in so short a time as Ashton. That the Ambassador appeared to hold Elphinstone personally responsible for what had happened was particularly galling for him. It wasn't as if Ashton had been working under his direction; London had simply notified him that he would be arriving on Saturday and would be contacting Pavel Trilisser. Head Office had also stated that his assistance would not be required in this matter.

Further humiliation had followed after the consular affairs officer had learned that Ashton had been arrested by the Counter Espionage and Security Service. Whenever there was a new development, he had been summoned to appear before the Ambassador like an errant fourth former dancing attendance on the Headmaster. He had never once been asked for his opinion, nor had his advice been sought; he had merely been shown the draft of the latest signal the Embassy was sending to the Foreign and Commonwealth Office. Since it was for information purposes only, his comments were not invited. He was however required to clear with Head of Chancery all signals referring to Ashton which he intended sending to Vauxhall Cross. Elphinstone therefore hoped relations were improving when Head of Chancery walked into his office late that afternoon to let him see the cable he had just drafted.

'Thought you'd like to know that Ashton is on his way home, George,' he said, and promptly sat down.

'That's the best news I've had all day.'

Things were not so cut and dried as he'd assumed before reading the cable. The consular affairs officer had been informed that Ashton had been served with a deportation order at 10.00 hours Greenwich Mean Time. However, instead of putting Ashton on the first available flight to the UK, the Russians were taking him by train to St Petersburg where he would be handed over to the British Consul.

'The Russians claim they are doing this for financial reasons,' Elphinstone said incredulously. 'They surely don't expect us to believe that the country is so broke they can't afford the cost of his air fare?'

'It's a smokescreen, George. The Russians want to do this quietly; they think putting him on a plane at Sheremetyevo Airport is too public and would attract a lot of unwelcome publicity. As you can see, Ashton wasn't too happy about the arrangement and demanded to see the consular affairs officer. The Russians had no objections and we were able to set his mind at rest before he was taken to the St Petersburg station.'

According to the timetable, Moscow to St Petersburg took five hours by rail but the train was often late and there was no guarantee it would arrive by 20.05 hours local. The Consul General in St Petersburg had been appraised of the situation and had been instructed to arrange onward movement to the UK from Helsinki either via Tallinn by air or from St Petersburg by road.

'I don't see when Ashton is expected to arrive in London.'

'That's hard to say, George, because so much depends on what time his train gets to St Petersburg.' Head of Chancery paused long enough to do a little mental arithmetic, then said, 'I think you could safely tell your people at Vauxhall Cross not to expect him before late on Wednesday afternoon.'

Acting on information received from the State Police, officers from the Miami PD had interviewed the manager of U Drive Cars who had rented the Chevrolet to the murder victim. At their request he had produced the agreement signed by Charles Barclay, which showed he was staying at the Fontainebleau Hilton on Collins Avenue. This was subsequently confirmed by the hotel management. When registering, Barclay had given 107 Schuster Road, London SW7, as his home address; he had also indicated that he would settle his account by traveller's cheque and had paid the room rate for two nights in advance. Recalling that instead of using a credit card, Barclay had put down four-hundred dollars in cash at U Drive Cars, the officers had asked if the deceased had placed any valuables in the hotel safe. On learning there was a small combination safe in each room, they had suggested the management should check out the one Barclay had been occupying on the sixteenth floor.

The discovery that the Brit had been travelling light with little more than a change of clothing did not greatly surprise the officers. Everything they had heard about the nature of the killing at the Everglades Motel on Route 84 had convinced them Barclay was a small-time crook who had overreached himself and had come up against somebody with a lot of firepower. They were however mildly surprised to find that the mini safe contained almost five thousand pounds in traveller's cheques.

The British Consul in Miami was informed of the latest development, and in turn passed the information on to the Foreign and Commonwealth Office with a copy to the British Embassy in Washington, DC. Responsibility for tracing the next of kin of the deceased rested with the Home Office. Hitherto, their ability to do this had been hampered by the lack of information. The passport number, date and place of birth were of little help when it came to ascertaining the last known address of Mr Charles Barclay. At first, that problem appeared to have been resolved by this latest communication. However, before acting on the information, one of the senior executive officers in the Home Office Police Department looked up the address in the *A to Z London Street Atlas*. There was, she discovered, no Schuster Road in SW7 or in any other postal district for that matter.

The journey to St Petersburg seemed endless. The train had left Moscow ten minutes later than scheduled and the crew hadn't attempted to make up for lost time. Although it was difficult to judge their speed in the dark, Ashton doubted if they were averaging much above fifty miles an hour. The seats were uncomfortable and the company he was keeping made him feel even more so. His minders were a couple of musclemen from the Security Service, neither of whom was prepared to tell him his name. Both men were in their late twenties or early thirties, almost as tall as himself but heavier and probably much fitter. They looked so alike, Ashton wondered if they were twins; mentally he referred to them as Tweedledum and Tweedledee. The fact that they gave short shrift to the vendors who plied their wares between stops was their one saving grace. Their studied aggression and the 9 mm Makarov self-loading pistols, which they carried in hip holsters and had no hesitation in displaying at every opportunity, ensured they had the compartment to themselves.

Ashton had no idea what instructions Tweedledum and Tweedledee had received before setting off but they had clearly been amended when the conductor handed them a telegram shortly after the train left Malaya Vishera. He couldn't understand why the Russians had decided he should be deported from St Petersburg when it would have been far easier to put him on a plane at Sheremetyevo Airport. The consular affairs officer who had visited him at the detention centre had had no qualms about the arrangement and had tried to set his mind at rest. The fact that his two minders hadn't bothered to handcuff him Ashton supposed was a sign the Russians were determined to play down the whole business, but a nagging doubt persisted even as they reached the outskirts of St Petersburg.

Ashton calculated they were roughly an hour adrift. He had only spent a few days in St Petersburg and that had been four years ago when the city was still calling itself Leningrad. Although none of the landmarks struck a chord with him, he could tell they had left the outer suburbs behind them and were nearing the terminus. They clattered across a branch line that ran eastwards in the direction of the Neva River and the apartment buildings thinned out and disappeared as the line cleaved through open parkland. Then, sooner than he had anticipated, the train began to slow down, its speed gradually falling away until they were barely crawling along. The end ramp of an island platform had only just appeared in view when the train came to a dead stop.

Tweedledum stood up and hauled Ashton to his feet.

'This is where we get off,' he told him.

'What are you talking about? This isn't the Moscow station.'

'You're quite right, this is Navalocnaja.' Tweedledee lifted Ashton's suitcase down from the rack. 'Moscow is unhappy about handing you over to the British Consul General at the terminus. Too many people there, so there's been a change of plan.'

Ashton was half dragged, half pushed out of the compartment into the corridor. Tweedledum opened the outer door, alighted on to the platform, then turned about ready to assist his partner should Ashton prove reluctant to leave the train.

Only the diesel locomotive and the first three of the fifteen cars that made up the St Petersburg Express had drawn into the station. As they walked towards the staircase which led to the subway below the tracks, somebody behind them blew a whistle and the train began to pull away. Two men were waiting for them at the top of the staircase. Appearances were not necessarily a reliable guide but neither one looked as if he were one of Her Majesty's representatives.

'Where the hell is the British Consul General?' Ashton demanded.

'We're taking you to him,' Tweedledee said. 'I don't know what you are worried about.'

Considering the odds were four to one, Ashton thought he had every reason to be worried, especially when he found himself wedged in like meat in a sandwich with two Russians in front of him and two behind. They went on down the staircase and walked through the subway to emerge in the station yard where a closed van was waiting for them. Nobody saw him climb into the back and, for all Ashton knew, nobody saw the vehicle move off.

CHAPTER 22

The van was a mobile prison cell; Tweedledee, Tweedledum and A. N. Other were therefore his jailers. Before he could leap out of the vehicle, Ashton had to get past Tweedledee and Dum to open the rear door. A. N. Other was surplus to requirements because a steel partition from roof to floor prevented him from attacking the driver. It also meant he couldn't see where they were going. To add to his sense of isolation, the side and rear windows had been blacked out with masking tape. The interior of the van was illuminated by a feeble blue light and ventilated by a wind-rotating fan in the roof.

For roughly fifteen minutes they travelled on minor roads, nearly all of them in a bad state of repair. During that time Ashton heard only three other vehicles, one of which overtook the van. When the traffic noise increased markedly after making a right turn, he knew they were on one of the main avenues. The more frequently they were caught by the lights, the more certain he became that they were heading into town and not away from it. Like a blind man he learned to see by using his ears. He came to recognise the distinctive hum of a trolley bus, the deep-throated snarl of a juggernaut and the pulsating rumble of a diesel-powered truck. He also listened to his three minders talking among themselves, hoping they might let something slip, but their conversation revolved around sport and women, when they weren't complaining about their low pay and lousy conditions of service.

The consular affairs officer from the Embassy had told him the newly established British Consulate was in Ploshchad Proletarskoi Diktatury. The trouble was Ashton didn't know how far that was from Navalocnaja station where he had been taken off the train, which made it difficult to calculate when they should arrive. Ashton stole another glance at his wristwatch and figured they had now been on the move for twenty-seven minutes. So when did he start worrying? In another five minutes' time or longer? More to the point, what was he going to do about it, if it seemed they had no intention of handing him over to the Consul General? One thing was clear: he could rant and rave at them all night and they wouldn't take a blind bit of notice. If he was going to escape, he had better make the attempt while they were still in a densely populated area.

Nothing wrong with that decision, executing it was the problem. The door handle was on the outside but, as he recalled, the driver hadn't locked them in. Had he done so, everybody in the back of the vehicle would be trapped in the event of a crash. And if the doors hadn't been locked for reasons of safety, they could therefore be opened from inside the van. The doors were secured offside by a vertical draw bar which engaged the recesses in the roof and floor. A cutaway section in the metal panelling which gave access to the locking bar had been temporarily blocked over with three-ply.

Tweedledee produced a packet of cigarettes, offered one to his partner and the third Russian, then dug out a gas lighter which refused to ignite. A. N. Other came to the rescue with a match. As he leaned across him, shielding the flame against the draught with a cupped hand, Ashton seized what was likely to be his only real chance to escape. Launching himself from the bench seat like an athlete competing in a 100-metre dash, he knocked A. N. Other into Tweedledum and hit the plywood cover with a clenched fist, breaking it in two. He clawed the wooden fragments out of the cutaway section, then grabbed the handle inside and yanked it down while fending off Tweedledee with his free hand. He tried to put his left shoulder to the door but the element of surprise that had given him a fleeting advantage had gone and suddenly he was locked in a wrestling match with two of the Russians. Somehow Ashton managed to deliver a hefty kick at the door as they hauled him away from it. Their own slipstream and a stiff breeze did the rest, plucking the doors wide open.

The headlights of a following vehicle illuminated the interior and the writhing bodies on the floor. Confusion reigned; Tweedledee yelled at the driver to stop. Tweedledum contradicted his partner and told him to go on. The driver obeyed both instructions in the order he received them, stamping on the brakes first, then flooring the accelerator just in time to avoid a multiple pile-up. Even with snow tyres, black ice on the road made driving at speed hazardous. The rear end slewed into the kerb where the wheels eventually found a purchase to send the vehicle careering towards the centre of the road, with every driver in their wake blaring at them on the horn.

Ashton kicked, heaved, wriggled, punched and bit in a desperate attempt to throw off the Russians who had pinned him to the floor. Freedom was only a foot away beyond the doors flapping wildly to and fro but he knew he wasn't going to make it because there were just too many of them on top of him. The van drifted back into the nearside lane and stopped; then the driver got out, ran round to the back and closed the doors.

Their van wasn't the only vehicle that had stopped. Several voices were raised in anger but who was saying what to whom was inaudible until the van driver yelled to them to fuck off and let the police get on with their job. Ashton reckoned he must have threatened the crowd with a pistol the way the altercation ceased abruptly. So far as he was concerned, this was only of academic interest, especially as Mr A. N. Other was hellbound on giving him a good kicking. Help came from an unexpected quarter.

'Leave the Englishman alone,' Tweedledum roared, 'I don't want him marked.'

'After what he's done to my mouth? Go blow it up your arse.'

'I told you to leave him alone,' Tweedledum said, and slapped A. N. Other across the face hard enough to make it sound like a pistol shot.

Ashton got up from the floor and sat on the bench.

'And I don't want any more trouble from you either, Mr Englishman.'

'Don't worry, I'm in no fit state to start another rumpus.'

'Are you all right?'

'Sure, no bones broken.' Just his pride dented.

'Why did you try to get out of the van?'

'I needed a breath of fresh air,' Ashton told him.

'No, you believe we are not taking you to the British Consul, but that is absurd.'

Absurd, was it? Ashton didn't think so. They had crossed the Neva; he had seen the river when the doors had been flapping. He had also caught a glimpse of the Peter and Paul Fortress, one of the few prominent landmarks he remembered from the last time he'd been in St Petersburg.

'The British Consulate is on Ploshchad Proletarskoi Diktatury,' he said pointedly.

'We know that,' Tweedledee informed him. 'Like we told you on the train, there's been a change of plan and the British Consul is waiting for you on the Finnish border.'

Garfield alighted from the Portsmouth Harbour train at Haslemere, waved his season ticket at the collector on the gate and walked through the booking hall into the dimly lit station yard. He wondered if Eileen would be waiting for him with the Metro; putting himself in her shoes, he wouldn't blame her if she wasn't. Their twentieth wedding anniversary had ended disastrously, thanks to Ashton. It wasn't only that he had had to go into the office at some unearthly hour in the morning; the fact was the crisis management team had been in session on and off all day.

There had been no question of returning to the Dorchester; Eileen had had to settle their bill with her own credit card and then get herself over to Waterloo and home to Churt. He had rung the house several times to make his peace with Eileen and on each occasion had got the answer machine. Of course he'd left several messages but she hadn't phoned back. Given the circumstances, staying late at the office could be seen as a kind of death wish but he had wanted to make damned sure Ashton was on his way to St Petersburg before he left Vauxhall Cross. Nothing, but nothing was going to come between Eileen and him that evening.

Garfield looked round the yard in a cursory manner and was about to head for a taxi when Eileen sounded the horn. Garfield thought he had reason to believe he was no longer in the dog house because he couldn't think why else Eileen would have bothered to meet him at the station. However, nothing in life was ever certain, especially where his wife was concerned. He told himself that tact and diplomacy were required in what could prove to be a volatile situation. Telling Eileen how pleased he was to see her was a good opening line; unfortunately Garfield botched it by adding that it had been one hell of a day.

'You don't think it's been any fun for me, do you?' Eileen added sharply.

'Good Lord no. I had to leave you to cope on your own.' Garfield frowned. Normally he wouldn't dream of telling Eileen what had happened in Moscow but in this instance, he decided she deserved an explanation.

'We got word from the Foreign Office that the Russians had arrested one of ours and for a while it looked as if the bad old days were back.'

'One of ours,' Eileen repeated acidly. 'Does this man actually work for you, Rowan?'

'In a manner of speaking.'

'What does that exactly mean?'

Garfield closed his eyes briefly. Eileen at her sharpest could match any Queen's Counsel at cross-examination. Three miles to Hindhead, another three to Churt; it was going to seem a long six miles.

'Well?'

The accused had made a big mistake in electing to go into the witness box and now Counsel for the prosecution was about to make mincemeat of him. He tried to explain where Ashton fitted in the nebulous chain of command and why he had felt responsible for Peter even though it was Hazelwood who had sent him to Moscow. But even Garfield recognised his reasons sounded pathetic and created the impression he was simply concerned to cover himself.

'Anyway, Ashton should have arrived in St Petersburg by now,' Garfield concluded lamely.

'So everything in the garden is lovely,' Eileen said, still a touch acerbic.

Garfield assured her it was and mentally crossed his fingers. Normally he didn't believe in tempting providence but this was one time he was prepared to make an exception. He even went so far as to blow his own trumpet, assigning to himself a much bigger role than he'd actually played in the affair. He did it to impress Eileen. However, it quickly became apparent that she was in no mood to be the admiring little woman and their conversation became even more strained so that it came as something of a relief when Eileen turned into the driveway of their house.

A creature of habit, Garfield liked to take a shower before changing into casual clothes. For him, it was the ideal way to unwind after a stressful day at the office. As had happened in the past, a well-established routine was rudely interrupted. He had just stepped out of the shower when Eileen yelled from the foot of the staircase that he was wanted on the phone.

'The bloody Mozart,' she added.

Garfield put on a towelling robe and ran down to the small parlour room off the hall which he used as a study. He barely had time to pick up the handset before the duty officer told him that Ashton was missing.

'What do you mean he's missing?'

'He wasn't on the train when it arrived at St Petersburg.'

The Consul General had contacted Head of Chancery at the Embassy in Moscow who in turn had spoken to the Counsellor in charge of the West European Department at the Ministry of Foreign Affairs. The Russian had professed to be equally surprised and had been unable to account for Ashton's disappearance. Major General Gurov, Moscow's Chief of Police, had heard nothing from his two officers and what was even more worrying had been unable to raise them on their mobile phones.

'What is Head of Station doing about it?' Garfield asked.

'The short answer is very little. Elphinstone says the Ambassador is now involved at the highest level and he's agreed to stay out of it.'

Garfield wasn't surprised. You could always rely on George Elphinstone to keep his head below the parapet when things began to look ugly.

'Has the Director been informed?'

'Yes, I rang him straight away.' The duty officer paused, then said, 'Perhaps I should have called you first but I understood Ashton had been tasked by the Director personally.'

'You did the right thing,' Garfield assured him.

'That's a relief.'

'What about Mrs Ashton? Has she been informed?'

'Not by me. I don't know if Mr Hazelwood intends to break the news himself.'

Garfield waited expectantly. Somebody would have to brief the Cabinet Office and he assumed Victor Hazelwood would do that, but it would be nice to be told.

'Is there anything else I should know?' he enquired tartly.

'Well, the Director is on his way to see the Cabinet Secretary, then I gather he will be coming into the office.'

'So am I,' Garfield said, and put the phone down.

He imagined Eileen would have plenty to say about it. She would ask if Hazelwood had sent for him and it might be necessary to tell a small white lie for the sake of a quiet life. Of course, had Victor needed him, he would have informed the duty officer or phoned him direct. However, sometimes it was politic to be seen to be doing something and, in Garfield's opinion, never more so than now.

Ashton glanced at the luminous face of the Omega and saw it was showing ten minutes to twelve. Almost three hours had passed since he had attempted to escape from the van and, allowing an average speed of thirty-five to forty, he reckoned they must have done at least a hundred miles. Judging by the noise level, he was fairly sure they had passed through Vyborg, the last sizeable town before the Finnish border, a while back, which meant they should arrive at the crossing point very shortly. The optimist in Ashton wanted to believe the Consul General would be there to meet him; the realist knew this was extremely unlikely.

That raised the question of what Tweedledee and Tweedledum and their two cohorts intended to do with him. If the Russians meant to kill him, they could have done so long before now. It was a comforting thought to nurture while they bumped over the moguls on the hard-packed snow that covered what had to be a minor road.

The van slowed to a crawl, turned right, started climbing, levelled out, made another right and then stopped. The driver left the engine to idle while he got out of the cab, walked round to the back and opened the doors. All Ashton could see was a vast expanse of snow and the unbroken line of a forest in the middle distance. There was no sign of life anywhere.

'This is where you get out, Mr Ashton,' the driver informed him in Russian.

'I don't see the Consul General.'

'He is waiting for you up the road.'

'So I am to believe he has come all this way from St Petersburg to meet me within spitting distance of the Finnish border?'

'No, this consul is from your Embassy in Helsinki.'

'That isn't what I was told three hours ago.'

'You were giving us enough trouble as it was,' Tweedledee said, chipping in. 'In the circumstance, I thought it best to set your mind at ease.'

'By lying to me?' Ashton snapped.

'But of course. Now please get out of the van. It is getting late and we would all like to go home.'

'Before I do, suppose you tell me the name of the diplomat?'

'I would also like to know his name,' Tweedledum said.

'Smith, Jones, Black, White: take your pick,' the driver said. 'We are lowly police officers, nobody in authority tells us anything.'

'They do things differently in your shitty town, do they?' Tweedledum snarled.

'You bloody Muscovites should try shutting your mouths,' A. N. Other told them.

The driver reached up, grabbed hold of Ashton's coat and tugged. At the same time, A. N. Other gave him a violent shove from behind. Taken by surprise, Ashton pitched head first out of the van and landed in the hard-packed snow, his outstretched right hand breaking the fall. The wrist folded under him as he rolled head over heels on the right shoulder. The sudden shaft of pain heralded either a greenstick fracture or, at best, a badly sprained wrist. Ignoring the injury, he scrambled to his feet and lunged after the driver but the man was too quick for him. By the time he got within touching distance of the van, the driver was already in the cab. The Russian slammed the gear stick into first, gunned the engine and took off, the rear end fishtailing.

The van shot down the slope, hit the road, and sideswiped the opposite snow bank as the driver made a belated left turn to head back to St Petersburg. The centre of gravity was all wrong and for a moment it looked as if the vehicle would tip over, but as Ashton raced after the van, it suddenly righted itself and drew away from him. His travelling bag sailed through the air, hit the road and burst open.

'Well sod you,' Ashton roared at the top of his voice.

He retrieved the scattered items of clothing and did his best to repack them using only his left hand while mouthing a string of Anglo-Saxon obscenities. The two red lights which appeared briefly in the distance told him the vehicle had stopped again and he assumed the driver had halted in order to close the rear doors. Since the Russians had made it clear that he definitely was not the flavour of the month, he saw no point in trying to catch up with them before they moved on.

Ashton had no idea where he was. Luckily there was no overcast and it was easy to locate the North Star from the Great Bear. He had to believe Tweedledee and co. were heading off in the direction of St Petersburg and that they had abandoned him somewhere in the Karelia region close to the frontier. If he was wrong about either assumption, homing in on the North Star could be a disastrous navigational error.

Although Finland had never been a member of the now defunct Warsaw Pact, the country had been of interest to Ashton when he had been the number two man on the Russian Desk. Apart from the historical background, the climatic conditions pertaining to the country were still fresh in his memory. In Helsinki, February was the coldest month of the year with temperatures averaging around minus 9 degrees centigrade, or 21 degrees of frost on the Fahrenheit scale. What previously had been a statistic was now a reality and the bitterly cold night air took his breath away. The raglan coat he was wearing afforded little protection against subarctic conditions and if a wind should really get up, he could fall victim to hypothermia. Ashton picked up the travelling bag with his left hand and set off at a brisk pace. Shortly thereafter, he started jogging; two miles up the road, he dumped the bag, convinced it was slowing him down.

Elphinstone could not recall an occasion when he had felt so helpless as he did now. On instructions from the Foreign and Commonwealth Office, the Ambassador had informed him that he had no role to play in ascertaining the present whereabouts of Peter Ashton. Nevertheless he had felt compelled to leave the diplomatic compound and return to the Embassy, as if by being there at his desk he was somehow giving Ashton moral support.

Ashton should have arrived in St Petersburg at 20.05 hours but his train had been seventy-four minutes behind schedule when it had finally pulled into the terminus. It was now 02.36 on Wednesday, 8 February, which meant he had been missing for a minimum of five hours.

Elphinstone told himself that the days had long passed when people whom the KGB regarded as enemies of the state could literally disappear without a trace, or end up in a mental hospital. The demise of the Komitet Gosudarstvennoy Bezopasnosti had not however made Russia a safer country to live in. One only had to recall what had happened to Tim Rochelle to understand why Moscow was the murder capital of the world.

Elphinstone felt his eyelids begin to droop; resting his elbows on the desk, he cupped his chin in both palms and happily surrendered. He was just drifting off to sleep when Head of Chancery walked into his office. The sound of his footsteps instantly aroused Elphinstone and set his adrenalin flowing.

'Can you spare me a minute, George?' he enquired politely.

'You've heard something?'

'Yes. I'm afraid things look rather dicky for your man.' Head of Chancery pulled up a chair and sat down, crossing one plump leg over the other. 'It seems the St Petersburg express made an unscheduled stop at Navalocnaja.'

The conductor and both locomotive engineers had been taken into custody and questioned by the militia as soon as it was discovered that Ashton was not on the train. The conductor had claimed that he had been given a telegram at Malaya Vishera, the last official stop before St Petersburg, and had been told to deliver it to the officers in the second compartment of the third car. He hadn't been given the names of the officers but he had been told exactly where to find them on the train. The conductor had been quite adamant about that.

'He was equally adamant that the man who'd given him the telegram was a colonel in the Security Service, said he'd seen his ID card and badge. This colonel told him to warn the engineers that the train would be making a brief unscheduled stop at Navalocnaja and that only the first three units should draw into the station. The two engineers confirmed his story.'

'Be a surprise if they hadn't,' Elphinstone said. 'After all, they had no reason to mistrust the instructions they'd received from the conductor. Or had they?'

'I doubt it, George. The chief engineer told the militia officers that he had been watching the platform at Malaya Vishera and had seen a heavily built man wearing a fur hat and top coat approach the conductor.'

'Even though it was a dark night and the train was how long?'

'Admittedly there were fifteen coaches but I understand the station is well lit.'

The second engineer had said that he'd seen a red light at the far end of the island platform as they drew into Navalocnaja. Complying with the instructions they had received from the conductor, his colleague had then stopped the train when the first three cars were alongside the platform. In his statement to the militia, the second engineer had also said he'd noticed that two men were waiting at the top of the staircase leading to the subway.

'The locomotive engineers were questioned separately, George. Both maintained that only three passengers got off the train and walked towards the staircase. They weren't able to describe any of the men other than in general terms but from the style of the clothes he was wearing, they were sure one of them was a Westerner. They didn't know whether the three men joined the other two by the staircase because the light changed from red to green and the chief engineer had to obey the signal.'

And that, so far as Head of Chancery knew, was how things stood at the moment. What he and the Ambassador found particularly disturbing was the fact that the two police officers who'd left Moscow with Ashton had also vanished.

'What do the Russians make of it?' Elphinstone asked.

'They believe Ashton has been kidnapped by the *Mafiozniki* and wouldn't be surprised if we received a ransom demand in the near future.'

For the theory to hold up, a staggering number of people must have been involved. To begin with, somebody in the Ministry of Foreign Affairs must have tipped off the *Mafiozniki* about Ashton and where he was going after being released from the detention centre. Then there was the bogus colonel from the Security Service, the two men at Navalocnaja, maybe Ashton's escort, and possibly the entire train crew, never mind the organising genius who had planned the whole thing. And would a Moscow-based *Mafiozniki* go into partnership with a firm in St Petersburg?

'I don't believe it,' Elphinstone said.

'Yes, it does take a bit of swallowing.' Head of Chancery uncrossed his legs and stood up. 'But take it from me, George, when you have been in this country as long as I have, you'll believe anything is possible.'

For the umpteenth time Ashton told himself that he had not yet reached the limit of his endurance, that to keep going all he had to do was put one foot in front of the other. It was, however, an assertion that was becoming increasingly difficult to believe. He had been on the move now for three and a quarter hours since the Russians had dumped him in the middle of nowhere. Back in the days when he had been in the SAS he would have covered nearly sixteen miles in that time in full marching order with a thirty-pound rucksack on his back. But that had been fourteen long years ago and it was stupid to pretend that he was still the same man.

If he had averaged three and a half miles in the hour tonight he would have been doing very well. But whatever distance he had covered, it still made a mockery of what the Russians had told him. The consular officer from Helsinki was waiting for him up the road, was he? Jesus, that was a lousy joke because the road he was on was leading him in and out of the pine forest and his strength was slowly ebbing away. Ashton recognised the danger because he had come close to death in similar circumstances on the Brecon Beacons during an escape and evasion exercise when the wind chill factor had got to him and lowered his resistance. He'd felt bone tired and had wanted nothing more than to find somewhere to shelter and go to sleep. Back then, an iron will had kept him going and he had lost none of that characteristic in the intervening years, Tonight it was reinforced by thoughts of Harriet, the child in her womb and Edward.

The ice road turned back on itself and emerged from the pine forest yet again. Ashton wondered if the man who had surveyed it had been as lost as he was. It was then he noticed the gleam of light over to his left. Could it be he was hallucinating? It was after four o'clock in the morning and who would be up at that ghastly hour on a winter day? Furthermore the ice road was taking him away from the source. He closed his eyes, counted up to ten and opened them to find the light was still there. Hesitating no longer, he left the road and struck out through the virgin snow. Forty minutes later, he was hammering on the door of an observation post manned by troops of the Finnish Army.

CHAPTER 23

The observation post Ashton had found was on the outskirts of Lappeenranta, a frontier garrison town which had become a thriving inland port following the construction of the Saimaa Canal. None of the soldiers on duty could speak English and knowing how the Finns felt about their powerful neighbour, Ashton had been reluctant to address them in Russian. The soldiers had reported his arrival to Garrison Headquarters and the language problem had been resolved when a German-speaking staff officer had arrived at the post to question him. The Russians had failed to return Ashton's passport when they had thrown him out of the van and the Garrison Headquarters had phoned the British Embassy in Helsinki to verify his nationality. Fortunately copies of every signal that had passed between Moscow and London had been sent to Helsinki and Tallinn from the moment it had been learned that the Russians intended to deport Ashton through St Petersburg. The Embassy's consular officer had therefore been able to confirm that Peter Ashton was indeed a citizen of the United Kingdom of Great Britain and Northern Ireland.

The Finns had looked after Ashton extremely well. The troops manning the observation post had stripped off his wet clothes and checked his face, ears, hands and feet for signs of frostbite before putting him through their homemade sauna. Wrapped in a thermal suit and looking like a Michelin Man, he had then been airlifted to the General Hospital in town, where he had been given a complete physical. His wrist hadn't been fractured, merely sprained and not badly at that.

He had tried to convince the doctors there was nothing wrong with him that couldn't be put right by ensuring he was on the next British Airways or Finnair flight to London Heathrow. Ashton had made the same point to the consular affairs officer when he had arrived from Helsinki to collect him and had got precisely nowhere. The Ambassador, supported by Head of Station, had insisted the Embassy's tame doctor should take a look at him to make sure he really was OK. It seemed that once the medics got their hands on you there was no escaping from their clutches.

By the time everybody was ready to admit he was fit to fly, the last flight to London had left. He had stayed the Wednesday night with Head of Station and his wife and had then caught the British Airways flight departing at 07.35 which had got him into London Heathrow a few minutes before nine o'clock. He'd arrived in borrowed apparel, looking like a refugee from a war zone and carrying what was left of his own clothes bundled up in brown paper. The junior member of the Russian Desk had been waiting for him at Terminal 1 together with Harriet, who had been carrying Edward on her back. Rowan Garfield's minion had had the un-enviable task of informing Ashton that the DG did not expect him to come into the office, which had provoked an acerbic comment from Harriet. She had become even more corrosive when he'd gone on to say that Mr Hazelwood would like to see him after morning prayers on Friday if that was convenient.

'The man is all heart,' Harriet had said, but the way Ashton saw it, his old guide and mentor didn't have much choice. It was odds on that the Foreign Office was pressing the SIS to hold a formal inquiry and Victor couldn't put it off until Monday just so that he and Harriet could enjoy a long weekend.

The inquiry was held in the conference room after morning prayers. In addition to Hazelwood, Peachey, and Victor's PA, who was there to record the proceedings, Ashton had anticipated that Rowan Garfield would be a member of the inquiry. To find that the Foreign Office had nominated Robin Urquhart to be their repres-entative was definitely a surprise.

'Shouldn't Jill Sheridan be present?' Ashton said looking at Hazelwood.

Urquhart shifted uncomfortably in his chair, looking up at the ceiling.

'Why?' Hazelwood asked.

'Because the information that reached me from Pavel Trilisser affects her department.'

'I think we'll deal with one thing at a time, Peter. For the moment we would like to hear your account of what actually happened.'

'It's a long story.'

'Take all the time you need,' Hazelwood told him. 'We're in no hurry.'

Ashton began with Katya Malinovskaya because she was the fulcrum on which everything turned. For the benefit of Urquhart and Clifford Peachey, he went through her curriculum vitae, and then explained why he had hired her. The first interruption came from Garfield, who wanted to know why he had been so anxious to trace the bartender of the Golden Nugget.

'Everyone was telling me that Tim Rochelle had been shot because he'd had the misfortune to be in the wrong place at the wrong time. Before I went after Pavel Trilisser I wanted to be sure the Russian Intelligence Service wasn't involved.'

'And were you?'

It was a tough question to answer. As it happened, he'd failed to get incontrovertible proof that the incident at the Golden Nugget was down to one of the local *Mafiozniki* gangs. Although Katya had been convinced that the men who'd raked her Mercedes with machine guns were gangsters, there was no escaping the fact that in trying to find the barman, she had sought help from her former colleagues in the Criminal Intelligence Division.

'Let's say there wasn't enough evidence to deter me.'

'Suppose we move on a bit,' Hazelwood said. 'According to the Russians you were arrested while dining with a major from military intelligence at the Ritz Grill on Arbat Street.'

'That's correct. The major called himself Nikolai Grigoryevich, claimed he had just returned from the Russian Embassy in Tehran.'

'His last name is Yakushkin.'

'I didn't know that, he omitted to tell me.'

'Who chose the rendezvous?'

'Pavel Trilisser. It was a last-minute arrangement; the meeting was set for seven o'clock and I only learned about the rendezvous when he contacted me pay phone to pay phone, shortly after 6 p.m.'

'And how soon were you arrested?'

Ashton gave the question some thought. The live entertainment had started fifteen minutes later than advertised and the Beatles lookalikes had been halfway through their second number when the headwaiter had shown Nikolai Grigoryevich to his table. They had then made small talk, the Russian advising him what to order from the menu before they got down to business.

'Forty, forty-five minutes,' he told Hazelwood.

'Do you think anybody followed you into the restaurant?' Urquhart smiled. 'With the benefit of hindsight, of course.'

'I did everything by the book and ran several checks to make sure I wan't being tailed. This was after I had sent Katya Malinovskaya on ahead.'

'Would she have had time to phone the Counter Espionage and Security Service and tip them off?'

Garfield again, and keen to deflect any accusing finger before it was pointed at Pavel Trilisser, whom he regarded as a priceless asset.

'At a pinch. But if she did tip them off, the Security Service had a funny way of showing their gratitude. One of their women officers took great delight in punching Katya in the stomach.'

'It's more likely they had Yakushkin under surveillance,' Urquhart said, venturing his opinion.

So far only Peachey had contributed nothing to the proceedings. Ashton got the impression he was content to sit there sucking on a cold pipe and looking wise.

'Were you ill-treated?' Hazelwood asked.

'No. I can't say what happened to Katya Malinovskaya and Nikolai Grigoryevich Yakushkin because I never saw them again after I was admitted to the detention centre.' The Russians had presumably been incarcerated in Moscow's Lefortovo Prison or somewhere even more sinister. 'I'd like someone from the Embassy to call at the security agency at 124 Gorky Street to see if Katya is back in circulation. If she isn't, I hope the Embassy will press for her release.'

'It would not be politic to do so,' Urquhart told him. 'The lady is a Russian citizen and was working for a foreign Intelligence officer.

We cannot meddle in what is an internal matter.'

'We owe her,' Ashton said fiercely.

'I was merely stating the Foreign Office view.' Urquhart smiled. 'I didn't say I agreed with it,' he added in a mild voice.

'Anything else, Peter?' Hazelwood asked.

'The Russians didn't return my passport. The consular officer in Helsinki had to issue me with a temporary one.'

'So we were informed. Having the original confiscated by the Russian Intelligence Service might even prove advantageous.'

Ashton reckoned he knew what Victor meant. Two years ago he had walked away from the SIS and although he had done one freelance job for the service before returning to the fold, his name had not appeared in the next edition of the Diplomatic or Blue List published by Her Majesty's Stationery Office. It was to have been reinstated in the 1995 list but if his interpretation was correct, this was now unlikely to happen. The list was a bit like *Jane's Fighting Ships*, a worldwide reference book which anybody could purchase. No Ashton in this book, no Foreign and Commonwealth Office connection, which made it much easier for the service to use him in a covert role in a foreign country – provided nobody thought of sending him into Russia again.

'Let's move on to the day you were released,' Hazelwood continued. 'When were you informed that you were to be deported?'

'About two hours before the train departed for St Petersburg. I demanded to see a consular affairs officer because I wasn't happy with the arrangement but he said there was nothing to worry about.'

'Which was far from the case,' Hazelwood said, prompting him to continue.

The junior desk officer who had met Ashton at Heathrow had told him they'd been inundated with signals from Head of Station, Moscow, but all the information they had received would have been provided by the Russians in the first instance. The moment he told them what had happened at Navalocnaja station and thereafter, he could tell from their expressions that they were getting a very different story from him.

'Relations between Tweedledee and Tweedledum on the one hand and the two men from St Petersburg on the other became more and more strained. After I had attempted to escape, the guy I had nicknamed A. N. Other wanted to give me a good kicking. Tweedledum wouldn't have it, told him I wasn't to be marked. When he refused to stop, Tweedledum slapped his face hard enough to make his teeth rattle.'

'Tweedles Dum and Dee,' Peachey said, suddenly coming to life. 'They were from the Counter Espionage and Security Service?'

'That's what I was given to understand and they had badges to prove it.' Ashton smiled lopsidedly. 'Of course we were never formally introduced.'

'Did they serve you with a deportation order?'

'No, that was done by an official from the Ministry of the Interior. They arrived after I had seen our consular affairs officer.'

'Major General Gurov, Moscow's Chief of Police, appeared to think they were his men and was alarmed when he couldn't raise them on their mobile phones.'

'Where did you hear that, Clifford?'

'From the Embassy,' Urquhart said before Peachey could reply. 'The information was given to Head of Chancery by the Counsellor in charge of the West European Desk at the Ministry of Foreign Affairs.'

Ashton gave a low whistle. He had been arrested by the Counter Espionage and Security Service, Internal Affairs had issued the deportation order; now it appeared the police and Foreign Affairs had been in on the act.

Hazelwood produced a Burma cheroot and lit it. 'Any comments, Peter?'

'I'm lucky to be alive. If everything had gone according to plan I would have died from hypothermia and exposure, which would have suited Pavel Trilisser down to the ground.'

'I refuse to believe that Trilisser was behind it,' Garfield said heatedly.

'Well, that's your problem, Rowan. I was the monkey on his back. If he could get rid of me, he reckoned it would loosen the hold the SIS had on him.'

'I would remind you it was Trilisser who contacted our Head of Station and not the other way round. How do you explain that?'

Ashton thought it had a lot to do with the information Yakushkin had brought back from Tehran. Although it principally affected the United States, the economic consequences for Russia were such that Trilisser had felt he had to pass the information on in order to cover himself.

'So why did he choose us?' Garfield demanded.

'We are the people who've been twisting his tail for almost two years. Maybe he hoped it would damage the so-called special relationship if the Americans dismissed the report as absolute rubbish. The fact is he decided to sever all connection with us after Tim Rochelle and his messenger boy were gunned down.'

'You can't possibly know that.'

'Naturally we couldn't allow him to get away with that,' Ashton said, riding roughshod over Garfield. 'So I was sent over to remind Trilisser that we still had our hooks into him.'

Garfield maintained it was pure conjecture and started to get overheated. Peachey tactfully suggested it might be helpful if they knew what Ashton had learned from Yakushkin. Then the phone in the conference room rang and there was a further eruption, this time from Hazelwood when the PA informed him the caller wanted to speak to Garfield urgently. Asked if he was aware that an official inquiry was in progress, the desk officer informed the PA that he had just received a signal from Head of Station, Moscow, which could affect the outcome.

'You'd better hear what he's got to say, Rowan,' Hazelwood said reluctantly.

What the desk officer had to say drew a series of grunts from Garfield, who also made copious notes on a scratchpad. After putting the phone down, it then took him a good minute to decipher his own handwriting.

'Well, don't keep us in suspense, Rowan,' said Hazelwood.

'The escorts have been found dead.'

'What, all of them?'

Garfield shook his head. 'Just the two men who left Moscow with you, Peter. One of them had been beaten about the face before he was shot. The Russians appear to think you had something to do with it.'

'Rubbish.'

'Full details of the incident have been sent to the Foreign and Commonwealth Office by the Ambassador,' Garfield continued relentlessly.

'All right, we'll meet again as soon as we've seen our info copy of the signal.' Hazelwood looked at Urquhart to see if that was OK with him and got an affirmative nod. 'Meantime, Peter, you can tell Jill what you learned from your source and see what she makes of it.'

'Right.' Ashton pushed his chair back and stood up. 'Whatever it is the Russians have told the Ambassador, it will still be a load of rubbish.'

'I quite agree,' Urquhart told the meeting. 'Forty-eight hours ago they were saying that Ashton had been kidnapped by the *Mafiozniki*.'

Although there was a murmur of agreement around the table, Ashton was aware that everybody was staring at the bruised fingers of his left hand.

'I punched a hole in a piece of plywood to release the door,' he said, and immediately regretted offering an explanation.

The senior executive in the Home Office Police Department who had discovered there was no such address as 107 Schuster Road anywhere in London had immediately asked the Passport Office to produce a copy of the application form submitted by Mr Charles Barclay. When the application form arrived two days later, it was obvious that the head and shoulders photograph bore no resemblance to the facsimile she had received from the consul in Miami via the Foreign and Commonwealth Office. It therefore followed that the man who had been murdered in the grounds of the Everglades Motel in Florida was definitely not Charles Barclay. It also raised the question why the real owner had not reported the loss of passport Number N386623E, assuming he was physically able to do so.

Acting on a hunch, the senior executive officer wrote to the Office of Population Censuses and Surveys at St Catherine's House. In response to her enquiry, she duly received a certified copy of an entry pursuant to the Births and Deaths Registration Act 1953 in respect of Charles Barclay born on 13 August 1963 at Ilford. In box 1, the date and place of death was 28 October 1994 at the South Western Hospital in Clapham North. Under occupation and usual address, the Deputy Registrar had typed, 'Warehouseman, husband of Dawn Marie Barclay, 34 Coronation Avenue, London SW4.' The cause of death was Coronary Artery Occlusion coupled with Severe Coronary Artery Atheroma certified by the Coroner after post-mortem without inquest.

As a result of the information, New Scotland Yard was requested to interview the widow and ascertain how the passport issued to her late husband had been found on the body of a murder victim in Florida. Coronation Avenue in Clapham fell within the boundaries of L District, which covered the London Borough of Lambeth. The nearest police station was in Union Grove where the Chief Superintendent in charge instructed the duty sergeant to assign the task to one of the constables on the day shift.

Dawn Marie Barclay was four years older than her husband and worked part-time in the local supermarket on the checkout. She was about five feet six, had dark brown hair, a pert-looking face and a figure that was a little too full for the miniskirt and sweater she was wearing. At least that was the opinion of the police constable who called at the house to interview her. He also thought she was remarkably friendly for a woman whose husband had died a mere three months ago.

Her house was a three-bedroom semidetached which formed part of a low-cost development built in 1937, the coronation year of King George VI. The property looked to be in good order to the constable and was well furnished, especially the sitting room at the back where the interview took place. Although too flashy for his liking, the leather three-piece suite was almost brand-new and had obviously cost a pretty penny. Other expensive items included a compact disc music centre, video recorder, wide-screen TV and a fitted Axminster carpet.

'Very nice,' the police constable observed.

'We thought so too,' Dawn Marie said and patted her hair. 'Only had the room decorated last summer.'

Barclay, he rapidly learned, had been her second husband and he had inherited the house from his mother. They had been married for just over six years when Charlie had snuffed it.

'Went as quick as that,' Dawn Marie said, and snapped her fingers. 'Just like his mother, the old cow.'

It didn't require much acumen to gather that there had been no love lost between the two women. Furthermore it was evident that until the old lady died, Charlie had been pretty much under his mother's thumb. She had controlled the purse strings, a situation that Dawn Marie had remedied following her demise. If the sitting room was anything to go by, the constable thought she had probably gone through Charlie's inheritance like a dose of salts and maybe landed him deep in debt as well. It was, he decided, a point worth keeping in mind.

'Listen to me going on like this,' Dawn Marie said coyly. 'You haven't had a chance to got a word in edgeways. What did you want to see me about?'

'There have been a number of burglaries in the neighbourhood recently,' the constable began.

'Tell me something new.'

'The villains hit on those houses where they know the occupants are out at work. We wondered if you had been done over?'

'Me?'

'They're in and out before you can bat an eyelid. They're after small stuff – cash, jewellery, the odd video – things like that.'

'I bet they leave a right mess behind them.'

'And passports, there's a ready market for them.'

Dawn Marie did a double take and smiled weakly.

'Really?' she croaked. 'Who would buy a used one?'

'Illegal immigrants, criminals anxious to skip the country.' The constable paused, then said, 'Your late husband's passport was found on the body of a suspected drug smuggler who was gunned down in Florida.'

'Come to think of it, maybe I was burgled shortly after Charlie died. I forgot to lock the back door before I left for the supermarket one morning and when I got home from work I had this funny feeling that somebody had been in the house.

'It won't wash, Dawn,' the constable told her bluntly. 'You sold the bloody passport. Now, all we want from you is the name of the guy who bought it and we'll walk away and you get to keep the money, if you haven't already spent it. So what do you say?'

Dawn Marie Barclay considered the suggestion for all of ten seconds, then gave him the name and address of the friend who'd found the buyer whom she could only describe in general terms.

Hazelwood had a quiet word with his PA and told her to be sure to phone him at a quarter to six with a bogus message from his wife, Alice, then returned to his office to await the arrival of Jill Sheridan. With any luck there would be no need for his PA to initiate the subterfuge but he wanted to leave at a reasonable hour after what had been a particularly difficult day, and Jill was apt to go on a bit. Ask her for an assessment and you were likely to get a lecture. He heard her footsteps in the corridor, put on a smile and greeted her cheerfully when she tapped on the door before walking into his office.

'I'm sorry I've had to put you off until now,' he said, waving her to a chair, 'but I dare say you know the reason why.'

'Word does get around, Victor,' she said with a faint smile.

Well, of course it did, even in a secretive establishment like Vauxhall Cross, and Jill had been closeted with Ashton. She would have asked him about his source and he would have told her what had happened to Yakushkin. The inquiry had reassembled at 14.00 hours after digesting the Ambassador's report to the Foreign Office and had adjourned three hours later, none the wiser and still undecided what interpretation they should put on the latest events in Russia.

'So what did you learn from Peter?' he asked.

'A lot of interesting stuff about a fifty-eight-year-old Iranian banker called Shahpour Bazargan who is dying of leukemia. Of course the man is not unknown to us.'

Here comes the first lecturette, Hazelwood thought, and sat back to enjoy a Burma cheroot while Jill recited a potted biography of the Iranian.

'Bazargan has been at the centre of power for years, so when he says the Ayatollahs are planning a massive attack on the US dollar, we should sit up and take notice. He claims that, with some help from the Cubans, Iran will be able to counterfeit hundred-dollar bills which will incorporate all the latest security measures and will be undetectable. Remember when I told you all about the rumours going the rounds in Tehran? How the Ayatollahs were preparing a very nasty surprise for the American capitalist hyenas, how the means of retribution would be ten times more destructive than any weapon yet devised by man? And how, best of all, it would be years before the Yankee imperialists realised just how much damage had been done to them? Well, I think this massive counterfeit operation could be their secret weapon.'

'I'll give you one thing, Jill, it's certainly a novel method of waging war.'

'Not really,' Jill said, and proceeded to tell him that the Nazis had attempted to undermine sterling during World War Two by counterfeiting five-pound notes.

'Nevertheless the printing, distribution and circulation of billions and billions of counterfeit dollars would be a Herculean task. It would take the Iranians years to accomplish.'

Jill had a ready answer for that argument as well, and reminded him what had happened when the Iranians had occupied the American Embassy. In addition to the hostages they had taken, they had seized sacks and sacks of highly classified material that had been put through the shredder. Each piece of shredded paper was no thicker than a strand of cotton and had been woven into an amorphous mass. Yet somehow the Iranians had unravelled the individual strands and pieced them together to make a complete document. As a result the procedures for destroying classified documents had had to be changed. After shredding, the waste material was now burned in an incinerator and the ashes raked out and flushed away with a high-pressure hose.

'I'm sure these Iranian fundamentalists have the know-how, and more than the necessary patience to achieve their aim.'

'Maybe.'

'I strongly recommend we should pass the information on to Washington.'

'As I recall, you told us the Americans had heard similar rumours about a secret weapon and regarded it as wishful thinking by the Iranians. Indeed, you yourself had no faith in our source whom you graded D5.'

'This is a different source, Victor, and there is a lot more flesh on the bone. I really do think we should send a liaison officer over to Washington.' Jill stole a glance at her wristwatch. 'Well, I've said my piece.'

And by implication the rest was up to him but he wasn't about to take issue with her.

'Indeed you have,' he said, 'and very informative it was too.'

'Well, thank you, Victor.'

Jill stood up, walked towards the door, then turned about.

'Regarding the Cuban involvement,' she said, 'I just wonder if Raúl Garcia Menendez and his five million dollars' worth of diamonds is part of it.'

CHAPTER 24

Publicity was the last thing the SIS wanted but that didn't mean they could do without a press cutting service. Unable to employ a firm like Romeike & Curtice for security reasons, the task was performed by the Head of the Security Vetting and Technical Services Division with the assistance of a clerical officer from the registry. The first thing Frank Warren did every morning was to scan the daily newspapers looking for any report or article which touched on the SIS or a member of the staff, no matter how obliquely.

When Frank Warren had taken over the task of running the amateur press cutting service from the pay department, Kelso had airily told him it was literally a five-minute job. It had become almost a full-time occupation when the press had learned about the triple slaying at The Firs. From the occasional snippet which was circulated in leisurely fashion to the DG, his Deputy and Assistant Directors, Frank Warren had found himself photocopying dozens of column inches for immediate distribution. For two days the multiple slaying had been the major news story, then interest in the case had steadily waned so that within a relatively short space of time it was no longer being reported. There had been a brief flurry of interest when the Hosein brothers had been arrested but all the information the reporters had had to go on was the police statement and there hadn't been a lot of mileage in that for them. The *Sunday Times* had come the closest to revealing the SIS connection when the editor had published a feature on the wartime exploits of Captain Gus Dukes who'd won the DSO, MC and Croix de Guerre while working for the French Section of the Special Operations Executive.

The newspapers and periodicals were ordered in bulk by the

Library and Research Department of the Foreign and Commonwealth Office and were delivered to Vauxhall Cross by the special
courier service each morning at eight o'clock sharp. As was their
usual practice, they split the task down the middle, Frank Warren
taking his share of the tabloids as well as the qualities. There was
nothing in Monday's edition of the *Express*, the *Mail* or the *Daily
Telegraph* to exercise him; it was only when he reached the centre
pages of the *Guardian* that his stomach turned over.

'Have you found anything, Mike?' he asked the clerical officer.

'Not a thing.'

'Wish I could say the same.'

Warren cut out the offending report from the *Guardian*'s Moscow
correspondent and made four photocopies for immediate distribution before pasting the original to a sheet of A4 paper. The
original went to Hazelwood, the photocopies to Peachey, Kelso,
Garfield and Peter Ashton, whose name did not appear on the list
of those who'd been informed, which he wrote on the DG's copy. A
phone call to Kelso's PA established that morning prayers were still
in progress; knowing this he stopped off to see Ashton before
delivering the press cutting to the high-priced help on the top floor.

'Are you a *Guardian* man, Peter?' he asked.

Ashton looked up from the file he had open on his desk. 'Sorry,
Frank, I didn't catch what you said.'

'I wondered if you'd seen the *Guardian* this morning.'

'Don't take it.'

'You do now,' Warren said and gave him one of the photocopies.
'I figure forewarned is forearmed.'

'So I've heard.'

'Just remember, you didn't get the press cutting from me. OK?'

'I've been a *Guardian* reader since the year dot.'

'Good. I'll get along and play postman.'

The article was the kind of journalism which in the UK gave
government ministers apoplexy because it was patently obvious that
some disaffected civil servant with an axe to grind had leaked the
information to the press. In the case of the *Guardian*'s Moscow
correspondent, it wasn't difficult to guess the identity of the source;
exactly who the source wanted to embarrass was a lot harder to

deduce. Ashton was still pondering that one when Hazelwood's PA phoned to say that the DG wanted to see him asap. For Victor, as soon as possible meant drop everything and come running.

'You're getting to be quite a publicity hound,' Hazelwood told him when he duly presented himself. 'And don't pretend you don't know what I am talking about.' A smile touched the corners of his mouth. 'Inscrutable is not a word Frank Warren is acquainted with; catch him offguard with a question he hadn't anticipated and you can read him like a book.'

'You want to discuss the article?'

'Yes. We both know the source has to be Pavel Trilisser; the question is, can you tell me what he's up to?'

'You should ask Rowan Garfield. The Russian Desk is part of his empire and he's got a high-grade team.'

'Rowan is a good assistant director and there's no one better at analysing hard facts but when it comes to second-guessing people, he is not in your class. Besides, you know Trilisser better than anyone else.'

Ashton wished he didn't. Ruthless, treacherous and devious were three adjectives which sprang instantly to mind whenever he thought about Pavel Trilisser. The man was highly intelligent and had been blessed with more than his fair share of luck, which was one of the reasons why, having been heavily involved in the plots to overthrow Gorbachev and then Yeltsin, he had come through both débâcles unscathed. And survival was what his latest actions were all about.

He had told the *Guardian* correspondent that the signal, which the conductor had delivered to Ashton's escort shortly after the train had left Malaya Vishera, had been a fake. The two men who had been waiting for them at Navalocnaja were criminals, not police officers, and they had kidnapped Ashton and his two escorts.

'Trilisser is very clever, Victor. Up to the moment we got out at Navalocnaja he tells the journalist these are the hard facts because the train crew saw what happened and he can't take liberties with their evidence. Thereafter, when there are no witnesses to contradict him, he says this is what I think must have happened and proceeds to lie his head off. Suddenly Tweedledum and Tweedledee are two heroes because they tackled the gunmen and sacrificed their lives so that I could escape. And he concludes by expressing the hope that the Russian authorities will be able to hear my story because my evidence is crucial.'

'I've read what the *Guardian* man says he was told, Peter. I asked what conclusions you had drawn from the article?'

'He's not after me this time,' Ashton told him. 'And he doesn't expect the British Government to send me back to Moscow so that the investigating officers can hear what I have to say about the incident. No, this whole business has everything to do with Major General Gurov, the Chief of Police. Gurov hates Trilisser's guts and would like to put him away for ever. Ask Rowan, he'll tell you the same thing.'

'I don't have to,' Hazelwood said, 'I already know it for a fact.'

'All right, let's take it a stage further. Gurov knows what happened at the Ritz Grill and he has a particular interest in the case because Katya Malinovskaya used to be one of his officers. So when he learned that I have gone missing with the two escorts, he puts it about that Tweedledum and Tweedledee are his officers. It's his way of exerting pressure on Trilisser. Gurov wants Katya Malinovskaya because he believes she can link Mr Yeltsin's special adviser on Foreign Affairs with Nikolai Grigoryevich Yakushkin.'

'That's a very interesting theory, Peter. Now suppose you tell me who is going to come out on top?'

'Pavel Trilisser,' Ashton told him without any hesitation. 'Katya is too scared to go up against him. The *Mafiozniki* have already paid her one visit; if they should call again at Trilisser's request, she fears it won't be her car they will riddle with bullets this time.'

'What about Yakushkin?' Hazelwood paused, then said, 'Assuming he's still alive, of course.'

'Well, I imagine the Russian Intelligence Service sent him to brief Trilisser about Shahpour Bazargan. That's something Trilisser can't deny but he can belittle the information he received and imply that Yakushkin then decided to peddle his story to a foreign power. What's more, he can make the allegation stick. I had two hundred and fifty pounds on me, which was Katya Malinovskaya's last payment for services rendered. The notes were sequentially numbered, which would look bad for Yakushkin.'

'You're right, Major General Gurov is no match for him.'

'There is one other thing,' Ashton said. 'I believe the information Yakushkin gave us is good.'

'Jill Sheridan is of the same opinion.'

'I also think we should share it.'

'She made the same recommendation, said we ought to send somebody over to Washington to liaise with their Intelligence Services.'

'And will you?'

'As things stand, there isn't enough meat on the bone to justify it.'

Hazelwood eyed the cut-down shell case on his desk and, as if motivated by the fact there was no ash in it, produced a Burma cheroot and lit up.

'But I would if we had something concrete to offer on the Cuban involvement,' he added.

Isherwood had chosen the Westminster Arms in Marsham Street because the pub lay within walking distance of his office. It wasn't quite so convenient for Brian Thomas but he hadn't complained; after the acrimonious way they had parted company a week ago, Brian would have been prepared to go to the ends of the earth to meet him again. 'This is the last favour I do for you' – Isherwood recalled what he had said and smiled ruefully. He had meant it at the time but there was something about the ex-Detective Chief Superintendent that made it very hard to walk away from him. Brian was irascible, exploitive and was forever calling in 'markers' that had already been repaid over and over, but he was utterly loyal to his friends and he counted anybody who had worked for him as a friend. It was also a fact that certain information had come to light which in Isherwood's opinion should not be withheld from the SIS.

Punctuality was another of his qualities; Isherwood had suggested they meet at one o'clock and Thomas walked into the Westminster Arms exactly on time. He looked round the crowded bar, his forehead creased in a worried frown until he spotted Isherwood sitting at a small table near the entrance, then his face lit up and he eased his way through the crush to join him.

'It's good to see you again, Paul,' he said awkwardly.

'And you.' Isherwood cleared his throat. 'I got you a round of ham and a whisky,' he added gruffly. 'Thought it would save time queuing up at the bar.'

'What can I say?' Thomas picked up the whisky. 'Except, here's mud in your eye.'

'And yours,' Isherwood replied automatically.

'So how are things, Paul?'

'Fox is dead, somebody emptied a magazine of 9 mm into him.'

Thomas gazed at him, his mouth half open in astonishment.

'Where did this happen?' he asked, recovering.

'In Florida at the Everglades Motel ten miles west of Dania. I couldn't find it on the map.'

'I suppose there is no mistake?'

'Absolutely none. There was some initial confusion because he was travelling on a passport which had belonged to a Mr Charles Barclay. It all came to light thanks to the efficiency of a senior executive officer in the Home Office Police Department who discovered the original owner had died of a heart attack last October. She passed the information on to the Yard and asked us to interview the widow. The lady also sent us a copy of the fax the consul general in Miami had sent to the Foreign Office which showed the head and shoulders photograph which appeared on page 3 of the passport. This went the rounds, starting with the National Identification Bureau.'

'But of course they couldn't put a name to him.'

Isherwood nodded. Fox hadn't been convicted since he was a juvenile and the NIB didn't have a photograph of him.

'Organised Crime made him as soon as the fax reached them.'

Thomas picked up the ham sandwich and took a bite out of it.

'Did Fox get the passport from Irwin?' he asked, his mouth still half full.

'Yes.'

'Can you prove it?'

'He was nailed this morning following an identification parade.'

'The widow picked him out,' Thomas said and took another bite.

Isherwood smiled. It was an assumption rather than a question but Brian happened to be right. Dawn Marie had told the police constable who had interviewed her that knowing how strapped she was for cash, a family friend had found a buyer for her husband's passport.

'Who put her in touch with Irwin, Paul?'

'A fence called Wally Quade. Apparently he used to do business in North London and moved south of the river when Irwin left the Force. Barclay was employed as a warehouseman and worked in a depository. There can be few better hiding places for stolen property than among the items of household furniture which people have put into storage. As you might expect, the buyer preferred to remain anonymous. Consequently, apart from the usual vague description, all that Dawn Marie had been able to tell the constable about him was that he had a deep voice, answered to the name of Jeff and, according to what Quade had told her, had been in the police. That clinched it for the Organised Crime Squad.'

'And what's Irwin got to say for himself?'

'Very little at the moment. Having been questioned on and off for a week, Irwin had become very blasé about the whole business and wasn't a bit worried when he was picked up again this morning. Got the shock of his life when Barclay's widow picked him out in a line-up. Right now, he is conferring with his solicitor in the hope of doing a deal with us.'

Isherwood finished the pint of mild and bitter he had been nursing ever since he'd arrived at the pub and then wiped his mouth.

'What have your people done about Novaks Promotions Incorporated?' he asked.

'I don't know. Ashton was out of the country and I told Peachey everything I'd learned from you. He seemed to think the police should handle any enquiries.'

'We talked to the FBI, told them we had reason to suspect Novaks Promotions was engaged in criminal activities in this country and asked what they had on the firm. That was a week ago. This morning they came back with the news that Novaks Promotions Incorporated was no longer in business.'

The janitor at the Seascape Center had told the agent from the

Miami field office that Novaks was a one-man operation and he understood Mr Novaks had moved on to better things in Chicago.

'He left no forwarding address,' Isherwood continued. 'The office had been stripped bare – no fax machine, no answerphone, no filing cabinets. Novaks didn't leave any debts behind him either; settled his bill with the phone company and paid the landlord three months' rent in lieu of notice. One day Novaks was there, the next he'd vanished into thin air.'

'When did this happen?'

'Around the time Fox gave us the slip,' Isherwood said.

Norden was back in Savannah, back in the house on East State at Wright Square in the Historic District, back with the lush who was known as the Broker. He was there at the behest of Mr Rafael Valdes, one of whose minions had phoned his apartment in Jacksonville yesterday evening to convey his master's wishes. Given any choice, Norden wouldn't have come within a mile of this snooty, well-heeled son of a bitch but you didn't ignore a request from Mr Valdes, especially after you had accepted a fifty-thousand-dollar retainer. So here he was, sitting in the same conservatory on the east side of the house watching the Broker pouring himself a large Jack Daniel's into a Waterford tumbler while he waited to hear why he had been summoned to Savannah.

'Sure you don't want to join me, Mr Norden?'

'No, thanks, like I said, it's too early in the day for me.'

'Ah well, *chacun à son goût*, as the French put it.'

'I'm impressed,' Norden told him sourly. 'Now suppose you tell me what I'm doing here?'

'My name is Joshua, but you may call me Josh.'

'And I'm still waiting to hear what Mr Valdes wants me to do?'

'My word, we are impatient, aren't we?' The Broker reached inside the drinks cabinet, took out a large brown envelope and returned to the wicker table.

'You may open it, Mr Norden,' he said, and sat down.

The envelope yielded a dozen colour prints which, with the exception of one showing a large colonial-style house, had obviously been taken without the knowledge of either subject. There was also a Cellophane packet containing five diamonds.

'The man is Howard Labbett, Executive Vice President in charge of production at Drax Incorporated; the blonde tramp wearing the indecently short skirt and blouse with the plunging neckline is his second wife, Cora.'

Labbett was in his fifties, had lost most of his dark brown hair and was about five feet nine. A spare tyre was beginning to show around the midriff which even his made-to-measure expensive clothes could not disguise. Norden estimated that the man was at least fifteen pounds overweight for his height.

'How old is Cora?' he asked.

'Twenty-seven, and my name is Josh.'

'I knew she was under thirty – looks young enough to be his daughter.'

He thought Cora was a showstopper, tall, long legs, curves in all the right places. A series of photos showed her getting out of a car and walking across the parking lot towards a large supermarket.

'What's the car?'

'A Maserati; must have set Howard back all of eighty-five grand.'

'The lady has expensive tastes,' Norden observed.

'Yes she has. The colonial-style house cost him a cool 1.2 mil. Four years ago, he could have written a cheque for that amount without turning grey overnight but now the poor slob is in hock up to his eyeballs and is falling behind on his loan repayments.'

Norden learned that thanks to her lawyers, Labbett's first wife had been well provided for. Apart from keeping the family home, the judge had split their joint assets sixty/forty in her favour. He had also ordered Howard Labbett to pay her twenty-five hundred a month in maintenance.

'What are the diamonds for, Josh? To make him feel better?'

'No, they are purely symbolic to remind Labbett of what is on offer.'

'Like five million dollars, Josh?'

'You're very perceptive,' the Broker said, and smirked.

The five million would be paid in diamonds, the same gems that Raúl Menendez had tried to steal from his uncle. Diamonds were easier to transport if you were planning to start over in another part

of the world. Also, a lot of people looked askance when presented with a hundred-dollar bill and you couldn't carry fifty thousand of them around in an executive briefcase.

'Mr Valdes would like you to call on Labbett.'

'Surprise, surprise.'

'He lives in Richmond, Virginia, 1371 Nine Mile Road . . .'

'Hold it a minute.' Norden took out a Biro and wrote the address down on the back of a print which showed Labbett emptying the mailbox at the bottom of his drive. 'OK, you got a phone number?'

'Area code 804, then 2212.'

'What about Drax Incorporated?'

'The factory is down on the James River off the Osbourne Turnpike. But check with me first before you go down there and I'll see if Mr Valdes has any objections.'

The Broker finished the rest of the Jack Daniel's, then contemplated the empty tumbler as if mentally debating whether to have another one.

'Negotiations have reached a delicate stage,' he continued, 'and we want to keep it under wraps.'

'Sure.'

'What Mr Valdes wants from Labbett is a firm date for completion. If he shies away from giving one, lean on him. We own the title to his property; that should give you enough leverage without resorting to physical intimidation.'

'That's out, is it?'

'You didn't hear me say so. It's a matter of judgement. OK?'

'Yeah. Listen, before we go any further, can I ask a question?'

'Depends what it is.'

'What do they manufacture at Drax Incorporated?'

'Quality paper,' the Broker told him without a moment's hesitation.

As Ashton knew only too well, all claims for reimbursement were anathema to Roy Kelso no matter how justified they might be. He therefore wasn't too surprised when the Admin king stormed into his office clutching MoD form 1771, which Ashton had submitted to the Finance Branch early in the afternoon.

'Is this meant to be a joke?' Kelso said, and waved the form at Ashton. 'Do you seriously expect Her Majesty's Government to pay for an entirely new wardrobe?'

'I wouldn't call it an entire wardrobe,' Ashton said calmly. 'The list consists of a few items which were lost or damaged beyond repair during my recent spell in Moscow.'

'You should claim on your own insurance.'

'Mine won't cover the loss.'

'That's your fault, you should have taken out an All Risks Policy.'

'I did, but there is an exclusion clause – acts of God, war, civil unrest. Your own people have looked at my policy and they say the company won't pay up.'

Kelso was momentarily thrown but he was not the sort of man to give up the struggle without a fight, especially when money was at stake.

'Your claim is in excess of five hundred—'

'Only by a pound.'

'Some of these items must have been part worn. When, for instance, did you buy the suit?'

'I'm not sure – eighteen months – two years ago.'

'Well, there is no way we are going to pay for a new one.'

Ashton had submitted a claim for a hundred and sixty pounds which he'd thought was not unreasonable. Kelso, however, did not share his opinion and slashed it by half, then moved on to the next item on the list, reducing the cost of replacing a Van Heusen shirt by two-thirds. He was just getting into his stride when Hazelwood's PA spilled everything with a phone call to Ashton, informing him that his presence was required upstairs.

The extractor fan which had been installed in the DG's office was having to work overtime to cope with the smoke-laden atmosphere to which Peachey was contributing with his pipe. Both men looked inordinately pleased with themselves.

'You're off to Washington, Peter,' Hazelwood announced cryptically as he walked into the office.

'To do what?' Ashton asked.

'Liaise with the CIA first, then possibly their Treasury Team. You shouldn't be gone for more than a week.'

303

'I don't understand; this morning you said there wasn't enough meat on the bone to justify it.'

'The situation has changed since then.'

'It has?'

'Yes. When Shahpour Bazargan spoke of a Cuban involvement, we all thought he was referring to the country. Right?'

'That was the impression I got.'

'Well, we believe the Cuban involvement is limited to Rafael Valdes and the organisation the family created.'

'Why would he want to go against the United States? America took his family in when they fled from Castro.'

Peachey removed his pipe. 'Remember what I told you about the Valdes family when you called on me at Gower Street? Remember I told you Humberto Valdes was killed in the Bay of Pigs invasion? I think he blames the Americans for Humberto's death and that's his motivation.'

CHAPTER 25

Ashton had got off to a slow start. From the way Hazelwood had talked, he'd thought he would have just enough time to go home and pack a bag before catching the first available flight to Washington, DC, which only showed how wrong he could be. Instead of an early departure, the following day had been taken up by a detailed briefing on Iran and an update on the current situation in Moscow from Jill Sheridan and Rowan Garfield respectively. There had also been a slight change of plan; having given it some thought, Hazelwood had decided that Ashton should forget about liaising with the US Treasury and funnel everything through the CIA.

He had finally departed on British Airways flight BA219, which had arrived at Dulles International Airport at 16.30, some forty-eight hours after he had been put on stand-by. Head of Station, Washington, had sent his deputy to meet Ashton at the airport and convey him to the British Embassy for yet another briefing. This time the subject was Joe Carlucci, a senior analyst in the Near East Division of the CIA's Directorate of Operations, and the man he would spend the next few days with.

Carlucci had spent his entire career in the Near East Division and was widely regarded as the agency's foremost expert on the region. Head of Station believed Carlucci had the ability to go all the way to the top, but was unlikely to do so because his superiors were reluctant to give him the opportunity to acquire additional skills, when he was doing such a grand job where he was. Iran was very much his bailiwick. Carlucci had got to know the country as a young man when he had been posted to Tehran in 1974 at the age of twenty-three. Extended in post for a further twelve months beyond his normal end-of-tour date, he had left Iran for a desk job at Langley a mere fortnight before the Shah had been forced into exile. By a matter of days he had escaped the fate of his erstwhile colleagues who had been held hostage for a total of 414 days after a mob of Islamic fundamentalists had stormed the American Embassy. As a result, he had earned himself the nickname of 'Lucky' Carlucci.

There had been a time when the nickname had attracted a great deal of quite unjustified disapprobation. In 1982 the CIA had feared the USSR was about to grab Iran's South West Oilfield. To help the United States repel such an invasion, the agency had recruited former soldiers of the Shah and organised them into five-man teams to strike at the Red Army's lines of supply. Subsequently the CIA had tried to convert the teams into high-level unilateral intelligence gatherers. The operation had been run from a base in Frankfurt and despite a warning from the Chief of Operations, Near East Division, that the CIA's radio communications were not secure, most case officers had continued to act as if they were. Carlucci had been the sole exception; his agents had survived because he had gone off the air and ceased transmitting. The other teams, whose case officers had failed to heed the warning, had eventually been rounded up by the Iranian authorities, tried and executed.

In order to re-establish contact with his agents, who had been the only eyes and ears the CIA had left in Iran, Carlucci had received permission to operate out of Dogubeyazit, close to the Turkish border with Iran. Ankara hadn't been too happy about the proposal but had finally agreed under pressure from the State Department. It had then taken Carlucci four months to set up a courier network which had stretched all the way to Tehran. Information from the friendly sources in the capital had taken at least a fortnight to reach him and was therefore sometimes out of date. However, this human intelligence had still given the agency a political insight which the spy in the sky satellite and the Signals Intercept Service could not deliver. Before meeting him, Head of Station wanted Ashton to know there was no greater living expert on Iran than the American.

The meeting had been arranged for 10.00 hours. Fifteen minutes before the appointed time, Ashton reported to the control desk at Langley, presented his identity card for inspection by the security officer and completed a visitor's proforma. In return he was given a clip-on plastic tag and an escort to make sure he didn't wander into a prohibited area.

Carlucci was aged forty-four but there was no sign of the spreading waistline that usually accompanied middle age. Ashton reckoned the American was about two inches shorter than himself and weighed less than a hundred and twenty pounds. He had jet-black hair, dark eyes and a swarthy complexion. Dressed in the right apparel, he would have little difficulty in passing himself off as an Iranian, something he'd probably had to do when he'd organised the network of couriers. Head of Station had warned Ashton that the American was also noted for his abrasive manner.

'So you're the guy who's going to tell me about Shahpour Bazargan,' he said when they shook hands.

'You've got it wrong,' Ashton told him. 'I've never met the banker but Yakushkin has and it's his story I'll be giving you.'

'Go ahead then, I'm listening.'

Ashton had been called on to give the same briefing so many times now he could have done it in his sleep. He related how Yakushkin had met the Iranian banker, then encapsulated the plan which the Islamic Revolutionary Council had hatched to destabilise the US dollar and send it into free fall.

'How do you guys rate Shahpour Bazargan?' Carlucci asked.

'He's regarded as an A1 source.'

'You can't get any higher than that. How about his information? Is it equally strong?'

Initially Jill Sheridan had thought his story was probably true, an evaluation which owed a lot to Shahpour Bazargan's previous track record. She had subsequently revised her assessment downwards after considering the problems of production and distribution on a massive scale.

'We think there could be something in it.'

'But on the whole it's little more than a rumour?' Carlucci suggested.

'You're putting words into my mouth,' Ashton told him. 'I wouldn't be here if we thought it was just hearsay of doubtful accuracy.'

'Right. I hear the Cubans are providing some sort of backup.

Leastways that is what London would have us believe.'

'We don't believe it's Castro's lot.'

'Is there another Cuba we don't know about?' Carlucci enquired acidly.

'Maybe there is down in Florida or haven't you noticed?'

Carlucci smiled. 'I asked for that,' he said. 'Put it down to my ulcer; it's been acting up lately.'

'And I've got a short fuse,' Ashton told him, 'so I guess we're both saying sorry.'

'Well then, let's call it quits and start over. The Cubans?'

'They're a family called Valdes. Once there were four brothers, now there's only two, one of whom is in jail doing twenty years for second-degree murder. The other is a corporate lawyer and is currently running the family business.'

'Let me guess – drugs and prostitution, yes?'

'Plus a few casinos and an offshore bank in the Bahamas.'

Ashton told him everything he knew about Raúl Garcia Menendez and the small fortune in diamonds he claimed to have salted away. He left nothing out from the moment the Cuban-American had sought refuge at the British Embassy in Santiago to his disappearance from the safe house and the three dead men he had left behind him. He took Carlucci through the entire chain of circumstantial evidence which had started the night a young woman called Debbie had walked into the Isle of Dogs police station and blown the whistle on Fox.

'It's a Jim Dandy story,' Carlucci said when he'd finished, 'but a vital link isn't in place. Let's assume Shahpour Bazargan is right and the Iranians are planning a massive attack on the dollar. Let's also agree Valdes wanted his nephew dead and hired a bunch of people to do it. But what have you got that puts Valdes in the same camp with Tehran? And don't give me the Hosein brothers.'

'I don't think we should dismiss them out of hand,' Ashton said mildly, but the American had got the bit between his teeth and wasn't listening to him.

'And there's another thing: even if Valdes can't forgive or forget what happened to his brother at the Bay of Pigs, why would he want to sink the dollar? That would be tantamount to cutting his own throat.'

'The family owns the Standard World Wide Charter of the Bahamas. It's possible he's already converted a truckload of dollars into yen and Deutschmarks.'

Carlucci was silent for all of twenty seconds while he considered the possibility before putting it aside. There was no way, he maintained, anybody would get anything out of an offshore bank, especially one owned by Valdes.

'It's still something to keep in mind,' Ashton pointed out.

'Maybe, though I can't think why Tehran would need Valdes. What the hell can he do for them? And the kind of operation they envisage will cost a lot more than a hatful of diamonds.'

'Suppose Valdes is using the diamonds to buy somebody who can supply the Iranians with what they need?'

The American went silent on him again, this time for a lot longer than a mere twenty seconds.

'I think you may be on to something,' Carlucci said and scribbled on his scratchpad. 'If you're right, a lot of people will want to call the shots on this one – ourselves, the FBI, Treasury – the Oval Office will have to lay down some ground rules before we get our wires crossed.'

'Sounds a good idea.'

Carlucci looked up from his notes. 'How long do you plan to stay over here?'

'I thought I'd stick around to the bitter end.'

'You've no reason to—'

'You're wrong, I've got four very good reasons.'

Ashton ticked them off on the fingers of his left hand. 'Sharon Cartwright, Gus Jukes, Harvey Yeo and Larry Rossitor. Nobody kills one of ours and gets away with it.'

Peachey fed a ten-pence coin into the machine, pressed the button for decaf with milk and waited for the cup to fill. The coffee machine near the lifts was a recent innovation, one of the very few initiatives Roy Kelso had implemented which had met with general approval. Taking care not to spill any of the steaming hot coffee over his hand, he removed the polystyrene cup and gingerly carried it back to his office.

With the exception of Jill Sheridan and himself, everybody else had gone home. Although there were no crises in the Middle East to detain her, Jill had stayed on, busying herself with a clutch of float files that had been circulated to her purely for information. Her apparent diligence had everything to do with the fact that she knew he was expecting a phone call from Ashton. In the short time he had known her, Peachey had grown to dislike Jill Sheridan. Although by far and away the best assistant director, she acted as if she continually had to prove it. Had it been anyone else, he would have said it was the old problem of a woman feeling she had to be twice as good as her peers in what was essentially a man's world. But Jill wasn't lacking in self-belief. She was driven by naked ambition and was imbued with a single-minded determination to rubbish anyone she saw as a potential rival for the appointment of DG when Victor Hazelwood retired. To this end, she was ruthless, devious and, when necessary, completely unscrupulous. The way she had used Sharon Cartwright was but one example of that contention. Jill Sheridan knew how to cover her back and by all accounts no one was more adept at cultivating friends in high places.

The call Peachey had been waiting for came through at 18.42 hours. The satellite link was so clear that Ashton could have been in the same room instead of four thousand miles away in the British Embassy on Massachusetts Avenue.

'So how did you get on with Joe Carlucci?' he asked as soon as they had exchanged the usual pleasantries.

'At first he was abrasive, later on he was almost friendly.' Ashton cleared his throat. 'I won't say Carlucci was a hundred per cent sold on our hypothesis but at least he's checking with various Intelligence and law enforcement agencies to make sure that no wires get crossed.'

'Well, that's something.'

'I told Joe I wouldn't return home until this whole business was finished.'

'But now you're having second thoughts?' Peachey suggested.

'Too right. The fact is the ball is very much in the American court and I don't see what I can usefully contribute.'

'You could tell them Menendez has been found.'

'Alive?'

'No.'

'You'd better give me the whole story.'

There wasn't a lot to tell. The sanitation department of Bradford City Corporation had decided it was time to do some in-filling on the rubbish tip and had dispatched a bulldozer to the site. In the process of levelling a huge mound of litter in the south-east corner of the tip, the driver had uncovered the body of a male caucasian.

'Menendez had been shot twice in the back of the head with a small-calibre weapon, possibly a .22 pistol.'

'We've got a positive ID on the body?'

'Not yet,' Peachey admitted, 'but the description Chief Inspector Oldfield gave us certainly fits Menendez. I think you can take the ID as read.'

'Right. It will be interesting to hear what Valdes has to say when he learns that his nephew has been murdered in England.'

'So what are your plans now?'

'I guess I will stay on for a while.'

'Fine. I will let Harriet know what's happening.'

'You will let Harriet know,' Ashton repeated with heavy emphasis. 'You're being just a little presumptuous, aren't you, Clifford? In case it has slipped your mind, I'm her husband, not you.'

Ashton severed the connection before he could protest. It was a monstrous suggestion because it implied he secretly lusted after Harriet. Peachey could feel the colour suffusing in his face and his hand trembled as he attempted to fill his pipe with Dunhill Standard Mixture.

'Can I trouble you for a moment, Clifford?'

He looked up, still flushed. Jill Sheridan, who else? She was wearing a russet-brown and white check skirt with a hemline that hovered around the knees. Without waiting to be asked, Jill sat down, crossing one leg over the other, apparently oblivious of the amount of thigh she had unwittingly exposed. Unwittingly? In the short time he had known her, Peachey had learned that everything Jill did was premeditated.

'What can I do for you, Jill?' he asked.

'Well, I know that, technically speaking, it is none of my business but I can't help wondering how Peter is getting on.'

She was right, it was none of her business, though Peachey didn't tell Jill so to her face. Half the art of being a successful interrogator was to know when to be silent.

'The thing is, Clifford, we have received certain information from Tehran which could be less than helpful to Peter . . .'

She broke off in apparent confusion and looked down at some mark on the carpet which was only visible to her.

'There is no easy way to put this,' she continued, 'and I would hate for you to get the wrong impression.'

'Please don't hesitate to be frank,' Peachey told her.

'Well, the fact is Peter has got a pretty short fuse and he can be very hard-nosed.'

She looked down again, this time at her hands resting on her lap.

'I should know, we lived together before I was posted to Bahrain.'

Little Miss Modesty, Peachey thought, but the effect she sought was marred by the amount of thigh she was showing. But Jill was right, it didn't take a lot to provoke Ashton, as he had discovered to his cost. He had never been able to understand what Harriet saw in him, and maybe that was half his problem.

'Help me, Clifford.'

'What?'

'I need your advice what to do about this latest input from Tehran. I shouldn't be saying this because it implies I'm criticising Victor behind his back, but I can't help feeling we should have sent someone more senior than Peter to liaise with the CIA.'

'Like you,' Peachey suggested.

'Why not? I am Head of the Mid East Department and it's possible the people at Langley might be less alarmed by the news from Tehran if they heard it from me.'

'What news?' Peachey asked.

'Shahpour died at least seven weeks before Yakushkin allegedly saw him, which makes the major's story a bit dodgy.'

'What's the strength of this report?'

'It comes from a reliable source.'

'So why haven't we heard about his death before now?'

'Because we only asked for an update on Shahpour Bazargan when Peter returned from Russia. However, the question is, do you want me to pass this information on to Peter or not?'

Peachey was only too aware of his limitations. He was first and foremost an MI5 officer on loan to the SIS. All he knew about the Intelligence setup in the Middle East was what he had been told when he was taking up the appointment of Deputy DG. He did not feel qualified to make a judgement of Solomon.

'I think we should sleep on it,' he said, taking the easy way out.

'I'm sure that's the right thing to do,' Jill told him.

Peachey had a feeling that somehow he had been outmanoeuvred. He wondered if Jill had gone back to Tehran requesting Head of Station to confirm the report, and if so, what sort of delay had this imposed? There was, he decided, only one way to find out. Tomorrow he would send for the officer in charge of the communication centre and ask to see the flimsy of every outgoing transmission to Head of Station, Tehran.

The Tavern on the Green was situated on the outskirts of colonial Williamsburg roughly a mile from the William and Mary College. Norden would have preferred somewhere less isolated but the restaurant had been chosen by Howard Labbett. At least Cora had said it was her husband's idea, though Norden was inclined to doubt it. The venue was about an hour's drive from Richmond and he believed Cora had reckoned the Tavern was far enough from home to minimise the possibility that one of Howard's colleagues, friends or neighbours might run into him at precisely the wrong moment.

Cora was the real shaker and mover. It was she who had phoned Norden at the Holiday Inn after he had mailed the five stones to the Labbett residence on Nine Mile Road. He had enclosed a calling card on the back of which he'd said where he was staying and for how long and who he was supposed to be representing. Norden had also made it clear that he expected Howard Labbett to call him between 6 and 8 p.m.

Cora had suggested they met for dinner at six thirty. Norden arrived at the Tavern on the Green fifteen minutes before the appointed time in the Ford he'd rented from Budget two days ago. Barely five minutes later a blue-grey Maserati swept into the car park, made a tight U-turn and then halted uncomfortably near his own vehicle, forcing him to slide down in the seat before he was silhouetted by the headlights. The driver stabbed the accelerator, giving the deep-throated engine one last flamboyant snarl before cutting the ignition. Two doors opened and closed with a satisfying loud clunk that spoke volumes for Italian craftsmanship.

Norden stayed down and listened to their voices gradually fading away. When the Labbetts were no longer within earshot, he slowly raised his head and watched them enter the tavern. Cora was wearing a hip-length fur jacket; knowing something of her expensive tastes, Norden was sure it was a genuine sable.

The Tavern was late twentieth-century fake Georgian – coach lamps with 60 watt bulbs illuminating the entrance, solid doors made of composite wood that had been stained to look like oak and a liveried footman to give the place atmosphere. Inside, a log fire in an open hearth provided almost as much light as all the candles on individual tables. Accosting the maître d', who was more conventionally attired than the footman, Norden pointed to the booth where the Labbetts were sitting and informed him they were his dinner companions. As he approached their table, Cora greeted him with a dazzling smile in contrast with Labbett, who merely gazed blankly in his direction.

'I'm Fred Norden,' he said, and shook hands with each of them in turn.

'The insurance agent from Mutual Benefit,' Cora said and held on to his hand a fraction longer than was necessary.

'The guy who is going to make a fortune out of us,' Labbett muttered sourly.

'All of us will come out a lot richer as a result of this deal, Howard.'

No two ways about it, Labbett had been drinking. The narrow width of the table meant he was close enough for Norden to smell the peppermints he had been sucking to hide it. Back in Savannah, the Broker had indicated that the Executive Vice President of Drax Incorporated might try to back-peddle; in which case it would be necessary to lean on him. Thus far, Labbett had given him no reason to believe he might be difficult but now it looked as though he was hitting the bottle, which was just as bad.

'Don't pay any attention to my husband,' Cora told him. 'Howard got out of bed the wrong side this morning and has been like a bear with a sore head ever since.'

'OK, let's order something and get right down to business.'

'Sounds a great idea to me.'

As he turned to signal a waiter, Norden felt the inside of her right leg press against his. At first, he thought it was purely accidental but when he moved his leg slightly, hers followed suit. It was a variation of footsie under the table but more exotic, more sexually arousing. Cora kept it up through the hors d'oeuvres, her eyes, hard and bright like diamonds, never leaving him while she nibbled a stick of celery, except somehow it wasn't an edible leafstalk she was chompimg. Then suddenly she invited her husband to say what they had in mind.

'It's like this,' Howard said, laying it on the line for him. 'Cora flies to Zurich on her own, takes delivery of the merchandise and has it authenticated. Once that has been done, she will bank the final payment and call me. Then the people you represent can take delivery of some high-quality paper. Two thousand pounds' weight to be precise.'

Norden thought they were both indulging in wishful thinking. Nobody in their right mind was going to part with five million unless the money was secured in some way.

'I'm your collateral,' Labbett said as if he knew what Norden had been thinking. 'Tell that to your bossman and then get back to me.'

'It stinks.'

'Take it or leave it. This is a once-in-a-lifetime deal.'

'And that's your last word?'

'It certainly is.'

Norden grunted. 'You guys had better deliver,' he said.

'Oh, we will.' Cora managed to drop her napkin and bent over to retrieve it. As she straightened up again, her right hand brushed the inside of his thigh and briefly fondled his crotch, inducing an erection the like of which Norden hadn't experienced in a long time.

'You can count on it,' she added.

CHAPTER 26

It took the communication centre less than two minutes to produce the flimsy of the signal which Jill Sheridan had sent to Head of Station, Tehran, requesting an update on the present whereabouts of Shahpour Bazargan. Convinced that Jill Sheridan was bound to raise the subject at morning prayers, Peachey had got the foreman of signals to make a photocopy of the flimsy. To his surprise, nothing was said about the untimely demise of the Iranian banker, not even after he had given a verbatim account of Ashton's meeting with Joe Carlucci. Although he had managed to catch Jill's eye a couple of times her only response had been an enigmatic smile. He'd assumed Jill meant to buttonhole Victor Hazelwood when the meeting broke up but instead of hanging back, she had left the conference room with the other assistant directors. It was almost as if their conversation of yesterday evening had never taken place. Completely nonplussed by her behaviour, Peachey followed Hazelwood into the DG's office.

'Has Jill told you the news about Shahpour Bazargan?' he asked.

'What news?'

'Apparently he died seven weeks before Yakushkin said he saw him. I don't know precisely when that was, but it does make his information seem questionable. Last night, Jill asked me what she ought to do about the report because in her opinion it wouldn't help Peter one bit.'

'And what advice did you give her, Clifford?'

'I said we ought to sleep on it.'

'Quite right.'

'Yes, well, I'm rather surprised Jill didn't raise the matter this morning.'

317

'She probably assumed you were going to discuss the situation with me.'

Given his known aversion to Jill Sheridan, Peachey thought it was unlike Victor to be so understanding.

'I think you ought to see this,' he said and produced the photocopy of the flimsy.

The date/time group showed that the signal had been dispatched on Friday, 10 February, at 17.10 hours Greenwich Mean Time, which was the day Ashton had been debriefed after returning from Russia. The text was short and very much to the point. In essence, Jill had asked for a bulletin on Bazargan's state of health and present whereabouts.

'I don't see what you're so excited about,' Hazelwood said after reading the flimsy. 'I would have been annoyed if Jill hadn't asked for an update.'

'Look at the signal precedence, Victor – priority. Wonder Jill didn't make it routine or even deferred.'

'I would have said she got the precedence about right. Maybe with hindsight Jill could have put it up a notch to Op Immediate, but at the time she had no cause to think anything was amiss.'

'I wouldn't bet on it.'

Hazelwood opened the cigar box, took out a Burma cheroot and lit it.

'Would you care to enlarge on that cryptic observation?'

'Why not? On Friday the tenth, Jill rated Shahpour Bazargan an A1 source and believed his information was probably true. In fact she was the one who advocated passing everything on to the CIA in the face of your scepticism. She was also the first to attribute the Cuban involvement to the Valdes family. However, come Wednesday the fifteenth, she begins to have second thoughts about the Iranian banker, most notably after Ashton had departed for Washington.'

'Are you saying she had heard from Tehran before then?'

Peachey shook his head. Whatever else she might be, Jill Sheridan was no fool. She might have sat on the reply for a few hours while she pondered what to do with the information but that was the absolute maximum. The signal from Head of Station, Tehran, would have been logged in at the communication centre and recorded by the chief archivist of central registry before it was ever passed on to the Mid East Department.

'You're right,' Hazelwood told him. 'Jill would be caught out in a lie if she fudged the date of receipt. The worst thing you can say about her is that, after thinking about it, she decided to temper Friday's enthusiasm in case there was a blip.'

'So what should we do about the report?'

'File and forget it,' Hazelwood said promptly. 'The news of Bazargan's death won't help Ashton. These days the Americans have to rely on their satellites and signals intercepts to know what is going on in Iran, so they're unlikely to have heard about it. Besides, we don't know when Bazargan confided in Yakushkin or how long the Russians sat on the information before Trilisser decided to pass it on. Yakushkin told Peter that he'd met the Iranian banker at the official opening of a new steel plant at Esfahan last May. It's possible he could have learned about the counterfeit operation any time between then and Bazargan's death.'

They had no way of finding out. Yakushkin had disappeared and Katya Malinovskaya's office on Gorky Street had been closed since the night of her arrest.

'Sounds like wishful thinking to me, Victor.'

'Perhaps it is.' Hazelwood flicked the ash from his cheroot into the cut-down shell case. 'But if the Russians have sold us a load of disinformation, what are we left with? A Mafia-type contract killing which we should have walked away from.'

Same location, same security routine, same office, same view of a massive parking lot with its backdrop of bare deciduous trees, pretty much the same sceptical attitiude from Carlucci. Ashton wondered why he had bothered to drive out to Langley to give him the news about Menendez when his only reaction had been to ask if the police had found the blue Transit as well.

'The whereabouts of the Ford van doesn't matter a damn,' Ashton said heatedly. 'If the vehicle turned up tomorrow, the discovery would have no effect on Valdes. On the other hand, the fact that the body of his nephew has been found on a landfill site in England with two bullet holes in the head might just rattle him, should he be asked if he can think of a possible motive for the killing.'

'One thing you should know about Rafael, the FBI has been watching the family for years and they haven't got a damned thing on him. The Bureau may suspect he is running the family business while brother Arnaldo is in jail but they can't prove it. As far as the law is concerned, Rafael Valdes is snow white; he doesn't even have a traffic violation. Tax him with nephew Menendez and he'll probably tell you he hasn't had much to do with him because they move in different social circles.'

'Menendez stole several million dollars' worth of diamonds from his uncle—'

'So you told me yesterday,' Carlucci said, cutting him short, 'but you can't prove it. That's no reflection on you guys. From what I hear, pinning anything on Raphael Valdes is an impossible task. He's never been seen head to head with a shady character. The thinking is that if he needs to hire a foot soldier, he does so through a middle man.'

'Like he might have done with Novaks?'

'It's possible.' Carlucci reached into the pending tray on his desk and passed a photofit likeness to Ashton. 'This was faxed to the Miami PD and the FBI by your Scotland Yard.'

'This is Novaks?'

'Allegedly. The photofit was composed with the assistance of a guy called Irvine.'

'His name is Jeff Irwin,' Ashton said. 'He used to be a detective sergeant in the Metropolitan Police, left the Force in 1989 to become a private investigator and security consultant. He was suspected of being on the take; we linked him to Fox.'

'So the Bureau told me.'

'Can I keep the photofit?'

'I don't see why not, it's only of passing interest to me.'

Ashton waited, hoping the American might have something for him but Carlucci was not forthcoming. So far, the flow of information had been all one way and he needed to do something about that.

'Did you get anywhere with the Oval Office? I mean, who's calling the shots?'

'We're out of it. The CIA doesn't operate in the US. We did when Nixon was in the White House but not any longer.'

'I don't recall you mentioning that restriction yesterday. Matter of fact, I formed the impression you'd got the bit between your teeth and were raring to go.'

'Wiser heads have prevailed since then. The demarcation lines have already been established and, like I said earlier, Valdes belongs to the FBI. And while we're on the subject, in answering our many questions, the Bureau told us Raphael has had no contact whatever with anyone who might have been representing the Iranians.'

'They are a hundred per cent sure of that, are they?'

'Every place Valdes owns or rents is under electronic surveillance,' Carlucci said, and proceeded to list them – the law offices in Tampa, Fort Myers, Miami, Boco Raton, Daytona Beach and Jacksonville, the house on Jekyll Island, Georgia, the apartment on New York's Park Avenue.

'I'm impressed.'

'He's also subject to physical surveillance.'

'Round the clock?'

'That's not always possible; Valdes has a large cabin cruiser and his own Lear jet.'

And sometimes, as Ashton knew from personal experience, a surveillance team could lose contact with their target through sheer bad luck. Technical failures were not unknown either; the electronic listening device which was a hundred per cent effective a hundred per cent of the time had yet to be developed. In the light of these factors, Ashton found it hard to accept the FBI's assurance that Valdes had had no contact whatsoever with the Iranians. He fancied Carlucci shared his scepticism.

'What did the US Treasury have to say?'

'Treasury?' Carlucci repeated as if he didn't know what Ashton meant.

'About the feasibility of a conterfeiting operation on a massive scale. I thought somebody was going to consult the Treasury about the sort of materials Tehran might need to carry it out successfully.'

Carlucci took out his billfold and produced a hundred-dollar bill.

'This is the new version,' he said. 'A lot of people don't like the design; they say it looks like Monopoly money with its bigger portrait of Franklin. What counts is the watermark; it's only visible when held against a light source and does not copy on colour printers. The official paper for the bills is manufactured by Drax Incorporated of Richmond, Virginia, and sold only to the Federal Government. It would greatly assist the Iranians if they could acquire a standard roll weighing two thousand pounds. Tehran would find it hugely expensive to manufacture their own paper but if they don't care what it would cost them, then they could do it using the genuine roll as a guide. Their problem is that the US Treasury's Secret Service carefully monitors the storage and transportation of the paper.'

'What about the company's personnel?'

'Everybody in middle management and upwards has been screened. They are all clean; there are no compulsive gamblers, no heavy drinkers.'

Something in Carlucci's tone of voice encouraged Ashton to probe a little deeper.

'All good family men?' he asked.

'Depends what you mean. Like every cross section of society, Drax Incorporated has got its share of gay men and women but that's all out in the open. The Company is one big family. So when Howard Labbett, the Executive Vice President in charge of production, split with his wife and family, he kept the board fully informed.'

'Getting divorced can be an expensive business,' Ashton said.

'Don't I know it, but Drax Incorporated say Labbett is doing OK – even though he does have a new wife to support.'

'I imagine he must be very well paid?'

'Oh sure.'

It occurred to Ashton that the American was saying one thing and meaning another. He also noticed that Carlucci's gaze was focused on the photofit he was holding.

'I don't know how this will affect your plans but I have to tell you the agency is taking no further action on your information.'

'Well, I'll just stick around for a while, take in some of the sights.'

Carlucci nodded. 'Don't do anything I wouldn't do,' he said, and pressed a buzzer to summon Ashton's escort.

The signal from Moscow was classified Top Secret, carried an Op Immediate signals precedence and filled the equivalent of two sheets of A4. It was delivered to Rowan Garfield at 17.10 hours who, before walking the signal along the corridor to Hazelwood, committed the text to memory so that he would be able to answer any questions Victor might throw at him. He did not bother with the PA who liked to think she controlled access to the DG. When all was said and done, he was an assistant director and status did have its privileges. Besides, the open door and the green light above it told him the great man was free. Nevertheless he still tapped on the door and politely enquired if Victor could spare him a few minutes of his time.

'Not more bad news, I hope,' Hazelwood growled.

Garfield told him that Katya Malinovskaya had surfaced at last and placed the signal on his desk, then sat down while Victor read the text. Before Hazelwood even opened his mouth, he knew what the first question would be.

'Do we know who Messenger is?'

Messenger was the blanket alias to conceal the real identity of an individual. Raúl Garcia Menendez had been issued with a British passport in the name of Raymond George Messenger by the British Embassy in Santiago before he was flown to the UK.

'Messenger is a British advertising agent based in Moscow,' Garfield said, 'the Deputy Head of Station recruited him approximately six months ago.'

'One of our patriotic part-timers,' Hazelwood observed.

Every SIS station around the world had its quota of willing helpers drawn from businessmen and retired expats domiciled locally. All had volunteered out of a sense of duty and a desire to do something for their country. They did not expect to be financially rewarded for their services and many of them never even submitted a claim for out-of-pocket expenses. Businessmen and women were occasionally wined and dined by the SIS when they passed through London but they were the exception.

'I assume we took a good hard look at Mr Messenger before he was approached?'

'Moscow Station had their eyes on him for some months and of course we checked with MI5 to see if he was known to them. That was when we learned he had done six years in the Intelligence Corps from '75 to '81 and had been trained as an operator, Intelligence and Security.'

This had been a tremendous bonus because it meant that Messenger had been cleared by positive vetting. At Garfield's request, the Armed Forces Desk at Vauxhall Cross had obtained his security file and personal documents from the army and he had immediately liked what he had seen.

'So he's not one of those people who get a vicarious thrill from being on the fringe of the Intelligence world?' Hazelwood said.

'Absolutely not.'

'Why did he leave at the six-year point, Rowan?'

'He was a corporal and, although highly recommended, was unlikely to be promoted to sergeant before 1984. The army lost a good man when he decided to leave.'

'Where did he learn to speak Russian?'

'That was a qualification he acquired in civilian life before he went to Moscow and set himself up in business. I wouldn't say Messenger is a first-class interpreter but he has a pretty fair grasp of the language.'

'Is that what finally tipped the scales for George Elphinstone?'

For a moment Garfield was nonplussed, then the penny dropped. There were strict rules governing the employment of people like Messenger. It was axiomatic that part-timers were never to be given a task which could put them at risk. In this instance, Garfield thought Head of Station, Moscow, was right to employ Messenger outside the normal parameters and said so.

'Did Elphinstone clear this with you?'

Garfield hesitated. As far as he knew, Messenger had been asked to check out 124 Gorky Street every morning and advise the Embassy accordingly. The premises had been closed for over a week but this morning Messenger had discovered that Katya Malinovskaya was back in business and had promptly used his initiative. He had persuaded the Russian girl to accompany him to his offices on Petrovka Avenue on the pretext that the place had been burgled twice in the last month and wanted to know how he could make the property more secure.

'George is a little short-handed with Tim Rochelle out of action,' Garfield said and left it at that.

'Did the army train him as an interrogator?'

'There was nothing in his documents to show he had attended such a course.'

'Well, he obviously has a talent for it,' Hazelwood said.

It was, Garfield thought, the understatement of the year. Katya had really opened up to Messenger. She had told him that, after 'The Englishman', as she had referred to Ashton, had been delivered to the detention centre, she and Yakushkin had been taken to the Lubyanka, which was still being used by the Internal Security and Counter Espionage Service.

'Ashton got that wrong,' Hazelwood commented, looking up from the Op Immediate signal. 'He thought they had probably been taken to Moscow's Lefortovo Prison.'

Katya Malinovskaya claimed that for the first forty-eight hours of her captivity she had been held in solitary confinement and treated with the utmost severity. She had been placed on a bread and water diet, deprived of sleep and questioned for hours on end. The velvet glove treatment had started on the morning of the third day when the leg irons and manacles had been removed. The guards had also brought her a hot breakfast of sausage, omelette and buckwheat pancakes with sour cream. Later that same day she had been moved upstairs to a holding cell, which meant that instead of sleeping on a stone floor, she had a bed of sorts, three blankets and access to a lavatory and washroom under escort. There had been no further hostile interrogations, only a low-key interview with an elderly-looking captain, who had asked her when she had made the acquaintance of Major Yakushkin.

'Surprise, surprise,' Hazelwood said drily. 'Katya tells him she had never laid eyes on Yakushkin before she was bundled into the prison van and he accepts her word.'

'You think she was lying?'

'Whether or not Katya is being truthful is beside the point and immaterial. The fact is Trilisser was looking for an excuse to release her; that's why the elderly captain informed her that she was only arrested on the say-so of Yakushkin. Katya is also told that the major is a basket case and was removed from the Russian Embassy in Tehran because of his increasingly odd behaviour.'

'Head of Station thinks that was all part of Trilisser's plan to discredit Yakushkin.'

'George Elphinstone lacks imagination,' Hazelwood said dismissively. 'But I don't suppose I need to tell you the real reason why Katya was taken to see Yakushkin at the Serbsky Institute of Forensic Psychiatry in Kropotkila Lane the day before she was released?'

Garfield managed a knowing smile. In his eagerness to deliver the signal to Hazelwood, he had merely committed the information to memory and hadn't thought to read between the lines. What was it Messenger had said about Katya? She was as jumpy as a cat on hot bricks – practically scared witless? Well, no wonder. She had seen the state Yakushkin was in and knew the same treatment awaited her if she ever deviated from the story the Internal Security and Counter Espionage Service had fed her.

'Committing Major Yakushkin to the Serbsky Institute was a smart move,' Hazelwood said. 'At a stroke, Trilisser removed the one man who could have put him in the dock and ensured that Katya Malinovskaya would keep her mouth shut. Major General Gurov, the Chief of Police, must be gnashing his teeth.'

'And have we fared any better?' Garfield asked.

'Despite everything, I'd still run with the information Yakushkin gave us, though what the Americans will do with it is another matter. On the debit side, I doubt if we will ever be able to manipulate Pavel Trilisser again. We twisted his tail once too often and damn nearly lost Ashton in the process.'

'And Tim Rochelle.'

'I hadn't forgotten him, Rowan.'

'Seems to me we come out of it rather badly if you take the Menendez business into account.'

Hazelwood didn't agree with him. Fox was dead, the Hosein

brothers had been charged with murder and Irwin, despite being co-operative, was looking at a long term of imprisonment for aiding and abetting a whole string of serious offences.

'It's still a bit of a Pyrrhic victory.'

'Some you win, some you lose,' Hazelwood told him. 'This is one which you have to walk away from and cut your losses.'

'What exactly does that mean, Victor?'

'It means I am going to send a signal to Washington recalling Ashton.'

Ashton checked out of Loews L'Enfant Plaza Hotel where he had been staying, drove across town to Alexandria and then headed south on Interstate 95. A little over two and a quarter hours after leaving Washington, he registered at the Shenandoah in Richmond. Carlucci hadn't told him where the Executive Vice President in charge of production at Drax Incorporated lived but that wasn't a problem. The telephone directory listed only one Howard Labbett. Finding the way to 1371 Nine Mile Road presented no difficulty either; from the gift shop in the hotel arcade he purchased a Rand McNally map of the city. What did exercise him was how he was going to spook Labbett without getting his head blown off.

CHAPTER 27

'Time spent on reconnaissance is seldom wasted' was one of the oldest maxims in the army. If he closed his eyes and listened intently, Ashton could still hear the plummy voice of the passed-over major who had drummed the adage into him when he had been a cadet in the University Officers' Training Corps at Nottingham. Years later he had seen that age-old piece of wisdom proved time and time again during the Falklands campaign. It was the reason why he had driven out to Nine Mile Road in the Pontiac he'd rented yesterday from Avis before going to the CIA Complex at Langley. What he knew about the Labbetts could have been written on the back of a postage stamp; running his eye over the property at 1371 while there was still an hour of daylight left could only increase his knowledge.

The Labbett house owed a lot to the antebellum school of architecture and Margaret Mitchell's *Gone with the Wind*, but Tara it wasn't. The house wasn't tall enough for the pseudo Graeco-Roman columns supporting the porch above the front entrance, and it created the illusion that the whole property had been compressed in a giant vice. But the feature which really killed off the old plantation theme was the adjoining treble garage which in no way resembled a coach house.

The house had been built on the crest of a slight rise. The neighbouring property on the west side of the house was a good seventy-five yards away, while that to the east was hidden from view by a belt of trees. There were no buildings on the opposite side of the street to mar the Labbetts' view and for all Ashton knew they enjoyed pretty much the same unspoiled outlook at the back of the house. To give the owners even more privacy, the developer had landscaped the front yard, planting shrubs and evergreens on the east and west boundary lines.

Although lacking the necessary local knowledge to put a price tag on it, the property looked expensive to Ashton, the kind of real estate that was unlikely to change hands under seven figures. Maybe that sum was within the reach of an Executive Vice President of Drax Incorporated but Labbett had two wives to support and surely that must stretch him financially? Or did the second Mrs Labbett have money? What proof was there that he was in debt up to his eyeballs? None whatever. Everything was based on supposition, including the fact that the Iranians needed to obtain a specimen roll of the new official paper being manufactured for the US Treasury if the counterfeiting operation was to be successful.

Acting on this premise, Carlucci had obtained a list of Drax executives, looked for a vulnerable insider and had picked on the Vice President in charge of production because after Labbett had been divorced, he had immediately acquired a new wife. But Labbett had been screened and pronounced OK by the Treasury. However, security procedures were never infallible; they could be undermined by complacency, human error or a lack of vigilance on the part of line management. Such lapses had occurred more than once in both MI5 and the SIS, and the Americans were equally culpable. For years the CIA had ignored clear evidence that Aldrich H. Ames was enjoying a life style way above what he could afford on his salary. It was therefore worth taking a good, hard look at Howard Labbett.

A blue-grey Maserati swept past Ashton, the offside indicator winking. At first he assumed the driver was signalling an intention to overtake a stationary vehicle but then the Maserati made a sharp left turn into the driveway of the Labbetts' house. As it did so, Ashton saw that the driver was a blonde woman in her late twenties or early thirties. Showing fine judgement, she touched the brakes, slowing the car just enough for the up-and-over door to respond to the radio signal. This enabled her to drive straight into the garage and park next to a dark green Volkswagen. Ashton watched her get out, walk round to the back and open the trunk to collect a large bag of groceries before going into the house. As the door began to descend, the second Mrs Labbett straightened up, turned about and gazed at him. They were too far apart for Ashton to see her features clearly but her rigid posture conveyed an air of hostility.

What now? Did he hang around until Howard Labbett came home? Or should he call it a day? And do what? Produce the photofit of Novaks and ask if she recalled seeing him recently? Nothing like the direct, blunt approach, but would it get him anywhere? Ashton drummed his fingertips on the rim of the steering wheel. If Howard Labbett intended to trade a roll of official paper for a fistful of diamonds, it was odds on his second wife knew what he was up to. And if snap impressions counted for anything, Labbett had got himself a very cool lady.

There was one further option: he could apply a little psychological pressure now to hot things up, then really turn it on when Labbett came home from work. Ashton started the engine, checked to make sure the road behind was clear, then executed a three-point turn and headed back towards Richmond. Three miles down the road a blue and white patrol car passed him travelling in the opposite direction at speed. A few minutes later he saw it again in his rearview mirror and wondered what had prompted the police officers to make a U-turn and come up behind him. He found out soon enough when the driver flashed his headlights and flicked the siren on and off. As he pulled over and stopped, the tannoy clicked on and a harsh metallic voice ordered him to get out of the car and place both hands on top of his head. It was the sort of order only somebody tired of life would ignore.

There were two of them, youngish-looking men bundled up against the cold in hip-length, double-breasted pea jackets that made them appear more intimidating than they already were. The driver stayed back with the prowl car, holding a revolver on Ashton while his partner moved in from the flank, taking care to stay out of the line of fire as he did so. Halting some ten feet away he ordered Ashton to turn about.

'You mind telling me what I am supposed to have done?' he asked politely.

The officer took a deep breath. 'Turn about. Do it now,' he roared in a voice that a good many drill sergeants would have envied.

Ashton gritted his teeth and did as he was told. Covered by his partner, the officer then handcuffed Ashton's wrists behind his back, undid his topcoat and subjected him to a none too gentle body search. Coming on top of his experiences in Russia, policemen were rapidly becoming his least favourite people.

'Whose passport is this?' the officer demanded.

'Mine,' Ashton told him.

'Where's it say that?'

'Try looking in the back.'

'Damned if you ain't right. Ashton, Peter, British citizen. Well lookey here, Lew,' he drawled, 'we've got ourselves a Brit.'

'Does that change anything?' Lew asked.

'Hell no, we'll still take him in for questioning. He's got a lot of explaining to do.'

'You should read him his rights then. We don't want to foul up on Miranda Escubo.'

'Never mind all that,' Ashton snapped, 'exactly what offence have I committed?'

It should have been a simple enough question to answer but the two officers made a meal of it, reciting statute after statute. Stripped of the legal verbiage, Ashton concluded he was being charged with the American equivalent of loitering with intent as applicable in Virginia. Neither officer would disclose the identity of the informant but it wasn't hard to guess who had made the 911 call.

The officer called Lew put Ashton in the back of the police car, leaving his partner to follow on in the Pontiac. The whole incident had lasted ten minutes. During that time, upwards of fifty vehicles had passed by, heading into or out of Richmond. To the best of Ashton's knowledge, not one driver had spared them so much as a passing glance. It seemed their little drama had been an everyday occurrence.

Norden walked into the Arrivals Hall at Richmond International Airport and made straight for the nearest bank of pay phones. He had been on the go from the moment he had left the Tavern on the Green shortly after Howard Labbett had delivered his ultimatum last night. He had called the Broker from his hotel room and hinted at a problem that needed to be quickly resolved; this morning he'd caught the US Air flight to Savannah departing at 06.30 hours.

After spending a little over five hours closeted with the Broker at the house on East State at Wright Square, he had still made the return flight leaving at 15.10 hours.

US Air had arrived on schedule and the time was now 17.46. Cora had told him they usually dined at seven because her husband always stopped off for a drink at his favourite bar in town on the way home from the paper mill. Norden found a vacant pay phone, fed a quarter into the slot and punched out 804-2212, confident that Howard Labbett wouldn't answer. The blonde tramp, as the Broker had seen fit to describe her, didn't keep him waiting long . . .

'Hi, it's me – Fred,' he said when she answered. 'I'm at the airport.'

'Where are you off to?'

'Nowhere, I've just got back.'

'I didn't know you'd been away.'

'I had to find out whether my associates would agree to your terms and conditions.'

'And did they?' Cora asked.

'That's something we need to talk about.'

'Howard won't be home before seven.'

Norden clenched the phone in a grip of steel. The bitch was acting coy, playing games with him as though he were a piece of string she could twist around her little finger.

'I meant you and me,' he growled.

'Well, that's a different ball game,' Cora told him in a voice full of innuendo. 'Where shall we meet?'

'Pick me up from the airport. I left my car at the hotel.'

'If you're thinking of taking me back to the Holiday Inn you can forget it.'

'I figured you'd know some place we could go.'

'Maybe I do.'

Damn right she did. He knew more about Cora than she could possibly imagine. The Broker had told him all about the former nurse at Henrico County General Hospital who'd married and divorced a Coca-Cola sales representative before she had snatched Howard Labbett from his first wife.

'So when can I expect you?' he asked.

'Give me twenty minutes.'

'I'll wait for you outside the terminal building then.'

'OK. Look out for a dark green Volkswagen, one of the original Beetles.'

'Anything else?'

'Yeah, I'll be wearing a fur hat.'

'And the rest?'

'That's for you to find out,' Cora told him with a throaty laugh, and hung up.

Norden put the phone down and walked away to kill a few minutes in the coffee shop. Cora Labbett was available; that was the coded message she had been sending him from the moment they'd met. Although not averse to accepting what was on offer, he wished he could be certain what the attraction was for her. It was easy to see why she had gone after Howard Labbett. Mistakenly, she had thought he was the crock of gold at the end of the rainbow. It had been her bad luck that the first Mrs Labbett and her attorney had practically had the shirt off Howard's back.

But the good tooth fairy was about to drop five million dollars into his lap, which should have made Cora a happy and contented woman. So why was she making a play for him? It sure as hell had nothing to do with his charismatic personality. Norden finished the mug of coffee and left, the question still unanswered.

He could have set his watch by Cora Labbett. He had phoned her at ten minutes to six and it was exactly ten after when she arrived in the Volkswagen. Opening the nearside door, Norden got in beside her and barely had time to fasten the seat belt before she pulled away from the kerb.

'What kind of answer did you bring back for me?' Cora asked. Norden thought it significant that she said 'me' and not 'us'. It seemed Howard didn't count. If that was the case, it could be she was planning to dump husband number two – but not for Norden himself. Cora had somebody else waiting in the wings.

'The people I represent were not happy about Zurich,' Norden told her.

'But you talked them round. Yes?'

'They agreed to meet you halfway.'

'Meaning they imposed certain conditions?'

'Yeah. Before you take off for Switzerland, Howard has to say when the stuff can be collected. They want an exact date.'

'No problem.'

'Secondly, one of their men will be holding your hand the entire time. He will be on the same plane to Zurich, stay at the same hotel in an adjoining room. He'll be a sort of bodyguard.'

'I hope you've got that job.'

Norden shook his head. 'I'll be handling things this end.'

Valdes was taking every possible step to distance himself from the operation but there was nothing new about that. The only time Norden had met him face to face had been on board his launch off Jekyll Island. On every other occasion he'd dealt with the Broker.

'Maybe we can do something about getting you the job?' Cora suggested.

'You can always try,' Norden said in a noncommittal voice.

Cora tripped the indicator to show she was turning left off Airport Drive on to Interstate 295. Shortly after crossing the Chickahominy River she made a right and followed a dirt road to a log cabin.

'It belonged to my dad,' Cora told him. 'He used to bring me here to go fishing when I was a little girl. We still use it occasionally even though it is kind of basic.'

Norden wondered who she meant by 'we'. Somehow he couldn't see Howard Labbett roughing it from choice. There was no power line; electricity was supplied by a diesel generator which Cora started without any difficulty. The accommodation consisted of two small bedrooms, a washroom, kitchenette and a living room furnished on simple lines. The lavatory was a chemical toilet out in the woods. Background heating was provided by three hot-air blowers placed strategically around the room. There was also a big open hearth and a pile of logs waiting to be laid in the grate. The cabin was not as cold as Norden had expected, which made him think she had been there earlier in the day.

'Can I get you a cup of coffee?' she asked.

'I've already had one at the airport.'

'Something stronger then?'

'What have you got?'

Cora removed her fur hat, shucked off the tweed coat she had been wearing and draped it over a rocking chair, then went into the kitchenette and opened one of the cupboards.

'I've got Jim Beam, Chivas Regal, Jack Daniel's—'

'Chivas Regal,' Norden said, interrupting her. 'No ice, no water.'

'Haven't got ice anyway.'

He heard her open another cupboard and assumed she was looking for a glass. When Cora reappeared with his whisky, he saw she hadn't bothered to pour herself a drink.

'I'm driving,' she explained.

'I had noticed.'

Cora gave him the glass of whisky, then curled herself up in one corner of the settee, both legs tucked under her rump.

'Why don't you come over here and sit down,' she said, and patted the nearest seat cushion.

'Maybe I will. I guess there's enough room for two.'

'I want you to be honest with me. Can Howard get away with it? I'm talking about the Treasury paper he'll be helping you to steal.'

'I can't tell you, I don't know how it's going to be done. I'm only a link man.'

'How it will be done isn't important,' Cora said impatiently. 'Soon as the theft is discovered, Howard will be the number one suspect.'

'So will every other vice president.'

He could tell it wasn't what she wanted to hear. Cora had her own opinion and was determined to share it with him. He had to understand that, for all his bluster, Howard was essentially a weak man. He wouldn't hold up under prolonged questioning and would cut the best deal for himself.

'I don't want to go to prison, Fred.'

'Neither do I,' Norden assured her.

'Promise me I won't go to jail.'

'I don't see—'

'Howard is a danger to us both.'

While he is alive, Norden thought. That was what she left unsaid, certain in her own mind that he would draw the appropriate conclusion.

'Maybe I can do something,' he said.

Cora was wearing a dark green button-through wool dress – very simple and undoubtedly very expensive. Tentatively, he reached out with his free hand and undid the one near the hemline. When she made no effort to brush his hand away, he continued until the dress was undone to the waist.

'Seems to me you already are,' Cora said as she straddled him.

Although the two patrolmen had been reluctant to let him go without a struggle, Ashton had rapidly become a major source of embarrassment to the Richmond PD. The woman who had reported him to the police had given the 911 operator a corrupted name and phone number. In an attempt to resolve the matter speedily, Ashton had suggested the unknown informant was probably a Mrs Labbett, which had proved something of a mistake. Unable to get a reply when they'd rung the house, the two patrolmen had driven out to Nine Mile Road only to find no one was at home. Thoroughly frustrated, they had concluded that he had deliberately wasted their time and they had wanted to press charges.

Ashton had done the only thing he could and played the diplomatic card, claiming immunity. Although the assertion hadn't secured his immediate release, it had persuaded the two patrolmen that he was out of their league and they had moved him onward and upward. The Police Department had no desire to be sued for wrongful arrest and had wanted to believe his story. A phone call to the British Embassy had finally removed any lingering doubts they might have had about him.

The Deputy Head of Station had been less than thrilled with Ashton. For one thing he'd only just got home after working late at the Embassy when the resident clerk had phoned to report that Ashton had been apprehended in Richmond. As a result, he'd had to turn round and go straight back to Massachusetts Avenue. He was also annoyed that Ashton had checked out of Loews L'Enfant Plaza Hotel without informing anyone or advising the SIS cell where he was going and for what purpose.

'We've had a signal from London,' the Deputy Head of Station had informed him in an icy voice. 'You've been recalled. I'm advising Vauxhall Cross that you will be on British Airways flight BA1850 departing at 09.40 hours tomorrow morning, so you'd better get your body back here pretty damn quick.'

From the faint smile on his lips, Ashton got the impression that the Borough Commander, who'd eavesdropped on their conversation, had not been too unhappy to hear him getting a roasting.

Free to leave at last, he collected his personal effects from the desk sergeant and signed for them. For some reason, the photofit likeness of Novaks, which had been folded in four and tucked inside his wallet, had been ignored by the arresting officers. It had been his passport that had attracted their interest. It had been issued the day before he had left for Washington to replace the one that had been stolen in Russia. In their eagerness to find something to charge him with, the two patrolmen had tried to maintain it was a forgery because the passport was so obviously brand-new.

Ashton buttoned up his topcoat and walked out of the station house into the cold night air. The Pontiac was parked between two blue and whites to the left of the entrance. Unlocking the doors, he got in behind the wheel, belted up and started the engine. It was only after he had reversed out of the parking slot and was edging into the traffic on Broad Street that he discovered that one of the patrolman had left his personal radio between the seats.

Up till that moment, Ashton had intended to pick up his baggage from the Shenandoah Hotel and drive straight back to Washington. The personal radio tugged him in an altogether different direction. He had never walked away from unfinished business before, and with Washington only a hundred miles from Richmond, he had plenty of time in hand. From the glove compartment he took out the Rand McNally map of the city and, using one hand, opened it up on the adjoining seat. Glancing at it now and again, he navigated his way to Nine Mile Road.

The up-and-over door of the garage was in the raised position. The blue-grey Maserati was still there but the Volkswagen Beetle had gone and a much-used Oldsmobile now occupied the third space. Ashton drove on slowly past the house and parked the Pontiac off the road beyond the belt of trees on the east side of the property where he hoped it wouldn't be seen. Alighting from the car he tripped the central locking and walked back to the Labbett residence.

CHAPTER 28

The lights were on in the hall, in the room immediately adjoining it and upstairs on the landing, otherwise the rest of the house at the front was in darkness. Ashton had a hunch that Mrs Labbett was the stronger character of the two and the probability that she wasn't at home could make his task that much easier. Even so, gaining admittance to the house would not be a pushover. The old Metropolitan Police warrant card might have fooled Labbett long enough for him to get a foot in the door but he had left that behind in the office safe and would have to improvise something. He took out his passport and folded the end cover back on itself so that his photograph and personal details could be seen, then cupped the document in his palm as if it were a badge of office.

The doorbell summoned a paunchy-looking man in his early to mid-fifties who'd lost most of his dark brown hair and whose features were also beginning to show signs of wear and tear. There was a strong smell of bourbon on his breath.

'Mr Labbett?' Ashton flashed the passport at him. 'My name is Peter Ashton, I'm from the British Embassy Defence and Liaison staff.'

'Yeah? Well, I'm not with the military, so you must have got the wrong address.'

'You are Mr Howard Labbett, Executive Vice President in charge of production at Drax Incorporated?'

'Yeah, yeah. What the hell is this?'

It was a good question and a difficult one for Ashton to answer. Joe Carlucci had steered him towards Labbett but only because he was thought to have financial problems and might therefore be open to bribery. Furthermore, it was entirely conceivable that Carlucci would not have named the Vice President had he not pressed him. In short, there was absolutely nothing to connect Labbett with Valdes, the Iranians or Novaks. The only thing Ashton had going for him was a smooth tongue.

'It's a matter of international security, Mr Labbett,' he said glibly.

'You're kidding me!'

'I know you've been screened by the FBI which means you are permitted occasional access to secret material.' Ashton returned the passport to the inside pocket of his topcoat. 'May I come in?'

'No way.'

'You're right to be suspicious, Mr Labbett. After all, you don't know me from Adam. Tell you what, why don't you call the precinct house on Broad Street and ask for the Chief of Police? He'll confirm I'm with the British Embassy.'

'You should see a psychiatrist, you need counselling,' Labbett told him and started to close the door in his face.

'I've got an even better idea.' Ashton put his left foot in the jamb and kept it there. 'Ring the CIA at Langley and tell the switchboard operator you want to speak to Joe Carlucci. Ask for his home number and don't let anyone fob you off—'

'Got your goddamned foot out of the way before I stamp on it.'

'Don't forget, you want Joe Carlucci. He's a senior analyst in the Directorate of Operations, Near East Division.'

'That's it, I'm through listening to your crap, asshole.'

Labbett was making all the right noises for an angry man but wasn't translating them into action. He was hesitant because he couldn't decide to what extent Ashton was bluffing. At least so Ashton hoped.

'Got off my fugging property.'

Still full of bluster and even more indecisive if that were possible. Ashton figured one more shove might push him over the edge.

'Have it your way, Mr Labbett,' he said. 'I'll back off and give you a breathing space to think it over. Say ten minutes. If after that time you still won't let me into the house, I'll leave and try again tomorrow. This time at the paper mill; that should make a lot of people sit up and take notice, especially the US Treasury.'

Ashton withdrew his foot from the jamb and walked away. Labbett didn't close the door on him even when he reached the bottom of the driveway, which made Ashton wonder who was bluffing who. The conundrum was answered to his satisfaction when he turned about on the sidewalk and the American quickly back-pedalled down the hall like a frightened rabbit retreating into a burrow.

Ashton turned to his right and continued on past the belt of trees on the eastern boundary, collected the personal two-way radio which he'd left in the Pontiac and then retraced his steps. When he turned into the driveway this time, a powerful security light clicked on to silhouette him against the dark background, the way a target is illuminated in an indoor firing range.

He had heard it said there were enough privately owned hand-guns, semi- and fully automatic rifles to provide every man, woman and child in the United States with their own personal firearm. If that were true, chances were that Labbett possessed an entire arsenal of weapons. Instead of being charged with manslaughter, any householder who shot and killed an intruder was more likely to receive a commendation or so the desk sergeant and arresting officers had gleefully informed him. Suddenly apprehensive, Ashton dipped into the pocket of his topcoat, switched on the two-way radio and turned the volume right down to eliminate the background mush.

The minutes ticked slowly by, each one seeming like five as he stood there motionless, caught in the glare from the security light. Although the traffic was a lot thinner than it had been when the police had stopped him on the outskirts of Richmond, the road was far from being deserted. The Volvo estate which passed the house heading west on Nine Mile Road was the sixth vehicle to have done so in the same number of minutes. All it needed was one driver to call 911 and the two-way radio in his possession virtually guaranteed he would find himself in serious trouble with the police. He checked his wristwatch, saw that the time limit he'd set had expired and was about to leave when Labbett appeared in the garage and beckoned him to come in.

'Forget it,' Ashton said in a loud voice. 'Go back inside and open the front door. That's the only way I am going to enter your house.'

'OK, have it your way,' Labbett told him, and turned on his heel.

Ashton smiled. Maybe he was getting a little paranoic but it would be all too easy for Labbett to shoot him and then make it appear that he'd broken into his kitchen. The police would be inclined to believe his story because he'd already been reported for loitering with intent. On the other hand, they knew no self-respecting burglar would dream of effecting an entry under the full glare of the security light and the body of an alleged intruder lying in the hall would therefore be harder to account for.

The front door opened and Labbett stepped outside.

'Happy now?' he asked.

'Ecstatic.' Ashton walked up the driveway and cut across the lawn.

'I guess you must think me a real s.o.b., Mr Ashton, but your story did sound kind of weird and we have our share of crazies in this neck of the woods.'

'I'd have been suspicious in your shoes,' Ashton told him.

'Anyway, I took your advice and called Langley and the people there put me on to Joe Carlucci. He said you were A OK.'

'That's a relief.'

'So what do you say we start afresh, Peter? It is Peter, isn't it?'

'Yes.'

'And I'm Howard. OK?'

The friendliness was overdone and jarred on Ashton. A neutral observer listening to Labbett welcoming him into his home could be forgiven for thinking Ashton was an honoured guest.

'This is what I call my den,' Labbett said, ushering him into a large room at the front of the house.

The den was roughly thirty feet by eighteen and was furnished with a pool table, a wall-mounted, giant-size TV screen, a wine-coloured leather-upholstered three-piece suite and a small bar with two high stools in the left-hand corner of the room near the door. There was also a display cabinet containing two sporting rifles and a pump-action shotgun. On a mahogany desk, an Apple computer shared the worktop with a portrait gallery of a voluptuous-looking blonde.

'That's my wife, Cora,' Labbett informed him without waiting to be asked.

'A very attractive lady,' Ashton murmured. He noticed there were no photographs of the children Labbett's first wife had borne him.

'She surely is. You want to take your coat off and make yourself comfortable while I fix us a drink?' Labbett went behind the bar. 'I've got Scotch whisky, gin, cognac, vodka and every kind of mixer you can name.'

'Just a soda water for me – I'm driving.'

'Hey, come on, fella, be sociable. One short won't do you any harm.'

It could however detain him longer than he'd anticipated and Ashton suspected this was precisely what Labbett wanted.

Cora Labbett took her eyes off the road for a split second to glance at the speedometer, saw the needle was hovering on sixty and immediately eased her foot off the accelerator. When you were caught up in a situation where every minute counted, it was all too easy to exceed the speed limit in a restricted area without realising it and the last thing she needed right now was some cop giving her a ticket.

She was in a mess – hair all mussed, lipstick smeared, both shoulder straps on the oyster-coloured slip broken and the pantihose ruined because Fred had ripped both undergarments off in his eagerness to shaft her. Had the mobile rung just ten minutes earlier than it had, she would have ignored the intrusive summons. However, at that precise moment they had been entwined in each other's arms completely satiated and she had instinctively leaned over Norden and, much to his annoyance, had grabbed the phone from her open handbag which had been lying on the floor by the couch.

'Switch the goddamned thing off,' he'd growled and had pinched her buttocks hard enough to make her cry out.

Norden had stopped hurting her the moment he'd learned who the caller was. At first Cora had thought Howard was agitated because he'd had one drink too many when he had stopped off at his favourite bar in town on the way home, and had been angered by the note she had left him in the den. Then he had told her about the ruckus he was having with a British Intelligence officer and from the description Cora knew it was the man she had reported to the police earlier on. If there was one thing she had learned as a nurse, it was how to deal with a hysterical patient and that knowledge had proved invaluable. Using all her expertise, she had calmed Howard down and got him back on an even keel. Once he was in a receptive frame of mind, Cora had told him exactly what he should do until she arrived at the house.

Norden had asked her very few questions and it had taken them less than four minutes to got dressed and be on their way. Back on Interstate 295 she had driven west for two miles before turning on to Creighton Road which took her into Richmond. She had dropped Norden off near the Holiday Inn and then made her way to Nine Mile Road.

Cora took one hand off the wheel, picked up the AT & T phone she had left on the adjoining seat and laboriously picked out the number of Norden's mobile.

'I'm almost home,' she announced when he answered. 'Where are you now?'

'About ten minutes behind you,' he told her.

Norden switched off the mobile and returned it to the glove department. He hadn't reached Nine Mile Road yet and was a damn sight more than ten minutes behind Cora Labbett. From where she had dropped him off in town, it had taken him longer than that to walk to the Holiday Inn, pick up the 9 mm Heckler and Koch pistol he'd left in the safe in his hotel room and collect the Ford from the parking lot.

He'd been involved in a couple of bad foul-ups during his time in Vietnam but nothing to compare with the one that was shaping up with the Labbetts. He wished he could walk away from them and the whole lousy deal but Valdes would never allow him to do that, even if he offered to return every dollar he had received. From where Valdes was standing, he knew too much. He had begun to have a bad feeling about the Cuban-born American the day they'd gone cruising in his launch off Jekyll Island. He had wondered then if the goons who worked for Valdes would put a bullet through his head and weigh his body down with chains before heaving it over the side.

Norden thought he must have had second sight that day because it had become more and more evident that his life expectancy would take a nose dive the moment Valdes took delivery of the merchandise produced by Drax Incorporated. He figured the Labbetts would be the first to go because once the loss was discovered, the Federal authorities would descend on the firm like a plague of locusts and the Vice President in charge of production was bound to be a prime suspect. As sure as night followed day, he would disappear shortly thereafter. Valdes had already taken steps to distance himself from what was going to be the biggest counterfeit operation in history and he wouldn't leave anyone alive who could implicate him. Even the courier who had delivered the semiautomatic pistol and silencer to Norden the day he'd arrived in Richmond was probably dead by now.

Cora Labbett had offered him a way out: dispose of her husband, split the five million and fall off the edge of the world. It was not an unattractive proposition but first of all it was necessary to deal with this unknown British Intelligence officer who had suddenly appeared on the scene. Norden picked up Nine Mile Road and headed east. Cora had told him to wait down the road from her house while she checked out the situation and decided if she needed his assistance. It sounded like a recipe for a fucking grade A disaster.

Labbett was on his second bourbon and branch water and was getting more and more garrulous by the minute. Ashton had no idea how much the American had imbibed on the way home but it had to be at least two, maybe three shorts judging by his slurred voice. Yet for all that his speech was impaired, he was still mentally alert and sharp enough to talk around the subject every time Ashton questioned him about Drax Incorporated. Everything he did confirmed an earlier impression that he was stringing him along until help arrived. Whoever Labbett had telephoned while he was waiting outside the house, it certainly hadn't been Joe Carlucci.

'Have you ever had any dealings with Novaks Promotions since you've been in charge of production at Drax?' Ashton demanded, interrupting another monologue.

'I can't say I've heard of them. Where are they located?'

'Down in Florida at Ponto Vedra Beach. The man who ran it used to have an office in the Seascape Center on Ocean View.'

'His business folded?'

'One day Novaks was there, the next he'd disappeared without a trace.'

'Leaving a bunch of angry creditors behind him?' Labbett suggested.

'No, as a matter of fact he settled all his bills in cash.'

'An honest man.' Labbett finished the rest of his bourbon and stood up.

'I'm going to have another,' he announced. 'How about you?'

'No, thanks, I'm driving. Remember?'

'Yeah, you did mention it,' Labbett said, and walked over to the bar.

'His first name is John,' Ashton continued. 'Claims he is a Canadian and probably has a passport to prove it.'

'Like I said, I've never heard of him. Maybe you should talk to the honcho in charge of our sales department.'

Labbett was confident, aggressively so, possibly because he was on firm ground.

'Novaks is undoubtedly an alias, Mr Labbett.'

'You're going all formal on me again, Peter.' Labbett rejoined Ashton and set his glass down on the low table between them. 'I guess that's second nature with you Brits.'

'Maybe. Can we get back to the subject, Howard?'

'What subject?'

'Novaks.' Ashton took out the photofit and placed it on the low table. 'Or whatever he calls himself,' he added.

Labbett glanced at the likeness and then quickly looked up. 'That's Novaks?' he asked in a voice that sounded on edge.

'Yes. It's how his accomplice in England described him. I think you should know that he's a very dangerous man. To our certain knowledge, he is responsible for the murder of five men and one young woman in my country.'

'Hey, just a minute, fella, are you implying I'm acquainted with this guy?'

'The young woman was tortured before she was shot in the head. Her name was Sharon Cartwright.'

'You are saying that I know this guy?' Labbett drank some of the bourbon and branch water and banged the glass down on the table in a show of anger. 'I just wish you would repeat that allegation in front of a witness because I would dearly love to sue the ass off you.'

'You may be about to got your wish,' Ashton told him.

There were certain vehicles which were immediately identifiable by the distinct noise of the engine and the original Volkswagen Beetle was one of them. Ashton heard the car before Labbett who made no attempt to disguise the look of relief on his face when the Volks swept into the driveway. After entering the garage, the driver gave the accelerator one last stab before cutting the ignition. The ensuing silence was broken by a low rumble accompanied by the hum of an electric motor as the up-and-over door began to descend. As soon as it was vertical, the locking bars engaged and the motor automatically switched off. The clack of high heels on the tiled floor acted like a tonic on Labbett; getting to his feet he walked towards the bar and opened the door into the hall.

'Hey, Cora!' he yelled drunkenly. 'Come on into the den, honey, we've got ourselves a visitor from Eng-al-and.'

'Well, keep him entertained while I make myself look presentable. I had to change a flat on the way home.'

'Goddammit, Cora, do as I tell you for once in your life. Never mind what you look like, I want you to meet Mr Peter Ashton right now!'

The bourbon had first made him confident, then garrulous and now belligerent; Ashton wondered how long it would be before Labbett turned violent.

'Did you hear what I said?' he shouted.

Cora entered the room, tight-lipped with anger, her eyes narrowed.

'Don't you yell at me, Howard,' she snapped, then turned to Ashton and switched on a radiant smile for his benefit. 'Your face looks familiar,' she said coolly.

'I was parked opposite your house this afternoon, Mrs Labbett.'

'That's right, you were driving a Pontiac. What have you done with it?'

'I left it farther up the road.'

'What the hell are you being nice to him for?' Labbett demanded.

'I called you into the den to hear the allegations he's been making about us before we send for our lawyer.'

'What allegations, Howard?'

'Your husband is mistaken, Mrs Labbett. I haven't accused him of anything.'

Ashton glanced to his right. His topcoat was draped over the back of the other armchair and he wanted to be in a position to grab the two-way radio if the need arose. Knowing any sudden movement was likely to alarm the American, he slowly inched towards the chair.

'I'm mistaken, am I?' Labbett pushed Ashton out of the way, picked up the photofit from the low table and waved it in Cora's face. 'Take a good look at this guy. According to Ashton he's a serial killer and we're supposed to know him.'

'I've never seen this man around here,' Cora told him calmly. 'Who is he?'

'Fred Nor— Novaks.'

Ashton was faced with two possibilities: either Labbett had let the cat out of the bag or else in his drunken state he'd simply got the name wrong. He got no help from Cora; her expression was one of complete bewilderment.

'I think perhaps I'd better leave,' Ashton said.

'You're not going anywhere,' Labbett told him.

For someone who was over fifty, unfit, overweight and half drunk, the American had proved surprisingly agile. While Ashton's back had been turned, Labbett had gone to the desk by the window, opened the centre drawer and armed himself with a Smith and Wesson .38 revolver.

'You stupid, stupid man,' Cora snarled.

'Shut your mouth.' Labbett cocked the hammer, then waved the revolver about as if the barrel were a pointer staff. 'Go get some rope and tie him up.'

'We need help.'

'Do it.'

'After I've called Fred,' Cora said and walked out of the room.

'You're making a big mistake, Howard,' Ashton told him when they were alone.

'I am? Seems to me you already have, fella.'

'Cora stopped to change a flat tyre. Right? So how come her hands aren't dirty? That's one question I'd ask myself in your shoes.'

'You're asking for it.'

'Of course I can see that Cora could have laddered her tights when she was jacking up the car but I'd still want to know why her slip is showing.'

'OK, that's it.' Labbett curled his index finger around the trigger and took up the slack.

Ashton closed his eyes. If ever there was a time when he needed to do some fast talking it was now but his mouth had suddenly gone bone dry. In a hoarse voice, he apologised over and over again for insulting Cora until finally Labbett calmed down enough to loosen the pressure he was exerting on the trigger. It was however only a temporary reprieve; Ashton knew he had to turn Howard round before Novaks arrived or he was a dead man.

'You ever heard of a Cuban-born American called Raúl Garcia Menendez?' he asked.

'No, and I'm not interested.'

'You should be. He stole five million dollars' worth of diamonds from his uncle and fled to England. The man we know as Novaks tracked him down and put a couple of .22 calibre bullets into his head.'

Without knowing how he had done it, Ashton could tell he had got through to the American. Unfortunately, the sea change had come a shade too late. Before he could really go to town on Labbett, Cora returned.

'Fred will be here in a minute or two,' she said.

'Yeah? I don't see the hank of rope I told you to get.'

'We don't need to tie him up, Howard.'

'Listen to me, both of you,' Ashton said urgently. 'As of now you're not in deep shit, but you will be if you let Novaks kill me. Remember Joe Carlucci, the CIA agent I told you to phone, Howard? He knew where I was going when we parted company. Jesus Christ, he pointed me in your direction.'

Ashton couldn't be sure that Labbett was even listening to him. He kept glancing at his wife as if he were seeking guidance from her. Then suddenly it dawned on Ashton that he was studying Cora's appearance, at the slip peeping below the tweed coat she was still wearing, the laddered tights and the love bites which were just beginning to show on her neck.

'You bitch, you've been with Norden,' Labbett said in an ominous voice. 'You took him out to that broken-down cabin near the Chickahominy River and got laid. He was screwing you when I phoned.'

'Don't be stupid.'

'Yeah, I'm stupid all right. I should have seen you had the hots for Norden the night we met him at the Tavern on the Green.'

Ashton didn't hear the car pull into the driveway, neither did the Labbetts. It was the clarion chimes of the doorbell which alerted them to the fact that Norden had arrived.

'That'll be lover boy; better open the door to him, Cora.'

As soon as she had left the room, Ashton took a chance and lowered his hands. As of that moment, his life expectancy could be measured in seconds and somehow he had to exploit the seed of doubt that he had planted in Labbett's mind.

'This is the last chance you'll get to save yourself, Howard,' he said quietly. 'So far as Cora and Fred are concerned, I'm not the problem, you are. They see you as the weak link in the chain. They know the FBI, the Treasury and just about every law enforcement agency in the US of A will be snapping at your heels the moment any of that high-quality paper goes missing from Drax. There's five million dollars at stake; people have been killed for a lot less than that.'

Ashton could hear voices in the hall outside the den and knew he had run out of time. He had no idea what Labbett would do in the next few seconds but suicidal or not, he sure as hell was not going to stand there and passively wait for Norden to put a bullet in his head. Ignoring the fact that Labbett was holding a gun on him, Ashton retrieved the two-way radio and concealed it behind his back as Cora entered the room with Norden.

'So this is the piece of garbage who's giving you trouble,' Norden said, gazing at him.

Ashton shook his head as if the whole thing were beyond his comprehension.

'Surely you are not going to stand there and allow lover boy to talk to you like that, are you, Howard?'

'You bet your sweet life I'm not,' Labbett said, and turned to face Norden, the Smith and Wesson levelled at his belly.

It was the opportunity Ashton had been waiting for. Directly above his head was a chandelier with thirty candle-shaped bulbs. Without pausing to take aim he hurled the two-way radio at the chandelier and then swinging round, launched himself at the couch and dived over it head first. The light bulbs exploded in a chain reaction which eventually tripped the fuse controlling the circuit and plunged the downstairs part of the house into darkness. As he crawled under the pool table, the Smith and Wesson barked twice and there was a hollow cough from a semiautomatic pistol fitted with a noise suppressor. Someone grunted, stumbled into the low table between the armchair where he had been sitting and the couch and fell heavily.

'Oh my God,' Cora wailed in a hoarse voice. 'You've shot him.'

'Is he dead?' Norden asked curtly.

'I'm not sure, I think so.'

'Well, look at it this way, it's what you wanted. It's happened sooner than we had planned, that's all.'

Ashton inched his way forward, crawling on his stomach to the other end of the pool table. He could see the cues lodged in the rack against the far wall some twelve feet away but if his eyes had become accustomed to the dark, the same applied to Norden.

'Have you found Howard's revolver?' Norden asked.

'I'm holding it,' Cora told him.

'Good. You stay where you are, we don't want any more accidents.'

'What are going to do, Fred?'

'The Brit's still in this room and I mean to take him out.'

Ashton could hear him moving slowly down the room towards the connecting door near the bottom. Norden was standing well back from the pool table; once he reached the door and cut off his escape route, he would crouch down to look under the table and that would be it.

If he attempted to arm himself with one of the cues, he would be shot down before he was halfway to the rack. The only weapons to hand were the balls in the rails directly beneath the pockets. Wriggling towards the nearest one on the left, Ashton carefully removed the only two balls which happened to be in the rail. What counted now was speed rather than stealth. Rolling out from under the table, Ashton sprang to his feet and hurled one of the balls at Norden, putting all his strength in it so that the ball was travelling at over ninety miles an hour when it left his right hand. Although tempted to go for the head, he aimed at the chest to be sure of hitting Norden.

Ashton didn't wait to see if he was on target. Labbett had tripped over the low table and he figured Cora had to be roughly in the same area. Whirling round, he let fly with the second ball and then charged towards the hall.

Norden was tracking Ashton with the Heckler and Koch pistol, lining him up for an oblique body shot as he ran away from him when a hard round object smashed into his right collar bone and broke it. The pain was excruciating and while he managed to got off a shot before he dropped the pistol, the bullet ricocheted off the far wall and buzzed around the room like an angry bee until it was spent. Bending at the knees, Nordon used his one good hand to feel around the floor for the Heckler and Koch semiautomatic. Cora screamed as the cue ball struck the edge of the low table a few inches from her face and a sliver of wood pierced her cheek to draw blood. Hugging the floor, she pointed the revolver vaguely in the direction of Ashton and squeezed the trigger. With her eyes closed, she never stood a chance of hitting him but at least the noise was impressive. In such a confined space, the .38 sounded like a cannon.

Norden had told her to stay put but in the heat of the moment that instruction went by the board. Aware that Ashton had gone past her Cora scrambled to her feet and went after him.

Norden closed his fingers round the pistol grip of the 9 mm semiautomatic and straightened up. Although Special Forces had trained him to be ambidextrous he had never been much of a shot when using his left hand but it wasn't necessary to be a marksman to hit a target at close range.

Cora fired on the move, shattering one of the bottles on the shelf behind the bar with her first round. The second flew across the hall and took a chunk of plaster out of the far wall. Then something hit her between the shoulder blades and her breastbone exploded.

Norden attached no blame to himself for what had happened. He had told Cora to stay put and the stupid bitch had disobeyed him and run straight into the line of fire. Of course it would have been necessary to kill her sooner or later; allowing Cora to got close to you was like snuggling up to a diamond-back. Moving forward, he stood over Cora and shot her in the head to make sure she would no longer be a problem.

'Two down, one to go,' he said aloud.

It didn't take Ashton long to realise he had made a bad mistake in choosing to go left in the hall instead of right. Two things had led to this error of judgement. The lights upstairs were on a different circuit and the one on the landing was partially illuminating the hall from the den to the front door. He'd also believed that Norden would nail him before he could open it and get clear of the house. So, with only a split second in which to make up his mind, he had decided to stick in the shadows and had ended up in the kitchen.

The tiled floor immediately betrayed his presence as it had when Cora had entered the house from the garage. Worse still, the door to the back yard was locked and the key missing. There was every possibility it was among the keys hanging from a row of hooks above the worktop of the kitchen unit but there was no time to find the right one by trial and error. The steel-plated connecting door to the garage hadn't been secured; opening it, Ashton switched the key from the kitchen to the garage side and then locked the door behind him.

Ashton doubted if the steel plate were thick enough to be completely bullet proof but at least it would make it more difficult for Norden to shoot off the lock while he looked for a way out. It was no use hoping the neighbours would raise the alarm. The nearest house was over seventy yards away and even if the occupants were at home the sound of gunfire inside the Labbett residence wouldn't have carried that far. There had to be a mobile in Norden's vehicle. He had arrived at the house a minute or two after Cora had called him and Ashton couldn't remember seeing a pay phone this side of Richmond.

However, the first thing he had to do was raise the up-and-over door and there, right in front of his face, was the fuse box. And on top of it somebody had thoughtfully left a flashlight. He reached for the flashlight and switched it on, then had second thoughts. It was all very well checking the circuit but if he used the electric motor to raise the up-and-over door, Norden would hear it and would be there on the driveway waiting for him. Every manufacturer knew that an electric motor could burn out at the most inconvenient moment and it should therefore be possible to raise the door manually, but could it be done silently? Ashton didn't think this was the time to find out. Instead, he circled the garage looking for anything which could be used as an offensive weapon.

The flashlight picked out a workbench the other side of the Oldsmobile. As he went over to examine it, Norden tried the connecting door, found it wouldn't open and put a bullet into the lock in an abortive attempt to shatter it. Ashton heard him back off, wondered what his next move would be and learned the answer to that question when Norden took a flying kick at the door. It was a tactic he repeated several times which led Ashton to think he was short of ammunition and was trying to conserve what little he had left.

The workbench was a treasure-trove of half-empty tins of emulsion, bottles of paint stripper, cleaning fluid, turpentine, putty, cleaning rags, a packet of candles, knives, tools of every description, and a short length of garden hose. Ashton collected all the bottles together and emptied most of their contents on to the concrete floor before setting them down close to the Oldsmobile. Then he removed the filler cap, inserted the length of garden hose into the petrol tank and sucked up the fuel to get it flowing. After he had filled all the bottles, he used strips of cleaning rag to make a fuse for each one, plugging it into the neck with a lump of putty. Since the Molotov cocktail lacked sulphuric acid and a small amount of calcium chloride, it would not explode on impact which meant he would have to light the fuse before throwing the bottle.

There was a packet of candles on the bench but they were of no use to him without a box of matches.

* * *

Norden took yet another run at the door and jumped into it, slamming the sole of his right foot against the lock. The kick jarred the broken collarbone again and triggered the usual wave of pain. The lock continued to hold and it was all too evident that there was no way he could physically break down the door. He couldn't afford to use the Heckler and Koch on it; the magazine only held eight rounds and he had already expended five. Then suddenly he saw a way round the problem and wondered why the solution hadn't occurred to him before.

He returned to the den and broke open the display cabinet. The shotgun and two sporting rifles were secured by a chain through the trigger guards which in turn was padlocked to a steel eyelet embedded in the wall. Acting on a hunch, he searched Labbett's body and found a bunch of keys in the jacket pocket, one of which fitted the padlock. He chose the Ithaca pump shotgun in preference to the sporting rifles, both of which were .22 calibre and didn't pack a large enough punch for the job.

In the bottom drawer of the desk he found a box of 12 gauge shells and painstakingly loaded the shotgun with five cartridges. By a stroke of good fortune the unique design of the loading and ejection mechanism of the Ithaca M37 made the shotgun easy to handle by people who were left-handed. Even so, loading the weapon was still a painful business for Norden.

One of the tricks Ashton had learned while attending the induction course at the SIS training school was how to hot-wire a car. For want of a match he'd simply bypassed the ignition switch on the Oldsmobile and, using the cigar lighter, had managed to light one of the candles at the second attempt after dipping the wick in petrol. The vapour from the high-octane fuel was a dangerous hazard but there were few safety measures Ashton could take other than leave the burning candle inside the car until the last possible moment.

He positioned the Molotov cocktails near the up-and-over door on the same side of the garage as the fuse box, then armed himself with a heavy monkey wrench in case Norden had locked his car and he had to break into the vehicle to get at the mobile phone.

Retracing his steps, Ashton opened the fuse box, threw the master switch and reset the blown circuit. As soon as he'd restored the power, he switched on the electric motor to raise the garage door and collected the burning candle.

A shotgun boomed, the connecting door rocked and a cloud of cement dust floated down from the ceiling. The second blast shattered the lock and sprang the lug from the housing. Ashton picked up one of the petrol bombs, lit the rag fuse from the candle and hurled the bottle at the widening gap between the door and the jamb. The bottle smashed into fragments and the high octane fuel erupted with a long-drawn-out woompf. Ashton picked up a second bottle and without bothering to light the fuse hurled the makeshift bomb at the existing conflagration. A river of flame ran back into the garage and snaked across the floor towards the workbench. From somewhere inside the kitchen, Norden aimed the shotgun at the gap and fired a third shell. The pellets were still in a solid mass when they struck the windscreen of the Maserati and blew it apart.

The up-and-over door was now sufficiently high for Ashton to duck under it while hugging the remaining three bombs to his chest. He returned for the candle, sidestepping along the inside of the wall with his back to it to give Norden little or nothing to aim at. The connecting door was now wide open and he could see that the burning fuel had spread throughout the kitchen, setting the table and the fitted cupboards ablaze. But there was no sign of Norden, which could only mean that, barring serious injury, he'd backtracked through the house to come in behind him.

Ashton grabbed the candle and shielding the flame against a faint breeze with his hand, went back outside. In what was virtually one continuous movement he picked up another bomb, lit the rag fuse and pitched the missile at the front door just as Norden was opening it. Although the bottle missed the target, it struck the wall a foot away from the door and showered the whole entrance with blazing fuel. Norden raised the shotgun in his left hand and got off a snapshot, then suddenly aware that both trouser legs were on fire below the knees, he retreated into the hall and slammed the door.

There was, Ashton decided, more than one way of raising the alarm. Winding up, he hurled the monkey wrench at the window the other side of the hall from the den with enough force to break it; then ran forward and literally posted the fourth petrol bomb through the hole. In a matter of seconds the room became a raging inferno.

Ashton ran back to the Ford Taurus and, to his relief, found that Norden hadn't bothered to lock the car. He opened the front, nearside door, ducked his head under the sill and instinctively looked in the glove compartment. Clutching the mobile phone, he backed out of the car and straightened up to find Norden advancing towards him, pistol in his left hand, the arm extended like some eighteenth-century duellist. One bomb left but inert because somehow he had managed to knock the candle over and it had gone out. Ashton ducked, seized the bottle, bobbed up and let fly at Norden, then turned about and ran for the belt of trees, jinking every few yards to present an unpredictable target. A pistol was essentially a close-quarter weapon with a high probability of error at ranges in excess of thirty yards. The noise suppressor would reduce the muzzle velocity thereby making the pistol even more inaccurate. He also knew from observation that Norden wasn't naturally left-handed. Even so a bullet came uncomfortably close before he reached the tree line and went to ground.

Although the Pontiac was no great distance away, Ashton decided to give the car a wide berth. Cora had known where it was parked and it was likely she had told Norden when he'd arrived at the house. That being the case, it was logical to assume the American would make straight for the Pontiac. Ashton planned to outwit him by doing the unexpected. Instead of retreating, he would circle the house and reappear behind Norden.

A car travelling west on Nine Mile Road gave Ashton the break he needed. Shortly after passing the belt of trees, the driver suddenly braked to a halt and spoke to Norden. Ashton couldn't hear what either man said and didn't care; getting to his feet, he made a dash for Labbett's backyard, using the trees as cover. As soon as he had put the house between Norden and himself, he switched on the mobile, extended the retractable aerial and punched up 911. He followed the same procedures he would have used in England, giving his name, present location, phone number and brief details of the incident. His English accent caused a few problems and he was obliged to repeat much of what he'd said. Even then the officer wanted him to confirm his location was definitely on Nine Mile Road.

'You heard me right,' Ashton grated, 'I'm at 1371.'

'We are in the process of responding to that situation,' the officer told him.

'You mean the incident has already been reported?'

'Yes, sir.'

Who by? he wondered. One of the neighbours or some motorist who'd passed the Labbetts' place earlier on? What did it matter anyway? Ashton thanked him and switched off the mobile and continued to circle the house.

The fire in the downstairs room off the hall had taken hold and spread to the upper floor. Gouts of black smoke were also billowing from the garage. There was no sign of the driver who'd stopped outside the house a few minutes ago but Norden was still around. He had turned back from the tree line and was hobbling towards the Ford Taurus, his right arm clutching the left shoulder. Although not visible, it was evident from his painful gait that he'd suffered a number of burns on each leg.

'Going somewhere?' Ashton shouted.

Norden raised the pistol and fired. They were almost a hundred and fifty feet apart and in his present state, he couldn't have hit a barn door at that range.

'You've got one round left.'

'That's all I need,' Norden told him.

Away in the distance, Ashton could hear the discordant wail of a police siren. 'It's over,' he yelled.

'I guess you're right.'

Norden closed his mouth around the noise suppressor, squeezed the trigger and blew off the back of his skull.

The two police officers who had arrested Ashton earlier that night arrived on the scene two minutes later. They were not exactly overjoyed to see him again.

CHAPTER 29

In the aftermath of the incident at 1371 Nine Mile Road nobody had been prepared to shake Ashton by the hand and tell him what a good job he had done. If the officers of the Richmond Police Department had had their way they would have locked him up and thrown away the key. In their eyes he had torched a two-million-dollar property, thereby destroying much of the evidence and hamstringing the police investigation as a result. He had also destroyed three automobiles, the most expensive of which was still the property of a finance company and the subject of an ongoing dispute with the brokers who'd insured the vehicle and were now refusing to pay up. Finally he had stolen and subsequently damaged beyond repair property belonging to the Richmond PD – viz. a two-way radio.

He had not been Top of the Pops with the US Treasury's Secret Service either, who claimed they had been worried about Howard Labbett for some time and had been keeping a watchful eye on his financial commitments which appeared to leave him overstretched. A few weeks before his death, the Treasury Secret Service had come to the conclusion that Howard Labbett could be a security risk and had resolved to put him under physical and audio surveillance. The Treasury had heard rumours of a massive counterfeit operation designed to undermine the US dollar but had no evidence of either a Cuban or Iranian involvement.

Furthermore the Treasury was not aware that Labbett had been suborned by persons unknown and was to receive five million dollars in return for his co-operation. They could only conclude that this might have happened before it was decided he should be kept under surveillance. In their opinion the Labbett case pointed to a lack of vigilance on the part of senior executives at Drax

Incorporated who should have seen that, with the cost of his divorce settlement and a new wife to support, he would be in financial difficulties. It was a point the Treasury intended to bear in mind when the contract with Drax was reviewed in 1997. Had this come to the knowledge of the senior executives at Drax, they too would have joined the list of people who were not enamoured with Ashton.

The FBI was a little sore with him because had Norden been taken alive, they could have used him to bring down Rafael Valdes. Of course they would have had to take Norden into the witness protection programme and there could have been no question of him standing trial for the murders of Gus Jukes, Harvey Yeo, Lawrence Rossitor, Sharon Cartwright and Ronald Fox. Naturally the Brits wouldn't have been too happy about it but in the end they would have accepted the situation. They always did. As it was, a valuable opportunity had been lost and they blamed Ashton for that. A law enforcement officer would have persuaded Norden to give himself up whereas Ashton had pushed him to the point where suicide had seemed the only option which Ashton thought was a pretty big assumption.

As any other Intelligence Service would have done in their place, the CIA vehemently denied they'd had anything to do with the fracas. Ashton may have been to Langley but that had been purely a liaison visit to exchange information on the Middle East. At no time had any officer raised the subject of a massive counterfeit operation directed against the United States by a foreign power. The agency had never heard of Mr Howard Labbett prior to his death, indeed they had no reason to. As an intelligence-gathering organisation, the CIA was not permitted to operate within Continental America and had never done so, at least not in the post-Nixon era. Ashton had not contradicted the claim when he was being questioned by both the FBI and the Treasury because you didn't betray your source. Besides, the day might come when it would be useful to remind Joe Carlucci he owed him one.

Head of Station, Washington, and his deputy had let it be known that they never wanted to see Ashton on their patch again. He had damaged the special relationship the station had enjoyed with the CIA, and the State Department had made its displeasure known to

Her Majesty's Ambassador Extraordinary and Plenipotentiary on what they regarded as unwarranted and unacceptable interference in the internal affairs of the United States. The Ambassador in turn had sent a full report to London, stressing how their efforts to establish cordial relations with the Clinton administration had been undermined as a result.

Whitehall had taken the report to heart and acted swiftly. The Secretary of State had demanded that appropriate action should be taken to discipline the offender and the Permanent Undersecretary at the Foreign and Commonwealth Office had written to Hazelwood to the effect that Ashton should be sacked. Fortunately, by the time Ashton returned to London after being questioned by officers of the Richmond PD, FBI and the US Treasury, much of the heat had died down. Hazelwood had gone to bat for him and instead of instant dismissal, he had been put on an adverse report which effectively killed any chance of promotion to Assistant Director he might have had.

Within the SIS it was felt the Menendez affair and its subsequent repercussions were best forgotten. The whole business had left a sour taste in Ashton's mouth; wanting to wipe the slate clean, he had presented Jill Sheridan with the original and duplicate recordings of their conversation when she had confessed that Sharon Cartwright had been working for her.

'Don't ask any questions,' he'd told her. 'Just destroy them.'

Jill had assured him she would, then asked if there was anything she could do in return. And he had told her that what really irked him was the fact that Rafael Valdes had got away with it unscathed. He had wondered in passing what the Iranians would do about it if they knew the whole story. The following evening Jill Sheridan had walked into his office and given him the name and home telephone number of the Chief of Intelligence at the Iranian Embassy. She had also told him how to arrange a clandestine meeting but on reflection he had decided not to follow it up.

Life gradually returned to normal. Over the next two months, Harriet got a little larger, Roy Kelso was allowed to withdraw his application for early retirement and Clifford Peachey introduced his 'stand alone' computer-based information system which was modelled on the one in service with MI5. No one outside Vauxhall Cross could access information on file or key in an input. This 'stand alone' system was also crypto-protected. As a further safeguard, material which could put the source at risk was withheld. In such cases, the officer seeking the information was automatically referred to the appropriate Head of Department who decided whether or not to grant access.

The system was up and running on Tuesday, 2 May. One week later Ashton decided to ask for an update on Rafael Valdes and received an extract of a report that had appeared in the *Miami Herald* on Thursday, 27 April, under the heading 'Prominent Lawyer killed in Mystery Bomb Blast'. The facts were simple enough: a young woman allegedly of Middle East origin had marched into his law office in Miami, convinced the staff that she had an appointment to see Mr Valdes and having gained admittance, had detonated a bomb concealed in her handbag which had killed them both instantly.

The report disappeared and was replaced by a message which read: PERSONAL FOR ASHTON. WHAT GAVE YOU THE RIGHT TO PLAY GOD?

When he tried to obtain a printout the screen went blank and he was unable to recall the message. He could not however erase the accusation from his mind.